"what a story!...vivid, almost magical, set in an alien place with unique characters embarked on equally alien and divergent goals. it was very readable, calling me back every time i had to lay it aside, in fact costing me one very late night, although there were some parts i would have preferred reading in the sunlight.

"i think it's a real winner."

—larry bond, international best-selling
   author of *vortex* and *the enemy within*

"the last segment of the madagascar manifesto trilogy is as poignant, terrifying and grandly moving as the two preceding it. i know of no other work dealing with the holocaust that treats this defining event of the twentieth century with such imagination and such brilliant inventiveness linked to deeply respectful scholarship. rounded off so splendidly in *children of the dusk*, the manifesto should now take it place among the very few works of our time that truly deserve the title *epic*."

—peter s. beagle, best-selling author of
   the last unicorn and *the unicorn sonata*

"with action, horror, and suspense, *children of the dusk* is a blockbuster world war ii novel unlike any other i've read before. it is a highly unusual and frightening depiction of a little-known aspect of the holocaust filled with startling details and eerie atmosphere."

—kevin   ng author
   of *the*

Children
OF THE DUSK

JANET

BERLINER

AND

GEORGE

GUTHRIDGE

Cover Illustration: Matt Manley
Cover Design: Michelle Prahler

White Wolf Publishing
780 Park North Boulevard, Suite 100
Clarkston, GA 30021
World Wide Web Page: www.white-wolf.com

Printed in Canada

ACKNOWLEDGMENTS

The authors wish to thank Robert Fleck for his editorial insight, hard work, and unfailing support and good humor, and Janet's mother, Thea Cowan, who was willing to remember, and whose oral histories brought life to this series. Also, of course, Laurie Harper of Sebastian Agency. She is the best agent anyone could have.

Individually, Janet wishes to extend personal thanks to Laurie Harper for her unfailing support and friendship, to her mother, to "Cowboy" Bob for his cooking, coffee, and caretaking, and to Dave Smeds for being the quintessential devil's advocate.

George wishes to thank Kay Addrisi, Eseta Sherman and George Harper for their valuable contributions.

to the survivors

PART I

"Everything that is really

great and inspiring is created by the

individual who can labor in

freedom."

—Albert Einstein

JANET BERLINER AND GEORGE GUTHRIDGE

Foreword

The island of Madagascar lies in the Indian Ocean, off Africa's southeast coast. It is the world's fourth largest island—the size of the Atlantic Seaboard from New York to Atlanta to the Appalachians. Having broken away from the mainland a hundred million years ago—perhaps, as some insist, as part of the continent of Lemuria—it developed a flora and fauna as unique as those of Australia or the Galapagos.

Madagascar's northern rain forests, the world's densest, teem with orchids and lemurs; the spiny deserts of the south are home to latex trees, whose sap causes blindness, and harpoon burrs, which tear flesh to ribbons. Until they were hunted to extinction, pygmy hippos roamed the land; there stalked the giant, flightless æpyornis, the elephant bird known as the *roc* in the Sinbad story and whose rare, semi-fossilized eggs are still found on occasion.

The island, only two hundred and fifty miles from the mainland, remained uninhabited until 500 B.C. Surprisingly, the first settlers arrived not from Africa but from Java (now Indonesia), three thousand miles to the east. These were the Vazimba, a race of bronze sailors who island-hopped their outrigger canoes all the way across the Indian Ocean only to drown in a gene pool when the peoples of what are now Mozambique and Somalia crossed from Africa to the rich island the Vazimba had discovered. As more Javanese arrived from the legendary Spice Islands far to the east, intermarrying gave the skin of many Malagasy a coppery color—though few islanders can trace their ancestry back to the original settlers.

Today the island suffers from overpopulation—especially along the central plateau, whose indigenous plant life has been burned off in an ecological disaster of staggering dimensions. Prior to World War II, Madagascar was relatively uninhabited. That, together with its being situated south of the oil-rich lands of the Red Sea and close to British shipping lanes between India and South Africa, brought it to Hitler's attention. In early 1938, he instructed Adolph Eichmann to collect material about the island for a "foreign-policy solution" to the "Jewish Question."

The idea of expelling Europe's Jews to Madagascar, then a French colony, did not begin with the Nazis; the proposal goes back at least as far as Napoleon. Between the World Wars, the idea was championed by

Britain's Henry Hamilton Beamish and Arnold Leese, and in the Netherlands by Egon van Winghene. The Joint Distribution Committee of the U.S. House of Representatives also toyed with the notion of resettling Jews to Madagascar.

In 1937, the Poles, who wished to encourage the emigration of large numbers of Jews, received permission from the French to send a three-man investigative commission—two of whom were Jews—to Madagascar to explore the possibility of just such a resettlement. In Berlin, the idea was greeted enthusiastically, especially by Heinrich Himmler, who wrote, "However cruel and tragic each individual case may be, this method is still the best, if one rejects the Bolshevik method of physical extermination of a people out of inner conviction as un-German and impossible."

Confident that Warsaw would quickly fall once Poland was invaded, in spring of 1939 Himmler called upon the S.S. and the Seekreigsführung—the Naval High Command—to test the waters of the Indian Ocean regarding what had become known as the "Madagascar Plan." There were more than seven million Jews in Poland. Czechoslovakia, annexed in '37, had over four million. Austria, annexed in '36, three million; Germany itself had five million. The numbers were growing beyond comprehension. *And had not the Führer promised to resolve the Jewish menace?*

Documented history of the "Madagascar Plan," which we have called The Madagascar Manifesto, ends there.

But what if—

On June 22nd, 1939, the *Altmark*, a steamer with a 178-meter length and a 22-meter beam, set sail from Hochwaldt Wharf in Kiel, in northern Germany. Though her secret, primary duty was to supply the German raider, the *Graf Spee*, her secondary, public mission was "humanitarian." She carried 144 Jews specially picked from Sachsenhausen, the concentration camp an hour's drive from Berlin, plus enough equipment and matériel for the men to begin building the requisite landing facilities for the planned exodus to Madagascar.

In charge of operations was Abwehr Colonel Erich Weisser Alois, whose military background until then appears to have consisted of guarding the mansion-headquarters of Nazi propagandist Joseph Goebbels. With Alois were forty Sachsenshausen guards under the leadership of one Major Otto Hempel, and Alois' own unit members: twelve German shepherds and eleven other trainers. (Alois was himself a dog handler, one of some note.) Also accompanying Alois was Bruqah, a Malagasy guide, and Alois' pregnant wife, Miriam Rathenau Alois, niece to Walther Rathenau, Germany's Foreign Minister during the early days of the Weimar Republic. Miriam's involvement was in great part due to the fact that a propaganda film was being made of the event, it was no accident that the *Altmark* set sail seventeen years, to the day, after Rathenau's assassination at the hands of anarchists.

The single significant military event on the voyage to Madagascar occurred approximately five kilometers off the coast of Lüderitz, Germany's Southwest Africa enclave. There, on September 1st, the day Germany invaded Poland, the *Altmark* rendezvoused for the first time with the *Graf Spee*. Captain Heinrich Dau, who would commit suicide the day after the war ended, waxed uncharacteristically emotional in the ship's usually carefully worded log:

> Spoke with Gustav Sophie [*Graf Spee*].
> Such a silhouette against the orange sunset!
> And on this day, no less, when the phoenix
> of the Fatherland has risen from the ashes
> of the Great War! In my rejoicing I brought
> the Jews topside, to tell them the news. This
> time their kind will *not* cost us the war!

Solomon Freund, a Judaic scholar and amateur linguist whom the other Jews called Rabbi, also had a diary entry that day—the only one he managed during the entire voyage—written (according to local legend) with a leaky fountain pen he discovered in a garbage can he was instructed to empty overboard, and on a scrap from *Der Sturmer*, the anti-Semitic newspaper he also found in the can:

> Sunlight at last. Saw Miriam. How
> beautiful she is! All ten diamond fruits from
> Tree of Life at once. Eyesight worsening.
> Got to hold on. For her. For us. *Graf Spee*.

The *Altmark*, renamed *Sogne* to further avoid detection of the oil and ammunition she carried for the *Spee*, reached Nosy Mangabé, a tiny island in Madagascar's Antongil Bay, on September 7th. Few Malagasy step foot on Mangabé, perhaps because of its history. Involved in a disastrous colony-attempt during the eighteenth century, it was later used as a small but secure base by British pirates with a taste for raping Betsileo women. Nosy Mangabé (to help the reader with pronunciation, the island is spelled *Mangabéy* in the novel) is a real island in the mouth of Madagascar's Antongil Bay. Mauritius Augustus Benyowsky built a bamboo hospital on the island during the late eighteenth century. Daniel Defoe studied the island as background to his writings, and the English pirate Captain Avery used it as a stronghold, probably because it is the source of numerous rare gems, including apatite, found nowhere else in the world.

Today, Mangabé is the world's only official refuge of the aye-aye, a lemur whose supposed powers of predicting death the Malagasy once feared so much that they killed the creature on sight. For the moment, the aye-ayes are safe on Mangabé.

Among the local tribes—the Betsileo, Tshimity, Antakarana—memories linger of the *Altmark/Sogne* expedition. However, perhaps fearing reprisal from some agency we of western civilization can only guess at, tribal elders speak of the attempted resettlement only in whispers, if they speak of it at all.

This is that story.

(We, the authors, beg the indulgence of those who read *Child of the Light* and *Child of the Journey*, and so might feel some impatience with our decision to reprise, in expanded version, the Epilogue of the latter as Chapter One of this novel.)

Prologue

Grasshoppers blackened the moon.

The Malagasy laughed delightedly and pointed what was left of his fist at the predawn sky. Abandoning his guardianship of the limestone crypt, he shrugged off his ragged, clay-colored loincloth. By the fading light of the stars, of glowworms, and of the last embers of the coconut husk fire, he began a sinuous dance of triumph. He moved around the moss- and ivy-covered totems that dotted the area, carelessly swatting at the mosquitoes and the rain flies that heralded a tropical downpour. When he tired of the dance, he removed a liana from one of the totems, wove it into a garland, and placed it on top of his grisly red and salt-and-pepper head like a crown.

He ran his misshapen fingers down the totem. Miniature zebu horns topped an arabesque of curling leaves. Carved lemurs balanced on one another's backs, looking outward with huge, whorled eyes.

The grasshoppers moved away from the huge egg-yolk moon, away from the Zana-Malata who grinned a toothless grin. *"Minihana!"* he shrieked. "Eat!" He opened the gaping pink hole where his nose and mouth should have been, pushed his tongue outward in the manner of an iguana, and drew a stream of glowworms into his throat.

He exhaled a burst of fire and chuckled at his own cleverness. Soon, he thought, it would be time for *lambda*, the dressing of the dead, and only he knew who waited inside the crypt. He and the tree frogs and the glowworms. Meanwhile, he could wait. Here, in isolation, time meant nothing to him—any more than it did to those who were buried in the *valavato*.

He moved around the totems that dotted the area. At his feet, a *dô* snake slithered away, carrying with it the soul of one of the dead who haunted the burial ground. Behind him, five short black men, eyes painted with white and black tar circles, bodies pulsating with a luminous white mud, appeared out of the rim of trees, cavorted a moment, and disappeared.

As if it, too, knew that changes were imminent, the rainforest chorus stopped. When only the bats sang *a cappella* in the damp tropical air, the fox-lynxes raised their long faces to watch him. The aye-ayes and the larger lemurs fled; the zebu sauntered down the hill, bells clanking hollowly and dewlaps swaying beneath their chins.

The Zana-Malata stayed where he was, listening to

the voices of the dead. Chief of all he surveyed, he stared down at the crescent coral reef three hundred feet below the burial ground. His keen eyes discerned the lights of a ship moving toward him. He glanced at the moon hanging over the horizon.

It was beginning. The ghosts were returning to Nosy Mangabéy, his island where the dead dreamed.

CHAPTER ONE

10 september, 1939

Sitting on the damp sand, Solomon Freund watched as lifeboats and launches traveled back and forth from the *Altmark* to shore. Some brought only men; others carried equipment and supplies loaded by the freighter's cranes and his fellow Jews. A large, awkward-looking raft, made of wood strapped onto empty fuel drums, was being readied to carry the small tank from the ship to shore. Knowing the German military, there was doubtless some order about the landing, but to Sol it seemed chaotic. He wondered cynically if Abwehr manuals contained explicit instructions for hacking a path through a rain forest.

Limited by his tunnel-vision, Sol tracked the boat

which brought Major Otto Hempel. The SS officer strode from the water, his wolfhound and nine-year-old Misha Czisça in tow. Reaching the beach, he looked out over the water with ill-disguised disgust. Sol turned back toward the ship and saw Erich Weisser Alois, Abwehr colonel, riding in the last boat. Erich. Despite his hatred, Sol could not avoid thinking of his childhood friend in the familiar. Head uplifted, eyes surveying the surrounding jungle as if he half expected natives to come rushing out and throw themselves at his feet with offerings of gold, Colonel Alois stepped from the launch. Behind him, two Jews carried his beloved German shepherd, Taurus, strapped to a hospital stretcher.

"We're going to have to cut a path to the top of the hill," Erich said. He turned to Hempel. "Give the Malagasy a machete." He nodded toward Bruqah, their coffee-colored guide. "After you've supplied all of your men with machetes, give the Jews the rest."

"The Jews?" Hempel asked. "Is that wise?"

"Are you questioning my orders?" Erich's voice was dangerously quiet. "Take one squad and lead the way. Use Bruqah to guide you. I am sure you will at least agree with that, since it is his primary function here," he went on, having apparently decided to downplay the matter of Hempel's insubordination. "Freund, stay with them and take care of Mir...the woman. Pleshdimer, you and Taurus bring up the rear." He raised his voice. "We are going up that hill." He pointed toward the jungle. "There will be no relaxation of discipline. For the sake of every Jewish life here, I will say this once, and once only. You are to use the machetes for creating a path. Look as if you see them as weapons, make one movement that smells of an attempt to escape, and we will shoot half of you Jews and let the dogs finish the rest. Now move it!"

Without so much as a glance at his heavily pregnant wife Miriam or at Solomon, he turned his back to them and waited to be obeyed. Hempel, obviously furious, strode toward the ridge of trees, his omnipresent companions trotting behind.

Bruqah, ever the Malagasy aristocrat though he was for the moment a guide, watched without comment or movement.

"Do you not fear them?" Sol asked him.

"Pah!" Bruqah spat onto the wet earth.

"Does anything frighten you?"

Bruqah threw his head back and laughed uproariously. "You ask questions like a small child." He helped Miriam to her feet. "What Bruqah fears you cannot understand. Not yet."

"Tell me."

"Bruqah only fears things of man and not of man," he said softly, all trace of laughter gone.

"You are right, I do not understand." Sol was reminded of the days in the farmhouse outside Oranienburg where he had first met Bruqah. The Malagasy had been assigned to prepare them for their journey and sojourn here. He was apparently studying botany at the university in Berlin when he was offered the job in exchange for transportation home. The more Sol had come to know Bruqah, the more convinced he was that the events were less coincidental than they appeared.

"We of Africa accept she mystery," Bruqah went on. "It is for Europeans to need understanding. Belief be truth here." Bruqah pointed his walking stick at a twig. "What be this, Lady Miri?"

"A twig," Miriam said wearily.

He tapped the twig lightly with his cane. A chameleon skittered into the underbrush. Bruqah smiled. "Come, Lady Miri. Come, we go, Solly."

Sol caught himself grinning. No one had called him that since he left his mother in Amsterdam. Seeing his smile, Miriam returned it with one of her own. He saw a glimpse of the young girl he had once known and felt a transient stab of hope as they entered the jungle. All his life he learned through riddles. His father had said it was part of the Judaic tradition. Perhaps by solving the riddles of this new land he would find answers to his old problems as well.

Sunlight gave way to the dark and dankness of the rain forest. Sol's physical discomfort was increased tenfold by his inability to see more than a couple of meters ahead. A high-pitched chittering spoke of living creatures disturbed by the human intruders, and around him, pinpoints of light flickered on and off, as if the forest were peopled by a million glowworms. Were it not for the moisture that hung in the air and covered him with a film of sweat, and the mold and moss that enveloped everything like a possessive lover, he might have been in the Black Forest.

Abruptly, the chittering stopped. A raucous sawing

began, followed by a series of deafening squeals which rose to a crescendo and shook the bamboo and ferns into responding. Leaves rustled and dripped and snapped back, ignoring his swinging machete. When he looked behind him, the forest seemed to have regenerated. He could hear the others, Jews and soldiers alike, fighting their way through the heavy undergrowth.

Ha-haai! Ha-haai!

Soft and shrill and mournful, the cry echoed through the forest, its sound so chilling it made Solomon's teeth ache.

He lifted his machete. Behind him, he heard the unnerving, metallic snaps of safeties being flicked off as, again and again, the sound came, piercing through the branches overhead.

A guard, panicked by the unfamiliar sound, opened fire.

Ha-haai! Ha-haai!

"Eeee-vil!" Arms raised, Bruqah followed the sounds with a shaking finger.

"Probably a harmless monkey," Hempel said contemptuously. "Stop acting like a bunch of children."

"There are no monkeys in Nosy Mangabéy," Bruqah said in a low voice, the veins pulsating in his neck as he strained to see up into the jungle canopy. "Not in all Madagascar."

"What was it?" Solomon asked.

"*H'aye-aye,*" Bruqah said, imitating the sound. He turned away from them and moved through the tangle of ferns and vines, parting the foliage with his walking stick and his machete. In an instant he had disappeared.

"Come back here!" Hempel shouted.

Bruqah returned, clutching his head, wailing and spinning as if he were performing a ritual dance. Gripping his face, ogling the newcomers to the forest, was a red-and-gold striped iguana the length of his arm.

"Do something, one of you!" Grabbing Sol's machete, Miriam chopped wildly at the bush ahead of her. She collapsed, crying, as Bruqah reeled toward her.

"For Christ's sake!" Hempel shouldered past Solomon. He tore the giant lizard from Bruqah and, holding it upside-down and squirming, cracked its back and threw it to his wolfhound, Boris. Pleshdimer, the Kapo who served as Hempel's manservant, crouched at the dog's side and grinned as it tore the reptile to pieces.

"Whatever's amusing you," Hempel said, "you might remember that one of these days you'll be glad to dine on that same meat."

"Are you all right, Bruqah?" Miriam asked in a small voice.

"I'm all right, Lady Miri." Bruqah signaled Solomon to come closer. "That thing." He stepped aside for a moment to allow Hempel and his machete crew to work past them. "*Liguaan*, like you," he told Sol. "She eye the future while she eye the past."

"How do you know…?" Sol stopped. He would examine the meaning of Bruqah's words later. Right now Miriam needed his attention. He helped her to her feet. She looked exhausted. He wanted to pick her up and carry her, but he was too debilitated; even with Bruqah's help it was all he could do to half-drag her along.

The climb grew steeper, the forest more dense. Layers of branches crisscrossed overhead. The leaves underfoot were slick from the humidity and lack of sunlight. Millipedes and beetles ran over their legs, stickers jabbed their arms, wet ferns, rough as a cat's tongue, stuck to the sides of their faces. Looking for ballast, they found themselves grabbing onto the yellow pitcher plants that seemed to flourish in the forest despite the weak light. When they did, a sticky syrupy substance erupted, bringing armies of flies and ants and mosquitoes against which there was no defense.

"Be careful," Bruqah said, when he saw them touching the pitcher plants. "For some people, pitcher plants dangerous. Make them breathe bad. Die, even."

Sol slapped at his neck and looked at his hand. On it lay a mosquito the size of an average fly. "Look at this thing," he said. "It's big enough to roast for dinner. We'll probably all need quinine, which doubtless our Nazi friends have brought along." If we don't die first from malaria, he told himself. "For the time being, we had better do what they say."

They resumed their climb. Eventually they found themselves in a boggy meadow. Only the lack of incline, the larger expanse of clear flat ground between trees, and the fact that those who had gone ahead of them were gathered together at the far end of the clearing, gave them any sense that they had crested the hill and exited the forest. Near them, leaning against a tree, was Hempel. "Wait here," he told Pleshdimer. "Shoot anyone who gives you trouble. I'm going to see what's beyond those trees."

After Hempel walked away, Sol helped Miriam to sit down, her back against a log. "Nothing happens without a reason."

He said the words out loud. He had to. For one thing, nothing short of his favorite rationale, which generally worked for him even under the most arduous circumstances, would stand a chance of reaffirming his faith. For another, the steady deterioration of his eyesight brought on by *retinitis pigmentosa* required—demanded—the reassurance of the sound of his own voice. As if knowing his hearing was unimpaired would somehow make the fact of his loss of vision bearable.

Now if I could only discover what those reasons were, he thought, life would begin to make sense.

Maybe.

Gasping after the hike up through the rain forest, he wiped his glasses and looked around as best his tunnel vision would allow. He watched the guards and his fellow prisoners...free laborers...file onto the relative flatness of the boggy hilltop meadow.

Dusk was descending, the sun setting behind the western edge of the dark overstory of foliage that surrounded the meadow. Night, he had been told, would come quickly in the tropics, almost like a curtain being rapidly drawn, but for the moment the side of the meadow in which Sol stood was cast in brilliant light. The air was so moisture-laden that the sunlight seemed to refract, lending the meadow an ethereal quality which was quite unnerving after the brooding darkness of the rain forest. He wondered how much of the odd light was due to the sunlight and humidity and how much to his own weak eyes. The disease had stolen all of his sight except for a circle of clarity, nearly devoid of color.

He wasn't going to be much use to himself, let alone anyone else, once blindness set in. When that would happen was anybody's guess; *that* it would happen was inevitable.

He moved his head from side to side to examine his new environment. Wreathing him in green, slender white-barked trees rose two hundred feet, where they spread their dense leafy canopy, blotting out the sky and perpetually dripping water. Curtains of gray moss, and creepers and lianas, hung down in a tangle from the trees; parasitic orchids sprouted from the trunks. At ground level, huge ferns, gleaming with moisture, grew higher than a man's chest.

Here and there, Sol intuited rather than saw a spot of color: the red acanthema blossoms, which Bruqah had warned them were deadly poison; the blue dicindra vine which opened in the early morning, closed up as the sun reached its height, and reopened briefly at dusk. His basic impression was that of a vast, oversized, gray-green world, an alien place, inhospitable to man.

By contrast, the hilltop meadow seemed almost congenial. Judging by the charred snags partially sunken in the marsh and by the singularly large count of dead trees, there were times of the year when there was relief from the wetness that hovered around them like a living entity.

At the far side of the meadow stood what Sol took to be a tanghin tree, at least judging from what he remembered seeing in Bruqah's crude drawings. Beneath the tree, a lopsided thatched shack, constructed of mud and wattle and pandanus palm fronds, stood on uneven stumps that elevated it a meter off the ground.

"Man who lives there carries storm in she heart," Bruqah said, misusing the personal pronoun as he almost habitually did. He sauntered closer to Sol, walking stick in hand, long, bronze-colored legs moving him with fluid ease through the meadow grass.

"Is he one of your people?" Sol asked, hunkering down next to Miriam, who was resting at his feet, her head against a log and one hand on her nine-months' pregnant belly.

Bruqah shook his head vehemently. "Zana-Malata can live only within his own self. Same as me. My people, Vazimba, no longer a tribe. We are like traveler's tree. We nourish Malagasy who need us."

Miriam opened her eyes and looked down the west side of the hill through a break in the foliage. She pointed toward another, smaller hill. "This island can't be more than five kilometers square," she said to Sol. "One of Erich's books called it two hills and an apron of rain forest."

Bruqah spread his arms as if to encompass the sun. "Once before, this island drowned in blood. Bruqah died, then."

"You mean your ancestors died," Sol said.

"I mean Bruqah," the Malagasy said quietly. "You know little, Solly. But you will learn…next time island drowns in blood."

Sol watched what looked like a ground squirrel poke a berry into its mouth, masticating with absolute concentration. The human intruders were of no concern, the food its universe. A deep envy overwhelmed Sol. How dare it be wiser than he, to know such single-mindedness of purpose? He must learn survival from such animals.

He looked around, assessing his friends and adversaries, who sat or stood milling in four groups. The largest group were his fellow Jews, one hundred and forty-two men who, against his better judgment, called him rabbi and leader. They had been plucked, like himself, from the degradation of Sachsenhausen, to be in the lead party for the Nazis' planned forced exodus.

Next in number were forty Nazi guards, also products of the camp, hand-picked for the expedition by Hempel, who had returned and stood with a hand on the shoulder of Wasj Pleshdimer, the murderer who in Sachsenhausen had been elevated to barracks guard. Both men appeared to be looking at something downslope of the shack. At Hempel's feet, his wolfhound whined. Also at Hempel's feet, leashed like the dog, was young Misha. A great sadness took hold of Sol, and he promised himself that he would find a way soon to communicate with the boy.

He looked at Erich, the man whom he had once called blood brother and, at Erich's insistence—

inventing a ceremony to match—a brother-in-blood. Why, Sol chided himself, had he never before considered the implications of that syntactic twist? For him, *blood* had meant kinship. For Erich it had meant...what? He claimed he had no family. His mother and father, though still living, were dead as far as he was concerned. Miriam was his by right of marriage but not love, and the child only possibly his, and that perhaps by virtue of rape. He loved his dogs and communed with them, or so he asserted, but they were hardly blood relatives. Still he did love them, all twelve of them but most especially Taurus, and he certainly felt affection for the eleven other trainers who made up his zodiac team. The Abwehr canine command had been selected by Himmler himself for the expedition, probably because Erich and his men had proven too powerful, and possibly too non-Nazi, for Reichsführer Himmler to allow them to remain in Germany any longer.

As for the Nazi Party, which so many officers loved as family, Erich Alois hated it.

Lounging in smaller groups among the others were sailors from the *Altmark*, the supply ship for Germany's indomitable raider, the *Graf Spee*. They would leave soon, Solomon was sure, and with them Tyrolt, the ship's doctor. Miriam was doubtless dreading that, for she would soon need medical attention. And Sol too needed Doctor Tyrolt. Not for his physical needs but for his psyche. Tyrolt alone among all the Nazis he had met was a man Sol felt he could trust.

Several dogs jumped up, growling, as two oxlike

animals, humped and sporting enormous dewlaps, huge ears, and curved horns, wandered from beyond the shack and into the clearing. Their appearance broke Sol's reverie.

"Zebu," Bruqah said, brightening.

Sol knew that the animals, while not sacred to the Malagasy, were the main measure of wealth among the islanders.

"*Zebulun*," he said to Bruqah. "Jacob's tenth son. Father of the tribe of Israel. What might he have thought of this place?"

Bruqah wasn't listening. He stood, hands on hips and head thrust forward. The mouselemur perched on his left shoulder also leaned forward. It was as if both man and animal were appraising the zebus' worth.

Pleshdimer raised his rifle and Bruqah's face went vapid with horror.

"No!" Bruqah ran toward the Kapo. "Please, no, do not shoot!"

Pleshdimer hesitated. Hempel squeezed his shoulder and the Kapo swung the rifle across his back and took off in a waddling run toward the animals. Waving his arms and yelling, he chased the zebus from the clearing.

Sol looked down at Miriam. He was about to tell her he would find her some water to drink when Erich came striding across the meadow and stopped beside them. Sol ignored him, affecting a studied nonchalance. Erich steered his gaze clear of all of them. "Will whoever lives there come back, Bruqah?" he asked, pointing at the lopsided shack.

"Of course." The mouselemur, which seemed to be

perpetually on Bruqah's shoulder, shifted position away from Erich. It clung to Bruqah's hair, its sad, dark eyes too large for so tiny a head. "All Malagash come back. Living or dead, they come. As Bruqah come back."

"Bruqah is Vazimba. His ancestors came from Indonesia," Miriam said, to Sol's surprise. He wondered how she could talk to Erich, after all he had done to her. "He told me that his people were Madagascar's first inhabitants."

Sol started to say something to Miriam, then stopped as it dawned on him that she was not speaking to Erich at all, not looking at him but through him. As though he did not exist. What had Bruqah called Nosy Mangabéy, back on the ship? *Island where the dead dream.*

He shuddered, wondering where the ghost that had inhabited him for seventeen years had gone.

"Vazimba, first race," Bruqah said. "Zana-Malata, last race." His teeth were bared in what could have been mistaken for a smile, but a hard look had risen into his eyes. "We are beginning and end, he and me."

"You know the man who lives there?" Erich asked.

"For too long." As if to end the discussion, Bruqah reached up to one side, plucked a fig from a tree, and handed it to Miriam along with a piece of wild ginger.

"Ha-haai! Ha-haai!"

Like spectators at a stadium, heads turned in unison to look in the direction of the sound, Erich's among them.

The cry came again from the northern edge of the surrounding forest, this time followed by the body of a creature that looked like a cross between a flying squirrel and the lemurs Sol had seen illustrated in the books about Madagascar. With the grace of a trapeze artist, the animal leapt from the overstory and landed on a beech branch entwined with lianas the size of a man's arm. Slowly, almost insolently, the creature raised its plumed tail.

"*Ha-haai! Ha-haai!*"

Sol stared at the coppery ball of fur. Its two enormous, sad-looking eyes seemed to stare back at him with human intelligence. Its tail was wrapped around the liana and its fingers gripped the branch.

As if carefully timing his action for maximum dramatic effect, Hempel unsnapped his holster and lifted and aimed his Mann. Misha seized the opportunity and scuttled toward the closest group of Jews, two of whom put their arms around him protectively. The wolfhound hunkered down in the grass and waited.

"*Ha-haai! Ha-haai!*"

The major smiled a tight-lipped smile and clicked off his safety catch.

"Don't shoot," Erich ordered, apparently fascinated by the creature.

Hempel did not immediately lower the Mann. The aye-aye, with almost human understanding, lifted its left hand and pointed at Hempel. It had a thumb and three fingers, the middle one of which extended far beyond the other two—fleshless as the finger of a corpse long dead.

"H'aye-aye have finger of death," Bruqah said.

The mouselemur on his shoulder squeaked and burrowed down, but the Malagasy did not appear to notice. He stood perfectly still, his usually placid features rigid with fear.

Commanding his wolfhound to stay, Hempel strode toward Bruqah. "Shut your mouth, or I'll kill you where you stand."

Something made Sol look back at the aye-aye. Its hand was still raised, its long bony finger extended toward the wolfhound, which had risen to its feet in defiance of Hempel's orders.

Back arched, snarling, Boris turned to face the trees.

Into the silence came a muffled roar, like the distant thunder of an approaching storm, followed by another. Clearer this time. Closer. Accompanied by the pounding of hooves through the underbrush and a blur of movement, a massive boar, head lowered, burst from the brush. In a lightning movement that defied the creature's lumbering bulk, it lifted the wolfhound high into the air and held it up there, a bloody trophy impaled upon one curved horn. Lowering its head once more, it shook off the dog's body, and raised its foot. A shot rang out. The boar looked up, snorted, shook itself, and trotted back into the forest.

Hempel walked over to his dog and nudged it with his boot. Like statuary imbued with life, the rest of the stunned watchers returned to movement. The shepherds, growling, tugged at their leashes, and the aye-aye, its business apparently finished, leapt back into the overstory.

"Dead?" Erich strode over to where Hempel stood,

gun in hand, and looked down at the wolfhound. Even at a distance, Sol could see that it was a bloody heap of fur and flesh.

"Might as well be," Hempel said. "Fat lot of good he will be to me now."

"Shoot him."

Erich issued the order without raising his voice, yet loudly and firmly enough to be heard over the shepherds.

Hempel turned to face him. "Who the hell are you to order me to shoot my dog?"

"I am the commanding officer of this operation."

Hempel paused, raised his gun, and aimed down at the dog. "For now," he said.

If he could shoot Erich instead, he would, Sol thought, watching the unfolding tableau. Miriam had told him about Killi, the dog Hitler had ordered Erich to shoot during the Olympics party at Pfaueninsel— Berlin's Peacock Island. Sol wondered if Pfaueninsel torchlights flickered, now, within Erich's brain.

But Erich was not looking at the wolfhound, or at Hempel. He was staring at a bare-chested, sinewy black man who had stepped from the shack and into the clearing. He was clothed in a ragged clay-colored loincloth that matched the red that peppered his curly white hair. As he stood surveying the newcomers to his domain, two animals with red fur and feline faces joined him, muzzles twitching.

There's more lunacy here than *The Cabinet of Dr. Caligari*, Sol thought, as the shepherds again started up their insane barking.

"The dogs, they care not for the fossas," Bruqah remarked.

Hempel swiveled and pointed the Mann at the newcomer. Judging from the look on his face, it would not take much to make him use it. Small wonder, Sol thought. Simply looking at the wiry black man was a challenge. There was a gaping pink hole where his nose and mouth should have been. The hand he held up to Erich in mock greeting was eaten away like the flesh of a leper. Dangling from his fingers like an offering was a large gray wriggling worm.

Seeing that he had Erich's attention, the man tilted his head. With some innate sense of drama, he waited just long enough to allow the horror around him to peak. Then his tongue emerged to envelope the worm and draw it down into his throat.

"Pisces, no!"

Pulling free from his trainer, who was apparently too caught up in the spectacle to hold firmly to the choke chain, one of the dogs bounded at the black man.

The fossas whirled around and darted into the underbrush. Reacting almost as fast, the black man leapt toward the hut and scrambled beneath it. The dog leapt after him, frenziedly digging his way under the structure.

Sol waited for the screams of pain which must come when a trained killer tears into the flesh of a man. He turned his head to look at Erich, then at the faces of the other watchers. Their expressions held varying degrees of expectation and horror.

From underneath the hut came a mewling

conciliatory cry, and the faceless creature crawled out on his elbows. Swiveling on his stomach, the muscles on his lean back glistening with his sweat, he reached underneath the hut and drew out the dog by its chain.

The dog lay passively where he left it, inert, defeated, head hanging limply.

Sol turned his attention back to Erich. A series of emotions played across his features: puzzlement, admiration, jealousy, and finally anger. Either the syphilitic's empathic abilities with dogs far exceeded Erich's own, or this was another demonstration of African magic at work.

The Zana-Malata stood up. The hole that had once been his mouth turned upward in a ghoulish imitation of a smile. Placing his hands on his hips, he bowed slightly as if acknowledging his victory. Sol heard Erich's dog, Taurus, whimpering softly from her stretcher; dysplasia—inflammation of the hip joint— had rendered her almost incapable of walking. Beside her, likewise bound to a stretcher, lay Aquarius, ill nearly to the point of death from the long journey.

One dog crippled, one near death from seasickness, one gored to death, one turned into a rag doll by some crazy Malagasy...and we've just arrived, Sol thought. Perhaps there is hope for escape after all.

"Bruqah!" Erich turned and shouted. "What the hell! Who—*what*—is that *thing*?"

"Zana-Malata."

"Leper?"

"Syphilitic." Bruqah gripped his crotch for emphasis. "By the looks of him, that thing turns twigs into something less benign than chameleons," Miriam told Sol with an edge of fear.

Sol started to reassure her but stopped when he realized that he felt much the same way. Apparently sorcery was endemic to Africa. He was sure they would find out soon enough what that meant to them. For now they both had to watch and learn.

"Let the dogs go!" Erich commanded. "Stop that bastard!"

Snarling, nine healthy shepherds leapt forward. From the encircling forest, varicolored birds lifted into startled flight. The screams of lemurs joined with the softly insistent shrill of an aye-aye hidden in the trees.

The dogs never reached their victim.

When they were close enough so he could surely feel their heated breath, the Zana-Malata crouched and patted the earth.

Sol watched in disbelief as the animals that comprised what was probably Germany's finest canine contingent stopped in their tracks and, in unison and panting heavily, crawled on their bellies to huddle like house pets around the man's feet.

Again, Sol witnessed Erich's struggle to understand the Zana-Malata's control over the dogs.

"How the devil—?" Erich asked Bruqah.

The Malagasy tapped his temple. "He like you with the dogs, Mister Germantownman."

Sol turned his attention back to the Zana-Malata. Ignoring the ruckus, the syphilitic made his way across the clearing toward Hempel. Either because he recognized the Zana-Malata as a potentially powerful ally, or perhaps because he, like the dogs, was an animal being controlled, the major moved toward him. Misha left what little protection and comfort the prisoners could offer and, knowing he would be beaten if he failed to stay close to the major, trailed behind, head down.

Motioning for Hempel to follow him, the Zana-Malata bent down and gathered the wolfhound in his arms. Seemingly without effort, he lifted the animal and carried it into the shack, leaving Sol to wonder if the heat had already affected his own brain and caused him to imagine the whole thing.

Pistol in hand, Erich burst past the dogs. They rose to their feet and shook themselves, disoriented. He leapt the shack's steps and slapped past the zebu-hide door, only to re-emerge moments later. For a split second he went rigid. His hand shot out as if seeking support, and his head snapped up.

"M-must have g-gone out a b-back way."

He waved the gun, but it seemed to be a motion without purpose. Sol waited for him to order dogs and trainers, perhaps the guards as well, into the surrounding rain forest to search for the man. Instead, he stumbled down the steps. "F-forget him, f-for now," he stammered.

Sol had not heard Erich stammer in fifteen years. Had the lightning petit mal seizure—finished almost the moment it occurred—had a greater effect on him than usual?

"W-we'll deal with him later," Erich told his troops. Confidence was returning to his face and voice, and his stammering was already less pronounced. "We have a military compound to build. W-we must always—*always*—keep our primary mission in mind."

Moving with an easy kind of grace despite the heat, the soggy earth, and the momentary physical lapse, he turned to look at the inhabitants of his new empire.

"Though I...I'm a man of action rather than words," he began, "I feel I should inform you of why you are here and what our plans are for you." He started a slow pacing in front of the men, who gathered together despite the animosity between the guards, sailors, and dog trainers. The prisoners likewise clustered, though apart from the Nazis.

"Four hundred years ago," Erich continued, "this tiny island, here in the middle of Antongil Bay, was the site of the hospital of a colony begun by one Augustus de Benyowsky, a Hungarian-Polish Count who attempted to civilize the local tribes...and wrote Madagascar's first constitution. Two hundred years after that, the island served as a base for British pirates. Later, it belonged to the French. Now"—he made a fist, showing his resolve—"it is the F-Fatherland's turn. What we create here on Mangabéy is only a beginning. Eventually, we will also p-penetrate the mainland." He turned his attention toward the prisoners. "Shiploads of Jews will follow you here. This is your new homeland." He looked at Sol. "Your Jerusalem—"

Sol stopped listening. Erich's desire for a benign dictatorship was pathetic. Even if he meant what he said, Hempel would never allow it. The Jews' hope for survival lay in Sol's recovering his wits and strength. He recalled the voices of his mentors, voices from visions he had experienced for seventeen years as the result of the dybbuk, the wandering soul, that had possessed him since that terrible day when he had witnessed the assassination of Germany's Foreign Minister, Walther Rathenau, a Jew, and Miriam's uncle.

Eyes closed, Solomon recalled the words of Beadle Cohen, his mentor: *Sometimes souls seek refuge in the bodies of living persons, causing instability, speaking foreign words through their mouths.* Such lost souls, the beadle had maintained, were unable to transmigrate to a higher world because they had sinned against humanity.

You must live his dybbuk's voices had told him. You have not yet fulfilled your destiny.

Survival, Solomon! Therein lies your duty! There are things to be done that only you can do. Only God has the right to order the universe.

God and not Hitler! he told himself bitterly. That madman and his insane designs on Madagascar had to be stopped. Hitler did not intend to make the island a homeland for Jews, a haven safe from a Europe that would like to obliterate them. It would not be a sanctuary but the world's largest prison camp. A place where Hitler could pen up Jewish assets and abilities and use them for his own evil ends. He remembered a joke Bruqah told him on the *Altmark*, which was no more funny now. Referring to a British pirate village that had once existed on the far side of Madagascar, he'd said, "This be the other side of Hell-ville."

How, Sol wondered desperately, are we to stop this insanity and escape at the same time?

"That awful man...the Zana-Malata!" Miriam

whispered, slipping a hand up into Sol's and clutching her belly with the other as she rocked back and forth. "This place! I can't make it, Sol. I hurt. I…I hurt, Sol."

Stooping beside her, Bruqah put his hand on her stomach and tilted his head as if he were listening to something or someone. "Your baby will come soon, Lady Miri," he said. "You must rest."

Sol sat down on the grass, and placed his hands atop Miriam's, on her belly. How many days before the baby arrived? "We will escape this somehow," he said. "But we need to learn the terrain first, and gain strength."

"You speak wisely," Bruqah said, standing up. "When time comes, I help."

"What will you call the…our…child?" Sol asked Miriam, seeking more than anything to distract her.

She looked into his eyes, and he could see her love for him through her pain. "Erich, if it's a boy," she answered. "I must. I am his wife, by Hitler's law. If it's a girl? Erich doesn't want a girl—"

"What name would you choose for our daughter?"

"She will be…Deborah."

The three syllables seemed to tumble from her lips and hang in the hot, wet air.

"Deborah," Solomon repeated dreamily. Then his body tensed and a cobalt-blue light engulfed the space around him.

A girl of about eight fights against thin ropes that bind her, naked, to a carved wooden post almost twice her height. She runs her fingers along its chipped designs. Perhaps thirty other intricately carved posts are grouped behind her, each topped with the skull of an ox. In the background, beyond a flickering fire, stand monoliths and menhirs that evoke Stonehenge. Then, as though a sound machine were turned on, her voice breaks through into Sol's consciousness as she twists in terror against the ropes. "Help me, Papa. Help me!" *she cries out.* "I am Deborah. Why do you not know me?"

The light faded and his body went slack as he emerged from the psychic flash, one he had experienced several times since the dybbuk had left him. The prophetic dreams of a visionary and psychic, according to Beadle Cohen. "Deborah, the prophetess and judge. The fighter who was instrumental in freeing the ancient Israelites from the Canaanites," Sol said.

Hope from a well Solomon had long since thought dry flooded his being. "Perhaps, after all," he said, "there will be a next year in Jerusalem."

CHAPTER TWO

"Deborah means 'bee' in Old Hebrew," Miriam said. It took her a moment to remember how she knew that. The information came from the mouth of Judith, whom she did not know—who probably did not even exist— yet whose presence had been haunting her in these last days of pregnancy.

"As there are no monkeys, so there are no common bees in all Madagascar," Bruqah said. "It is fitting name for first woman—"

He seemed to be talking to himself, Miriam thought, assuming him to mean the first Jewish girl-child born in this place.

"How would you know that meaning?" Sol said, frowning at her. "You have not studied such things."

"Judith told Emanuel—"

"Miriam!" Sol shook her reasonably gently. "What

could you know of what Judith said? She was the woman in one of the visions the dybbuk brought *me*."

"Perhaps the dybbuk got bored with you and decided to vacation with me for a while." She made no effort to hide her weariness or to disguise the edge of impatience that took hold whenever Sol spoke of the dybbuk. His belief in its existence inside of him and, now, in its disappearance from him, was immutable. It was also his business. On the other hand, it had caused more than enough trouble for both of them over the years.

Seeing the hurt and confused expression in his eyes, Miriam immediately regretted her lack of self-control. The truth was, she *had* heard what she had heard where she said she had heard it; still she knew that Sol hated her propensity for making caustic remarks in the midst of travail. It was the ex-performer in her, she supposed. The defense mechanism of the singer-dancer that had inured her from the lust and insults of Berlin cabaret audiences who had known she was Jewish, and therefore legally available for rape...if only alcohol could help them overcome cowardice long enough to climb onstage. Sol surely understood that veneer. He had one himself, only he called it *philosophy*.

Distracted by introspection, she at first ignored an unfamiliar buzzing that was attempting to penetrate her consciousness. When it became so intense it was almost a thrumming, she looked upward to find its source. All that she could see against the canopy of tree and sky was Bruqah, staring with fearful eyes toward the outer fringes of the rain forest.

She made a lethargic attempt to push herself to her feet.

"Get down!" the Malagasy yelled.

Even as the words left his mouth, a dark cloud emerged from the surrounding forest and spread across what little sun remained. The shadow touched Miriam and she squinted upward. Panic set her heart racing like waves against the shoreline as the darkness deepened. All human sound stopped in the clearing as heads and eyes turned upward.

A quiet whirring began high in the air. Starting *pianissimo*, it grew rapidly into a crescendo that drowned out the incessant calling of the lemurs and chittering of the birds. Mesmerized, prisoners, guards and dogs watched the dark cloud move toward them. When it looked as if it would envelop them, the guards came to life, pointing their carbines this way and that.

"The hand of God," Sol said quietly.

As if in answer, the sun went black, and Miriam realized the cloud was alive.

Grasshoppers swarmed in from all sides, the cloud so thick that guards and prisoners alike danced and batted and cursed the deluge of whirring, maddening, gray-green wings. Sol threw himself across Miriam, who could not stop herself from whimpering with fear as the insects, some as long as fifteen or eighteen centimeters, alighted in her hair and on her face.

"Get them off me, Sol, get them off!" she yelled, batting at them to no avail.

He fought them, but it was a losing battle. They invaded his clothes, and then his nostrils and ears. He tore at his shirt and hair. Around him, Nazis jerked like marionettes. The dogs howled and leaped and snapped, or ran in terrified circles.

Sol brushed the insects from Miriam's face but he was unable to stop the horde. He hugged her, covered his head, and squeezed shut his eyes. Miriam did the same, aware of grasshoppers on the bridge of her nose, exploring her nostrils, fluttering against her eyelids.

Suddenly she felt Sol go rigid. His arms felt like iron around her body.

"Not here! Not now!" she thought, knowing immediately that the trauma of the swarming had triggered a psychic episode, and that the darkness behind his lids had exploded with cobalt-blue light. When she felt his body go slack, she knew that the vision held him in thrall. For as long as it did, he would be useless to everyone, especially to himself. Dybbuk or no dybbuk, he would always be a visionary, able to glance into the future.

Not that it did anyone any good, Miriam thought. The visions always seemed out of context until the event was upon them.

She felt Sol thrashing on top of her and pushed him off her belly. The vision had apparently ended, she thought, curious despite her skepticism and her fear of what was happening around—and on—them.

"Solomon?"

The word emerged as a whisper. Sol rolled fully off her and looked around. He appeared to be dazed by fear and by the spectacle of the meadow, seemingly so benign when they had emerged from the track that ran up the rain-forested hill, acrawl with myriad insects. Most of the grasshoppers had settled and were eating. Now and again a few whirred into the air, only to alight again on the closest solid object. The Nazis and prisoners were brushing themselves off, the insects suddenly listless after the fury with which they had arrived. The guards wore sheepish expressions, a result, apparently, of their cowardice before something as innocuous as grasshoppers, disturbing though they were in a swarm. The prisoners picked off the insects gingerly, unafraid, unhurried. After all, what was an insect after what they had endured in the camps and during the long, dark voyage in the *Altmark*'s hold?

The dogs shook themselves and pranced about like pups, sniffing the intruders. Except we are the intruders here, Miriam thought.

"Solomon?" she asked again. "What did you see?"

"A blue fog broken by sentry towers," he said. "Within the fog, people moved amorphous as ghosts. I felt ringed by darkness, by the fog, and by the moving bodies that stayed at the center of my sight, like players on a stage. Then bats winged past, hundreds of them, smelling of oranges—"

"Bats?" Miriam shuddered.

"I was holding a machine gun. I could feel the vibration of it. I squeezed the trigger, once, twice, three times, unable to stop, and laughed as spent cartridges flew from the weapon. Below, people shrieked and swore, and always there were the bats, soaring into the line of fire, bursting like balloons—"

He stopped, and she realized he was not looking at

her. She followed his gaze and stared upward, transfixed, past the foliage.

Sweeping in arcs across the waning light were fruit bats. She had seen them in the half-light of predawn, when the *Altmark* weighed anchor in the lagoon. They had hung like black lingerie from the trees just inside the forest perimeter, and Bruqah had regaled her with tales of what delicious stew they made, pungent with the odor of the fruit on which they gorged.

But they had not come to gorge on fruit.

They had come for the grasshoppers.

Grateful for his protection, Miriam allowed Sol to cover her head with his arm as the bats wheeled down to feast. Though she knew they had not come to hurt her, this was hardly her idea of a day at the Tiergarten.

She closed her eyes.

When she opened them, her fear having given way to curiosity, she saw that the grasshoppers were still feeding on the grasses, oblivious or uncaring that they in turn were being eaten.

"I'm all right now, Sol," she said.

He removed his arm from her head and started to rise. As if on signal, the insects took flight. The flurry, followed by the bats again taking wing, nearly bowled him over. He sat down hard on the ground.

Miriam chuckled. "I don't mean to laugh at you, Sol," she said, "but this is all too crazy for words. What else can one do but laugh?"

When the last of the bats had flitted away into the shadows, she turned over and sat up. She felt amazingly calm as Bruqah helped her to her feet.

"I suppose you're going to tell me those were the spirits of the dead on this island where the dead dream," Miriam said, her voice almost jocular.

"Perhaps," he replied, "they be *messengers* from the dead."

She shook her head in exasperation and brushed herself off. Bruqah took hold of her wrists.

"You are bonded to the child you carry, Lady Miri," he said seriously. "Bruqah is bonded to this land." His eyes searched hers. "Maybe you chase away ghosts, you and Solly and the baby. But do not think the grasshoppers they come by—how do you call it—by coincident. Nothing happen by accident here."

Sol nodded, and Miriam felt the echo of her own earlier musings. Maybe Solomon was right. Perhaps there *was* a reason for everything, and if so, perhaps this insanity *would* eventually make sense.

But all of that notwithstanding, right now it was not reason that she sought. What she really wanted was a hot bath, a loofah to scrub away some of her weariness, and a real bed with a real mattress.

All of which, she thought, labeled her—and not Solomon—as the ultimate dreamer.

Chapter Three

Erich stood in the middle of the compound, watching the Jews use block and tackle to hoist logs for the three sentry towers. Other Jews were building the tall crib that would serve as a water tower. The camp would never survive on the meager spring at the bottom of the knoll.

He was oddly proud of the efficiency of the Jews, managing to complete so much work in two days.

The Jews!

Next he'd be calling Hitler the Savior. Had he allowed the Party, with its insidious and constant propaganda, to infect his mind like those idiots had at the Passion Play at Oberammergau? He had gone there for solace and, he had told himself, spiritual healing after those sleepless nights in the Black Forest where he had taken his advanced Abwehr training. Someone in the audience had whispered "Berlin" when *Bethlehem* was mentioned, and suddenly the program had taken on new meaning. By the time Christ was raised upon the Cross, people's eyes had become bright with anger and resolve. It hadn't taken genius to read their faces. The Jews had killed Him, of course. It was always the Jews. The audience, though, would not let that happen again. *They* would not crucify the new Messiah, for if the audience had its way, there would be no more Jews.

No, he thought. He might have been gullible then, but not now, when he knew the *real* Hitler. Not the public man who stood on the Reichschancellery balcony and fluttered his hands like small birds, as Solomon's papa used to say. The one who thought nothing of insisting that a young Abwehr officer—who may not have loved the Party, but certainly his country and his Führer—put a bullet in the brain of his favorite dog, the only unwavering friend he had ever known. All because Achilles had bitten one of their screeching Pfaueninsel peacocks. What had the Führer expected, when the damn thing was strutting around like a long-lashed transvestite whore?

As for Taurus, Killi's daughter, he had begun to live with the morbid feeling that she was nearing the end of her capacity to survive in this unrelenting heat and humidity. The dampness aggravated the existing inflammation in her hips; an open invitation to disaster. Her disability had increased markedly since they'd arrived—though perhaps the defect simply was more noticeable now that the animal was free of the ship's confines.

With only minor satisfaction, he watched the log floor of the headquarters tent being emplaced. Next to it stood the medical tent, the first structure to be finished. He wanted to visit Taurus, to comfort her, but to go to the medical tent could mean seeing Miriam, and he didn't want a confrontation. Instead he reached out, as he had done so many times, and touched Taurus's mind with his own. A dull throbbing grew in his hip as he took some of her pain onto himself, trying to ease her burden for a short time. How he detested his inability to help her more!

Angered, his thoughts returned to the people who had sent him here. He would show them all, Adolph Hitler included, he reassured himself. He would oversee the building of the base camp here on Mangabéy, and the creation of the docks at the mouth of the Antabalana River, over on the mainland. He would stand with his zodiac team of trainers and shepherds and watch the first voyagers of the greatest exodus in history disembark from the ships from Europe. But Madagascar would not be another concentration camp. As far as he was concerned, his charges were colonists—not slaves or prisoners. If every one of them happened to be of the Jewish faith and that satisfied the Reich's larger plan, so much the better.

Come what may, he would spit in the Führer's eye. Whatever Hitler wanted he would get, but not the way he wanted it. He, Colonel Erich Alois, would see to that. At the top of the list was presenting the head of Major Otto Hempel on a stick. On the beach on a stick, turned toward the East, so the son-of-a-bitch could watch the sun rise each morning while the flesh rotted off his face. He would crush them all. All. Whatever it took.

Erich lit a cheroot and watched the match burn down. Deliberately, he let it singe the unfeeling flesh of his damaged left hand. He stared at the skin, fishbelly white ever since his fingers were caught in a falling sewer grate during childhood. Despite the lack of full use of his hand and by virtue of his unwavering regard for what it meant to be a soldier, he had risen in the world of perfect Aryan men; by unfaltering compassion for the animals that were his charges, he had ventured close to the heart and soul of Germany. Had it not been for that night on Peacock Island, he might have become Hitler's personal security. As it was, he had come so close that Himmler, fearing the heat of an encroaching new power, had named him head of the Madagascar Plan and shipped him off to Africa, hopefully to be forgotten.

Well, they would find out that he wasn't to be discarded that easily, but first he had to cure this weakness of his for compromise.

Thinking of the Jews, *his* Jews, as colonists, was fine in the long term, but perhaps not immediately expedient. Hempel must not know his larger design, or the major would be on the radio to Himmler. Then it would be Erich's head on the stick.

Along with those of all the colonists.

He and his trainers were all that stood between Hempel and the colonists' slaughter. The major had no more wanted an African assignment than he himself had. Why Hempel had not turned it down was a mystery.

Because he wanted to kill the Jews?

Ridiculous, Erich thought. Hempel could have done that much more conveniently in Sachsenhausen.

Erich came to the same conclusion he had come to each time he'd posed the question: Hempel was in Africa because of him. That and some other agenda which had not yet come clear. Meanwhile, Hempel would try to kill the colonists—for himself, for Hitler, for the Reich. For whatever sick reasons he gave himself. Like the good people of Oranienburg; Erich had watched them last April, spending Easter sunrise stoning Jews for Jesus.

With Hempel in charge, the killing here would surely include Solomon Freund. Include Miriam...and the child.

My child, Erich thought.

Mine!

Regardless of what Miriam claimed. What did it really matter if she said she was emotionally and spiritually married to Solomon Freund. She was legally *his* wife.

The child is mine, as is Miriam. As they all are.

Mine to save.

Mine to use.

Feeling a great deal better, he noticed Solomon coming toward him, threading past colonists carrying fence posts across their shoulders. Till then, he had tuned out the noise around him, a skill he had developed with some deliberation. He prided himself on his concentration. The lesson had been easily learned once he'd understood that it was merely a matter of priorities. Like a frog after a fly, or a dog sleeping while cabaret music blared from the Victrola, he tuned in only what was necessary.

Pity Solomon had never developed that trait, Erich thought, looking at the man whom, during his younger and impressionable years, he had considered his brother. Lanky nearly to the point of emaciation, despite Erich's having come to loggerheads with Hempel to assure the colonists had sufficient rest and food and fresh water. Large hands incapable of real work, only of holding books or of stocking shelves in the tobacco shop their fathers had co-owned. The mind of a philosopher or a fool, if those were not the same thing. Erich snorted, appreciating his own humor.

Solomon looked around the compound as if he were searching for the comedy. "You find something funny in all of this...Colonel Alois?" He tagged on the title as if it were an after-thought, yet quietly enough that it was clear that he remained fully cognizant of his place as a Jew in the Nazi hierarchy.

"You don't?"

"What could possibly be humorous about building an advance camp for what we both know to be a sham?"

"That's precisely what makes it so funny. All this effort for what Himmler will almost certainly never allow. Not unless we can convince Hitler himself of the wisdom of going through with the plan. It's like the old question: If six men can dig a hole in sixteen hours, how long does it take three men to dig half a hole?"

"There's no such thing as half a hole."

"I think that's why I liked you. You were always able to figure out my riddles. What a pity you seem unable to use that mind of yours for anything *important*. You're an enigma, Solomon. An enigma. This operation reminds me of when I was beginning my military training, back at Berlin *Akademie*. We'd dig a hole, the officer in charge would toss in a cigarette, we'd fill up the hole and have to dig up the cigarette. No shovels the second time, only our bare hands. Then we'd fill the hole again. Most of the other cadets took the exercise as hazing, but when I'd finished filling the hole I realized what an important lesson I'd learned: I'd arrived back where I had begun, but now I knew where I'd been…and who I was." He gazed off toward the rain forest, where a parrot was cawing. He had kept one of the cigarette butts. Kept it for a long time afterwards. Whatever had happened to it? he wondered.

He rubbed his chin and, feeling the stubble, realized he had forgotten to shave. "Did you want to talk to me about something in particular," he asked, "or is this just a social visit?" Again he chuckled at his own cleverness.

"I've come to you with a…" Solomon lowered his voice, "a request from my people."

"What is it you want, vichyssoise and a fine Rhine wine for dinner? An evening at the Paris Follies?"

"This is a request for something that is likely to increase the men's productivity."

"Appeal to my Germanic sense of order and efficiency, is that it?"

"I too am German...Herr *Oberst.*" An even lower voice.

Whatever was left of Erich's benign mood dissipated. Sol's arrogance in calling himself a German angered him. "You are a Jew, Solomon Freund. A shopkeeper's son and a Jew."

"Yes, Herr Oberst. I am subhuman. I am feces. Offal that should be washed from the earth."

"Don't give me that Sachsenhausen crap, Solomon! This is *not* a concentration camp!"

"I'm trying to find the route to your heart, Erich, assuming you still have one," Solomon said in a quiet undertone. "You hold all the cards, and we both know it."

"That's how life is, Solomon," Erich responded. "Complicated, and not often fair. If you are expecting anyone to care—"

"*You* care, Herr Oberst. You care whether or not this operation succeeds. And you care about us. Us *Jews.* Deep down, you care."

"If that's your assumption, by all means continue to delude yourself. It's your right as a Jew." Erich had begun to tire of the game. "Just tell me what you want, and I'll consider it."

"Thank you."

"I said *consider* it," Erich said sharply. "Now what is it?"

"Sundown tomorrow begins Rosh Hashanah, the Jewish New Year. We wish to hold a short service at sundown, at the start of our High Holy Day, and an even briefer one at sundown the following day. We would need the Torah—"

"You're asking for permission to hold a religious service, a *Jewish* religious service, during a German military operation?" Erich started to correct himself to *Nazi* military operation, but decided he did not want to give Solomon the benefit of knowing that he made the distinction. "This joke of yours is less than funny, Solomon. First you fuck my wife, and now you want to fuck up my colony. *With* my permission, no less."

He watched with pleasure as the blood drained from Sol's cheeks, his face suddenly as white as when he'd emerged from the hold of the *Altmark* and into the tropical sun.

"This is not about you and me," Sol said at last. "It is not about Miriam or the child. This is about the men. This is about finishing the building of the compound exactly the way you want it. And on time. My people will work better if they are shown some humanity."

Erich tried to stem his rising fury. Almost unconsciously he found himself unsnapping his holster and folding his fingers around the clean, hard feel of the Walther's walnut grips. It took considerable will to let loose of the pistol and resnap the holster. "You ever touch Miriam again, I'll kill you." His gaze burrowed into Sol's with an intensity he could not control. "The child is mine, Solomon. Do you understand that?"

Sol looked at the ground, not replying.

"Do you understand that!"

"Yes. Oberst."

"Now get back to work. I don't care how you do it,

you and your Jews, but get my compound built!"

With an expression of defeat and exasperation, Sol executed an about-face and strode off. Like it or not, you will learn who is king here, Solomon, Erich thought. You will have to acknowledge that, as you will finally have to acknowledge the true parentage of the child.

In an effort to set the incident aside, at least for the time being, Erich reassessed the state of the encampment. He told Pleshdimer, who was overseeing the completion of the headquarters tent, to make sure that the Jews bladed the deck evenly; he didn't want everything lopsided—his bed and operations table, especially—in what would be his command post and his home for God only knew how long. Pleshdimer saluted but Erich didn't return the gesture. He would not .waste the recognition on someone not truly a soldier, particularly one whom Hempel had illegally made a corporal because the fat Kapo had a knack for finding succulent boys for the major to bugger. As far as Erich was concerned, Pleshdimer should have a machine gun shoved up his ass and the trigger pulled.

The man gave him the creeps. Slit the throats of his two young daughters, people said. Hung them from a rafter so that they would bleed into pans, which blood Pleshdimer fed to his prized sow. For that he had been sentenced to Sachsenhausen and placed in charge of honest, hard-working men whose only crime was that they had been born Jewish. Come to think of it, he saw why Hempel appreciated the Kapo. They were two of a kind.

Where was Hempel, anyway? He should be supervising all of this. "Kapo! Where is the major?" Erich called out at the fat man's receding back.

Pleshdimer glanced furtively at the Zana-Malata's hut, just beyond the perimeter of the camp. "I don't know, Herr Oberst."

Idiot, Erich thought, and headed toward the hermit's shack. Halfway there it occurred to him that perhaps he had not been entirely wise in instructing the Kapo to tell the prisoners to do *anything*. Who knew *how* he would go about enforcing the command?

By now, Erich was no more than a dozen meters from the hut. He could see Hempel's boots, resting against the outside wall. Suddenly he did not wish to venture closer. He hadn't seen the Zana-Malata since their arrival, and didn't want to. The syphilitic had made a fool of him and the dogs, no denying that.

"Major Hempel!"

After several moments the major emerged, pushing through the zebu-hide door and descending the three shallow steps. He did not bother to salute, or to excuse his lack of boots. He was chewing vigorously.

"I am giving the Jews permission to hold a religious Service," Erich said. "It will boost their productivity." He felt instantly annoyed at himself for rationalizing his actions. "Tell your men not to interfere with the proceedings."

To Erich's surprise, the major offered no objections. Not even a look of disdain. His face remained bland, as unruffled as his silver hair. Erich found himself glancing from the major's forehead to the armpits of his army blouse. The man never seemed to sweat, despite the withering humidity.

"My men have been without fresh meat for weeks," Hempel said. He pulled a piece of cartilage from his mouth, examined it, and tossed it away.

"There was plenty of meat aboard the *Altmark*—"

"I said *fresh* meat," Hempel interrupted. "Aboard ship, everything was canned."

To emphasize his remark he lifted a brow and gazed over Erich's shoulder—he was more than a head taller—toward the edge of the rain forest, where one of the zebus was tied to a stake. The animals had drifted in and out of the meadow, but Erich could not recall having seen one tethered.

He weighed the request. "Am I to take it that the beast belongs to your syphilitic friend?"

Hempel shrugged, as if he either did not know or did not care.

"Go ahead," Erich said, "but any ownership problems are your responsibility. If you know who owns the animal, arrange for some kind of payment."

Not that he really cared, Erich thought. The Zana-Malata had embarrassed him: taking the man's cow—or whatever—would be just punishment.

With two fingers, Hempel signaled to a guard who was lounging, a rifle in hand and a straw in his mouth, beside three prisoners installing metal bands on poles. The soldier pulled the weed from between his lips and started running.

Pandemonium ensued. Within seconds half-a-dozen guards were galloping, yelling, toward the zebu. Befuddled, it simply stood and watched them come on, swinging jouncing carbines off their shoulders. Behind them trundled Pleshdimer, belly flopping, eyes glistening like huge fat globules.

He and the guards formed a semicircle around the animal, which stood without moving, apparently torn between attack and an attempt to break her tether and make a run for it. When none of the men moved closer, she returned to cropping the nearly barren ground on which she was hobbled.

Hempel checked the action on his Mann, glanced at Misha, who had thrust his head out of the door of the hut, and reholstered the weapon. He looked as if he were about to stalk toward the zebu, but instead he went back to the steps and called the boy to come to him, using the same tuneless whistle with which he had commanded his wolfhound.

CHAPTER FOUR

Misha heard Hempel's whistle, but he did not move. Despite having watched the Zana-Malata and Hempel dine on the wolfhound the night before, and again today, he had not come to terms with the fact that he was expected to act as Boris' replacement.

"A mongrel like you should consider this an honor," Hempel had said, placing the dog's collar around the boy's neck. "Boris was every bit a thoroughbred, presented to me by Himmler himself. He would consider you a poor replacement."

Misha tugged at the collar. His fingers came away with several dog hairs stuck in the cracks of his broken nails. He pulled the hairs out and blew them away.

Coughing the dry, hacking cough that had started almost from the moment Hempel put the band around his neck, though the collar didn't feel all that tight,

Misha wiped his hands on the sides of his raggedy pants. From his crouched position he could see through the gap between the zebu hide and the door frame. He had heard the conversation between Hempel and Erich, and knew what was to come. He could only guess at what the major's mood would be afterwards.

Though the hut was dark and stank of food, the fact that he was alone provided a few moments of relief from the constant expectation of bad happenings. The only other time he could think was at night, when Hempel slept and Misha lay awake, going over the list of good things and bad things that had happened to him in his life, making sure the balance was still all right. Some nights he went over his plans for killing Pleshdimer; others, he mapped out in exquisite detail several alternative plans for killing Hempel. And he had added the Zana-Malata: alive, on the bad side; dead, on the good side. Not that the Zana-Malata had done anything bad to him. Yet. He must be waiting, like Pleshdimer had done. When Misha was at the camp, Pleshdimer had treated him like the other prisoners. Better, maybe, once Hempel *adopted* him. That hadn't changed until they were out of the camp. Then the major started to reward Pleshdimer by allowing him to hurt Misha.

Pleshdimer wasn't allowed to do the *thing*, but that didn't mean much because it wasn't what the Kapo wanted. Tying Misha down and hurting him with the edge of his knife, that was what he wanted. Being mean. Threatening him. Making him scared.

How he hated all of them, Misha thought, edging outside because he had no other option. He couldn't pretend to be asleep, because Hempel had seen him glancing through the doorway. If he tried to stay inside, Hempel would come to drag him out, or worse yet send Pleshdimer to get him. Besides, the Zana-Malata would be back soon, and just looking at the syphilitic made Misha want to vomit. He sensed that the black man was evil, not just ugly.

There was hating and hating, Misha decided. The one kind was for a reason, like the way he felt about the people who had taken away his parents. And Pleshdimer and Hempel. Anything about them was automatically on the bad side of the list.

Then there was hating like the way he felt about Boris, which had little to do with the wolfhound and almost everything to do with its owner. True, he had never especially liked Boris, but he knew that was from how he felt about Hempel and not from any particular dislike of the dog. Perhaps, had the animal been properly trained like Taurus and the other shepherds, it might have been more receptive to children; it might even have communicated with him, or he with it. He had certainly felt sorry for the dog when the boar gored it. To hear Boris' roar of pain followed by a cry of helplessness and then silence had chilled him.

And to end up being cooked and eaten!

He couldn't really hate Boris after that, Misha decided, as he pushed through the zebu hide and blinked in the light.

"I was calling you, Misha," Hempel said. "Come. I want you to be present for the first flowing of island blood."

Chapter five

The entire series of events was staged and unmilitary, Erich thought as he watched Misha come out of the hut in a half-crouch. Hempel motioned for the boy to follow as he strode toward the zebu and its would-be killers.

Erich started after the major but was stopped in his tracks by the trainer he had nicknamed Fermi. The man approached him, holding a closely choke-chained Pisces at heel at his side. The dog kept glancing toward the zebu and the guards but made no attempt to pull his trainer in that direction. His obedience pleased Erich, after the display of insubordination with the Zana-Malata when they had arrived.

Fermi looked down at the red dust on his boots. "The guards have been talking all morning about killing the zebu," he said in a quiet tone of respect. "Fresh meat would be fine, especially after the weeks on the ship. I would like to make certain there will be portions for us and for the dogs."

"What makes you think I would neglect my animals or my trainers?"

"You have a lot on your mind, sir."

Erich was flabbergasted at the intimation that he could overlook his primary responsibility. His primary love. "You and the dogs will be taken care of," he said, somewhat more angrily than he had intended.

Fermi glanced up. "Thank you, sir." He saluted and made his way toward the kennel area.

Removing his cap, Erich wiped his forehead with the back of his hand. In this heat it was no wonder the dogs were suffering, he thought. But suffering was one thing, brain fever another. Though they didn't have that, the danger of its happening was real. Already they were irritable and uncoordinated, not at all the fine corps of healthy animals he had loaded onto the ship. He could only pray that they would make the adjustment soon, or he would find himself in charge of a ghost unit.

"Does it really take that many men to kill a tethered animal?"

Erich turned, startled to find Miriam behind him and annoyed that he had not heard her approach. He prided himself on being aware of what was going on, not only around him, but anywhere nearby. Of thinking like a dog, he had told people when he was young. "Don't you start in on me as well," he said.

"Oh yes, by all means, let the boys play. Maybe you should dust off your javelin and join them."

My javelin, Erich thought, wondering what had become of that. He'd been so proud of his skills with it as a youth, had even fantasized about participating in the Olympics, and he'd come close, too. Miriam walked toward the doomed animal. He wondered if she expected him to follow. He did so. He would not join in the sport, as she called it. He had never killed for sport. In fact, he had never actually killed anything. Except Grace, Taurus' grandmother, who was nine-tenths dead by the time he'd used his javelin to put her out of her misery. And Achilles, of course. Taurus' mother. He had killed her. But that wasn't by choice, either. Not his choice. That was Hitler's doing. Erich was merely following orders, as any good soldier must.

If only Miriam could understand that. Solomon, also, but Miriam most of all.

He watched her move toward the zebu. The cow about to be killed seemed to draw her irresistibly, as if it needed her presence to dignify its slaughter. She stood slightly apart from the guards, who had lined up in front of it like a firing squad.

The animal kept feeding, pulling up her head every now and again to stare at her executioners, as if she defied them to look her in the eye.

"Let's not ruin the meat," Hempel said, striding up. "Just one of you will do. Johann?"

"Sir?" the blond radio operator asked.

"You're the youngest. Put a bullet through her brain."

"Yes, sir!" The youth raised and sighted his Mauser. Erich felt a brief though undefined satisfaction when Miriam turned away, momentarily shutting her eyes.

The shot sent birds twittering from the forest.

The cow bellowed and staggered in a circle, head turned around nearly to her back as though she were troubled by insects along her spine. Her protest rolled through the morning and set the dogs howling. Then she toppled sideways, as if she had been pushed over by some enormous force. Her legs stiffened even as she dropped and her head nodded twice against the ground; her tail slapped once, and she lay still.

Johann grinned and lowered the gun. A hush fell upon the pasture and the surrounding ring of forest. Erich could see the animal clearly: ribs prominent, rheumy-eyed, covered with flies. Shouting, the guards pulled out daggers and threw themselves upon the beast, laughing as they slashed the belly and gutted her. Pleshdimer squirmed among the others like the largest member of a litter, squealing as he tore out the upper intestines. They gleamed like sausages. He drew them toward his mouth, as if he could not wait for the cookpot before he gorged himself, then changed his mind and wrapped them around his neck like a boa.

C HAPTER SIX

"A pretty killing, you think?"

Bruqah knew that to the foreigners' ears—all but Miriam who understood him intuitively, and Solomon, who was learning to do so—his words, spoken in his melodic voice, often acted contrapuntally to his meaning. Eventually they would all understand, even Colonel Erich Germantownman. Understand and remember.

"You walk with the grace of a man who hears secret music in his head," Miriam said, as if the dancer in her had suddenly become acutely conscious of her clumsiness.

Bruqah smiled, acknowledging the compliment. As always, he carried his polished, carved, lily-wood walking stick, and the mouselemur sat at the nape of his neck, clinging to his hair. He was shawled from shoulders to waist in his white *lamba*. Already taller than everyone else, it created the illusion he wanted—that he towered above them. They were so easy to trick, these foreigners, he thought. They drew fast and faulty conclusions because doing so was less tedious to them than thinking. By creating the assumption of magic for themselves, they rendered his skills as a master illusionist superfluous. He had appeared with the mouselemur no more than twice before they took to whispering of it as his familiar. The same was true of his appearances and disappearances...as if from nowhere, to nowhere. They never quite felt his absence and always anticipated his presence, which was just the way he wanted it.

"I tell myself this Rosh Hashanah of Solomon's must be of great concern to you. Must be, or you would not encourage this sacrifice," he told Miriam.

"Killing the zebu has nothing to do with what the Jews want," Erich butted in. "The guards know nothing about the Holy Day."

Bruqah smiled again, condescendingly this time, and brought the mouselemur around against his chest. He stroked its fur and ran his fingers along the thick tail that tapered abruptly at the end like the nib of a fountain pen. The creature made stuttery, appreciative sounds.

"I think they know. I think they know more than you think, Mister Erich Germantownman. You are full of death, you Germans. Yes, I think they know." He pointed toward the Nazi flag, which dangled—as though wilted by the humidity—from the first pole the

Jews had erected, one near where the gate was being built. "Even your flag is the color of death. We Malagash wear red and black as shrouds."

"So do we, since the Nazis came to power," Miriam said.

Bruqah shifted his gaze back toward the zebu. The animal's master had allowed it to overgraze. He pointed toward the cow's barren patch of ground. "All over Madagascar...the same." He allowed his anger to enter his husky voice. It was simple, yet no one seemed capable of understanding: they burned the forests for the *savoka* to grow, then grazed the zebu until even that grass was gone. He shook his head sadly. "I was once the worst offender."

"You?" Miriam asked.

Until the trees taught me, Bruqah thought, and I learned from the lemurs. All of which took lifetimes. "There is a saying. *Omby milela-bato, matin'ny tany mahzotra*—the zebu will lick bare stone, and die in the earth it loves." He ran his hand from the mouselemur's head to its tail, causing the tiny animal to shudder with apparent joy. "We Malagash measure our worth by our cows, but we allow them to kill the land that is our mother...and theirs."

"We Germans measure our worth by—what, Erich?" Miriam said in an ugly tone, looking at the butchered zebu with undisguised disgust. An apparent wave of pain, reflected in her face, passed over her. "By our...our scientific accomplishments?" Her breaths began to saw. "Or our industrial efficiency?" She shot Erich an angry glance. "Or by our capacity for killing?"

"You weren't always this harsh, Miriam." Erich's voice trailed off. He stared past them, as though something held him motionless. Neither was it a sight that gave Bruqah pleasure.

At the edge of the rain forest stood the Zana-Malata, holding up the head of Hempel's huge wolfhound. Bruqah watched Erich carefully. He saw him glance from the dog to Hempel and back. Rather than revulsion, the colonel's face held an expression of anticipation and something tantamount to envy. He wants the major's head on a stick, and the sooner the better, Bruqah thought.

"I wasn't always hard and you weren't always a Nazi," Miriam said.

The words were barely out of her mouth when her eyes rolled backward and her knees buckled. Bruqah stepped forward, but Erich was closer to her. He caught her as she collapsed. She winced and, clutching her belly, doubled over in pain.

"I am ashamed to be part of the human race," she said in a whisper. She looked at Bruqah, and the animal wrapped around his neck. "Small wonder you hold lemurs in higher esteem than man." Glaring at Erich, she straightened up and pulled free of him.

"Concerning some men," Bruqah said, "I could not agree more."

Chapter Seven

"The guards do delight in death," Erich said.

"Don't all Nazis?" Miriam asked.

With what he felt was great self-control, Erich refrained from making an angry retort in the face of her insolence. He watched a zebu foreleg being drawn down like a lever while the meat was sliced near the socket. Someone produced an axe, and a hacking against bone began. Why don't they just quarter the cow and be done with it, he thought.

"I need to sit," Miriam said.

She stared at the grass for a moment as if examining it for crawling things, then, holding onto Bruqah's arm, sat down. He stood over her like a bodyguard—the two of them apart and yet together in a way that Erich envied. Away from the compound, he felt closer to her, less restricted. He experienced a territorial need to defend her, as if Bruqah represented a threat. He was worried about her, in much the same way that he was worried about Taurus. They were his; they belonged to him. He had brought few enough possessions with him to the island, so it made sense to him that he would want to ensure that the ones he had brought were not endangered.

He started to say something to Miriam, but saw by the set of her mouth that anything he said would only trigger more harsh words. Turning on his heel, he walked toward the hill that he had been wanting to explore. It lay at the other side of the pasture, a fair enough distance away from the encampment that he thought it might afford him a place to be alone when he needed to think things through without constant interruptions.

In no mood to encounter anyone, he skirted the meadow and the Zana-Malata's hut by taking a trail through the jungle on the steeper, northwest side of the saddle formed by the island's two hills. En route, he distracted himself by trying to identify some of the flora and fauna he had read about in the books he'd passed on to Miriam. According to those, the rain forest abounded with life, yet he had seen comparatively little of it. He could only conclude that his eyes were not yet trained to see through Madagascar's disguises—the way his stomach was not yet trained to digest the figs and wild ginger he had eaten, forcing him to drink half a bottle of schnapps during the night to quiet his stomach cramps.

Erich began to climb. At first he found himself

fascinated by the series of tall, carved, wooden posts which, judging by the curved zebu horns at the top of each one, were the burial totems he had seen pictured in his books about Madagascar. A few were taller than his head, but most were chest-high and about the size of his bicep in diameter, stuck like ornate needles in a green pincushion. He found them beautiful and odd and could not but wonder who might be buried beneath them.

Slowly his interest gave way to fatigue. As his calves and thighs started to feel the strain of the climb, he regretted his lack of a machete and thanked whoever it was who had forged the existing narrow path to the top. If this was to become his hill, his refuge from the problems of Hempel and Miriam and the Jews, there would have to be a wider path. And, he thought wryly, he had better rid himself of the thirty-one-year-old city-boy weakness that had developed in his muscles since the demands of rank and family had curtailed his daily workouts. He would take Miriam's advice, he decided, ignoring the spirit in which it had been given. He would fashion himself a javelin and use that and daily walks up this hill to get into shape.

He put his arm back, took several long strides which carried him through the last of the trees and onto the top of the hill, and threw an imaginary javelin. The action felt good.

Very good indeed.

He leaned against a heavily sculpted totem and saw that there were more than two dozen of them, each bearing the skull of an ox. At the crest of the hill stood a stone menhir—what looked like a three-sided rock house dug into the hillside. The roof was a huge stone slab overgrown with moss. At the northwest corner stood a larger totem. It, too, bore the skull of an ox, this time crowned with a woven liana garland.

He examined it up close. He could make out miniature zebu horns, curling leaves, carved lemurs standing on top of one another's backs and looking outward with enormous eyes.

He put out his hand to touch the totem, and quickly withdrew it as the thought occurred to him that the syphilitic had probably forged the path and woven the garland. Automatically, he turned full circle to make sure that the hideous black man wasn't standing somewhere watching him. Assured that he was alone, he forced himself to relax.

He resolved to order Hempel and his men to open and examine the crypt, for who knew what buried treasure might lie inside. It could even contain some key to the true story of his hero, Count Augustus Benyowsky.

Standing on the crest of the hill, Erich watched the tropical evening prepare to swallow the *Altmark*. By morning, the ship would be gone, on its way to rendezvous with the *Spee*, which needed "mother" to feed her oil and pick up prisoners, British seamen from the *Africa Shell*—her third victim sunk south of Madagascar. He felt little regret that they were leaving so soon. He had only been on the island for two days, yet he felt oddly at home.

If only....

He looked down at the area he had chosen for the base camp. The encampment was roughly the size of a soccer field. The far corner had been set aside for the Jews, some of whom were still at work emplacing the tall posts of an eastern sentry tower. Others, barehanded, strung barbed concertina wire across the fences they had just completed. As for electrifying the fences—which Hempel was trying to insist upon—there were other, more urgent uses for the generator when they got it up and running. First and foremost, it had to be used for lighting the compound at night and for pumping water into the water tank if the rain could not keep it full.

He turned his attention from the compound to its second flanking hill, a second knoll. The hill itself was starker and narrower than this one and looked almost like a natural chimney. It was shielded by a canopy of trees alongside the sheer limestone cliff that formed its western edge. The natural camouflage made it a perfect southeast sentry post for the encampment. He'd have the Jews cut a road up the back and build a breastworks, an easy job, once that Jew, Goldman, finished welding the armor plate to the front of the small tank as a blade. The *kleiner Panzerbefehlswagen*, with its machine gun and armor plating, would serve as bulldozer and, later, as a deterrent to any would-be attackers from the main island. So it had proved to be a good idea after all, bringing the tank instead of the obvious equipment. Proved that no one, not even Otto Hempel, could be wrong about everything. Of course, Hempel had wanted to waste precious cargo space on a large raft-barge to bring the tank ashore. Erich had found the much simpler solution of using the emptied fuel drums from their resupply of the *Spee* to make a raft much like the floating bridges they'd built in his Wandervögel days.

Which left only the plane, in terms of large equipment. There was certainly no place on this little island for a landing strip, so the Storch had been retrofitted with floats. It would take off from the lagoon. That was Hempel's domain, as were the reconnaissance flights which had to be made over the mainland.

Yes, Erich thought, he could be happy here, if only Taurus were not taking the climate so hard, and if only he could avoid conflict between his trainers and Hempel's men, and the major's syphilitic friend, and....

Putting the question of Miriam and Solomon aside to examine later, along with his assessment of Hempel's true motives in accepting this assignment, he looked across the meadow at the trainers, exercising their animals while Taurus lay helpless in the medical tent. Picturing her haunches swaying like the butt of an overweight old woman, he cursed the responsibilities that separated him from the dog. Yet, guiltily, he admitted he was also thankful for the whirlwind of duties. Achilles' execution was merciful compared to what he was watching her daughter endure.

The pampas of Argentina yearned for the likes of his shepherds! Maybe he should use the seaplane for escape. Take the dogs and the baby, and let the rest rot. From what Perón had told him, Buenos Aires seethed with women beside whom Miriam was a dishrag.

Yet despite his desire to leave, Mangabéy Island seemed to speak to him in tongues he understood. It was his, in a way the Rathenau estate could never have been.

Gazing at the horizon, he tried to imagine with what newborn hope Benyowsky must have stood on this same hill and peered over the aquamarine bay that was to become his kingdom—the site of his *heldentod*—his hero's death. After the white suffocation of Siberia, the Hungarian must have been enraptured by the green lace shawl of rain forest and swamp. It was here, on Mangabéy, that he had built a block-and-bamboo hospital to quarantine those of his men who suffered from smallpox. Here, he found rest from the rigors inland…until he was forced to open the veins of his beautiful French wife, to bleed her of malaria.

Or maybe the other version was true, the one that had been as much in his dreams as in Benyowsky's diary. Erich had dreamt about the ships *Peter* and *Paul*—which the Count and his fellow prisoners had stolen in Vladivostok with the aid of Aphanasia, the warden's daughter. Barred by France from founding a colony on Formosa but given a go-ahead for Madagascar, he had sold the leaky vessels in Canton, where Aphanasia had expired of a fever. Then Benyowsky sailed to Paris, to fetch his French wife. In the dream she had become a ballerina with the Stuttgart and was on tour in Paris. He had seen them sailing into Mangabéy.

Erich struggled to recall the rest, but the memory eluded him. He lifted his hand and with an index finger surveyed the shoreline, until he located the mouth of the Antabalana River. There, in 1776, Benyowsky declared Madagascar independent and, inspired by his friend Benjamin Franklin, wrote its first Constitution. He could feel the Count's presence, flickering pure and transcendent in the gathering evening, like the light of the fireflies that sparkled along the meadow's edge. Even the bats, wheeling and diving and soaring, seemed like black, winged offerings in the Hungarian's honor, and the very frogs seemed to chorus his name: *Ben-yow-sky, Ben-yow-sky, Ben-yow-sky.*

He shut his eyes, the better to recall one of his favorite scenes in the Count's diary. He could see it clearly: three thousand Sakalava warriors, in a circle according to region and rank, prostrate at the Hungarian's feet. He could hear the drums pounding as dancers swayed in the moonlight, see the Count and the King of the North slicing open their left breasts with an *assegai*, throwing the spear aside, sucking each other's blood and swearing fealty while the warriors rose to toast Benyowsky with clay chalices brimming with the blood of freshly killed zebus.

Ampanandza-be! they cried.

"Chief-of-chiefs!"

Ampanandza-be!

"We have returned," Erich said in a low, strained voice as the warriors' yowling echoed through his skull.

Learning about the Count and knowing that he,

Erich, was coming here, had been more than enough inducement for Erich to do his homework.

So what *had* he learned, outside of the obvious, he wondered.

That the rain forest of northeastern Madagascar— the world's densest—was home to the Betsileo, and scattered groups of Antandroy and Tstimileo also lived there, as did the Tanal, the warriors legendary for their ferocity. That together, the tribes could prove a formidable force, and with the probable exception of the Tanal were known to unite against a common enemy. Hadn't Benyowsky said in his diary that thirty thousand northeastern Malagasy had gathered to pay him homage? The Count was given to hyperbole, but the point was not lost on the colony's European financiers: the tribes could come together, and quickly, in support of a new venture. Or against it.

What was most frequently said of the Count was no exaggeration—that his greatest talent lay in turning enemies into friends.

Erich sensed rather than heard a soft whimpering. He cocked his head and listened. Convinced that it was Taurus calling out to him for help, and angry at himself for wasting time better spent, he rushed down the hill and across the marshy ground toward the compound.

Chapter Eight

Miriam awoke in a stupor and gazed blankly around the medical tent, her eyes bleary and puffy. She remembered heat shimmering on the meadow; guards, with knives drawn, descending on a fallen zebu; sudden light-headedness. Right at this moment, she had no active memory of how she had made it back after watching the nauseating display of bloodlust in the meadow.

She lay there concentrating and bits and pieces returned to her. Like fragments of a dream, they did not fully add up, yet she had confidence that ultimately they would. She saw herself sitting on the grass; Bruqah's singsong voice and kindly hands held her safe and she did not pull away.

"What do you wish to say to me, Bruqah?" she'd asked, looking up into his eyes.

"We believe the dead speak softly through the voices of the unborn, but only some can hear them."

The rain forest had seemed close, as if the pasture and compound had shrunk. She felt protected by it. Sunlight had seeped into the verdant growth. Where before she had seen only darkness, she saw slim unbranched trunks, speckled with light and latticed with tree-fern, and lace-fans of lichen and moss.

There is a way through the forest, Bruqah's eyes told her. Hempel's men dragged the zebu carcass toward camp, leaving a wet, fly-ridden trail. Pleshdimer pranced along, a clown in a parade, the intestines around his neck like a boa, and she'd felt ashamed to be part of their human race...

With effort she sat up. Her flesh felt clammy. A medical gown, damp with sweat, clung to her skin. Someone had undressed her, probably Franz, the corpsman. Certainly not Erich, whom she vaguely recalled having seen striding toward one of the hills.

He was doubtless angry at her for something, and if not at her directly, then at himself for loving her.

She put up her hand to her face as if it still stung— as if the handprint were even now upon her cheek where the bastard had slapped her while they were aboard ship.

And why had he hit her?

That one was easy to answer, she thought. Because she'd lost patience with the whole lie and admitted her love for Sol. As if Erich hadn't known that all along. The question that was far less simple to answer was why his hitting her had been unexpected; she had long known of his uncontrollable temper, his violence, his subsequent remorse...so seemingly heartfelt, so ultimately shallow.

Not only had he hit her, he'd hit so hard that she had immediately begun what proved to be false labor. In the midst of contractions, she had begged Erich not to hurt Solomon.

"I won't kill him, if that's what you mean," Erich had said, looking at her with a scorn he had in the past reserved only for the likes of Otto Hempel. "I'm going to let him get as close to you as he can before I take you away from him. Forever." His look of contempt had darkened. "I can live with a marriage of convenience, but not with being made a fool of!"

Since then, with each passing hour, she had grown increasingly sick with apprehension. It wasn't just the pregnancy or the mind-numbing heat that was making her ill; it was waiting for Erich's anger to resurface. Someday, she knew, he would drop his pretense about wanting to help the exiled Jews, however much he might currently believe in the façade, and act out his hatred of Sol. If that meant killing everyone to rationalize his revenge, so be it. He had the capacity for such a thing, though he swore that violence repelled him. In reality, it was violence in others that he loathed, not his own.

In an effort to stop the replay in her mind, she pushed aside the mosquito netting, grabbed her hairbrush from the bed stand, and began to brush with firm and practiced strokes. How Erich had loved to look at her, she thought, loved to stroke her legs and hair.

Especially her hair. How she hated that hair, right now! ...lank and sticky against her skin. She hacked at it with the brush but, quickly enervated, let her hand drop to the sheet. She sat staring down at the brush, too emotionally drained even to cry.

From beyond the screen separating her cot from the rest of the tent she heard the dogs' whimpering. Scissors, she thought. Corpsman's kit.

She swung her legs over the side of the cot·and struggled to stand. The action, though minimal, made her head swim. The tamped-earth floor felt cool against her bare, swollen feet, but only momentarily relieved her stupor. She took off her gown and put on a cotton slip-dress. Giving up, she grabbed the hand mirror from the bed stand and stumbled forward.

The two sick dogs who were her tent companions lifted their heads as she neared. For now, they were the only patients in the tent other than herself. Two other patients, showing the onset of malaria, had been quarantined in their tents. Several prisoners were also suffering from illnesses and accidents, but Erich had given in to Hempel's demand that they be treated in the wired-off Jewish sleeping area the guards had named "the ghetto."

Miriam gave Taurus, craning up the farthest, a scratch on the ear, and looked around. Except for the mess tent, the medical tent was the largest in the compound. One screened-off corner, with pallets for flooring, served as a scrub area and held the trestle table that would be her delivery table. Though she was frightened about delivering in such a remote area, she felt confident with

Tyrolt. The ship's doctor was gentle, caring, and obviously skilled from his years of mending men at sea, despite his lacking all the academic training a city physician might possess.

She found the corpsman's bag beside the microscope and rummaged among tubes and tools and gauze until she located the scissors. A mosquito droned near her ear; she batted at it hard enough to kill a horsefly. Damn things! Despite her request that the flaps be left open in the hope of a breeze, the tent was a bug-filled hothouse. Petroleum jelly smeared on the cot braces helped keep crawling insects out of her bed, but the flying bugs ate unremittingly. No matter how she arranged the cot's mosquito netting, insects found a way inside, especially the vicious gnats the soldiers called no-see-ums.

She leaned on a pallet that had been left propped against a tent pole, positioned what passed as a mirror between the slats, and gripped a clump of hair. Taurus whimpered and put her head down, looking up with woeful eyes. Miriam stared into the mirror, at a blotchy, puffy face she barely recognized. Had pregnancy changed her so much, or was it the awful voyage and this heat, this terrible heat?

Or just being married to Erich Alois?

She snipped—hard. Hair dropped into her lap. She cut again, and the second clump seemed to fall in slow motion. She felt faint and sick to her stomach at the same time.

Taurus nuzzled her head against Miriam's hand. "Poor thing," she said, dropping the scissors. She glanced over at Aquarius, who was making a feeble attempt to get into the act. "And you," she said gently. "You aren't going to make it, are you?" Erich's dog was in horrible pain from dysplasia, but it was Aquarius, unable to recover from seasickness, that was dying. Miriam listened to the breathing. Hers, theirs. Taurus', raspy but regular; Aquarius', a rattle. She felt sorry for Ernst Müller, Aquarius' trainer. The man was so upset by his animal's condition that he'd become hysterical the last time he had visited, and been ordered from the tent. She had seen the hurt in Erich's eyes when he had had to do that, and wondered anew how any one man could love so much and hate so much at the same time.

If only it weren't for the child, she'd even now be with Sol.

Or maybe she wouldn't be on this island at all. Maybe none of them would. With Juan Perón's help, and without Erich's knowledge, she had finagled Sol's release from Sachsenhausen and onto the ship bound for Madagascar. Getting herself on board was no problem as long as Erich believed the child she carried was his.

As to which of the two men was the natural father, she had no idea. She and Sol had been secretly married, not by civil decree but in the sight of God, before Sol left for Amsterdam. Her civil marriage to Erich had come later, when he told her that Sol had been captured and sent to one of the camps. She'd believed she needed someone with influence in the Party to keep Sol alive.

New fury filled her. She retrieved the scissors and

chopped at her hair again. If this would relieve the heat and Erich's ardor, she would crop herself bald.

She stopped and shut her eyes. Block out the world, she thought. Let me faint——

——*She is lying on stone, her ankles fastened by straps. Shallow depressions in the stone fit her form perfectly. As though made for her. She turns her head, and beyond the open door she sees tiny gyrating men, dancing as jerkily as marionettes. Sweat streams off her forehead as contractions roll through her with a pain she swears aloud she cannot endure. Not one more——*

The baby kicked hard, drawing Miriam out of her dream. If indeed it had been a dream. In a state of semi-awareness, she tuned in to several conversations that seemed to be taking place around her. She had heard a few of the voices before, at other such moments, though where she could not at once recall. Emotionally, she had a sensation of *déjà vu*, that sinking sense of eavesdropping on the past, and yet it did not seem truly to be her past. She was bathed in sweat and filled with a new fear. Judith, Emanuel, Lise—the names were linked by only one thing: Solomon's dybbuk-inspired visions.

As a lover and a friend, as a wife and a *Jew*, Miriam knew she should, *must*, consider Sol's visions real—both the ones inspired by the dybbuk, which appeared to be happenstances in some kind of universe that paralleled their own, and the psychic flashes, the glimpses into their own futures, to which he had become so much more prone since the dybbuk had left him.

Had not Beadle Cohen called him a visionary? Had

not Rabbi Nathan, internationally recognized for his writings about the Kabbala, confirmed this?

Had they not both said that he had been possessed by a dybbuk—a wandering soul seeking atonement for sins it had unintentionally committed while alive? But when Nathan tried to exorcise it, the dybbuk was already gone. Only the visions remained. Haunting Sol.

And now me, Miriam told herself in terror. And now me.

She shook her head. She could not fall apart, not with the baby to consider. Besides, her trials were nothing compared to what Solomon and the other prisoners had endured.

One way or another, she would figure this out. "Right, Taurus?" She scratched the dog's head again.

Taurus looked at her with dark, velvety, pain-dulled eyes and responded with a whimper. She tried, and failed, to wiggle from the box. Miriam stood up and, clinging to a tent pole for balance, looked out through the green netting at the encampment. A light rain had begun, more mist than drizzle and completely unlike the previous quick tropical downpours that had struck with the swiftness of a passing cloud and ended as quickly. She stepped outside and lifted her face to the mist, as if she were welcoming a lover. The slightly cooler air enfolded her like a huge sweaty hand. The grass will like this, too, she thought, noticing that a considerable amount of grass was gone already, tramped down to spongy, red laterite soil as the men worked. During the time she had been in the tent—an hour or so, she guessed, looking toward the dusky sunset sky, its clouds the color of dirty gauze—the prisoners had finished putting up the northern fence. Taut barbed wire twisted between rolls of concertina wire. It was beginning to look like Sachsenhausen.

Then she heard the quiet cadence of Hebrew coming from near the spring, and she felt her spirits lift.

"Dog food would taste better than what they've been feeding us!" a voice called from the direction of the mess canopy.

"Couldn't taste worse! I can hardly wait for that zebu to be ready."

She jumped as a guard pounded his mess kit against the garbage bucket for emphasis and metal clanged against metal.

"Dog food? Those goddamn shepherds eat better than us," one of the men said, loudly enough for everyone to hear.

Several others with Mausers over their shoulders formed a knot around him, dangling their kits by the handles like a group of armed beggars.

As usual, it occurred to her with a kind of perverse pleasure, she did the opposite of what Erich would have wanted. She pushed through the men and, conscious of the hard lust in their eyes, entered the mess tent. What sexual innovations, she wondered, could they think up for a woman nine months pregnant!

The smell in the tent added to her nausea.

The cook strode forward and joined in the complaints. "It's that damn canned meat! How do they expect me to cook decent *Klopsen* with canned meat? Tonight, at the party, when we eat the cow, you'll taste cooking." He pressed together the tips of his fingers, kissed them noisily, and waved them in the air. "Once the generator's hooked up for refrigeration, all the food will be fine. Just like the Sturmbannführer says."

He walked away and stood, spoon in hand and arm against the tent pole, watching the Jews.

"He used bad meat on purpose. I'm sure he did," one of the men said under his breath.

Surely there's something in there that they like to eat, Miriam thought. She looked across at the supply tent, which held enough food to keep the nearly two hundred men fed for three months, until they learned to live off the land and on what the prisoners cultivated. It occurred to her that food was not the issue. *Boasting* was. These idiots were actually *boasting* about the hardships they were enduring. Good German soldiers, priding themselves on hardship. On hardship and on victory, no matter what the price.

Uncomfortable beneath the lewd stares from the guards, she crossed her arms beneath her breasts and looked apprehensively toward the knoll. While she was inside the mess tent, darkness had fallen with the rapidity of a stage curtain. She could just make out Erich half-striding, half-running toward the encampment. Over to one side, she noticed the ship's doctor and the unit corpsman, in earnest conversation, walk slowly in her direction.

"Don't worry about the delivery, Franz," she heard Tyrolt tell the corpsman in a hushed voice. "You'll do fine. I feel terrible having to leave her like this, but orders are orders. The *Altmark* must be gone by morning. Not that I'll be sorry to be away from this heat."

Leave? Miriam felt rising panic. The corpsman was pleasant enough, but he was no physician. She had thought—been told—that Tyrolt and the *Altmark* would still be around when she gave birth.

"She's more *blutarm* than I would have expected," the doctor went on, "but anemia is common under these circumstances. Make sure she eats red meat, and get rid of that man Pleshdimer. I know he's been helping out, but he has no business in a medical tent."

So the blood workups *were* more than mere precaution!

"I won't be able to bother the Herr Oberst unless it's an emergency. Even then one must be very careful unless it is a problem regarding the dogs."

Tyrolt looked around, and then replied quietly, "A fourth of this company treat dogs like humans, the rest treat humans like dogs. It makes me damn glad I'm navy. Your job, Franz, if you're half the humanitarian I think you are, is to bring what sanity you can to this craziness by giving the woman your utmost. She needs rest, proper food, and loving attention. Keep the Rottenführer and that goddamn syphilitic away from her. I saw them peering around the screen at her while she slept. Imagine waking to those two!"

He spotted her in the semi-darkness.

"How are you feeling, Miriam, and why aren't you resting?" he asked, in his gravelly voice. He smiled at her, and she returned his smile. She liked this tall, skinny man, with his Kaiser Wilhelm mustache and ever-present five o'clock shadow. He had made the long sea-voyage bearable for her, and along with Bruqah had helped her keep body and mind together following Erich's blow-up. Maybe Tyrolt did lack some of the experience and fancy academic training of a city physician, but he was gentle, caring, and obviously skilled. If only the *Altmark* were not sailing so soon, or if at least she had some guarantee that he would be on it when it returned with fresh supplies and, according to the plan, a new load of Jews.

"How do I feel? Hot, scared, irritable, and not a little terrified. What about you?"

"I feel...apolitical." He put an arm affectionately across her shoulders. "And more than a little philosophical. But then I usually do...which is doubtless why they've kept me so long at sea. I'd bore my patients to death if they didn't have to listen."

Releasing her, he stood back and looked at her carefully. "Your hair," he said. "What did you—"

"I cut it. It's *my* hair!"

Tyrolt chuckled. "Seems reasonable to me," he said. "I trust the Herr Oberst will not be too upset."

Miriam shrugged. She had bigger things to think about, like what it was going to be like giving birth here, with only Franz, an inexperienced corpsman, to help. The guards' stares drilling into her back made her feel all the less secure. Whom did they hate more, she wondered, the Jewish prisoners, or the Jewish wife of the colonel in charge of operations?

Not that she was Jewish anymore, according to the Reich. Hitler had decided that she had been "orphaned at birth and *stolen* by the Jews." She was a Rathenau, he said, only by name, not blood.

An unlikely charade, but not all that uncommon. One of Hitler's top generals had been Jewish, she was aware; his heritage had likewise been changed by official decree. Political and military need overruled prejudice when the situation warranted. She had consented to the decree, even to the making of a propaganda film in which she renounced Judaism "and all its evils," not only to save her own life and possibly Sol's, but also to put herself in a position where she might help other, less fortunate Jews.

Many of the prisoners did not consider her Jewish. "Better death than denial," she had heard whispered. And the guards, she was sure, considered her just some "Jew whore masquerading as a German."

As for Hempel's opinion of her, she thought, seeing the major walk into view, that could doubtless fill a book. He was flanked by Captain Dau from the *Altmark* on one side and by Misha on the other. Slapping his billyclub against his palm, he ambled across the compound. Immediately, some of the guards formed behind him. They were Totenkopfverbände—members of the Death's Head Unit—and the ugly looks on their faces showed they wished to live up to their name.

"Disgraceful," Hempel said. "I have never seen such behavior in an officer. Babying *Jews*. Pandering to their every demand. A religious service! What next?"

"Alois told me, 'A holy Jew is a happy Jew,' whatever that's supposed to mean," the ship's captain replied. "Well, I've washed my hands of it. I've no authority here over how he trains his animals, two- or four-legged, but it won't go unnoticed in my report, I can assure you of that. I tell you, it borders on treason!"

"He crossed that line a long time ago," Hempel said stiffly.

Almost involuntarily, Miriam linked her arm through Tyrolt's and put her head against his shoulder. She needed someone strong to keep her from lashing out at Hempel. Yet she could not help but continue to wonder what motive really lay behind Erich's orders that the Jews be treated humanely—as long as the work progressed on or ahead of schedule. She wanted to credit him with compassion, but she could not quite convince herself that he hadn't long since shed whatever modicum of it he might once have had. Could he think it possible that she would give her heart to him if he demonstrated some newfound ability to love?...or had he transcended that particular need and replaced it with some new conceit?

Maybe it was much simpler than that. Perhaps he had become afraid enough of the wrath of *his* God that he was willing to go to any lengths to obtain forgiveness, even if it meant infuriating Hempel into killing them all. Or could *that* be his purpose? To make *certain* that Hempel killed all of them?

"I can't stand this a minute longer," Miriam said. "I want to join Sol and the others."

"You can't, my dear, and you know it," Tyrolt whispered to her, looking down at her seriously. "No matter how much you'd like to." Casting a furtive glance in Dau's direction, he added, "Forgive me for saying so, but of late your feelings have become transparent."

He was right of course. She could no more join the other Jews than Erich could renounce the Party. For Sol's safety, the child's, her own, she must remain in Erich's custody for...how many more months—or years?

Hempel and Dau strode past them. Tyrolt left Miriam's side and faced the two officers, causing them to pause.

"You should not judge Herr Oberst Alois too harshly." Tyrolt lifted a brow, as if to indicate to the two officers that he wished his words to be given careful consideration. "People with the hope of freedom outwork slaves at a ratio of something like five to one."

Dau looked at him blankly. "Is this a medical opinion? If not, keep your heretical ideas to yourself, Herr Doktor." He turned to Hempel. "I shall take my farewells, Herr Sturmbannführer. I look forward to hearing that you have the encampment running and a good water supply secured. No doubt I will be one of the first to know, since once you have fulfilled the initial part of the plan I'll be ordered back here with new supplies and," he laughed, "old Jews. Funny, isn't it, how they all look old to me."

Hempel flipped his half-smoked cigarette toward Tyrolt's shoe and, advancing, glared as he ground it out with the toe of his boot.

"Rottenführer Pleshdimer!" he yelled.

The Kapo hurried from the kennel area. "Heil Hitler!"

"The Oberst said the Jews would be allowed their

filthy rites provided each day's work is completed up to then, is that not correct?"

The Kapo smirked. "Ja, Sturmbannführer!"

"The area was not properly policed." With the toe of his jackboot Hempel pointed toward the cigarette butt.

The Kapo saluted and lumbered off toward the Jews. The men took no notice, but from the gloom of the rain forest, a dozen eyes reflected the waning light. Probably lemurs, Miriam thought, her heart pounding with anger at Hempel. If the forest creatures weren't careful, their curiosity would earn them the stewpot.

Absently she scratched a mosquito bite on her arm. When she stopped, there was blood under her nail. "These damn bugs," she said. "No matter how I arrange the netting, they find a way inside. If you are still worried about my iron count.... And they'd better keep that fat Latvian Pleshdimer away from me," she said irritably. "I can't stand the sight of him. Last night I heard him outside the tent, mumbling about *Kalanaro* coming. God knows how long he stood there, staring at me. He and that hideous Zana-Malata."

She wanted to add, but did not, that Pleshdimer reminded her of Hitler's personal physician, that revolting Doctor Morrel who had performed the conception-date tests. Even Eva Braun, who doted on the Führer's every word about who and what were excellent, had told Miriam she found Morrel dirty and disgusting.

"Let's go over to the medical tent," Tyrolt said. "I want to give you a thorough examination.

Tomorrow...." He paused. "I have duties that will keep me aboard the *Altmark* for a while."

"I overheard you," Miriam told him. She took a deep breath to quell her rage and the threat of tears, and wondered why God could not keep Tyrolt on the island for a few more days.

CHAPTER NINE

"I examined Miriam as thoroughly as I could under the circumstances," Tyrolt said, speaking quietly to Erich as they headed toward the compound gate. "She should be able to manage. Physically. Just keep Pleshdimer and that syphilitic away from her, or she's likely to have a nervous breakdown." He hesitated. "And be sensitive to her condition when you see what she's done to her hair."

"Her hair?"

"She chopped it off. I can't say that I blame her, in this heat."

"What about Taurus?" Erich asked, almost as if he hadn't been listening. He had sat with his dog during Tyrolt's examination of Miriam.

"I am not a veterinarian, Herr Oberst. I have told you that before. You know the animal has dysplasia. You also know that there's little help in such cases. I could try a shot of morphine, but the results would be temporary, at best...."

They had reached the compound gate. Tyrolt put out his hand. "I almost forgot," he said. "Captain Dau sends his greetings."

"And I mine." Erich shook the man's hand. "Heil Hitler!"

"*Sieg* Heil!" The doctor smiled wryly.

Erich watched the physician head down the broad path that wended to the beach. Not a veterinarian. Then what good was he?

He caught sight of Pleshdimer strolling toward the mess tent. "Rottenführer!" he called out.

The corporal glanced anxiously toward the medical tent, and Erich saw the Zana-Malata scuttle like a beetle toward the concertina-wire fence. Maybe Tyrolt was right. He'd have to keep a closer eye on those two, and on Hempel as well. Worried about Taurus, he'd neglected a primary rule: In the chess game of life, stay at least six steps ahead of an adversary. He had already allowed Hempel too many moves since the wolfhound's death.

He increased his pace to catch up with Pleshdimer. "I could use a cup of good German coffee," he said as pleasantly as he could, falling into step with the corporal.

"Shall I bring you one—sir?" Pleshdimer avoided his eyes.

They reached the opening to the mess tent. Erich watched the men toss tin plates and army-issue cutlery into a large cast-aluminum tub. The clang of metal against metal was the only sound in the mess; gone was the usual raucous laughter of camaraderie between guards and sailors. The guards stood in line on one side of the tent, the trainers at the other, each group glaring. "I'm sorry to have missed the farewell dinner for the *Altmark*," Erich said in a slightly too-loud voice, trying to relieve the tension. Pretending to ignore the men's antagonism toward one another, he used a hotpad glove to lift the lid of the largest pot. "So that's how zebu smells. Gamier than a cow, but still beef."

"Shall I dish some up for you, sir?" the cook asked.

"I'm not hungry," Erich answered. "Whatever is left is to be split between the dogs and the Jews."

Hempel's men stiffened and a few of the trainers smiled.

"Do you have a problem with that?" he asked the guard closest to him. The man stared stonily ahead. "Good. And while you're about it, make sure the Jews' netting is in place. We have no need to deal with a mass outbreak of malaria."

"The Sturmbannführer will object, sir," Fermi said.

"To what, the food or the netting? I will inform him of my orders myself. I suppose I will find him with his new friend—"

"Eating the leftovers of the wolfhound, which he seems to prefer to this," the cook said.

He obviously bore no fondness for Hempel, Erich thought, before the meaning of the words took shape.

"He *ate* Boris? Are you saying the man *ate* his dog? If this is a joke—" He remembered Hempel emerging from the Zana-Malata's hut chewing, recalled the cartilage he had pulled from his mouth. Erich had assumed it was lemur, or some other local animal.

"As you say, it was *his* dog...*sir*," one of the guards said.

Without a further word, Erich strode out of the tent toward the Zana-Malata's hut. He found Hempel seated alone at an open fire. Probably the same spot where he roasted his wolfhound on a spit, Erich thought, with a feeling of sick disbelief. He wondered at which point in his grief the major had conceived of the idea to consume the animal.

Grief?

Erich thought about Taurus and the sympathetic pain that seized him whenever he visited her.

The campfire sputtered, sending sparks among the stars, then another figure appeared. At first he thought it was Misha or Pleshdimer, but with a sense of nervous anger, he realized it was the Zana-Malata. The major continued sitting with his head down.

Staying out of sight, Erich observed the black man. Tertiary stage syphilis, he guessed. Bruqah as usual had been enigmatic when mined for information, with that infuriating habit of speaking in riddles and losing his syntax as it pleased him. However, a picture had emerged of the Zana-Malata tribe, if one could call it that. Mulatto outcasts, ostracized because of the congenital syphilis nearly all of them carried. The disease was a legacy from their European-pirate forefathers, William Kidd among them, who had made Northern Madagascar a base of operations.

The gnawed mouth with its pink, frilly flesh; the rheumy eyes; the black skin taut over cheekbones or so loose it hung like fruit-bat flesh from toothpick arms...the effect made Erich's skin crawl. How could lovemaking lead to such horror?

Hempel's knife glinted and he handed the Malagasy a strip of meat.

Erich felt his breath catch in his throat. He knew that something more than a dining scrap was being passed between the two silhouettes, something that demanded more than courtesy or congeniality. Given to a subhuman, no less.... Erich fought the urge to draw his pistol and put a bullet in each of the figures before the fire.

Time enough for that, he decided. When and if matters were set right, or perhaps went very wrong, he would not hesitate to kill. Especially someone like Hempel.

"Herr Sturmbannführer," he called out.

Hempel looked up.

"The following is not a request. It is an order. I have instructed your men to give the Jews mosquito netting at once. I have also ordered the cook to split the leftover zebu meat between the Jews and the dogs—"

"You ordered *my* men—" Hempel rose to his feet. "How dare you. *I* control them. *I*—"

Erich turned and stalked back to the HQ tent. He chased the young fool Johann away from the radio for the night, pulled a bottle of schnapps from the crate in the corner, and sat down.

Drunks like his father disgusted Erich. He himself could handle alcohol, and at that moment he needed a drink. Just a shot, to settle his nerves. Maybe two.

CHAPTER TEN

"Heave!" Pleshdimer bellowed.

Sol drove his shoulder into the narrow, green-barked log he was using as a lever. Just a few more centimeters, he thought, as the generator moved, almost into place.

Helping to maneuver it up the road from the ocean had been like toting his own prison up the hill. Everyone sweating and swearing—insects bombarding them in the barely breathable air beneath the forest canopy. The tank had done the pulling at that point, Sol and the other men on the detail scurrying to keep thin logs under the generator as it moved. Pleshdimer, like a minor god Hempel had deified, was up on the back of the tank cajoling, complaining, threatening.

Now that they were so close to finishing, the tank had been removed and they had only the strong backs of himself and his fellow Jews to emplace the machine.

"Again!" Pleshdimer bellowed. "Push, you scum!"

Half a dozen men grunted and metal groaned, and at last the generator stood square. The Kapo came forward, brushing dirt from his hands. He was grinning. "We hook her up tonight!"

Electricity was essential, Sol thought. Erich had said so.

Of course, he had no plans to electrify the fence around the Jewish sleeping area. He had assured Miriam of that, and she in turn had told Sol.

He eyed the fences with angry resignation. It was as though reality had been born with the rise of the moon, and the barbed wire coils on the fence seemed thick and formidable.

There were too many other uses for the power. In the morning the *Altmark* would sail, and communications would need to be established with German operatives in Italian-held Ethiopia, who would relay messages to and from Berlin. Water had to be pumped from the spring into the encampment's water tank. The camp would need lights—particularly searchlights. But the fences would only be electrified if it became necessary to keep out intruders.

"Or to keep us in," Sol said under his breath.

"What'd you say?" Pleshdimer growled.

"Not a thing, mein Kapo."

Sol stepped from beneath the tarp and waited in the shadows cast by the tent for one of the guards to escort him to the supply tent for a toolbox. He found the ritual of getting needed supplies to be one of the compound's more interesting ironies. The guards rarely retrieved things themselves, even if they were the ones who intended to use them. Since no Jew could be trusted with tools, getting something as simple as a screwdriver required at least two men—one with a finger on a trigger.

"Can't you work without making a racket!" Erich slapped the inside corner of the tent.

Pleshdimer saluted the canvas. "Heil Hitler!"

"The hell with that! Just keep it quiet!"

"But we're...," the confused Kapo looked at the guards, who were smirking, and lowered his arm, "providing power, Herr Oberst."

"What you're providing me with is one hell of a headache. Who's out there, anyway?"

"Pleshdimer, mein Oberst." He added, a pride-filled smile breaking across his face, "Rottenführer Pleshdimer!"

Solomon noted with surly amusement how the Kapo had adopted the rank Hempel had given him even though no pay or uniform or induction had been effected. A corporal in the SS menagerie? Hah!

"You take your garble, Rottenführer, and drown it."

"Ja, mein Oberst," the Kapo quietly replied.

"*Now!*"

With a morose flip of his hand, Pleshdimer dismissed the men. Solomon walked to the sleeping area with a triumphant jounce to his step. After saluting the guard at the gate and being frisked, he sprawled across the matted grass and listened to the birds and lemurs, his face washed with sun. He did not even mind when a cobalt-blue haze enveloped him——

——As if in a fog, he sees Miriam lying naked and in labor, legs spread and knees up, on what appears to be a stone slab with carefully hollowed depressions for shoulders, buttocks, heels.

Candlelight reveals cobwebs above her. Beyond her feet, a skeleton in an army officer's uniform slumps in an oval wicker chair suspended from a chain.

The candles gutter. A breeze from beyond a rough-hewn doorway swirls the fog within the stone chamber. She squints against the candlelight, trying to raise up off the stone and prevented from doing so by the straps at her ankles and wrists.

He can see through the doorway, now. Beyond lies a gentle, grassy slope bordered by thicket. At its top, tall stones seem to be reaching for the moon. There are posts among them, carved totems topped with what look like buffalo horns.

Papa? Help me, Papa!

A girl is tied, naked and struggling, to one of the totems. He can see the face clearly, etched with anguish, her hair hanging in tangles down past her nose. She blows at the hair and renews her struggle with her bonds.

Three figures, man-shaped but hunched, wearing animal skins, stalk laterally across the slope, knives at the ready, moving toward the girl.

Papa!——

As swiftly as it had come, the cobalt-blue haze dissipated. Refusing to dwell on the prophetic meanings of the vision, Sol closed his eyes and strove to keep his mind blank but for the trill of the rain forest. With

Bruqah's help, he had learned to distinguish the calls of the white-headed *Tretreky*—a vanga—from the warbling *Poretika* and the omnipresent starlings, but there was no way to pin down the birds' German names without begging Erich for books, something he was loathe to do. Bruqah's facility with German did not extend to winged creatures.

Except for *Spatz*.

In Berlin, the Malagasy had seen people feed the sparrows and had been amused that food would be wasted on an animal that people did not eat. His amusement was compounded by learning that Sol had fed them so regularly that Erich had—much to Sol's dismay—nicknamed him *Spatz*.

As if awakened by birdsong, a nocturnal lemur, not yet settled after its night of roaming, took up the melody of the rain forest. Its voice sounded shrill and lonely—though Sol was sure his perception was colored by Bruqah's explanation that nocturnal lemurs tended to be solitary animals, while those that prowled by daylight were social and sounded quite different from their night brothers.

Far to the left, another lemur answered, its caw piercing the drone of the cicadas. There followed the tinkle of a music box playing "Glowworm."

"*Glühwürmchen, Glühwürmchen, Glimmre, Glimmre,*" Sol sang quietly. No matter what else happened in his life, he would never be able to hear that music without replaying the first time he had seen Miriam. The first time Erich had seen her. The night they had both fallen in love with the beautiful and charming fifteen-year-old niece of Walther Rathenau as she performed at KAVERNE, the nightclub her wealthy, socialite grandmother had opened next door to the Freund-Weisser tobacco shop.

How extraordinarily beautiful she had been, Sol thought. Not that she was any less beautiful now, just older, wearier.

He blinked open his eyes and sat up to find the canvas-covered area around him filled with activity. He realized his reverie had been deeper and longer than he'd supposed. Squinting in the direction of the music, he saw Bruqah, *vahila* in hand, seated cross-legged in the path that ran between the Jewish sleeping area and the main fence.

The Malagasy listened intently to the music box, then plucked out a reasonable rendition.

"Must you?" someone asked.

"Maybe some of us enjoy the music," a different voice said. "Close your ears if you do not wish to hear it."

The *vahila* and music box lifted Sol on a wave of sentiment and set him down, like a castaway, in a Berlin separated from the real world. He lay for a moment beneath his eiderdown, in the bedroom whose ceiling with its three cedar beams hovered in the haze of life without his glasses. He'd been young, then. At least he saw himself that way. He tried to manipulate the memory—to cast himself a dozen years later, Miriam beside him, but to no avail. Dread and doubt ticked loudly in his mind, and he found himself eyeing the Malagasy suspiciously.

What motive, he wondered, lay behind Bruqah's

apparent devotion to Miriam and, to a somewhat lesser extent, to Sol? The voyage—a free ticket home—that much was understandable. But Miriam had said that the Malagasy had refused all offers of money, and not only from Erich, but from her as well. So what did he want? After all, the instant Erich set foot on Nosy Mangabéy, he was invading Bruqah's country, unless Bruqah was truly a collaborator intent on some future, greater reward.

In which case, befriending Jews made no sense at all.

Sol scrutinized the *vahila* player. Bruqah was so engrossed in his attempt to imitate the music that he scarcely looked up from the strings except to stare disconcertedly at the box and try another chord. After a dozen measures, he frowned and shut the box lid. He reached beneath his *lamba*, removed a small ring-tailed lemur from next to his stomach, and tucked the box in its place. Squinting toward the dogs, who were pacing and yapping nervously, he patted the lemur on its rump to shoo it toward the fence. It went hesitantly, constantly looking back, like a raccoon loathe to give up food found at a campsite. At the fence it lifted its tail and, as if aware that the shepherds were chained, sauntered with a diffident air between the wires.

"I awoke him too early. He is social, that one."

"Like you?" Solomon asked.

Bruqah laughed lightly as he placed the *vahila* across his knees. "*This* Bruqah neither alone nor part of a pack. I be traveler's tree."

"You refresh whoever needs help," Solomon said rhetorically. He knew the traveler's tree legend. Symbol of all Madagascar, it provided water and sustenance to those who might otherwise perish.

Bruqah shook his head. "Not willingly."

When he looked at Solomon, the Malagasy's eyes were so deep with meaning that Sol felt fear ripple up his back, as though he were arching like a cat.

"He who thinks Zanahary, the Prince of Creation, made land solely to serve man will awaken to find himself buried beneath it," Bruqah said.

"Then why are you here?" Solomon asked in a hush. "Why do you stay with us now that you're..." To his chagrin he found it difficult to say the word. "Now that you're home," he managed.

Bruqah leaned forward, thumb and forefinger of his right hand outstretched as though he meant to reach between the wires and snare Solomon's nose—a child's game. Instead he carefully took hold of a barb and turned it to and fro, as though in scrutiny.

"Fence is *fady*," he said.

Fady. Taboo. There was no longer music in his voice, and the glimmer in his eyes had gone from flat to fierce. Solomon realized the *fady* that Bruqah now referred to was not the *fady* of which he so often spoke. *Fady* to eat white on Wednesdays, *fady* to sit with the feet extended toward the east, *fady* for a woman not to wear a skirt. This *fady* was of a different, deeper quality. More basic, Sol sensed. And not just to Bruqah.

"Why is it *fady*?" Solomon probed. "Because Nazis strung it?"

Confusion showed in the Malagasy's face. "Your people strung it, Rabbi. Are you also Nazis?"

"You know what I mean. Don't play coy, Bruqah." Sol cautiously put a hand atop Bruqah's fingers, on the wire. "Why is the fence *fady*?"

"Lines turn the forest back—and black," Bruqah said.

"You talk in riddles." Seeing that the remark appeared to trouble the Malagasy, Sol added, "...my friend."

"I am supposed to. I am *mpanandro*—an astrologer."

Sol tightened his hold on the Malagasy's hand. "Tell me, *mpanandro*, what the stars say about why a Vazimba named Bruqah befriends *Vazaha*—we Europeans."

"If I told you, would you believe? Sometimes, stars lie." Bruqah's thin lips twisted into a wry smile.

"More often, astrologers are charlatans."

"There is that."

Out of the corner of his eye Solomon saw Pleshdimer approach with his enormous bucket on his shoulder, as if bound toward the kennel area to feed the dogs.

"Tell me!" Sol whispered.

Bruqah's eyes flicked in anger toward the Kapo, then turned in earnest toward Solomon. "You have dwelled in dreams too long not to know the answer, Rabbi. Why does a traveler's tree grow beside a path? Why are some men *fato-dra*, bound by blood, or the spirit of the newborn dead restless until it is exalted through the feast of *tokombato*?...*Fa fomba vao*, because it is custom. I know not how else to answer you, Rabbi." Leaning closer to the fence, he said, "Would your temper be untroubled if I told you I seek the child?"

"My child? Mine and Miriam's?"

"Yes, if it be your child."

"But why would you want the baby? I don't understand."

"And you call yourself 'Rabbi'!"

"I am not a rabbi. Nor have I ever claimed to be. It's just an honorary title that the others—"

"In that case, you are a fool."

Glaring, Bruqah drew back as Pleshdimer came to stand between them. "Buggering each other through the wire?" he asked Sol. He lifted a shoulder-high strand. "When she's hot, we'll let you Jews close as you want to the fence."

"The Oberst"—Sol had started to say 'Erich'—"won't stoop to that. He knows we are men of our word."

"Not a Jew born that can be trusted," Pleshdimer said soberly and a little sadly as he set down the galvanized bucket. On top of a pile of what looked like skinned rats lay an undercooked, reddish-gray haunch, days old and crawling with maggots. Sol's stomach wrenched.

Bruqah looked at the animals in the pail in horror. "Lemurs!" he said.

The Kapo picked up a stringy hunk of meat. Drooling as he chewed, he lowered himself to a sitting position and wiped his mouth with the back of his hand. "I would offer you some, Rabbi, but it isn't koshered." He laughed uproariously at his own cleverness, pulled an uncooked lemur breast from the bucket, and offered the meat to Bruqah. "Want some of your own kind, monkey man?"

"Zanahary did not create His creatures so you could fill buckets," Bruqah said.

"It's not for *me*, *Neger*." Pleshdimer patted his ample belly. "Sturmbannführer Hempel *personally* sees to it that I get the best meat. Nothing is better eating than dog, except…" He winked and snorted. "…except woman." Nodding toward the kennel area, he used his teeth to twist off another enormous bite, and dropped what remained into the bucket. "The shepherds dine fancy tonight!"

He stood, lifted a leg to fart loudly, and sauntered along the fence. Sol stayed inside the sleeping area and moved laterally to keep up with him. "Does the Oberst know about this?" he asked. "Do the trainers know you're feeding the dogs lemur?"

Pleshdimer picked meat from between his rotted teeth, and worked his jaws as if to exercise them.

"Why should they care what goes in those dogs' mouths and comes out their butts?" he said finally. Belching, he ambled across the grass, leaving Solomon to clutch the fence.

Well, let the dogs eat the lemurs and each other! Sol thought. The shepherds weren't any concern of his and, besides, the meat was probably good for them. Why should Erich care? Why should he, Sol, care even if Pleshdimer did give them something that wasn't proper or—he mentally grimaced—or kosher. As far as he knew, the only thing that differentiated those dogs from the ones at Sachsenhausen was the hand controlling the choke chain.

He gripped the fence so tightly that the wire cut into his palm.

…*the hand controlling the choke chain.*

Erich's hand.

His was the hand that controlled the wireless key, with its connection to Berlin and the *Sicherheitspolizei*; held the lifeline of the hundred and forty-some Jews, including the one in the womb...if indeed the child was the progeny of Jewish parents.

His papa's voice came to him from the past: "*There is no such thing as being half Jewish.*"

He thought for a moment about what he had just seen and about the uses to which he could put the information. If Erich did not know what the dogs were being fed, reporting it could possibly put him in Sol's debt. Even if he did know, telling him could do no harm. Either way it was a sign of good faith that might ultimately stand the Jews in good stead.

"Jew wishing to exit on an errand!" he called out as he ran toward the guard at the gate. "Jew begging permission of his betters!"

Erich had made certain concessions to keep the guards happy.

After Sol explained that he had important information meant for Erich's ears only, he was allowed to walk alone toward the HQ tent, the guard's glare drilling into the back of his neck. Of the Jews, only Sol had the freedom to move about the camp with relative ease. The soldiers—even the trainers—resented it, and in a way Sol couldn't blame them. He *was* an enemy, after all. When not pulling guard duty, the soldiers stacked their rifles tripod-style in front of their tents. And the supply tents, crowded with boxes of ammunition and weapons, were within reach if a man bent on destruction were not carefully watched. Once the generator was in full operation, the radio could transmit messages to French forces at Diego Suarez or to the capital, Antananarive, if HQ could be accessed for a few minutes. Even Erich's gun—

"A gift for you, Rabbi." Bruqah's voice was low and emotional as he emerged from the latticework shadows cast by the sleeping-area fence.

Sol glanced furtively to see if the guard was watching. He was. The man shifted nervously from one foot to the other.

"If it is not important, may *dô* snakes slide from my ancestors' eyes!" Bruqah said, passing his hand across Sol's and leaving something metallic in Sol's palm. The shape was familiar, but he dared not look down, for fear the guard would come running.

"It was in the box of music," Bruqah whispered. "Lady Miriam say it yours. Germantownman would love to possess it, I think."

Suddenly the shape made sense. Sol passed his thumb across the object, his mind immediately a-tumble with painful memories.

Papa's medal.

"That's an Iron Cross," he whispered. He wiped the mud from both sides and ran a fingertip down it. He could feel the inscription, etched into the back so lightly that the casual observer would miss it.

He remembered how Jacob Freund had gone over the original engraving, cutting deep into the metal for fear someone might attempt to delete it.

Solomon seized Bruqah's wrist and wrenched the Malagasy closer. "Where did you get this!"

"Germantownman take it from music box drawer. He say, 'This was my father's.' Lady Miri say he lie."

"Erich told you this was his?" The depth of Erich's self-deceit made Solomon feel weak. Suddenly, the world of Erich Alois made sense. By taking the Iron Cross Sol had left with Miriam, Erich had rid himself of one father and given birth to another. He no longer had to think of himself as the son of a guttersnipe raised to entrepreneur by a Jew. He was reborn out of his own Imperial-German imagination, his patriotic heritage fashioned as easily as he had forged a new surname. Born Erich Weisser; reborn Erich Alois to ingratiate himself with Adolph *Alois* Hitler.

"This belongs to me," Sol said quietly. He gripped the Iron Cross and squinted toward the headquarters tent.

He heard an undercurrent of sound beneath the noise of the generator and the jungle. It seemed to emanate from along the fence. He looked in alarm toward Bruqah, who put a finger to his lips.

"Look!" Bruqah whispered.

Along the perimeter of the fence stood a gathering of lemurs, too numerous for a single group. Sol had seen them move through the forest when he and other workers had cut the jungle's slender trunks to build the compound, but he had never seen them like this, prancing around with eyes as huge as eternal questions.

"My friends," Bruqah said, smiling. He scanned the

forest. "Me and lemurs share a past. We the same, me and these," motioning back and forth with a hand. Lifting his eyes, he looked intently at Sol, "Dreams be mirrors, and mirrors dreams, Mister Rabbi. You must dance there…among your dreams."

A whirlwind of images swirled out of Sol's memory. "I know you, Solomon Freund," a Gypsy said. "I am a dancer in the dwelling place of dreams." An old blind man with a lemur called an indri asked him, "Are you a dog-headed boy, Solomon? Is that what your dreams say?"

Solomon looked at the Iron Cross. "Who are you, really, Bruqah?" he asked. "Can you help us…help me?"

"Only man who help himself win battle, Sollyman," Bruqah answered, turning toward the last rays of sunlight. "Child will come soon," he said. "The Kalanaro have been waiting."

Solomon spotted the natives in the fringes of the jungle. As black as the Zana-Malata, they were pushing forward through the foliage, coup-coup machetes and *assegais* in hand. They looked like small warriors, bodies pulsating with smeared mud in the sudden darkness of dusk.

For a moment Bruqah stared earnestly toward Solomon. "Luck to all, Rabbi. Danger find you, you find island's hill," Bruqah whispered in a hurried staccato. "Burial place. Sacred with lemur soul. Even Germantownman would not disturb."

The Malagash turned away. In seconds he had disappeared into the blackness of Solomon's peripheral vision.

"Come back!" Sol rasped, turning to follow the other, but he could not find him. He noticed, instead, that a guard had left the gate and was starting toward him. Being caught with the medallion could mean death. Who would believe that he had acquired it by means other than theft?

The HQ tent. His only chance: hide the cross, let Erich discover it. Sol hurried on, pretending to be oblivious to the guard's presence.

As he neared headquarters he heard a voice slur from the medical tent beyond.

"Can you ever forgive me?" Erich asked.

Sol approached the HQ tent with the elaborately played respect one would expect from an underling...from a Jew. Cap clutched in armpit, head bowed, shambling steps. He raised his knuckles to knock quietly against the tent post holding up the front canopy. And all the while, his ears were tuned to the voices in the medical tent.

"It's not my forgiveness you really want, Erich," Miriam said.

"Solomon's?"

"Your own."

"Would Solomon follow your lead—if you could find it in your heart to forgive me?"

The cold muzzle of a rifle touched the nape of Solomon's neck. "Move, or I'll kill you."

"Would you want him to forgive? Would you debase yourself so much, Erich Alois?" Miriam said. "It would surely be debasement in your view, would it not?"

Solomon stood with hands lifted, the medallion

clenched in his palm, as the guard walked in a semi-circle, faced Sol, and peered into the HQ tent.

"The Herr Oberst isn't here," the guard announced, eyes narrowing with suspicion. "Not the radio operator, either. *No one*." He moved around Sol with the cautious wrath of a cur sniffing a rival. "Just what did you think you could get away with here, Jew?"

He jammed the barrel into Sol's gut. Sol doubled over in pain but managed to keep the medal concealed.

"Get back to your sty! Sturmbannführer Hempel will hear about this!"

"The Oberst is next—"

"Silence!" The guard swung the rifle butt-first, missing Sol's forehead by a centimeter.

Sol staggered toward the sleeping area. He hesitated as he entered the gate, allowing the guard time to kick him because a boot was better than a bullet, and crumpled, groaning, onto the matted grass. As he lay with his face in the sod, trying to wheeze air into his lungs and drive out the fear and humiliation, he wondered if he should get word to Erich about the incident. The colonel's orders had been explicit: no beating or berating of prisoners unless they deserved it. The problem was that Sol could not say anything without revealing that he'd overheard the conversation in the medical tent, and Erich was not beyond killing him for being privy to his weakness.

The pain subsided and the guard drifted into shadows to smoke a cigarette. Sol crawled over to the edge of the fence. He felt the paralytic fear instilled in him in Sachsenhausen. The only difference was that here the unfinished construction made in-compound movement relatively easy.

Then a knee bore down against Sol's back and a guard gripped his hair, forcing up his head. Grinning, the guard slapped the flat of his bayonet against Sol's cheek.

"Did you summon them, Rabbi?" the man said, directing Sol's vision to the lemurs. "You and your Jewish sorcery?"

"Stick him!" another voice said.

The guard lifted the weapon. "What, and spoil the fun? The Sturmbahnführer has plans for him."

CHAPTER ELEVEN

Erich thought he remembered Taurus calling him sometime during the night. Remembered staggering to the medical tent, collapsing to his knees before the dog and wrapping his arms around her warm neck, mentally begging her to forgive him for bringing her to this terrible place. He remembered standing over Miriam, she lying beneath netting as hazy as a wedding veil.

"Can you ever see it in your heart?" he thought he had said.

After a long silence, she had answered, "Someday, perhaps. If you think my forgiveness would help."

"And Solomon?"

"What about Solomon?"

"Would he follow your lead?"

"Do you believe he could? Would you really want him to?"

He awakened to a false dawn heavy with humidity. It made his sinuses swell and brought on a headache behind his eyes. When he dragged himself out of the chair he'd slept in and looked outside the tent, there seemed to him to be a sheen to the air, as though the sky had fractured and fallen. He winced and closed his eyes, wanting nothing more than to shut himself in for the day—alone with his military books and maps, the smell of dusty canvas, and what was left at the bottom of the bottle.

"Bastards," he said, with the triumvirate of Hempel, Pleshdimer, and the syphilitic clearly in mind. "We'll see about you after the dogs and I get through with you."

He had no intention of using his dogs for guarding the Jews. That was the job of Hempel's...*boys*, as Miriam was fond of calling the guards. Erich had never seen the dogs as guard dogs, but as sentry dogs and combat troops. With Taurus and Aquarius out of action, he was loathe to do much training; the dogs needed to acclimate to the heat. Much to the anger of the guards, he had placed the dogs and the trainers on light duty.

A hand touched his shoulder "It's the animals, sir! Come quickly!" Fermi's voice sounded like a megaphone.

Suddenly fully awake, Erich followed the trainer. He felt himself running as though through glue to the kennel area, a feeling of renewed despair sticking like sweat against his skin. The trainers were each struggling to bring a raging shepherd under control. Pisces had wrapped his chain around his run-pole and was up on his hind legs, straining against his bonds, jaws snapping and eyes filled with frenzy. Snarling, Gemini was sprinting the length of her run with such force that each time she reached the end she was thrown off her feet and lay squirming and growling, tugging her head against her collar.

"They're fevered, sir. I think this damn humidity's got to them." After great difficulty Fermi managed to snap a choke chain onto Pisces' collar and lift him to the dog's full height, temporarily controlling the animal while Erich, squinting against the urge to sleep, clamped Pisces' jaws together and slipped on a muzzle. "Feel his nose, sir! Hotter than a nipple on a French whore. All the dogs' are."

Shivering and gnashing his teeth against the leather restraint, Pisces abruptly twisted from Erich's grasp and insanely pawed the air as Fermi fought to control him.

"It's not distemper, is it?" Fermi was clearly worried.

"They wouldn't all have it." Erich's voice sounded outside himself. He realized he was watching himself as if from a distance. "You see?" He knelt and lifted the upper gum, revealing the canines. "No pink froth." He anxiously searched the forest. "Something outside the compound has them riled. The Kalanaro, maybe?"

"Kalanaro, sir?" asked Holten-Pflug, Sagittarius' trainer, a chubby staff sergeant with a boyish face.

"Those pygmies with the glowing face paint." Erich silently cursed himself for having spent the night with the bottle. He tried to think about the Kalanaro as he rose to his feet and peered around the jungle perimeter. He thought he recalled digging through books from his footlocker earlier in the night. He had found no mention of the Kalanaro in the military literature or the supplemental guides. He had counted eighteen tribes—plus the Vazimba and Zana-Malata, who functioned as individuals rather than in groups. In his mind's eye he remembered demographic maps; he had even found the location of the Mikea, a tribe so small and mysterious that they had been considered mythical until a decade ago.

The Kalanaro were not among the eighteen.

They were not listed among the sub-groups: the clans and moieties. Nor among the lists of non-Malagasy peoples inhabiting the country.

Bruqah had proved no more enlightening. "Kalanaro," was his only answer. "They not hurt you. They be spirit-guardians of Madagascar."

"Spirits, my ass," Erich had said, but the Malagasy had refused to say more.

Returning to the moment, he said, "No, I don't think this has anything to do with the Kalanaro. The dogs all seem to be straining toward the main gate."

"What, then?" Fermi asked, going to help Virgo's trainer.

"I'm not sure," Erich said over his shoulder.

Virgo struggled in the trainer's arms and gnashed her teeth. Her eyes bulged, but at last, within his loving arms, she briefly settled, whining and quivering. Erich followed the dog's gaze. She was glaring past the ghetto and the compound gate—glaring toward the hut.

Emerging from the doorway, the Zana-Malata stepped aside as several guards filed out and, in a mob, headed toward the compound. Hempel was in the lead, with Misha trotting alongside, leashed by a choke chain. The syphilitic followed. The two guards at the gate snapped to ready arms and saluted when Hempel entered.

Nostrils flaring and eyes so intense they seemed about to pop from her skull, Virgo renewed her frenzied, deep-throated growl. From the medical tent, he heard Taurus. Trying to tell him something.

That's it, isn't it, girl! When I was at the crypt, you sensed trouble and wanted to warn me.

More guards had emerged from their tents and were joining Hempel, several swacking truncheons against their palms as, a mob now, they marched toward the Jews.

"Let the dogs go," Erich said.

Totenkopfverbände: Death's Head Unit. He'd show Hempel what death was all about!

"Sir?" Fermi questioned.

"Do as I say!"

Fermi looked from his commander to the oncoming mob, and then suddenly, like the precision squad that they were, the trainers sensed their predicament at the same time. They were weaponless but for the dogs. Between themselves and their rifles, stacked outside their tents, were Hempel and his men on the one side and, on the other, over a hundred and forty Jews who would tear any German soldier apart if they had the chance.

The guards began to chant. "Kill the Jews! Kill the Jews!"

With perverse pleasure Erich saw the faces of his men

harden. He had trained them well—though they were untried in battle, he was sure they could be as savage as the dogs. Fermi's face shone with fierce delight as he unmuzzled Pisces.

The Jews, seeing two packs of jackals doing battle over hunks of meat—them—started running around within the sleeping area and yelling to one another, searching for anything with which to defend themselves.

"Release...now!" Erich commanded. Then, mentally, he ordered the dogs to restrain the guards.

Slavering and crazed, ten of the twelve dogs of the zodiac raced indiscriminately toward anything that moved.

"Get the guards!" Erich screamed.

"KILL JEWS!" the guards intoned.

Instead of responding like Erich's trained killing machine, the dogs behaved like sharks in a feeding frenzy.

"Herr Oberst!" Holten-Pflug shouted above the din. "The dogs' water dishes! It looks like someone's dribbled blood—!"

No wonder the shepherds were going crazy. Having tasted blood, they wanted more. Now controlling them would be a thousand times more difficult.

"Who fed my dogs blood!" he called out when he was near enough for Hempel to hear.

Hempel's men stopped their approach and grew silent, all except Pleshdimer, who shouted, "I did!"

Erich felt heat rise into his cheeks. "Shoot that man," he said to the guard closest to him.

The guard did not move.

"Rottenführer Pleshdimer is SS, and thus not subject to your orders." Hempel withdrew a cigar from his pocket and moistened it by drawing an end over moist lips. "None of the guards are. You are Abwehr, we are Totenkopfverbände." After lighting the cigar with a match, he held the red end before the mouth of the Zana-Malata.

The syphilitic encompassed it with gnarled flesh that once had been lips, and inhaled deeply, a look of pleasure entering his eyes.

"You may do as you wish with your shepherds and Abwehr chimps," Hempel said, "but my unit is *mine*."

"Then command your unit to conduct the execution. Or do it yourself. You are still subject to my orders."

With his holster strap unsnapped and one hand on the grip of the Walther, Erich glared at the Zana-Malata, who must somehow be responsible for this insurrection. Hempel was crazy, but he was not stupid, certainly not stupid enough to pull this kind of maneuver so early in the game. Play the professional, he reminded himself. If they see chinks in the armor, they may crumble the castle.

He drew his pistol and kept the weapon steady as he pointed it at Hempel. "Or do you intend to disobey your commander, Sturmbahnführer?"

Hempel smiled a reassuring smile, as though he intended to gather Erich in and grace him with his confidence.

"So you are, officially," Erich said in a tight, hard voice, "disobeying a direct order?"

"That is correct."

Erich's finger tightened on the trigger.

Puuuh.

The Zana-Malata had craned his neck so that his head was level with the gun when he blew the smoke ring. Tinged with blue fire and writhing with worms, it floated around the barrel and fastened onto Erich's flesh. His skin burst into flames. He screamed, fired, and dropped the pistol.

The bullet went wildly astray.

Slapping at his good hand with his dead fingers, he tried a roundhouse kick at the Zana-Malata. Off balance, he missed.

"We each have our units to command," Hempel said.

"We'll see about that! Guards, arrest those three!" he shouted, trying to be heard above the barking and growling. When no one moved to obey, he added, "They're to be shot for treason against our Führer!"

The men did nothing. It was as if they did not even know that he was there. Disregarding the pain in his hand, he grabbed a tall man by the shirt. "You heard me! Arrest them!"

The guard stared past him, making no effort to respond.

With the back of his dead hand Erich struck the guard across the face. Blood burst from the man's nose. Erich looked at his hand in horror. Oh my God, I've struck an enlisted man.

The man appeared hardly to notice. From somewhere close by, Erich heard again the sound of rubber against flesh. He swore to himself, pushed past the guard, and headed for his tent—and his MP-38 submachine gun. He would take all of them on himself, he thought irrationally. Behind him, he heard Hempel issuing orders and speaking to the Zana-Malata.

"Our revered Herr Oberst has struck an enlisted man," he said. "Calm the dogs, my friend. You men are dismissed. We have won."

You have won nothing yet, Erich thought. What he needed was more manpower. A guerrilla force. The Kalanaro, perhaps, who were forever popping up with that bird-shit on their faces like targets in a shooting gallery. But he wanted mercenaries who would act like soldiers, he thought, not like a bunch of gibbering monkeys.

The "sit and wait" military order, he figured, was not a Führerbefehl—a direct order from Hitler, not to be questioned—but had come from Goebbels. As a field commander, he had a certain latitude. The guards were young and, in their demented way, idealistic; they wanted to do battle, not oversee Jews creating a matriculation center in the middle of nowhere. Promise them that they could march on Antanarivo, the capital nestled in the country's cool, central highlands, and they would abandon Hempel like fleas from a dead dog. The takeover of Madagascar with a handful of untested German troops and support from local tribes, that would appeal to them.

He burst into his headquarters tent and grabbed the submachine pistol.

A few of his trainers and their dogs—all of whom were to be trusted since they were Abwehr—could stay behind to maintain the island base camp, with its superior radio and secure position. They would also provide protection for the corpsman and Miriam and the child. Erich would take Taurus and the rest of the trainers and shepherds.

As he turned to leave he spotted the bottle of schnapps, not quite empty from the previous night.

One drink, to settle his nerves. As he poured the amber liquid, it occurred to him that playing the hothead was what Hempel wanted of him. Well, he wouldn't fall into that trap. Otto Braun had taught him to disappoint his enemies. The secret of guerrilla warfare, Braun had said, was to out-think your adversary.

He sat down and put his feet up on the desk. Drinking the alcohol he had poured, he reached out, drew aside the tent flap, and saw that the compound was clear. The Jews had settled down again, the dogs were back in the kennel area, the guards had dispersed. Hempel was surely stewing in his own juices right now, upset that the young colonel had proven too cool-headed to rise to the major's bait.

He settled back again, chuckling at his wisdom, and closed his eyes, imagining his troops marching into Antanarivo, the windows of the city's whitewashed buildings open, women waving flowers and men cheering.

CHAPTER TWELVE

Misha pretended he was somewhere else, not on a log beside a fire pit outside the Zana-Malata's hut, but on his father's knee in an easy chair in the tiny apartment off the Ku'damm.

In his imaginings, his father, a rabbi, was reading to him again about how Abraham did not hurt his son but prayed to God, and about how Abraham knew Sarah and also knew things about Hagar who had a son named Ishmael and slept by a well. He told himself that when the story ended it would be bedtime, and his father would shut the book with a dramatic snap and kiss him goodnight. Misha would be ushered off to bed by his mother, happy that life was good.

The boy could only sustain the illusion for a short while before reality intruded. He shifted position, straddling the log and using his hand to tug at the leash so that he would have more room. With his other hand he pulled bark from the log, wondering what he could do to cause something bad to happen to Hempel, like a fire to consume the hut while the major slept.

When they were in the hut together, the Zana-Malata dawdled at similar things, using roots and sticks and powders and impressing Hempel with the uses he found for them. Surely *something* could happen if he, Misha, kept working at it.

The Zana-Malata was only the second black man he had ever known. He didn't like him, but not just because he was ugly. His papa had taught him that no man was ugly unless his heart was evil. Ugliness, like beauty, papa had said, was something that lay beneath what was visible.

How unlike Bruqah the Zana-Malata was, the boy thought. Hempel said the Vazimba was just another nigger African, no more trustworthy than a hyena, but he was wrong. Bruqah was wonderful.

The Zana-Malata eased from his sitting place and, leaning forward, seemed to pull a thimble from midair. He passed it three times around the perimeter of the smoke, eyes closed serenely, appearing to savor the smell. He put his face into the smoke and slowly slurped from the thimble, then offered it to Hempel, who had squat-crawled forward, his hand on the black man's back. The thimble was still full. Hempel took it and looked at the Zana-Malata with solemn eyes before he drank, tipping his head back and tossing the liquid toward the rear of his throat, like Misha had seen his real father do sometimes with schnapps.

Hempel handed back the thimble to the Zana-Malata, sat on the ground, and laid his head against the log. He looked up at the stars and sighed contentedly. "Do you know," he said to no one in particular, "that I once stood in a sleet storm all night at parade-rest, without a coat, just because I knew that Reichsführer Himmler would sometimes look down from his window? There must have been a hundred of us, men of all ages, and we kept up the vigil without ever planning it among ourselves or debating whether we should continue once we'd started. It was during a winter solstice celebration, at Wewelsburg Castle. After a book-burning. God what a night that was!"

He stretched out his arms, seemingly lost in thought. Misha watched him. He didn't know what to think about Hempel anymore. He remembered hating him, but lately he didn't feel anything at all except shame. He had learned to separate himself from the pain and hatred that had at first overwhelmed him when the major did the *thing*.

"Bring me some wine, boy," Hempel said, letting go of the leash attached to Misha's collar. "On second thought," he picked up Erich's Walther from where it had been lying in the grass, emptied out the bullets, and placed the gun between Misha's teeth, "the Oberst is certainly asleep in a drunken stupor by now. Sneak this into his hut and bring back whatever's left of that good schnapps he's been drinking."

Misha dropped the gun, which was far too heavy for him to carry in that manner. "Pick it up and carry it,"

Hempel conceded. "If he wakes up while you're in there, don't speak to him. And be quick about it."

Obediently, Misha set off through the tall grass that bordered the hut site. "I said be quick," the major called out, and threw a rock at him.

He wouldn't go any faster, Misha thought. If it meant more rocks and worse, which it surely would, that was the way it was. He knew it was a small rebellion, but it was enough to lend him the courage to stop en route to the compound and dig up the zebu horn the guards had left after they hacked up the animal. It had looked so much like the shofar that the cantor had used at his father's High Holy Day services that he had buried it at the base of the tanghin tree, hoping to get it to Solomon in time. That way, though he couldn't be there himself, he'd be there in a kind of way.

He tucked the Walther into his waistband, and holding the shofar in his hand headed around two prisoners who stood between him and the HQ tent.

"That damn leash and collar. We should take it off," one of the prisoners said, reaching for Misha.

The other man grabbed his friend by the wrist. "Don't be a fool!" he said. "You think it would make things better for any of us? You think it would make things better for the boy?"

Misha held up the horn. "A shofar," he said, coughing, his voice hoarse from disuse. "For Herr Freund."

The first man took it from him. "I'll make sure it gets to the rabbi," he said.

Misha saw tears glisten in the man's eyes. He made a weak attempt at a smile and went on his way, guided by the quarter-moon which hung in the sky like a grin and shone down on the Panzerfelswagen which Goldman and Bruqah were working on. He remembered Hempel saying that it should be used to blow the hell out of the devils they would encounter on the mainland, and Colonel Erich saying...he could not remember what the colonel had said.

"Halt or I'll shoot!"

The boy patted his waistband to make sure the pistol was there, and lifted his hands. The guard who had called out to him lowered his rifle and Misha went into headquarters, which he knew doubled as the colonel's sleeping area and the radio center. It was much smaller than he had expected, and very messy.

Colonel Erich, seemingly fast asleep, lolled over a bottle.

"So what'd ya come for," he said, opening unfocussed eyes. "Hempel send you to beat me with the dog leash?"

He chuckled, and his head flopped around as though he could not control it. Then he lay down, stretched out, dropped the bottle, and began to snore.

Standing there in the moonlight, Misha felt truly separate from Hempel for the first time in months. He felt a part of himself return, the way he had felt when, after his parents were taken, he had worked for Miriam in the underground. A message runner whose world was Berlin's alleys and sewers. He tried to remember how he had felt during those headlong flights through the city, threading through crowds, hearing his footsteps echo down deserted alleyways, his socks constantly down around his ankles. If only it hadn't been his mistake that had gotten Herr Freund arrested!

Don't dwell on it, he told himself. Don't even think about it. He's not here, now.

But the fear and the memory of pain caught in Misha's throat and stayed there. Hurrying, he placed the pistol beside Erich and picked up the bottle. It was almost empty. For a moment, he felt again as he had while working for Miriam and the underground, strong and invincible.

Until Erich sat up, put both hands on his own forehead and, turning his face toward the ceiling, began to laugh. Loudly, with such drunken force that the sound sent Misha rushing from the tent.

CHAPTER THIRTEEN

"This," Hempel said with a calm that Erich knew belied his seething, "is an outrage."

Erich placed himself between the major and the Panzer, jockeying slightly whenever Hempel tried to step around him and get to the tank.

The major did not frighten him, Erich assured himself. Maybe years ago in Berlin, around those campfires on Lake Wannsee, when he had feared that the Freikorps-Youth leader might not like him; but no more. Fears of the likes of Otto Hempel had died when his boyhood died...whenever that was.

Behind him, Goldman again fired up the arc welder, adding a shower of sparks to the brilliance of the morning. Erich did not turn to look. He smiled inwardly as Hempel flinched. Only from the welding light? Erich wondered. Or because Goldman—a Jew, no less—was cutting and welding on the major's toy.

Putting on a blade. Turning a tank into a bulldozer.

He thought of cutting off the tank's barrel, just to spite the major—like a proud soldier with his dick sawed off—but he dared not push the changes too far, too fast. There were the volatile guards to consider. The previous day had shown him how tenuous was his position with them—if indeed he had not dreamed the whole thing.

Besides, who knew what Malagasy might attack Nosy Mangabéy once word spread of the German invasion, however small? Madagascar was French, and even those tribesmen who held no love for the Frogs—which, he assumed, would be most Malagasy—might not take well to any more foreigners on their beloved red-clay soil.

"Next time you have some question about my orders, you will come to me, your superior officer, for your directive." Erich looked up into Hempel's cold gray eyes. "Is that understood?"

Not a flicker of emotion showed in the eyes. The blankness unnerved Erich.

"I will do my duty...Herr Oberst."

"I will see that you do, Herr Sturmbannführer." Erich spoke slowly, articulately. "There is a stone gravesite atop the western hill, where the Jews are working. A crypt of some sort. Have one of the Jew...Jewish details open it up. I wish to determine the hill's potential as a pillbox to guard that flank. If the crypt seems appropriate, begin the fortifications. Send ten men. I shall join you later for the opening of the tomb."

"Ten *men*? Or ten Jews?"

"Ten total."

"Then two men and eight Jews."

"Whatever. Dismissed, Herr Sturmbannführer."

Hempel saluted stiffly. Without emotion he stepped back and did a smart about-face. As he walked toward the Jews' sleeping area, he lifted an arm and snapped his fingers. Three guards, carbines in hand, came running from near their tents at the other side of the compound.

Erich marveled at their loyalty, but wondered how effective they would be as real soldiers. Herding and clubbing Jews at Sachsenhausen was hardly equal to fighting the French and British in the trenches. Not that he himself had done any real soldiering, or that fighting for the Nazi Reich could ever be an honor. *The height of my life was my time in the trenches*, Adolph Hitler had written. Erich would fight, and well, he assured himself; and willingly. But not for Hitler. He would fight in the hope that the past would return, that a new Kaiser would be proclaimed.

He remembered Solomon's pewter Hessian soldiers and a sense of nostalgia filled him. How courageous each had seemed, lined up on his bedcovers around the hills of his knees. When he'd played with them with Solomon, he would lift a cuirassier or foot soldier and peer at it so intently that the uniform would appear to take on color and the face, expression. How could the farm boys and city toughs who followed Otto Hempel possibly compare? How far Germany had descended!

"Herr Oberst Alois? Ready for your inspection, sir!"

Goldman stood at attention, his welding mask

crooked in his arm, the look in his eyes—or so Erich thought—one of respect. Or was he deceiving himself? he wondered. One could never tell with Jews.

Now I'm sounding like Hempel.

He moved around the machine, pretending to inspect the welds but unsure what he should look for. Who but a master welder or engineer could determine without testing if the blade arms, made from two of the tank's side plates, would not buckle at the first full load? He would need a whole motor pool of machinery to create a full-fledged landing facility on the mainland, once base camp was well-established here on Mangabéy, but for now the converted Panzerfelswagen would do. It would have to.

He stepped back as more men gathered. Jews on in-compound duty, mostly, and a couple of trainers with their dogs, which sat panting against the morning heat, watching curiously. The guards avoided the converted tank, walking out of their way to keep from crossing too close.

Erich caught himself on the verge of praising the Jew, and sliced short the near compliment by declaring, "See to it that it's perfectly maintained. I'm holding you personally responsible!"

"Yes...sir!" Goldman all but smiled.

Erich relented. "Good job," he said. "Is there some small favor I can grant you to show my...the Reich's...gratitude?"

"The Torah, sir," the man said without hesitation. "We need it for the service tonight."

"I will see to it," Erich said, remembering that Sol had asked for it when he'd requested the service, but without the vaguest idea where it had been placed.

As if Goldman had read Erich's mind, he said, "I believe it is in the black man's hut...sir."

"*Where?!*"

"You kick the bejesus out of jungle with this, Mister Germantownman!" Bruqah said, popping his head out of the turret. He grinned and slapped the machine.

As I would like to kick the bejesus out of you for perturbing my land, Erich thought he saw the Malagasy's eyes say. He wondered if Bruqah had been inside the tank the entire time Goldman was welding, but that too became secondary as the Panzerfelswagen rumbled into life, spitting blue exhaust.

"I drive you!" Bruqah shouted.

Erich leapt onto the machine, ready to tear the Malagasy's head off, but no sooner was he close than Bruqah clutched his wrist. The African had amazing strength for one so thin, Erich realized. The grip was near to cracking his bones.

"I good driver," Bruqah said in a voice just loud enough for Erich to hear. He gave the guards, emerging from beneath the mess canopy, a broad, theatrical grin.

Erich pried the Malagasy's fingers from his wrist. "Where on Earth did you learn...?"

Bruqah continued to grin at the guards. "German Southwest Africa, where I learn to speak German. War with South Africa. Many, many battles."

Erich knew about Bruqah's having lived in the German protectorate where he had earned or was given a trip to Berlin. Botanical study at the university, or some such thing; until now, Erich assumed it had been political, an excuse to train another African operative. How and why Bruqah had left Madagascar, Erich was uncertain. He made a mental note to try to find out. Perhaps Miriam would know. She and the Malagasy had been close aboard ship. Too close, in Erich's estimation.

"I take you…how the North Americans say? Around the blockhead. We take Lady Miri, too, maybe? Or does Mister Germantownman plan to lazy around here all day like a pet lemur?"

Erich stood on unsure legs as Bruqah dropped back into the turret and drove the machine toward the gate, the soldiers parting like a sea. "Pretty good ride, eh, Germantownman?" the Malagasy shouted from inside.

The tank lumbered around the compound, kicking up dust and grass.

"We go back for Lady Miri, like I say?" Bruqah asked. "Ride she and baby?"

"No," Erich said. But an image of Miriam as a young girl, riding with him on the Ferris wheel at Berlin's Luna Park, induced him to change his mind. Soon Miriam was propped as comfortably as possible on the Panzer.

Standing in the turret, Erich directed the driving. It was a heady feeling, as though he were leading an armored charge. His headache, lately a regular morning event, became a tolerable throb, and he did not let the sight of Solomon being marched off with a detail of woodcutters spoil his festive mood. Everyone merely had to be patient, himself most of all, he decided.

Things would work out for the best, if the Panzer was any indication. Who but a Jew could see a plowshare in a sword? *That*, if for no other reason, was why the Madagascar Experiment would succeed!...because he, unlike blind fools such as Hempel and Hitler, understood the value and purpose of the Jewish people.

They had three months to secure Mangabéy as a base of operations and build a dock and receiving station on the mainland, at the mouth of the Antabalana River. If they failed, Goebbels would send no more Jews.

Well, he'd meet the deadline with weeks to spare.

He leaned nonchalantly against the turret as Bruqah drove the machine across the compound yard, and signaled for the gate to be opened. Then they were in the meadow proper, spewing chaff and dirt as Bruqah ran in the *savoka* stubble alongside the forest.

Erich motioned straight ahead, feeling like the commander of an armored division going into battle.

They neared the Zana-Malata's hut.

In an inspiration born of hate, Erich banged his fist against the turret to get Bruqah's attention. "There!" He pointed toward the hut. "Go there! Knock it down!"

The tank stopped. Bruqah ground the gears, but the machine only wheezed and sat still.

"What's the meaning of this!" Erich yelled.

"Zana-Malata protect his home." Bruqah cranked up the engine again and jammed the tank into gear. Within meters it stopped again.

Erich grabbed the Malagasy by the edge of his *lamba* and, surprised by his own strength, fairly yanked him from the driver's seat. Bruqah arose choking, flailing his arms ineffectually against his assailant. Erich jumped into the driver's seat and positioned himself. How to begin? he wondered. It angered him that, despite his years in the military, he had no working knowledge of armor. As a member of the Abwehr, the intelligence sector, he'd had less opportunity for combat training than did a line officer, and even most of them lacked specialized skills regarding most weapons, but it infuriated him that he knew so little. He hit the accelerator. The tank ran in reverse. He braked, left the machine in idle, and climbed from the turret.

"Take us home," he said to the Malagasy, who was reclined across the top plating.

The words were scarcely out of Erich's mouth when, from inside the hut, there came a piteous screech of terror so penetrating that it rose even above the noise of the tank. At first he thought it was a dog, or one of those fox-lynxes that intermittently emerged from the rain forest. Fossas, it had said in one of the books he'd brought. He had a footlocker full of books. Madagascar, tactics, *The German Shepherd Dog in Word and Picture* by Rittmeister Max von Stephanitz. The one book he'd had since boyhood.

A moment later Misha's small form hurtled from the hut, rose to all fours, and crawled toward the smoking ashes of the fire pit. A simmering anger displaced Erich's sense of bravado.

Jumping down from the tank, he stalked over toward the boy. The child swiveled and backed up, bare feet stepping through the fire pit, face distorted with such terror that one might have thought the tank was chasing him. The taste of bile swilled into Erich's mouth—residue of last night's drinking, he assured himself; as a soldier he could stomach *anything*.

Except for a dog collar, and a pair of ragged, cut-off pants, the boy was naked. Furious, Erich flashed back to his own youth and his years in the Freikorps, with Otto Hempel as the youth group's leader. He remembered the night he ran away from home and came across Hempel and two boys who were no more than children. He remembered the man's grunts, and the snap of a whip against one boy's fleshy pink buttocks in that Ku'damm alleyway.

"Come here, Misha," Erich said, his hatred of Hempel rising to new heights.

So terror-filled a moment before, the boy's face became suddenly, inexplicably blank. He ceased backing and bowed, mechanical as a tiny wooden monkey held between two sticks. "I am a filthy Jew not fit to kiss your feet," he said. The dog paws danced against his chest. Tears brimmed and began trailing down his cheeks. "Filthy and not fit!" he said again. Coughing, he lowered his face, striking the top of his head with angry fists, as if attempting to beat his own brains in.

"Stop it!"

"…to kiss your…feet!"

"Stop it, I say!" Erich seized the boy by the shoulders and shook him.

"…to kiss your feet…*sir!*"

The boy's eyes rolled up and he slumped sideways.

Erich caught him by the waist, and the child doubled over like a sandbag. Lifting him up, Erich started for the hut, then changed his mind and carried the boy to the tank. Hempel's property or no, the child was *not* going to endure again whatever had just transpired in that shack. The hell with Hempel: a man who did not own his own soul had no right to own anything else.

Then he remembered the Torah.

He handed the boy to Bruqah and strode quickly toward the hut. As he drew near, a pungent odor of overripe oranges hung in the air. He saw one of the Kalanaro creep up to peer beneath the doorway's tanhide and watched him retreat, whispering and pointing, as another joined him, nodding excitedly. Seeing Erich, they skittered away behind the tanghin tree—pygmies with heads like hairy coconuts and mouselemur eyes too big for their faces, shining black as boot polish. Their lurking and scuttling along the edge of the *savoka* gave him the creeps, but he renewed his intention to find out if they were trainable.

Wrenching aside the zebu hide, he entered the hut, squinting against the smoke rising from the brazier. As his vision cleared, he saw the major seated on a mat and bent over the Torah that had been carried aboard ship and used in the documentary being made by Leni Riefenstahl, Hitler's favorite propaganda-film producer. The silver scroll-caps had been pried off. Hempel held one; the Zana-Malata, the other. The syphilitic was wearing a breastcovering of crocodile skin trimmed with tufts of bright feathers. He sat in a crude raffia chair, legs apart, his breechcloth lumped in his crotch.

He cackled as if in response to something Hempel had done, and bent to slurp a mouthful of sea urchin that overflowed his other palm, gumming the soft meat like a toothless crone. After licking his fingers, he raised the scroll-cap and chortled.

"*Prosit!*" Hempel toasted, lifting the second silver cap. With his other hand, he picked up a stick and stirred the contents of a large cast-iron pot that sat among the brazier's coals. Steam and an aroma reminiscent of Grand Marnier drifted from the pot.

Hempel inhaled deeply. "Flavored with fruit bat. At first I found the idea revolting, like something out of the Middle Ages, but it's delicious."

Smiling, he looked up at Erich through bleary eyes that reflected the brazier's glow, and lifted the liquid-filled scroll cap. "*Rano vola,*" he said. "The national drink. They add water to the leftover rice that sticks to the bottom of the cooking pot, and boil it."

He sipped, then with forefinger and thumb lifted out a sauce-covered wing. Popping it into his mouth, he crunched down on the tiny bones, smacking his lips. "Just what we should do to your Jew friends. Use them as flavoring. Do you know how sweet human fat smells?"

He laughed and, closing his eyes, flared his nostrils in mock anticipation. "But pardon my manners, Herr Oberst." He gestured for Erich to sit down. "Pull up a mat. Luncheon in Madagascar is a delightful event."

Finishing the drink, Hempel put down the scroll cap and, ducking his head to the Zana-Malata's lap, used the edge of the breechcloth to dab his lips, which sent the syphilitic into renewed gales of laughter.

Straightening, Hempel held up a hand as if to halt an accusation before the senior officer had a chance to speak. "No, Herr Oberst. Not drunk. I have never in my life been drunk, nor shall I ever be. I am merely *contented*."

He stretched up an arm and ran his fingertips along the Zana-Malata's dark, chafed cheekbones, like a photographer sensing the spirit in his model before a session. "He's shown me my dreams."

Erich's stomach turned, and he fought to contain his anger. The major needed a straitjacket, he thought. Insubordination was no longer the issue; evidence for a firing squad lay at his feet. Taking the Torah could be construed as theft, a capital offense on a combat mission.

Looking from the Torah's de-jewelled sheath to the tiny pyramids of sapphires and pearls that gleamed in the sockets of the water buffalo skull in the corner, Erich asked, "By whose authority have you stolen and desecrated Party property?"

Hempel laughed sarcastically. "By yours and God's, or do you consider those to be one and the same?"

"You disgrace the uniform of the Reich."

"And you, Herr Oberst? I assume you have come to reclaim the Torah in order to loan it to the Jew vermin so they can practice their unholy rites—within a German military installation, no less!" Hempel was grinning, but his eyes narrowed as he spoke. "For your information, you gave permission for the killing of the zebu, and insisted that righteous payment be made to the owner." He pointed at the Zana-Malata and then at the Torah. "Owner, payment. It was what he wanted. I merely delivered it to him. Now if you have nothing more pleasant to say, I suggest you leave."

"Not without the Torah," Erich said. "And you might as well know that I am taking the boy, Misha, with me, too. You have buggered him for the last time."

His right hand settled on his pistol grip and unsnapped the holster, expecting and hoping that Hempel would try to hit him with whatever it was he was holding. He tensed his forearm for a block and used his peripheral vision to locate Hempel's forward knee. That was where the bullet should go. It would drop him nicely, but would not greatly delay the court martial. A good lesson for the troops.

To his astonishment, Hempel merely shrugged.

The devious bastard was doubtless playing with him, Erich thought, wanting him to believe that he had won so that he would be caught off-guard by his attack...when it came, and whatever it turned out to be. He had a feeling it would pay him well to watch his back.

Without a further word, Erich picked up the Torah and the scroll caps, and left the hut.

He found Bruqah gazing toward the shack. "Zana-Malata gather magic like bee gather honey." He straightened his *lamba* and slid back down into the turret, eyes flashing toward the colonel. "Mister Erich—

Germantownman be wise to hold she temperament from now on."

He clanked down the hatch and started the engine.

Erich looked at Miriam, who was holding Misha. The boy was skinny enough that, despite her bulk, she could cradle him on her lap. Erich hoisted himself up and, sitting down on the slitted plates above the engine, stroked the boy's head.

"Misha," he said softly.

Looking over his shoulder, Erich told Bruqah, "Drive up the hill." It would be good for Miriam and the boy to be up there away from the compound. Besides, he wanted to be present when they opened the crypt, which should be any time now.

The Panzer growled and snorted and turned on its treads without forward motion. The child's eyes opened suddenly and fearfully, and his body stiffened. Thinking that the boy might fall from Miriam's lap, Erich put out a hand to steady him. Miriam pushed it away with a strange motion. Though her eyes were open, he got the disquieting sense that she was asleep; smiling serenely, she placed forefinger and thumb under the boy's brows and lowered the eyelids as one might those of the dead.

CHAPTER FOURTEEN

"Into the cage, *Hundescheiss*."

Clutching at tufts of grass, Solomon crawled toward the tiny prison. He found the cage and jerked open the door with a clattering of chain.

He pulled himself inside and sat as he had done so many times at Sachsenhausen, head scrunched down against drawn-up knees. Hempel kicked him to make him move farther in, then slammed and chained the door.

Do what you must to me, but stay away from Miriam, Sol prayed, wondering why he imagined that his words could have any meaning for the God who seemed to have deserted him all over again. At that moment, it seemed to be as unlikely a possibility as that of an appeal to Hempel having any effect.

Any *positive* effect, he amended his thoughts.

"See how much good your precious Torah will do you sitting out here in the sun," Hempel said, adding, "and I remind you again that you can thank your friend, the good Herr Oberst, for this little holiday." The guards who had hastily built the cage laughed.

Sol heard a familiar metallic grating as Hempel checked the magazine of his pistol. He fought the dread that threatened to overcome him. Again it's come to this, he thought. So much of my life dependent on Erich's actions.

His heart beat wildly, pounding against his chest. Don't let the hate crowd out hope, he told himself. Surely Erich will save me, as a matter of pride, if nothing else.

He heard Hempel and his men walk away, still laughing.

Sol's tension abruptly uncoiled, and his body sagged with helplessness. Slipping from around his legs, his arms fell to his sides. He thought he heard himself mumbling a prayer, but he hadn't the energy to listen or stop. His mind seemed incapable even of subvocalizing the words, yet his lips kept moving. Insects buzzed and bit him and ran up his arms and legs, seeking his sweat.

Deborah, the blazing sun beat out on his head. *Deborah*.

The name came to him on the humid wind, rustling the grass and touching him so tenderly that he felt compelled to repeat it. "De-bor-ah." Tongue against frontal palette, a brief compression of lips, a tiny outrush of breath.

The whispered syllables gave him such reassurance that he opened his eyes despite the pain and disorientation, but instead of the compound and the hut, he saw cobalt-blue light pinwheel before him——

——*Amorphous figures move about him in a pulsing blue haze.* Unfamiliar hands grip him. He squalls for the woman who lies nearby, wanting her love.

Mama, he wants to say, but can only wail.

White, ragged, fearful heads leer down from the edges of the fog. He sees zebu skulls. In the corner of a hut.

A thousand needles stab his eyes, but Solomon squints harder, concentrating his focus, his face thrust as much as possible between the bars.

In a glimpse immediately overwhelmed with blue pain, the haze lifts——

Zebu skulls! In the corners of the hut!

Was he seeing into the future again?

The breeze wafted against his face, cooling him enough to allow the pain from the beating he had received at Pleshdimer's hands—and Hempel's instructions—to penetrate. Intruding into the pain came a renewed maelstrom of blue——

——*Fingernails as long as talons tie a length of wire around a blanket of cypress palm*——

——*Through the door of the Storch, he sees Hempel raise his Mann*——

——*The Zana-Malata rushes toward a baby wrapped in cloth*——

"Leave her alone!" Sol screamed, shaking the bamboo bars.

For a moment the talking in the compound, the tinking of hammers against metal, the sawing in the jungle, all ceased. The only sound in the universe seemed to be the thunder of his anguish.

"Deborah! My God! Miriam!"

Tears of fury burst from him and he ground his knuckles against his eyes, hating all the agonies they'd witnessed. "Do something, Erich!" he ranted. "Prove to the world that you've got some courage."

His body slackened against the bars and he cried, his breaths an angry rasping. When his anger was spent, his normal vision—poor though it was—had returned. He saw bamboo and grass and wire, and an orange sun, and he could hear the dogs yapping and yowling, pacing back and forth on their runs like expectant fathers.

"Erich," he whispered. "Take care of Miriam and the child."

You must dwell among your dreams, the wind whispered back.

It was Bruqah's voice, but it reminded him of something deeper in his past. He smelled ginger cakes and apple-peel tea, and he thought he heard the crunch of autumn leaves underfoot. When he squinted upward, the sunlight seemed to have coalesced into a tunneled steep of stairs with a red-orange orb at their end, and he felt as if he could hike through the sky and unlock the sun, a vault containing the power of his meditations and memories, if only he were willing to confront the moon and his nightmares as well.

"Miriam," he heard his lips tell him, as his muscles tightened and his body convulsed, a single spasm. His self stepped away and he fell into a state that was neither vision nor delirium, but something at the same time newer than the infant Miriam was carrying and more ancient than the universe itself...

He labored up the stairs and into the heavens, following a Gypsy's call, holding onto bamboo rails that were the scrolls of the Torah and Zorah so that he would not stumble or turn back. The compound and the island and the Earth fell away behind him, while around him the ten stars of the Kabbalah shone in a night sky. As he neared the moon, he heard voices, increasingly distinct, greeting and gently admonishing him for not having traveled skyward sooner. His father was there, and Hans Hannes, his friend from the camp. Rabbi Czisça was there, too, an older version of Misha. Their souls—all of them—danced joyously within a Bushman's moon.

He hesitated, fearing that if he stayed here for even a minute he might never return to the world that he knew. Unready yet to leave it, he stretched out a trembling hand and touched reality—and a halo of cobalt blue——

——"*I don't think Wilhelm worked for the SD for the money,*" a woman's voice says. "And I never accepted his explanation about his becoming a spy simply because he was German. I'm sure he lived in Tehran because the morphine content of Iranian opium was thirteen percent, five percent higher than that in Beijing, where he'd formerly been living."

Solomon looks around. He is in a large cell with a small window which is higher than his head. Five other people are in the cell: a muscular black man in raggedy shorts, withdrawn into a corner and staring listlessly at his scarred left calf; a gray-haired woman leaning against a wall and smoking a cigarette; a man in a fez, standing behind a hurdy-gurdy; a young woman in a Siit pilgrim robe, kneeling beside an old man who wears a tattered woolen coat and has an ancient carbine across his thighs.

"Then the war broke out," the young woman continues telling the old man, "and Wilhelm found himself in what was probably the most isolated capital in the world. He so wanted to be part of the conflict!"

The old man tilts up the carbine and starts cleaning it with a rag. "Sounds like he was addicted to being addicted."

The elderly woman flips her cigarette onto the straw floor and grinds it out with the toe of her shoe. "Talk! All you two do is talk!"

The younger woman grabs the carbine and shakes it. "What would you have me do? Talking stills the pain! I was raped—God only knows how many times." Her voice abruptly lowers, and her face becomes a mask, eyes pale and distant. "But that pain is nothing compared to what I feel about having—"

"I harbor more than a little guilt myself," the elderly woman says in a shaky voice.

Holding his back as though he has bursitis, the old man rises. "Let's face it, we were fools."

"Except him." The elderly woman nods toward the black man, who is silently crying. "He alone among us is truly innocent."

The hurdy-gurdy man, head lowered in a look of shame, sluggishly turns the handle of his machine. The metal fingers, hitting at the wrong speed, play "Glowworm" out of tune, flat and funereal.

Solomon gropes through the blue light as though the air can be parted like a curtain. "Wanda," he hears himself say to the younger woman. He gazes at her thin, almost childish body and eyes made vapid with woe. "Wanda Pollock."

He steps forward and puts a palm on the older woman's shoulder. "I'm dreaming," he says.

"A wiser Solomon would know otherwise," she quietly replies.

"For over twenty years I've heard a woman crying. 'My soul is dirty, let me die,' she'd say. That was you?"

The elderly woman nods.

"And you, begging for borscht and ginger tea?" he asks the man in the ragtag coat whom his dreams called Schutze Margabrook.

The old man turns and gazes blankly toward the moonlight streaming between bars of the window as Solomon moves past the hurdy-gurdy and stands, hands clasped, over the black man, as though he were beside a grave. "I dreamed that from you the evil ones took the sinew that had made you a human gazelle."

Eyes brimming, the man does not lift his head. The hurdy-gurdy man stops playing.

"Dreaming," Solomon says again.

"Dreams are mirrors, and mirrors, dreams," the old woman says softly. "Perhaps you're still asleep in your bed on Friedrich Ebert Strasse."

"We've waited all these years for you to face your Self and touch the truth," Wanda interjects.

"And what is that truth?" Solomon asks.

She gives him a slight, condescending smile as her attention appears to drift. "German troops raped me after they took Warsaw. I escaped to Pinsk, where Russian troops raped me and shipped me to Siberia. Later I was sent to Iran. When the KGB discovered I was living with Wilhelm, they let forty soldiers gang-rape me, hoping to learn things about him that I didn't know. For four days, until he was able to rescue me."

"The truth," the elderly woman says in a voice filled with regret, "is that a child is about to be born whose soul is a dybbuk's. A dybbuk who is collaboration made manifest."

"A dybbuk you must vow to kill."——

——"Oh my God, they've killed you."

Solomon blinked and saw someone crawling rapidly toward him through the grass. As he neared, Sol could see that it was Max, a man in his early twenties. He looked over his shoulder to assure he was not seen.

"I'm alive," Sol whispered hoarsely. He thrust a hand between the cage bars to wave Max away. "Get back to the others. The Nazis'll shoot you if they catch you roaming about."

Max drew near and stopped, panting fiercely. "No one's paying attention to us. Even the sentries aren't watching." He stabbed an index finger toward the nearest tower. "The rest are all down at the east end, with their rifles ready. Look! See them?" He pointed toward the far edge of the perimeter, beyond which stood the Zana-Malata's hut. "And there, just outside the jungle. Do you see them?"

"The Kalanaro?" Sol asked.

Max nodded.

At the east end, someone fired a shot in the air, and Sol watched in disgust as the Nazis hooted and jumped about in triumph when the Kalanaro disappeared into the bush.

"It's this place." Max looked around timidly at the jungle. "This Africa. It isn't real."

"I think there are probably some pretty strange things in Africa," Sol said. "Things no whites will ever understand. But this...." He too looked around, though more in anger than fear. "This isn't Africa. This is Europe—transplanted."

Yet his mind wasn't on his words. He was mulling over what Max had said. Where among the camp shadows, he wondered, did reality end and illusion begin? And was that the demarcation—if one existed—between his dreams and his wakefulness?

"Why do the Nazis hate Jews?" Max asked abruptly. He turned onto his side and watched the spectacle at the far end of the camp as though he were lazing on a village green, listening to a summer ensemble. "I've been thinking about that a lot, lately. They can't all think we were responsible for the death of their Christ. They've officially renounced Christianity anyway. They know we fought alongside them in the Great War, and surely they all can't be so blind as really to believe that 'subhuman' business. Look at what we've done, Rabbi! The schools we've founded, the Nobel Prizes we've won, the courts...." The ease left him, and his face squinched with incomprehension.

He stared at the sky, apparently too saddened to express himself in words any longer.

"They don't hate the Jews," Sol said.

"*What?*" Max eyed him with suspicion. "And to think I called you 'rabbi'!"

"This time the persecution's no purge or pogrom. Those days died out with the Christian kings, who wanted to kill us only if they couldn't convert us. In their minds, our religion posed a threat to the world's salvation. What Beadle Treichzat termed a 'rational' hate. Like hating an enemy."

Squinting, Sol could see the white-splotched faces of the Kalanaro slowly emerge from the foliage. "With the birth of modern dictators, we've become the focus of an *irrational* hatred. Like being afraid of the dark. The Nazis don't hate us—they fear us. They don't want to convert us to National Socialism, they want to exterminate us. We represent reason and scholarship and justice, the very things the Fascists and Communists must burn from the globe if their ideologies are to survive. We're the finger-pointers...those who remind the world's conscience that 'Thou Shalt Not.'"

"Moral law," Max said, eyes brightening with admiration as he picked up the thread of Sol's logic, "versus the law of the jungle." He squeezed Sol's hand and smiled. "I shall find the Oberst and request your release," he said. "If they want someone in there, let them take me. You are needed here."

He smiled one more time and, turning, crawled away on his belly like a guerrilla.

Chapter Fifteen

Bruqah maneuvered the growling tank along the track that now pierced the rain forest and ran up to the gravesite. Erich looked out over the foliage into a sun that appeared to have been dipped in Miriam's rouge and hung in a sky colored by her blue eyeshadow. Directly above him, cirrus clouds the color of beaten copper feathered the sky. Watching as the glow dulled and the deep aquamarine bay took on a crinkled sheen, he asked himself why he had never noticed such things until Miriam came to live with him.

Came to live with him?

Hardly the right words—but he had put his bitterness behind him, he was sure of that. The days when he worried about her emotional outlook toward him—and did demeaning things to win her approval—were part of a world gone mad. Love took many forms, myriad faces; what she felt toward him would change when he showed her how high he was capable of rising above the Nazi miasma.

The tank reached the bottom of the saddle between the two hills and angled up the second slope, the forest once again enclosing the machine as though in a tunnel. Sunlight filtered between fronds, dappling the machine and making the leaves spangle. Branches scraped along the sides or swooped low as if to decapitate him. The tank growled and jolted as its blade shoved aside felled trees and brush. He supposed he should exult in how rapidly and efficiently the Jews were opening up the forest, but he found himself surprisingly saddened by the neat roadways and new clearings the axes and blast cord created. The rain forest gave him the boyish delight of secret places, secret things, mysteries begging to remain unsolved. Perhaps his decision to have the Jews broaden the larger of the two paths that led from the hut to the *valavato* had been unwise, even if it had made military sense. He would have preferred to keep the hill more remote. His place, except when it was needed to defend against attack.

Abruptly, the tank stopped.

"Look there, Mister Germantownman."

Bruqah's voice sounded icy. Ducking a branch, Erich looked down to see the Malagasy, eyes rigid with fury, pointing into the thick of the forest. Ahead, behind layers of greenery bursting with orchids and snaked through with lianas, Erich could discern the shapes of the Jews, working amid the undergrowth. The *thuk thuk*

thuk of machetes and axes rose above the idling of the engine. Though he could make out a guard standing with his gun across an arm, he could hear no voices, no shouted commands or other harassment. He felt gladdened that the guards seemed to be obeying his orders regarding the Jews. *You do not train a dog by beating it*, he had reminded Hempel's men.

"Looks fine to me," Erich said.

Bruqah lowered his hand, but his angry mien did not change.

Startled—the Malagasy usually was so easy-going—Erich followed Bruqah's gaze into the brush. His eyes were directed toward something much more immediate than men clearing the jungle. He tried to figure out what it was, but flowers and ferns kept drawing his attention, softening his resolve as if their colors were infusing him with their beauty. "Tell me!" he ordered at last, exasperated.

The Malagasy shook his head as though in disbelief, climbed from the driver's seat, and dropped to the ground. He walked into the foliage, moving with the grace of a lemur.

Erich swore under his breath and went after him, pulling apart brush the Malagasy had passed through seemingly without effort. Veils of moss brushed against his face with the mockery of a woman's hand. A liana's large inflorescences scraped like grotesque fingers across his shoulders.

In a grotto of undergrowth swarming with mosquitoes and so suffocatingly hot that sweat burst from beneath his hairline in itchy rivulets, Erich caught up to Bruqah, huddled, head down, before a totem no thicker than a woman's wrist. It was broken off at an angle about a meter above the ground. The Malagasy had his eyes pinched shut and his face was drawn with emotion.

"You promised, Germantownman," he said in a sad voice. "You said island's past would be persevered."

"Pre*served*," Erich corrected testily, rummaging among the shattered branches and forest duff for the rest of the totem. To Bruqah, each mention of the past seemed inviolate. No sense arguing with the Malagash over the loss of an artifact; he *had* made the statement, which was meant to be taken in a broader context. The hill abounded with hidden markers radiating in an indecipherable pattern from the taller ones surrounding the limestone crypt site at the hilltop. Destroying a few was unavoidable as the necessary paths and clearings were cut.

"Here it is." Erich held up the length of totem he had found. The broken end had sheared off strangely. The lily-wood totem was cleanly broken, as though it were shale. It looked as if percussion, instead of the blast itself, had severed the stick. He guessed that the forest—capable of intensifying blast waves as well as blocking them—had caused the break: an effect similar to that of an opera singer shattering crystal.

The totem otherwise was not damaged. Its arabesque of curling leaves reminded Erich of the intricate, petal-like candles so popular at Easter. A more representational series of carvings—lemurs balanced atop one another's backs and looking at him with huge, whorled eyes—formed the middle. A set of miniature zebu horns, common on other totems he'd seen, adorned the top.

"You want me to have it put back together?" Erich asked. "Some of the Jews are excellent craftsmen."

"The damage is done."

Best to let the matter drop, Erich decided. If Bruqah did not want the totem repaired, it would make a good walking stick. Erich tried it out for size as he pushed back toward the tank. Just the right height and heft. It gave him a feeling of balance and power. No wonder, it occurred to him, the members of Germany's Old Order had relished such things.

From behind him came a screech, and Bruqah emerged onto the track, a ring-tailed lemur riding merrily on his back, its arms around his neck. He was climbing back onto the tank when Pleshdimer came waddling toward them, waving his arms as he stumbled over cut but uncleared brush and tree trunks. "Herr Oberst, come quickly. Time for the uncovering!" the Kapo said breathlessly.

"Surely all the surrounding brush hasn't been pushed aside already!" With an irritable gesture toward the downed trees among which they were standing, Erich added, "Look at this!"

Pleshdimer hunkered down his head, like a turtle retreating into its shell, and gazed greedily from the tops of his eyes. "Good enough, the others say, mein Oberst. Plenty of time for clearing after the uncovering's done."

The protuberant eyes, the oily lips, the neck's rolls of fat filled Erich with disgust. He followed slowly.

Increasingly narrow and confined, the path enclosed them. Soft, spiky stamen of crimson browneas dusted Erich with pollen as he ducked through the last of the foliage and into the sunlit gravesite.

He had expected to see the two guards sitting and smoking on the crypt's grass-covered mound while around them the Jews carried away the brush and saplings they had delimbed. With its towering, delicate totems of mahogany and lily wood, this was no place that the tank could plow through after the initial clearing was done. Work here had to be slow and methodical—no blast cord, no mistakes.

Instead, the guards were digging as madly as the Jews, looking not in the least resentful.

A great scallop had been dug out along the front of the grave, exposing the stone entrance. Erich intended the crypt to be a pillbox—his west-end protection. It would have a good view of the bay and an excellent field of fire toward the crescent-shaped lagoon below, where the Storch was parked.

Pleshdimer waved a finger toward the digging. "The jungle told me we'll find gold and treasures inside," he said.

"The jungle," Erich repeated. "What next—voices from a burning bush?"

"He thinks he heard the wind whisper," Bruqah said softly, coming up behind Erich. The Malagasy's eyes glittered impishly. "Ravalona's resting place has been so long forgotten, my patience grew weak-willed."

Erich grinned. Seeing the guards shoveling frantically gave him perverse pleasure. According to Bruqah, the grave was empty—of bones, not just gold—a fact Erich had emphasized before any of this had begun.

"This only crypt on Mangabéy," Bruqah said. "Many more over there." He pointed toward the mainland. "Fancy. One has big airplane," he stretched his arms wide, "like dead man ride in life."

The crypt they were about to open was unadorned except for the surrounding totems and a shroud of mossy grass that did not seem indigenous to Mangabéy. It was built, Bruqah had said, as Ravalona would have wanted it; she was said to have appreciated simplicity above all else. Perhaps that much was myth, Erich thought, an outgrowth of the sadder part of real history: a native princess captured, along with her maidservant, during the slave trade and shipped to the island of Mauritius. What had perhaps begun as a kidnap-and-ransom attempt had ended in tragedy, for the young woman had died of a fever and never returned home. Her body had gone unclaimed, despite Benyowsky's efforts to rescue her alive and, that having failed, to retrieve the corpse.

The guards had apparently not heard Erich's words regarding the tomb; or, at least, were not heeding them—a small slight, but one of many. Whispered innuendoes, eyes that went blank during salutes, personnel switches on his posted duty rosters because *Hempel* had approved the change, or claimed to.

Let them dig, he thought. Maybe it'll teach them to listen.

Shovels scraped limestone. The chiseled, discolored

blocks emitted a fine yellow dust that sprinkled across the upturned red soil each time a guard brought a blade down the side of the crypt to dislodge dirt. The guards spoke in rapid whispers, their eyes avoiding Erich's; they swore and shooed away Goldman when he asked if the white rocks at the bases of the totems were to be kept or cleared. With a small smile and a nod Erich indicated that the rocks were to remain, and Goldman resumed his work.

That was the difference between the guards and the Jews, he decided. The former were paid not to think; the latter never stopped, as they had proven in the camps by staying alive.

Aristida bunch grass had grown in the long, unbroken vertical line of rock that indicated a door in the crypt; the tomb had not been opened for a very long time. It occurred to Erich that that was a good thing, though he was uncertain why. Perhaps because he too liked his history inviolate, he thought.

The grumble of the Panzer interrupted his reverie. The tank came crashing through the underbrush, bending and then snapping saplings. Resolutely Erich stalked toward the machine and signaled for a halt. The tank stopped. Bruqah poked up his head.

"Were you not told to leave this machine where it was?" Erich demanded. "You complained about the ruination of the hillside artifacts, yet you endanger the tall ones here."

Bruqah shrugged. "Damage already done," he said. "I forgive you." He climbed down and put a hand on Erich's shoulder.

Erich shrugged it off. "Where did you leave Miriam and the boy?"

"Misha awoke. They walk a bit to here." Bruqah disappeared down the turret and shut off the tank, which stopped idling with an angry huff. The Malagasy walked over to where the entrance was being uncovered.

Bruqah pulled up a lump of grass and, holding it by its knot of dirt and roots, ran his fingers through the coarse strands as if through a head of hair. "The dead inside tomb dream of daylight," he said.

"Are you attempting to provoke me?" Erich asked in a low voice. "You said the tomb was empty."

"Except for longing." The Malagasy placed his hand upon the stones, a wistful look creeping into his eyes. "To be buried away from home is to be lost. When body cannot come to family burial grounds, stone is raised beside highway or main path so soul can find way home." He stopped and scratched his head, as though searching for words to match complex thoughts. "For common man is enough," he went on, "but for Vazimba...." He stopped again. "People given untruth after Ravalona die. Servant said Princess soul enter Count. People bow at him. French soldiers come—"

"I know the rest," Erich said. Benyowsky was by then without power. Learning the truth, the people fled from him and he was killed by his friends the French—and did not rise from the dead three days later as he'd promised.

"Crypt was built in hope that queen come home," Bruqah said. "She come soon."

"She died a hundred and fifty years ago," Erich said. "As you measure time."

The guards, fingers crammed into crevices and backs bent in effort, were attempting to open the stone entrance. Waving his arms for work to cease, Bruqah approached them. The guards moved aside tensely and suspiciously.

"He'll claim you have to know magic words," one of them mocked.

Bruqah gave him a patronizing smile. From somewhere beneath the *lamba*—a pocket, Erich supposed—he pulled out a piece of gristle. "Witness, *Zanahary*," he said to the sky, "this offering from a tender and well-raised zebu killed only yesterday."

Closing his eyes, he tossed the meat high into the air. It came down among a group of Jews, who dodged it. The guards broke into nervous laughter.

Bruqah took out a second piece of meat and held it up in his palm. He swung his hand to and fro, as if toward the corners of the earth, saying, "Witness, O ancestors. Though we cannot mention you all by name, yet all are included in this prayer! Do not make yourselves spirits without homes. Save your children from witchcraft! Bless we all!"

He cast the meat at the feet of the nearest guard, who backed up apprehensively.

"Witness, O Earth. We give to you because you give to we."

The calling of the birds and insects and the breathing of the other men pulsed in Erich's ears, and in that instant he was transported home. Father Dahns genuflected before the altar, bronze figures of Mary and Joseph looked down from their niches at a little boy standing wide-eyed between his parents while they likewise genuflected, he gripping their hands and wondering about the Holy Mother and her carpenter husband.

"Damn you," Erich said under his breath as the Vazimba sat down on his haunches, head bowed, arms limply hanging.

"What? No more mumbo jumbo?" a guard asked, leaning against the stonework. A boa constrictor slithered out between his legs, its back reticulated with red and orange, and the young soldier cried out, dancing aside as though trying to stamp out a fire. He shivered as he watched the animal sidewind into the taller grass.

"*Dô* snake," Bruqah said. Crossing quickly through the grass, he cut off the snake's departure. Finding feet in front of itself, the serpent lifted its head, burrowed forward, and coiled once around an ankle. The Malagasy looked at Erich and, teeth clamped together, grinned widely as he lifted the leg, the snake dangling. "They vessels of the souls of the dead," he announced.

"I thought you said this crypt was empty," Erich said again, and immediately felt the guards' angry glares.

"I am not *always* right, Mister Germantownman." Bruqah pulled the snake off his leg and, after holding it out at arms' length to appraise it, shucked it, curling, off his arm and dropped it unceremoniously amid the weeds. "Open it, we find out."

The guards quickly jumped to and pried at the door

with all their strength. The stone moved easily, surprising the men and throwing them off balance.

He's nothing more than a poor man's magician, Erich thought, less able than the syphilitic but probably also less evil. He stared down the guards and strode toward the tomb. They looked away to avoid his eyes.

Moving sideways through the narrow door, he entered the crypt. Cool darkness swathed him, bringing a sense of relief after so much humidity. For a moment he stayed still, drinking in the calm and feeling wonderfully separated from the world outside, with all its heat and tempers.

"Bring me a flashlight," he ordered finally, half-expecting that, when he flicked it on, he would see Solomon peering up from the musty blackness, arms cradling a terrier in the sewer hideout of their youth.

Instead, the light revealed a moldering corpse in a soldier's uniform, reclining in a raffia and mahogany chair suspended by frazzled ropes from the ceiling. Erich could see that the body was rotted. Gray flesh mottled with age had given way to brown bone along the cheeks and nose. The eyesockets were empty except for dark pulp at the bottom of the round. The lips were gone, the teeth uneven.

Erich accidentally nudged the chair as he moved closer to examine the body. The head nodded forward, chin against chest, what was left of the wig nearly slipping from the skull. Over a shirt of heavy muslin the corpse wore an embroidered dress coat, threadbare with age, wrist-length sleeves ending in cambric ruffle showing their tatter, the coat's once-gleaming metal buttons glinting dully in the light. Tiny buckles at the kneecaps embellished the black-velvet breeches. The bottoms of the legs, tucked beneath the rest of the body rather than dangling, were outfitted in close-fitting high boots and gaiters decorated with white, woven cloth.

"Benyowsky," Erich guessed in a low breath. His heart pounded with such excitement that his usual fear of the dead seemed to vanish.

The dank low-ceilinged room proved to be empty save for the near-skeleton and three small ceramic bowls, scrimshawed with blue ships upon a blue floral sea. The bowls sat upon a stone pallet which protruded from a side wall and was perhaps meant as a resting place for a body. The floor was also stone, though furred with a fine, wet moss. When he touched it, Erich made a face and brushed his hands clean against his trouser leg.

Bruqah entered.

"You know who that is," Erich said, sensing the Malagasy's lack of surprise.

Bruqah picked up a wrist as if checking for a pulse, and set the arm down again.

"I thought you said Benyowsky had been buried at the *far* end of the bay, near the mouth of the Antabalana River," Erich accused.

"*Entombed*," Bruqah corrected. "Not *buried*. And please to remember my people remove and re-shroud the dead whenever the *lambamena* needs replacing— or when living spirits feel the need."

"For Malagasy dead, yes, but for Europeans?"

Bruqah moved slowly around the corpse, scrutinizing it. "Was Count never Malagasy? Had he no roots in this our land?" He looked at Erich. "Was he never *Ampandzaka-be?*"

The words chilled Erich. Just the dankness of the tomb, he told himself. He drew his shoulders closer together, crossing his arms. "Someone brought the body here. Who would go to such trouble?"

"Zana-Malata awaits return of soul of princess."

"And you?" Erich asked, as the guards peered in the doorway. Erich lanced his light toward them. "Out!"

Muttering, they withdrew.

"I, too," Bruqah said softly. "I, too." More loudly, he added, "Body faces east, where spirits of our ancestors rest. Legs are tucked. Forbidden to extend feet to east. Carefully done, all right."

"Someone went to a lot of trouble," Erich said, hesitant to divulge his suspect for fear Bruqah might disagree—and whatever small sense Erich had made of the matter would unravel.

"Count has waited long years for his woman to return. He yearns for her, I think. He knows her near, I think."

"You know too much," Erich said sternly. "Or at least you think you do."

Using the flashlight as if it were a lance or staff, he ushered Bruqah from the tomb. Glancing back, as the lamp passed the bowls, he thought he glimpsed rice and what looked like chicken fat within two of them, but subsequent sweeps revealed only that the bowls were empty. He emerged, squinting, into the light and heat of the day.

"We want to look," a guard said. "See for *ourselves*."

Erich gave him the light, and the two guards crowded toward the crack. "If I find you've touched him or searched his pockets, I'll court-martial both of you," he warned.

He sent the Jews packing, shovels over shoulders. When the guards exited the grave, he dismissed them as well, and told Bruqah to go and find Miriam and the boy. Alone at the site, the world, even this new world, seemed very far away.

Everything was going to work out fine, he thought. And if all else failed, there was always Plan B: the Storch that waited at the lagoon below. The problem there was that Hempel was the only person on hand who knew how to fly. Plus, the Storch was only built for three; he didn't know if a fourth passenger would be possible. Who would be the other passenger?

Miriam?

Could she ever be happy, knowing they had left Sol behind? Taurus?

From far below, an engine coughed and purred into life, as if responding to his thoughts. Erich stood up and looked down into the lagoon, where Hempel was conducting his daily check of the plane's engine. Sunlight sparkled off the Storch's fuselage. At this distance, the plane looked like a toy.

Erich wished he'd had the time and foresight to learn to fly. In Berlin, he had thought escape would mean boarding one of the rubber boats that, hooked together, would form the pontoon raft they would build to ship the Panzer and other heavy equipment to the mainland.

That was then.

He realized now that losing oneself among the jungles of northern Madagascar or among the human jungle at Antananarivo, the capital, would be insufficient. He would have to abandon his former existence altogether, which meant putting distance between himself and Mangabéy as quickly as possible. Ergo, an airplane.

This airplane.

He strode up the dirt mound and sat down on the crypt's grassy top. Obeying the admonition about not extending his feet, he kept his legs tucked. The hair of graves, he thought, recalling a poem he'd once read. He broke off a handful of blades, bent one in half and tried to make a whistle. Managing to squeak out a spluttery sound he looked around guiltily, fearing he'd been seen or heard, and tossed away the grass.

CHAPTER SIXTEEN

Misha lay on the grass at Miss Miriam's feet, feeling outside of himself, seeing himself, happy that for a while there had been no pain except the heaviness in his chest that made him want to cough all of the time. He thought about what he would want to be when he grew up; that is if wishes were horses and he still lived in Berlin and still lived with his parents. It was a game he played when he wasn't thinking about how he could kill Hempel and Pleshdimer.

Today the answer was easy.

He'd be a magician, like Jean-Jacques Beguin. Papa had taken him to see Beguin, and afterward he, Misha, and Papa had talked about whether Beguin could really read people's minds. His papa said there were only two kinds of magic, the real magic of God and the false magic of men. Misha wondered if his papa was right.

Maybe there was also a third type: God's magic given to men.

"Mishele, what are you thinking?" Miriam asked.

He started to answer, but his words were cut short by renewed coughing.

"That's a nasty cough," Miriam said. "When we get back to the medical tent, Franz must give you medicine—"

"No," Misha said quickly, remembering the burning stuff that the Zana-Malata had given him. "To cure your cough," Hempel had said. Only it hadn't cured a thing, and it had given him terrible nightmares. He remembered the Zana-Malata, face streaked with glowing white slashes, tilting Misha's head sideways and up and pouring a thimblefull of fiery red liquid between his lips. When some had dribbled from the corner of his mouth, the Zana-Malata caught it up with his index finger and forced it back inside his mouth. He choked, and the syphilitic's watery eyes mocked him. The man had pinched Misha's lips shut to keep him from spitting up. He'd gagged, but could not pull away.

The fire had filled his veins, making his skin burn as though from the inside and yet giving his body an easy, drowsy feeling at the same time. It was as if he could take a razor blade, slice open his flesh, and step out of it, like a clown passing through a papered hoop and into the ring of the Berlin circus. His mind had sped up the more his body slowed. He had seen images: two fossas watching him from the hut's corner; the skull of a water buffalo, stubby candles burning in its eye sockets.

He remembered lying on the floor of stripped saplings, a breeze fluttering the edge of the zebu-hide door, and then the hut dissolved. The walls shimmered, wavered, undulated into air. He'd felt himself floating above the meadow. The forest canopy blended into a crenelated green cap covering each of the island's two hills, and around Mangabéy white wavelets shuddered against black and tan shores. The bay was aquamarine, shiny as satin and underlain with the dark irregular shapes of reefs and ledges. Farther beyond, the broad crescent of rain-forested land rose felt-green up steep slopes, to lap at pinnacles that jutted above the jungle canopy like peaks of a ragged crown. He was free. He remembered closing his eyes, feeling the sun against his cheeks and the wind in his hair, and thanking the Zana-Malata and the fiery drink.

Then he was back in the hut. The good, warm feeling was gone and the Zana-Malata stood over him. He wore a rattan hat, brimless, its fringes dancing darkly in the shaft of sunlight that penetrated the hut's dark interior. Misha had felt like crying. But he would not cry, he never cried. On the morning after he left the fire escape where Papa had secreted him and climbed back into the shambles that had been his home before the Gestapo broke in, he had promised himself he would never cry until he and Papa were united once more. Still, he'd heard the whimpering in his own throat and felt the trembling as the Zana-Malata squatted before him, seized his wrist, and brought forth a short dagger he had been holding hidden against his side.

The Zana-Malata had pulled him slowly forward.

He'd allowed himself to be drawn like an object at the end of a rope. The black man's eyes had flickered and he'd brought the dagger tip against Misha's neck and cut into his flesh.

Laughing all of the time.

Laughing...

They were sitting in the shade, but the combination of heat and inactivity was making Misha drowsy. In a few minutes, he was fast asleep and dreaming—of Hempel, and Pleshdimer, and the Zana-Malata. In his dream, he lay on Miriam's lap on the jouncing tank, watching the clouds and wondering if he were not in fact up there, watching some other boy lying on the machine as it plowed across the meadow.

"We should go, Misha," Miriam said, shaking him gently.

He looked around. He was seated amid daisies and tall grasses. Through a break in the surrounding foliage he could see down to the shore. Shadows and sun flicked across his face, and he felt himself sliding into sleep again.

"Lady Miri, Misha, Germantownman say it time to go."

Bruqah's voice filtered through the bushes. Misha stirred lazily.

"Go, Misha. Tell Bruqah I could use his arm to lean on."

Misha stood up and offered Miriam his arm. She smiled and thanked him, and they moved in the direction of Bruqah's voice. They found him easily, and he took over the role of escort, motioning to the boy to go ahead. Misha could see the tank through the foliage and ran toward it, but he was seized by a fit of coughing and tripped over a rotted log overgrown with passion-flower vines and covered with thornbugs and zebra butterflies. Picking himself up, he saw that he had stumbled into a grove of pitcher plants, as whitish-yellow and velvety as a midsummer moon. The remains of beetles and ants floated in translucent syrup.

Looks like honey, he thought, poking his finger into the stickiness above the plant's curled lip. He licked it off.

His pleasure at its sweetness lasted only a moment. He began staggering in a circle, gargling and gasping for breath. He could see Erich racing toward him from one side, and Bruqah from the other.

"What is it?" Erich demanded. "What!"

Misha could not answer. He pointed toward his mouth; the gagging grew more pronounced, and he fell to the ground.

Erich gripped Bruqah by the wrist. "What the hell!"

"Faking," Misha heard a guard say. "I've seen similar tricks."

"They pulled stunts like this back at camp, we'd pee on their faces," another guard said. "*That* brought 'em around."

Misha wheezed so heavily that it sounded to him as if he had an entire string orchestra locked inside his chest. He could see Pleshdimer waddling toward him.

"Stay away from him," Miriam said, placing herself between Misha and Pleshdimer. She knelt awkwardly and took Misha's head in her lap. He looked up at her fearfully.

"Oh God, what's that on his face? Some kind of a rash."

"You're going to be all right," Erich said softly.

Terrified, Misha quivered and lay still. He could hardly move, but he was fully aware of what was going on around him. Bruqah squatted and pressed his fingers against the boy's throat, testing for a pulse.

"Is he...?" Miriam asked.

"Dead?" Bruqah shook his head. "Sometime easier, that. Dead forget pain." Looking up at Erich, he said, "Get water."

"Give him your canteen," Erich ordered over his shoulder.

No one moved.

"Water!"

"Here." The guard held out a canteen begrudgingly. Erich tore it from the man and started back toward Misha.

Bruqah put a hand on Erich's, halting him. "Water good?"

"How the hell do I know! Of course it is!"

"It not *Rano valo*, but it do, if Erich-man say it be pure," Bruqah said.

"You heard me say it is," Erich replied angrily.

Bruqah lifted the canteen from Erich's grasp.

"Now what are you doing!" Erich burst out.

"What I must," Bruqah said. "Am I not *mpanandro*-Vazimba...an astrologer? I warn Sollyman, pitcher plants most bad for some people."

Standing before the pitcher plants, he bowed his head. Then he extended his hand and, mumbling words Misha could not comprehend, sprinkled water into each of the elongated cups.

Erich grabbed Bruqah by the hair. "What the hell do you think that's going to do to help—"

Miriam put a hand on his wrist and he let loose of the Malagasy who ministered to the last of the section of pitcher plants, letting the water dribble across his tilted palm and into the cup. The mumbling never ceased.

"What happened?" Misha sat up and inhaled noisily.

Bruqah stood, grinning, and lifted the canteen as if in a toast. "Spirits happy now," he said. He drank deeply and smacked his lips. "Incantations make Bruqah thirsty."

He handed Misha the canteen. The boy drank deeply.

"Even the rash is gone," Miriam said. She hugged Misha to her.

"I feel fine, now," he said.

Taking him at his word, Erich led the way to the tank. They settled themselves, Misha again on Miriam's lap at her insistence.

He was sitting awkwardly upright when they passed the hut and, looking the other way, he saw Herr Freund, in a cage like an animal at the zoo.

"Stop," he said, jumping up and stepping right on Miriam's foot. "Please. Stop."

Erich looked in the direction of Misha's finger. "Stop the tank," he shouted.

He jumped off the machine at a run. Misha followed

close behind, leaving Miriam sobbing and clutching at Bruqah who had emerged to find out what was going on.

"Not to worry. I bring Torah," Bruqah yelled.

Then they were at the cage and the Herr Oberst was issuing orders, and there was arguing, and finally Herr Freund was released. His skin was bright red and blistering.

"Who did this?" Colonel Alois asked in that loud whisper Misha had heard his own papa use when he had gone beyond anger.

The question was at first met by silence. Then Herr Freund looked right at the Herr Oberst.

"Who do you think did this? He thought he was punishing both of us," Herr Freund said.

"Come with us," Erich commanded.

Then Misha was in Bruqah's arms, the colonel in front, pushing back the flaps of the medical tent to admit Sol and the rest of them. The corpsman was inside with the sick dogs. He was the man called Franz, who used to sneak him chocolate and bread during his Sachsenhausen days.

Through half-closed eyes Misha saw Miriam, Franz, and Bruqah move toward the supplies, gathering things. Bruqah left, saying he was going to gather petitboom and Christmas-bush leaves so that they could boil them up and make tea for the boy's cough.

Erich hovered close, and there was angry pain in his eyes. He glanced toward the others, as if to assure himself that they were not watching, and with his fingers combed back Misha's hair.

"Otto Hempel won't hurt you again," he whispered. "I'll see to it."

Misha shook his head. "I have to go back, Herr Oberst," he said.

"No!" Miriam took hold of him and held him so tightly he could barely breathe. "I won't let you return to those...those monsters!"

"I must," Misha said, when she loosened her hold.

He wanted to tell her why, but somehow he knew that if he did his resolve would weaken. No matter what they did to him, Hempel and Pleshdimer and the Zana-Malata, being near them would make it easier for him to do what he had to do.

In his mind's eye, he conjured up his list.

Kill, it read next to each of their names.

Kill.

CHAPTER SEVENTEEN

Miriam looked at the sleeping boy. He blinked and twitched, but the soporific was working; in all probability, he would not wake for hours. Sleep would not dispatch the trauma he had endured, nor would it change his mind about returning to those animals, but at least he would be away from it for a little while.

She closed the mosquito netting around him and, after nodding thoughtfully toward Franz, went outside the tent to join Erich. He stood smoking a cheroot, looking off toward the west.

"Hempel has got to be stopped," he said. "Somehow I've got to break him."

"The whole operation has to be stopped," Miriam said. "This entire Madagascar insanity."

"What alternative would you suggest? Leave all of Europe's Jews in Hitler's hands, and let him annihilate them?"

"Things will be different here? Everyone will be penned on the island, with no way to escape. At least in Europe there's the chance that they can flee *somewhere*."

"Once the bulk of the Jews have left Europe, Hitler will have fulfilled his promise to the German people to cleanse the continent of them. And he'll have what he really wants—the property they leave behind."

"You Nazis are all alike...simplistic answers for everything."

He tilted his head and blew a long stream of smoke. "You haven't been yourself, lately. The voyage, the pregnancy, getting settled here. I'll treat your remarks accordingly." He looked at Miriam and narrowed his eyes. "But don't overstep too often, Miriam Alois. You may find yourself on the wrong side altogether."

"When have we ever been on the same side?"

He lifted an insolent brow as if condescendingly letting her rant, and returned to smoking his cheroot.

A runner stopped at the gate, raised his arms, and let the guards frisk him. Panting, he marched toward Erich. It was Max, youngest of the prisoners other than Misha. During one of several brief conversations, he had told Miriam that they had arrested him when he'd gone to get help for his wife, about to deliver. He had never learned the fate of his wife or unborn child, for he had refused, despite torture, to reveal their whereabouts. Due to her own condition—and perhaps, Miriam had to admit, to his exceptional good looks— he had a special place in her heart. She found herself smiling at him as, gasping, he saluted and delivered his message.

"I got permission to look for you at the crypt, but you had already left, Herr Oberst, sir!"

"And? Why did you wish to speak to me so urgently?"

"To tell you what they had done to Solomon Freund, sir."

"Rest easy, young man," Erich said. "Your rabbi has been released. Tell me, did you see Sturmbannführer Hempel on your travels up and down the hill? Has he assessed the hill as a forward post?"

"I would not be privy to such information, sir. The last time I saw Sturmbannführer Hempel he was headed down the other side of the hill, toward the lagoon. He left Kapo Pleshdimer—Rottenführer Pleshdimer," Max did not try to mask his disgust, "in charge."

Miriam could see that the young man held a certain amount of real respect for the colonel, despite the Nazi uniform. There was no denying that conditions here on Mangabéy were infinitely better than in Sachsenhausen, and much of that was Erich's doing.

And mine, she thought. If he only knew how much.

An explosion went *whump* from the far hill. They must be back clearing the last of the forest around the crypt, Miriam thought.

Erich listened intently, as if expecting to see part of the forest fall, even from this distance. Those birds that had not taken flight earlier rose into the air. As if satisfied that the explosion was part of the clearing and not some insurgency, he relaxed and stuck his head inside the tent. "Bruqah! Outside! I need you to drive the tank!" he said.

The Malagasy almost instantly appeared. "You need Bruqah? Who fail make machine go forward?"

"Just get in the goddamn tank."

"Erich?" Miriam said. "I wish to go back with you."

Erich scowled at her. "Forget it. Not in your condition. This isn't the Autobahn, you know."

"You are going to the crypt. I need to see inside it."

She had realized by now that somehow she had lost the memory of a part of the day and replaced it with another of the bizarre waking dreams—visions as Sol called them—that had come to her with increasing frequency since their arrival on the island. Something told her that the roots of this one were to be found inside the tomb. Had it not been for Misha's unfortunate run-in with the pitcher plant, she'd have asked to be taken inside the crypt when they were up there earlier in the day.

Without much effort, she reconstructed what she had seen in her mind's eye…

She lay on stone, her ankles fastened by straps, shallow depressions in the stone fitting her form perfectly. As though made for her. Sweat streamed off her forehead as the contractions rolled through her with a pain she swore she could not endure. Not one more. Then she turned her head, and beyond the open door she saw tiny gyrating men, dancing jerkily as marionettes….

"Please, Erich," she said. "Franz can stay with the boy."

"Very well, then," Erich said. "But you are not to blame me if this overtires you. *You*, whatever your name is, ride in the tank with us. Make sure my wife rides safely."

"Yes...sir, Herr Oberst!"

Miriam wondered if the young man's enthusiasm were the result of helping her or of riding rather than walking. There *were* some things best left unknown, she decided.

Bruqah drove slowly, the tank barely bucking on the deepest ruts. This time, being on the machine gave her a particular excitement she had not experienced since girlhood, the kind of pleasure she had known when one day she, Sol, and Erich rode bicycles to the *Siegessäule*—the Victory Monument—and later that afternoon, drenched from a sudden rain, had broken into the abandoned Belford mansion and within five acres of underground wine cellar had pretended to be knights-and-lady. Erich had been Tannhaüser and she Lady Venus; she could not recall what role Sol had elected, except that he had surprised them all by winning. That was the first time she had seen him when the ghosts came....

It was all too long ago to belabor.

She forced her attention upon the moment and caught a glimpse of what it was like to play toy soldier. Perhaps, she thought, the attraction of the military *wasn't* just killing.

"This is absolute foolishness," Erich said suddenly, when they were halfway up the hill. "Stop the tank, Bruqah, we're going back. I don't have time to waste.

I've already inspected the crypt and I've the building of the dock to oversee. Max, help Miriam off this thing. Then Bruqah and I will head down the hill."

Bruqah did as he was told.

"Erich...," Miriam said, her anger rising.

"I've made my decision."

She could see by his expression that he would brook no argument. When they arrived back at the gate she allowed Bruqah and Max to help her to the ground.

"Tell me what you found in the crypt, Bruqah," she said, keeping hold of his hands as he leaned over the edge of the tank.

Quickly, almost in a whisper, Bruqah filled her in. "Some say Count never try to bring her here. Even he never know her, some say. But one thing every man know for damn sure: she die of fever, and never return. Not even for *lambdamena* ceremony."

"The dressing of the dead."

He looked at her with a pain-filled expression. "We wait rebury her, one day."

Miriam sensed Erich's growing impatience, but did not want to cut Bruqah short. "I'm sure that will happen."

"Anything possible. Everything have reason. Mister Sollyman specially know that." He shrugged as if to relieve himself of an emotional burden. "I run same risk when I not in Madagascar. There is place for my bones in crypt at kidney lake where alligators carry ancestors' souls. I am woman and man, both. My people need my soul, else blood run thick again. Aye-aye say—"

He shuddered, clearly afraid. He was always so proud and strong that Miriam was loathe to let go of his hand.

"Bruqah! Let's go!" Erich said.

Miriam chuckled at the great army commander needing a Malagasy to operate his modern machinery.

The tank pulled away, leaving Max to escort her to the medical tent. Feeling the need to walk after Erich's brusque treatment of her, she sent him on alone into the compound and meandered down a path that led toward a copse of slender trees.

She found herself in a tiny clearing, almost a grotto. There was a well-worn bench and the grass was tramped down, as though the place were often used. She sat down, thankful to take the load off her feet. Letting her head tip back, she breathed in the humid air and looked up toward the bowl of deeply blue sky. She felt strangely at peace, despite the heat. And despite the larger, terrible questions: birth, survival.

She thought of the maze of events that had brought her here, and of her own manipulations of those events. She'd relied on her friendship with Juan Perón, who had so adored her when he had first danced with her, when she was young and beautiful and optimistic. She wondered fleetingly what he would think of her now, with her chopped-off hair and ungainliness. It was still a mystery to her why Erich had never said anything about her bout with the scissors. Even Sol had said little except, "It will grow back."

Which was probably what her Uncle Walther and Perón—or Domingo as she had called him, using his middle name—would have said. They had indulged her, the two of them. In those days, he was a young attaché to the Italian embassy, and she was being groomed by her uncle to enter the political arena. "Half Jewish and, soon, all woman—now *that* will set the Reichstag on its ear," Uncle Walther had told her. Not that she'd ever wanted to be anything but a performer.

Perón, still wanting to please her many years later, had requested that Erich Alois be placed in charge of the Madagascar Experiment. Or at least in charge of initial operations. Himmler had surprisingly acquiesced. He had approved, as well, her accompanying her husband, and signed without hesitation an order releasing one Solomon Isaac Freund, Jew, fluent in French and experienced in accounting, to be interpreter and supply clerk with the advance party.

She had deluded herself into thinking that Himmler's decision was based on Erich's qualifications. After all, Erich and his trainers were in charge of security for Goebbels' headquarters, and there was word that his expertise in security and his genius for dog training might land his zodiac team the coveted job of guarding Hitler himself.

Only weeks later did she learn that Himmler had approved Perón's request out of political, not military, expediency. Regardless of Hitler's having declared her "without Jewish blood," she remained Jewish in Himmler's eyes. And she was the perfect ploy. Goebbels, with Himmler's blessing, had hired Leni Riefensthal to make a propaganda film, with Miriam in a title role. *Pregnant wife of Colonel Erich Alois—*

stolen from the cradle by Jews and raised by the traitor Walther Rathenau, once Germany's foreign minister—is now bound for the African island of Madagascar. The island is the remnant of the sunken continent of Lemuria, home of the great winged Roc that attacked Sinbad. There she would serve husband and Fatherland, as in his compassion the Führer created a homeland for the Jews.

The documentary would play to teary-eyed audiences in the Reich's theaters—more likely in theaters all over the world. Like her first film, when the young and beautiful Frau Alois—who no longer felt young or beautiful—renounced Judaism and all its evils and placed a wreath on the graves of the young anarchists who had assassinated her uncle.

To save Sol.

To keep her love alive.

She sighed and closed her eyes, wishing she could forget. The baby kicked. She smiled and placed a hand on her belly. The Nazis had taken her mansion and her money, and severed her career. They would not have the child. Or Solomon, if she could help it.

"Deborah," she whispered, repeating the name again and again. Feeling the child move as had happened each time she'd spoken the name aloud. The child was a girl, she was sure of it, a girl-child aware of the mother who bore her.

Images began to bombard her. She gave in to them——

——Again, she lies on the stone hearth, the shallow depressions fitting her form perfectly, as though carved for her. Her belly rolls like the sea. She stares at it in horror. The baby is coming, the pain jerks her head back, and still the unnatural rolling of her belly continues. Through the doorway she sees pygmy dancers, whitely glowing, undulating. An eternity passes before the pain lets up enough for her to move. A hand with nails like claws touches the outside of her thigh. In horror she looks down her body, but the hand darts away. Behind the rows of guttering candles there is a blanket-draped figure.

An elderly white woman wearing bifocals, her safari hat wrapped and tied under her chin with a bright yellow chiffon sash, enters the stone room. She reaches out for Miriam but does not touch her. Her hand, the same hue as her khaki jacket and pants, remains suspended in air, as if she fears to touch the woman on the dais.

"You have choices, Miriam," she whispers. "Your child is bringing you one reality. You do not have to accept it."

"Who are you?" Miriam asks, struggling to rise above the pain.

"I am Judith," the woman says. "Dr. Judith Bielman-O'Hearn."

"Thank God," Miriam gasps. "A real physician."

"Not a medical doctor," Judith says. "An anthropologist. I work with the Falasha—the Black Jews of Ethiopia. Hitler has plans for them…uproot them from their ancestral home and send them here to Madagascar. Mussolini has approved the idea. As has Stalin, with the Ukrainian Jews."

The pain is excruciating. Miriam screams, wishing the woman would help her or go away.

"I have come to warn you of the Malagasy. He wishes to control the child."

"The Zana-Malata? I wouldn't let that...that creature—"

"Yes, he is evil and power-mad. He confuses the dybbuk in your child with the soul of Ravalona—"

"The *what*?"

"The dybbuk that was in Solomon was in his seed...."

Before Miriam can fully comprehend what she has heard, Judith says, "But it is the other one, the one called Bruqah, of whom I speak. He knows the child is not a vessel for Ravalona, but fears what the false belief that it is will do to his people. It is he whom you should fear."——

——*Tekiah.*

The first note of the shofar sounded—long and melancholy. In ancient times, it had summoned Jews to battle.

So the Juterbourg farmer had succeeded in fashioning a shofar out of the zebu horn Misha had found, Miriam thought, glad that the trumpeting had broken the spell of the vision. For a moment all other sounds ceased. The guards' talking and clatter, the dogs' barking and baying, the lemurs' and insects' chittering in the jungle that surrounded the hilltop pasture on which the encampment sat—all stopped, as if man and beast recognized, for whatever reason, the traditional call to worship on this Rosh Hashanah, the first day of the Jewish new year.

Sundown had surprised Miriam again. Already it was almost dark and the cooler evening air pressed against her skin like a soft hand. She half-ran toward the encampment, hampered by her bulk. In the southeastern corner, beneath the limestone knoll that served as the fourth sentry tower, she could see the prisoners gathered around Solomon, heads bowed but bodies upright in defiance of the four machine guns that were trained in their direction.

Miriam felt her heart sink as Pleshdimer grinned at her in passing and lumbered toward the Jews. The bowed heads did not seem to notice him coming, but from the rain forest, a dozen eyes reflected the dying sun. Lemurs, probably. If they weren't careful, their curiosity would earn them the stewpot.

Shevarim. The second note. Broken. Mournful.

If only she could attend the service, but having "officially" renounced Judaism, anything contradicting that would bring down Hempel's wrath, much less Erich's.

Or maybe it wouldn't.

Their beloved Führer Himself had defined her as Aryan. Even on a remote Madagascar island they could not obviate His orders and live without fear. She was safe, surely.

"When, Solomon, will we find a way to live together in some semblance of normal life?" she whispered.

Perhaps, she thought hopefully, she could watch the service from a distance, yet close enough to put herself among the prisoners should Hempel and his ilk decide to interfere. Were she in danger, Erich would be more likely to intercede on behalf of the Jews.

She shook her head, chiding herself for her

assumptions and angry with her self-centered attitude. She had the baby to consider, she reminded herself.

Besides, what right had she to think herself welcome in the company of a congregation of men who had survived Sachsenhausen!

CHAPTER EIGHTEEN

Teruah.

The third note of the shofar sounded—sharp, staccato, expressing the pride and the pain and the hope of Solomon's people. This time, the forest animals replied as if in counterpoint.

Looking over the bowed heads of the huddled Jews, Solomon remembered the last important time he had stood at the *bimah*. His bar mitzvah.

What an event that had been for him and for his family.

Now, he stood before the others near the narrow spring that ran over the cliff from the embankment. Standing to one side were the few men who no longer believed that their God listened when they prayed. Above him, pointing down at the piece of cloth he was using as a *yarmulke*, was a machine gun. Beyond the prisoners, two of Erich's dog trainers held Krupp machine pistols, while half-a-dozen others stood beside their dogs, fingering the choke chains nervously.

In obedience to Erich's orders, Hempel's men kept their distance.

"*Baruch Ato Adonoy, Elohaynoo Melech Ha'olom,*" he intoned after Goldman, serving as cantor, lowered the shofar. *May the Lord make His countenance to shine upon you and bring you peace. Amen.*

Sol kept his voice hushed. No sense waking the dead—or at least those who, priding themselves on spreading death, were morally so.

"For obvious reasons, I'm going to keep this brief," he began. "We are here today to honor a beginning. For us, this Rosh Hashanah is more than a New Year and a time of remembrance and judgment. As Jews we must examine our past wrongs, where in deed and thought we have failed our Father...*land,*" he added, glancing uneasily toward the men with the dogs. "We stand here beneath the eyes of He who created us; our actions and conduct must serve not only as an example for those who follow us, but also as the springboard—the base camp— for the fact that they *will* follow...*if* we not only obey"— *our consciences,* he wanted to say—"but work as men possessed."

He continued with the sermon, keeping it short yet striving to ensure that his fellow prisoners understood his message, both explicitly and implicitly. On this Holy Day, his people prayed to be included in the book of the righteous who would live one year more. Even the dead, it was written, prayed for the living. This holy day was when the Jew reviewed his history and prayed that he would find contentment and hope in Jerusalem. Such was the dream of all Jews since the Diaspora. So this wasn't Jerusalem, but it also wasn't Sachsenhausen. How bittersweet that they had reason to give praise to Adolph Hitler.

Sol had carefully thought out the sermon. He wanted to be certain that a subtle but clear message underlay his words, one conveyed by inflection and nuance. The fact was that ultimately each of them would have to decide in his own heart whether he should work with the Nazis—compromise with evil—to build a sanctuary here for European Jewry. He, Solomon, knew of Hitler's plans to transform Madagascar not into a homeland for Jews but a ghetto where he might pen up Jewish assets and abilities for his own ends. The Führer wanted to rid the world of Jews, but keep at hand what they could give him. The list of Jewish achievements, especially in industry and science, was endless; even a madman such as he would not be so foolish as to give that up. A Nazi-dominated Jewish island off the east coast of Africa would guarantee ongoing use of the ideas and human energy the Jewish people possessed; it would also protect Fascist oil interests in the Gulf states, ensure Italian imperialism in Ethiopia, and break up British shipping lanes between India and South Africa.

The notion of a Jewish homeland on Madagascar had not originated with Hitler. Napoleon had considered it; Bonnet, France's Foreign Minister, had supported such a plan; the Poles had sent a contingent to Madagascar to study the matter. But Hitler clearly had a greater design, if he intended to go through with the project at all. Hadn't he said as much to Rathenau way back in '18?...*pen the Jews on Madagascar, and use them like dogs*.

Right now, on tiny Mangabéy island—an area of land almost as small as the infamous Alcatraz, in the United States—the plan was but a seed. Solomon and the other prisoners could help assure the survival of European Jews, in a world grown insane with hate; but in building what Hitler wanted, they would run the risk of supporting what he might do on Madagascar. Should they attempt to create a sanctuary—or sacrifice themselves and sabotage the mission?

His personal history drove him toward the latter course, which was not surprising after his many years of studying the texts of the great Kabbalist, Isaac Luria. Luria had believed that *galut*, the exile of the Jewish people, was a reflection of the self-imposed exile of God Himself, who withdrew to make room for the world.

How much simpler it would be, Solomon thought, to believe as many Kabbalists did that *galut* was a condition of a universe in need of redemption, rather than a circumstance imposed by man. So firm were they in that belief, that many of them went into exile by choice, both seeking expiation and in order to participate in what was thought of as the divine exile.

He spoke of that in his sermon. With enemy ears trained upon his words, he could not talk much about their present reality. Had he been able to do so, he would have said that if Hitler lacked a destination to which to send European Jewry, he would be forced into compromise, however self-serving. For how else might he deal with the millions of Jews with which he must contend now that he had invaded Poland and annexed Austria and Czechoslovakia? And he would not stop there. It hardly seemed possible that even he could hope simply to kill them all.

The prisoners kept their heads down as Solomon spoke. Not only in reverence and to avoid arousing suspicion, but also because each mulled the questions, considered the ramifications—and remembered home and loved ones. Dare they throw away whatever chance they had to see those loved ones again, in exchange for the pitifully small reward of *possibly* keeping Madagascar out of Nazi hands? Even if the project failed, should Germany attack France it was likely that Madagascar, though nominally French, would side with Hitler. There was considerable Nazi sympathy here, as there was in South Africa. Solomon knew there was another variable, one each man could not avoid considering, though none would ever admit having thought about it: Solomon Freund, whom they had chosen to act as rabbi, was or had been involved with Miriam Rathenau Alois. Misha, who had worked for her before his capture, had told them that. She was *here*. The women they loved were…where?

If they were even alive.

Nearing the end of the service, Sol signaled Goldman to take over the reading from the Torah. That night they would share in the eating of the head of a fish, so that they would all be heads and not tails in the year to come; tomorrow, singly because they had not dared to ask permission to gather again as a group, each man who still believed would cast away his sins against God beside the stream.

For now, he must ready the bread they had saved and the honey they had gathered—symbolic of their joy and gladness in the Lord.

Deep in thought, he did not immediately see Miriam standing near the outer fence. Seconds later, panic rose in him, though not at the sight of her there, or of the half-a-dozen Kalanaro armed with spears who danced, and glowed, in the dusk.

What caused his pulse to quicken was the sight of Dr. Judith Bielman-O'Hearn, standing large as life at Miriam's side. He could see her clearly in the sentry tower's spotlight.

Sol blinked and tried to focus with weak eyes, wondering if this could be another of the visions that had plagued him since childhood, the visions that had become so much more terrifying after he had witnessed the assassination of Miriam's uncle.

But there had been no cobalt-blue light to presage this vision, as there had always been before; and, despite the shadows and his eyesight, the woman's figure had a clarity to it that had never been true of his amorphous ghosts.

The Kalanaro leaped and cavorted and spun in silence, brandishing their weapons, their heads like hairy coconuts, their eyes charcoal-rimmed and too big for their faces. Mouselemur eyes.

Forcing his focus, it became apparent that the Kalanaro were covered with a white substance that appeared to pulse and wink—

"You all right, *Reb* Solomon?" the man next to him asked, placing a light hand on Sol's arm.

"May you be written down for a good year," Solomon said, choosing to use the traditional Rosh Hashanah greeting in the hope that it would lend him strength.

"Prisoner three-seven-seven-zero-four!"

Hearing his Sachsenhausen number, Sol jerked his attention to the left, moving his whole head rather than his eyes to compensate for his lack of peripheral vision. Pleshdimer, his fat carp mouth downturned in a sneer, stood beside the spring.

"I'm talking to you, Jew!"

Solomon shoved the bowl and bread into the nearest man's hands, raced toward Pleshdimer, and snapped to attention. Erich had ordered the Kapo not to speak to the prisoners in a derogatory manner, but Sol knew that beneath Pleshdimer's fat was a strength that could break a man's neck like a twig. Erich's orders or no, it was life-threatening to treat the Kapo with anything but the greatest show of respect.

Sol saluted. "Yes, Herr Kapo Pleshdimer!"

"Herr Kapo Rottenführer Pleshdimer!" the man bellowed into Solomon's face. "I'm army now, you know."

"Yes, Herr Kapo Rottenführer Pleshdimer!" Were the pygmies still there? Sol wondered. Were they watching? Was Judith?

He glanced from the corner of his eye; as usual he

saw only dark gray where his eyesight failed him. He turned his head, slightly. The dancers were gone.

Judith was gone.

Pleshdimer hit him.

The punch came from the side. Sol heard a cartilaginous crackling in his left ear even before he felt the pain. Then something roared through his head and he slumped sideways to his knees, struggling to hold himself up with his right hand.

Pleshdimer kicked him beneath the chin, snapping Sol's head backward and catapulting him onto his shoulder blades. He lay there, schooled by the terrible lessons of Sachsenhausen into knowing he had to arise immediately or face further punishment.

"You will look at me when I speak to you, scum!" Pleshdimer boomed from above.

He squatted and stuck a cigarette butt between Sol's lips, then scooped up red mud from beside the spring and mashed it against Sol's mouth, rubbing hard with the heel of his hand.

Solomon managed to rise to his knees and struggled to stand, careful not to spit out the cigarette nor wipe off the mud. Let no man refuse what gifts Wasj Pleshdimer gave; Solomon had learned that the hard way, too.

"Yes…Herr Kapo…Rottenführer…Pleshdimer, sir," Sol forced himself to say. He felt blood coming from his left ear, trickling down beneath his collar.

"What's going on here!"

He looked up through eyes half-shut in pain to see Erich striding toward him, pistol in hand. He's going to shoot me, Sol thought. So be it. He would not again endure what he had been through in Sachsenhausen. He would not.

"This Jew scum…disrespectful! Disobedient!" Pleshdimer lowered his voice toward the end, as if suddenly less sure of himself. "I found this!" He pointed, shaking with anger, at the cigarette butt hanging from Sol's lip.

Erich took the butt and flipped it away in disgust. He cocked the pistol, glared at Sol—and abruptly swung the barrel toward Pleshdimer. "I don't care what you found! You ever touch one of my Jews again without my consent, I'll tear your eyes out and stuff them down your throat."

"Rottenführer Pleshdimer did not find the offensive item." Major Hempel ambled into Sol's tunnel vision. "I did. Captain Dau and I discovered it days ago near the mess tent—obviously, and probably purposely, overlooked by your *colonists*." The major said the last word as though it made him want to spit.

"Are you saying that the Jews improperly policed the area?" Erich asked.

"I have yet to see them maintain *any* part of this camp to *my* satisfaction," Hempel replied.

"We both know what your standards are, Herr Sturmbannführer." Erich spoke with equal animosity. "Jew blood to fertilize the flowers. Jew flesh as fodder for pigs. Except this isn't Sachsenhausen. We have no prize hogs here on Mangabéy." Erich barely came up to the major's lapels. Without tilting up his head, he looked into Hempel's eyes with a withering glare that made the major look small. "A Jewish child to warm your bed," Erich continued. "*That* you have had here, and at the boy's insistence will have again." Erich holstered his gun. "That is my one concession to you," he said. "Watch yourself, Herr Sturmbannführer, or you'll be left without any concessions."

"Don't threaten me, Herr Oberst."

"No threat, Herr Sturmbannführer. A promise. Your proximity to Himmler means nothing to me here. My orders to create this camp came directly from the Führer himself."

"Through Reichsführer Himmler," Hempel reminded him.

"It matters little which postman delivers an envelope," Erich said. "Only who signed the letter."

As if fighting to save face, Hempel switched subjects back to the original point of contention. "What about the cigarette, Herr Oberst."

"What about it."

"I believe you will find many more butts by the mess," the major said in a raised voice. "Ones your precious *Jews* failed to police."

Solomon glanced toward the mess and saw two or three of Hempel's men, watching the proceedings, flip cigarettes to the ground. Before looking back at the confrontation, he caught a glance from Miriam. Her stance reflected raw fear, though whether for him or herself he could not tell. He did know that if Erich lost this or any other fight with Hempel, it would be the beginning of the end. Erich held the better hand, but he was running out of cards. Hempel was not one to be cowed, and if Erich failed to have the prisoners police the area again at once, he would in effect be countermanding his own orders regarding the Jews keeping the camp spotless.

"Herr Oberst! Herr Sturmbannführer!"

Johann, the radio operator, burst from the HQ tent, waving a piece of paper. Solomon knew the type well: young, Aryan, eager to please and to rise in the ranks of the Party. He was blond and boyish, with that youthful enthusiasm Solomon had in the past decade too often seen translated into Nazi fervor.

"Our troops have laid siege to Warsaw!" the boy called out.

The fact that Hempel took the note and did not give it to Erich, the senior officer, did not escape Sol's attention. He was sure that Erich noticed the slight, but the colonel remained aloof, almost implacable, as if fully expecting the major to pursue the matter and report to him in turn.

Hempel visibly brightened as he read. "Seems the prayers of your Jews are in vain." He handed Erich the message. "The Reich is unstoppable."

"Your implication concerning the Jews is obscure, Sturmbannführer." Erich scanned the message. "As always."

"Then perhaps you are not aware that your Jew dogs are committing sacrilege," Hempel said evenly.

"Sacrilege?"

Hempel touched the top edge of the paper with an index finger. "Subhumans bowing before a dead god on the eve of the Reich's triumph!"

Drawn by the announcement, Hempel's men began gathering. They watched Erich as hungrily as they had the zebu. Solomon knew Erich's dilemma had suddenly worsened. If he allowed the service to continue, he would appear to be elevating the status of the Jews above that of the Reich; stop the prayers, and Hempel had won an easy round.

Erich stepped back and lifted his head in what was clearly a poised, staged effect, like that of a great orator. He seemed to be calm, but Sol knew Erich Alois was steaming.

The colonel looked from man to man.

"You've no answer?" Hempel asked.

Erich put his hands in his pockets and rocked back on his heels. He was not the relaxed, intuitive thinker that Solomon himself was, but one who either arrived at a conclusion from a logical base—or spun off into anger. Sol knew from long experience that Erich's control at this moment was a fragile thing.

"I do not believe I was asked a question, Sturmbannführer," Erich said, his contempt evident.

A nonplused Hempel opened his mouth to reply, but Erich shrugged and stepped toward Solomon, who straightened as rigidly as a statue. "Free laborer Freund," Erich said, "you are to close your service tonight by praising the Fatherland and praying to the fiction you call God that this latest German endeavor will bring its rightful due. Is that understood?"

"Ja, mein Oberst!" Sol knew he must do everything within his power to keep Erich in control. If that meant vowing eternal allegiance to the Reich and to Erich

Alois in particular, he would acquiesce without a second's thought. Had he not, after all, once licked horse manure from Hempel's boots back in Germany, to keep himself alive? Humiliation meant little. Once endured, he merely locked it up in some small part of his psyche he never re-examined unless forced to do so. It was the physical humiliation he could no longer abide...and not just his own. Watching the torture and slow, painful dying of friends was so much more horrific.

"When you are through, you will personally lead a detail to scour this compound for cigarette butts."

"Ja, mein Oberst!"

"Dismissed."

Solomon did an about-face, stepped up before the other Jews, formally summoned them to arise, and standing at attention guided their voices in prayer. Learning to weed substance from irrelevancies, he thought. A light rain, more mist than drizzle, had begun. It made Miriam's clothing cling to her skin.

"That was a trick," Hempel was saying behind him.

"Any fool knows that Jews are too devious to be duped," Sol heard Erich say, his voice receding.

Solomon smiled at Otto Hempel's minor defeat. That's one for you Erich, he thought—and one for the rest of us.

PART II

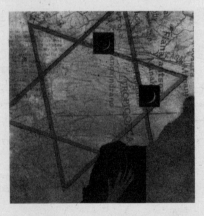

"THOSE WHO PROFESS TO FAVOR FREEDOM, AND YET DEPRECATE AGITATION, ARE MEN WHO WANT RAIN WITHOUT THUNDER AND LIGHTNING. THEY WANT THE OCEAN WITHOUT THE ROAR OF ITS MANY WATERS."

—FREDERICK DOUGLASS

Chapter Nineteen

Erich grew increasingly edgy throughout the next days. Hempel had not made any move to avenge himself for having lost out to him about the Rosh Hashanah service. Except for the detail roster, followed by minor complaints—the kind of thing all commanders had to endure—the days following the Rosh Hashanah service had been uneventful. That Hempel would take his revenge was a certainty; what form that revenge would take was anybody's guess. This business of making Erich wait for the other shoe to drop had become part of a pattern.

The two of them had faced off twice. Erich had emerged one morning to find the Jews digging a trench around their quarters. The major had apparently come up with some unbelievably stupid idea of having them actually move into and sleep in the trench. Not only were there vocal objections to the idea of preparing the ground for what looked like a mass grave, but there was the question of standing water in a tropical environment—a perfect breeding ground for mosquitoes and all manner of disease-bearing insects and fungi.

He had put a stop to that immediately, with surprisingly little resistance from the major.

There was also the matter of electrifying the fences around the Jewish quarter. He had consistently told Hempel that he would not countenance this, yet perhaps doing so would allow vigilance to be relaxed a little, giving him more free time, or at least relieving some of the mental pressure. The generator could certainly handle the extra load: he was glad, for the first time, that he had agreed to take the behemoth, despite the difficulty they'd had—even with the tank for assistance—dragging it up the hill.

For now, what was weighing most heavily upon him was his concern for the dogs, the two sick ones, particularly Taurus, but also the others. Despite his best efforts, they were not responding properly to him or to the trainers. He knew they missed the leadership of Taurus, but that was not enough to account for their constant vacillation between restlessness and sluggishness.

He, too, felt restless and sluggish. Mostly, Erich decided, he was bored. By the time he went to bed and fell asleep, cradling a bottle, he had filled his day with what seemed like a thousand things—none of them relevant to him. Miriam provided no companionship.

She acted drugged half of the time and disinterested or angry the rest. Although as their officer he felt close to the trainers, he had no real friends among them, and drinking alone was hardly a substitute for camaraderie.

"I wish to speak to you about the fence, Oberst."

Erich had arisen at dawn despite a hangover and was standing in the center of the camp, watching the Jews ascend the water tower to continue filling the tank. He braced himself as the major approached, but Hempel appeared surprisingly at ease.

"The matter of the fence has already been discussed," Erich said.

"Insurrection will come from the inside!" Hempel said. He pointed toward Solomon, who was emerging from the medical tent and heading toward the Jewish sleeping quarters. "Just look at how lax your security is. That Jew...number three-seven-seven-zero-four...coming and going as he pleases. Like he's at some kind of social event."

That Solomon might have spent part of the night ministering to Miriam renewed Erich's anger, but he struggled not to show it. "How is it you recall his number so easily, Herr Sturmbannführer?" Erich asked. "Have you *interest* in him? His name is Freund. Solomon Freund. And no, we will *not* electrify the sleeping area." Erich made a final decision. "What danger exists comes from with*out*. Did you not see those two Kalanaro, dancing and taunting us from the edge of the forest last night? Not that you spend enough time in the compound to worry about security! You don't give a hog's damn about security, Sturmbannführer. All you care about is Jews. And that goddamn Zana-Malata."

"Do not use his name in vain, Herr Oberst. Don't you...dare!"

Hempel abandoned all pretense of congeniality. Giving Erich a hard smile, he turned on his heel and was gone.

Wishing he had forbidden Misha to return to Hempel, Erich strode to the medical tent. He greeted Miriam indifferently and went over to the dogs. Taurus' condition remained unchanged, but Aquarius lay with his head hanging over the edge of the grass-filled box Müller had fashioned. The dog's ragged panting boomed in Erich's ears.

"Misha," Miriam muttered.

"Sir, my dog is dying and no one is doing anything to help," Ernst Müller said, entering the tent. "There must be something...."

Erich defined Ernst in simple terms: dog trainer; brother to Ursula Müller, the schoolgirl who had taunted half the boys at *Goethe Gymnasium*, Erich among them. Her conduct had caused her brother much pain.

Maybe that was why Ernst loved his dog so much. Why Erich and all trainers loved their charges. Because the love was simple, without pain. Without reproach.

Aquarius' breathing grew louder and more ragged, as if the dog were trying to suck the tent sides in and out, struggling to draw the dusk into weakening lungs. Then he gasped—a bellowy exhale that ended in choppy breaths. And stopped breathing.

Memories from the training center in Berlin assailed Erich. Aquarius, the most respectful and obedient of all the dogs, approaching his food dish with doe-eyed gratitude. First to conquer the horizontal training ladders at the estate; everyone so happy that Ernst yelped with joy and threw his hat high in the air. The dog leaping from the apparatus to grab the cap in his mouth, leaping into the sun....

Ernst stooped before his dog, arms around the animal, crying.

"Stop it," Erich said softly. "Get a hold of yourself."

Müller shook his head.

"You think I don't know what you're going through?" Erich's voice rose in pitch. "You don't think I've lost a dog before?"

"I don't care...what you think." Ernst spoke in cobbled, sawing breaths. "You're not...me. You're not...any of us, no matter what...you say." The corporal raised his head and added quietly but sincerely, "You bastard. You brought us here. You'd like everyone to *think* it was Himmler's and Goebbels' idea to bring us to this hellhole," he said after a moment. "Maybe even you believe that. But you wanted it. You wanted to prove yourself. Prove *us*. The *team*. But we're not a team anymore, are we, Herr Oberst! Hempel's wolfhound...dead. And now Aquarius...dead."

Erich turned away to stare outside.

"Perhaps you're the one who should get hold of yourself, Herr Oberst," Müller said.

"Under the circumstances I will overlook your words," Erich said. "Have the body of your canine soldier ready for a memorial service in exactly," Erich checked his watch and turned to face the corporal, "one hour. Is that understood?"

Apparently in no mood for military etiquette, Müller simply nodded.

"Heil Hitler," Erich said.

"Heil...," Müller lifted himself to his feet and returned the salute even less enthusiastically than it had been given. "Hitler."

Erich ducked through the tent flaps and was almost bowled over by the syphilitic, who pushed past him and went straight to the dog's side.

"*Chien...chien...beau.*"

Müller made a fist and lifted it menacingly in front of the Zana-Malata's deformed face. "Go. Away." His fist shot out. The Zana-Malata caught it in his claw. Gaining superior leverage, he wrenched Ernst's arm to the right, forcing the trainer to his knees. Then he pushed Müller back and, stepping over him, went outside.

Rubbing his arm, Müller returned to Aquarius, gently stroking the dog's ratty coat, mumbling to himself.

Embarrassed by the man's grief, yet understanding it only too well, Erich went outside and watched the trainers move about the kennel, feeding and brushing their charges. He saw the Zana-Malata depart the compound and head toward his hut. Hempel's habit of spending every off-duty moment with that revolting syphilitic, listening to his babblings with the deference due a fellow officer—that would cease, Erich decided. The chain of command structure on Nosy Mangabéy would be strong, even if it meant cutting away certain links.

Ernst exited the tent, returned with two more trainers, and exited again. Erich's hip was hurting him after being near Taurus, so, satisfied that preparations were being made, he went to his tent for a breakfast pick-me-up. He told himself that he would review his maps, review in detail the logistics of moving to the mainland once Nosy Mangabéy was secured, but instead he sat with bottle in hand, staring into a corner.

An hour later, as per his orders, rifle shots rang out— three trainers firing volleys atop the limestone knoll, at the back of the camp. The guard at that post leaned in undisguised rancor across his machine gun, as if to avoid the dog handlers who had invaded his territory.

Erich barely made it there in time. He could see Miriam in the distance, picking orchids from the overhang of jungle against the fence. "For Aquarius," she had said, "I'll put them on his grave." He had not argued. The flowers befitted a dog of such strength. After all, was not *orchid* Greek for testicle?

Dogs and masters formed a gauntlet. Erich stood at the one end, reading a passage from von Stephanitz that praised the breed's loyalty and intelligence. Müller, tears rolling down his cheeks, stood erect beside the dead dog. Nearer the spring, Pleshdimer stood at attention, holding a leash; from the corner of his eye, Erich could see Misha at the end of it. While part of him wished that he had ordered the boy to stay in the Jewish quarters, another part hoped that Misha would successfully rid all of them of the triumvirate.

When the memorial service was over, Müller requested that he be allowed to bury his dog in private. Erich readily agreed. He had been thinking about what he could do to help assuage the grief of both the dogs and their trainers. The answer he had come up with would work better without Müller around, acting like a spare part.

"Holten-Pflug!" he called out. The trainer ran forward. "It's been far too long since we properly exercised the dogs," Erich said. He was about to suggest that they practice the Zodiac, when his attention was drawn to a group of Kalanaro. They were moving around in the last shadows of the morning, which lay near the track leading to the beach.

He pointed at the natives. "What do you say we bring in some of those black monkeys?"

"Yes! Sir!"

Holten-Pflug scurried to gather the other trainers and the dogs. Erich lit a cheroot, one of his last. He would have to ask Bruqah to provide him with whatever the island could supply in the way of a smoke. Liquor, too. Realizing that he had moved from sipping to solid drinking, he had counted bottles. There was no way that he had enough to last until Nosy Mangabéy was secured, the dock built at the Antabalana River, and the next major shipment of Jews arrived. At the rate at which he was emptying bottles, he would have to speed up the timetable—or build a still.

"That a kill order, sir?" one of the trainers asked, when they had all gathered together.

"Not this time, I think," Erich said. He contemplated

the request, remembering the night that Taurus had drawn blood from a whore's wrist on the streets of Berlin. He found the memory satisfying, and that frightened him. "Search and seizure will do it," he said, looking toward the jungle. "I really just want to try to talk to one of them." Not that he had the slightest idea what language the little buggers understood. If the team succeeded, he would have to enlist Solomon's help. Or Bruqah's.

He watched the nine dogs and trainers fan out. Then, on impulse, he raised his voice. "If you meet with resistance," he said, "you have my full permission to kill."

Chapter Twenty

"Do not do this, Mister Germantownman," Bruqah said, stepping more hastily than usual out of the jungle.

The trainers looked at him, then at Erich. There was a sadness in them and in the dogs, Bruqah thought, but like good and proper soldiers, they had put aside their grief and looked ready to begin whatever maneuver their commander ordered.

"Search and seizure," Erich repeated confidently.

Dogs and men moved toward the Kalanaro, who disappeared at once into the rain forest.

Erich glared at Bruqah. "Don't you ever do that again," he said, his voice tense with anger.

"Do what, Germantownman? I did not do anything. I merely advised. Is that not my job?"

"Your job is to give advice when asked, not to interfere with my orders. Besides, I don't see the big problem. There seems to be an endless supply of the little bastards."

"They be like rain forest. You cut, it come back more and stronger." Bruqah did not allow his voice to reveal how appalled he was by Erich's callousness. The full truth was that the chase itself would antagonize the Kalanaro, but they would not be captured. The dogs and men would thread their way down the hillside. Reaching the mangroves and the tiny strip of beach, they would erroneously conclude that their quarry had paddled to the mainland, and return here frustrated with the insects and the fruitlessness of the search. "Jungle sometime like alligator. She like to swallow men and dogs." He grinned, deliberately showing his teeth. "Swallow Kalanaro too, maybe."

"We'll find them," Erich said.

"Maybe. They be glowworms. Here, yet not here. Sometime you no-see-um. Other time they full of light." Bruqah remained placid, his smile in place. The Kalanaro were perfectly able to take care of themselves, and the thought of agitating the Germans charmed him. The trainers were a different matter. He thought of them as apart from the others, and could not revel in their frustration. He had seen too much futility for that: burning off the central highlands for planting, then watching the thin red soil wash to the sea; warning his people not to hunt the giant flightless birds and pygmy hippos, gone now from the face of the land; pain piercing his heart each time a Malagash slaughtered an aye-aye because he feared its power.

"So you're telling me that we can't find them?"

Erich's temper had cooled. He looked more amused than angry.

"I saying you do not wish to find them, maybe."

"Obviously what you are not telling me is more important than what you have said."

"Ob-viously." Bruqah had trouble pronouncing the word.

"I think that in future I should only ask you what I do not want to know." There was a hint of a smile in the colonel's eyes, as if the verbal sparring pleased him. "You will be surprised to hear that I believe you," he said. "But this time it does not matter if they find nothing. Sometimes it's the looking that's important. Sometimes, that is more than enough."

With a wave of his hand, the colonel turned his back on Bruqah and walked toward the road that led to the beach. Watching him, the Malagash admitted to himself, albeit reluctantly, that there were things he liked, even admired, about the Germantownman. It was just a pity how rarely those things surfaced; for had they done so more often, Erich might have been worthy of saving.

CHAPTER TWENTY-ONE

"Herr Oberst."

Erich awoke as Fermi entered the tent. The trainer looked worried.

"Forgive me for disturbing your rest, sir, but we have seen no sign of Ernst since the burial. Some of us are worried about him, sir."

"He is undoubtedly somewhere mourning the loss of his friend." Erich made no effort to hide the bottle that lay on his cot. "Give him until tomorrow. If he hasn't returned, we'll search for him. Dismissed."

Fermi did not move.

"I said, dismissed."

"Pardon me, sir, but we have already searched for him."

"Did you look around the syphilitic's hut?"

For the first time, Fermi hesitated. "The major and

the black man seem to be celebrating something in there," he said.

"I still say give him until morning." Erich sounded less convinced. "This is a small island, but there are any number of hiding places."

Fermi saluted and left. Erich uncapped the bottle and took a swig. He tossed and turned for a while, but an uneasy sense of foreboding kept him awake and, finally, drove him outside and in the direction of the Zana-Malata's hut. If those sons-of-bitches were celebrating the dog's death....

He was working himself up into a new round of hatred. He knew the fury that burned in him was not the cold bright anger that so often helped to clarify his thinking. Lately, he felt that clarity only sporadically. It came and went like the racing clouds that alternately obscured and exposed the orange tropical moon. The anger he was experiencing was reckless and dangerous, but he didn't care.

Behind him, the dogs' baying became more insistent, as if the animals' display of grief had reached a new plateau. It unnerved him until he decided the sound symbolized what military life was all about. What his dogs possessed and some human soldiers too easily forgot.

Devotion.

Discipline.

He gave a perfunctory salute as he went through the compound gate. The Kapo passed him with a gruff "Heil Hitler." Erich did not bother returning the salute, but watched in distaste as Pleshdimer headed toward the dog yard, head cocked to make room on his shoulder for his load. Probably more lemur meat, Erich guessed. The syphilitic seemed to take special delight in providing the dogs with the dietary change—as if there were a rivalry between him and that lemur-loving Bruqah.

To hell with them both. Just so the dogs got fed and stayed healthy. He didn't want to go through another memorial for one of his shepherds. Ever.

The sound of raucous laughter greeted him as he pulled aside the zebu-hide and entered the foul-smelling hut.

"Why, Herr Oberst," Hempel said, as if he were addressing an honored guest. "Do join us. Come. Sit down."

"I am here on official business," Erich said. "It has come to my attention that...what in God's name is that?"

"This, Herr Oberst, despite its crust of dirt, is the egg of the elephant bird, the *æpyornis*, which dwarfed the ostrich. Didn't they teach you *anything* in your precious Reichsakademie? Think of it—the largest bird known to mankind, and the Malagasy hunted it to extinction without giving the matter a second thought." He paused as if for effect.

Then he said, "We, the strong, must do the same to every Jew."

He placed the egg lovingly on a plank next to three porcelain bowls whose sides depicted a blue ship sailing into a floral sea.

"If we hold true to our *vision*," Hempel made a fist

for emphasis, "there won't be a Jew left in the world. And, unlike with the bird, it won't be a shame."

Hempel's eyes shone and his voice rose, all trace of inebriation gone. "We are the strong. It is our birthright that we use the weak to our advantage." He waited for a moment, as if expecting Erich to agree.

When Erich did not react, Hempel gave a condescending smile and, with an usher's gesture, bade Erich to move closer. "Let us put aside our small differences, Herr Oberst, and break bread together." He drew open a palisade of strung bamboo Erich had thought was the left wall, but which he now realized was a curtain. "My mentor says we cannot partake of the truth of this great green land until we dine—in its depths, shall we say."

The Zana-Malata laughed, kicking his legs and slapping his chest, as the curtain was swung open its final meter.

Erich blanched.

Misha was huddled in the corner, next to a shovel. He was stroking Aquarius' huge, furry head, its melancholy eyes open and staring. Part of the animal had been skinned, and one hind leg had been cut off.

"If you dislike stew, I'll cut you a fillet," Hempel said. "Or some ribs, perhaps?" He drew a knife from a sheath on the wall. "Anything but the heart. The master says to eat the heart only at dawn, though for an honored guest such as yourself...." He eyed Erich with a mix of alarm and amusement and replaced the knife in its sheath. "You all right, Alois? The cooked meat has been bled and koshered. We wouldn't want to upset your Jewish playmates."

Erich pushed the child aside and sank to his knees beside the mutilated animal.

"Müller buried this dog." He looked at Hempel with unadulterated loathing. "You dug up the animal."

"Perhaps the boy did, Herr Oberst. Have you considered that?"

"And upon whose orders!"

"Why feed worms if you can feed the human spirit?"

"Take that shovel," Erich pointed toward the wall, "and re-bury the dog. Then burn this hut to the ground and report to my tent for summary court martial."

As he enunciated the words, Erich glanced over at the soil-encrusted shovel. Bending, he examined the dead animal's fur. Except for splatterings of blood, the hide was clean.

"This dog was never buried."

Hempel chuckled. "I said *perhaps* the boy dug it up. I never said he actually did so."

Standing, Erich drew his pistol. It felt extremely heavy, and he wondered, absurdly, if Hempel saw that he was shaking. "Where's Ernst Müller? I haven't seen him since...."

Hempel took a cigar and a wooden match from his breast pocket and lit the match by scratching it across the pistol grip of his holstered Mann. Biting off the cigar end, he spat it between Erich's boots.

"Where's Ernst!" Erich screamed.

"He had...objections...to our decision." Lighting the

cigar, Hempel inserted the lit end into the mouth of the Zana-Malata, who encompassed it and inhaled deeply, a look of pleasure entering his eyes.

"*You murdered Müller because he wouldn't let you eat his dog?*"

"Don't have a tantrum, Herr Oberst." Hempel smiled reassuringly. "The worms are dining well. The balance has been maintained."

Erich aimed his Walther between Hempel's eyes and, leaning forward carefully, removed the major's weapon from its holster and tossed it toward the door. It hit the zebu hide with a *thoop* and fell outside. "I will give the free laborers an hour of prayer at sunset tonight and again tomorrow." A surge of power mixed with Erich's rage. "They'll thank God for delivering you into my hands."

He released the safety.

Hempel lifted an arm casually, as if to ease the pistol aside. "It is you who loves the Jews, Erich Weisser," he said sincerely, as if wondering why his commander could possibly be upset. "Unless you want your coming newborn similarly infected with Jewish contagion, I suggest that as soon as he is born you move mother and child here to the hut, where they can be safe." He opened his hands with the charismatic innocence of a salesman. "Once we obtain the power of the Kalanaro, we'll burn out the Jewish corruption. Until then...."

A bullet's too clean a death for this monster, Erich thought, his finger tightening on the trigger.

Puuh.

The Zana-Malata made a short puffing sound, and

Erich swung around to face him, pistol raised. A halo of lavender flame rose from the syphilitic's gaping mouth-hole. The smoke ring fastened around the barrel of the Mann and tightened around Erich's hand, burning into the flesh as it had done the last time with the cold heat of dry ice.

Screaming, Erich got off one shot before he dropped the pistol. The bullet tore through the raffia a few centimeters from the Zana-Malata, who threw back his head and guffawed as Hempel stomped a jackboot down on the Walther.

"Don't you ever learn? Forget it, *Weisser*." Hempel picked up the pistol, fastened the safety, and tucked the gun in his belt. Placing the lit tip of his cigar in his mouth, he inhaled as deeply as had his mentor. With a triumphant *puuh*, he released a similar circle of lavender fire toward the ceiling. "We each have our units to command." He smiled obsequiously. "There's no reason we can't work together."

"We'll see about that!" Erich staggered through the doorway and, tripping on the steps, fell to his knees in the grass. Starting to rise, he reached for the Mann that lay at arms reach.

A black foot stepped onto the pistol; a speartip touched his jugular.

Above him stood two Kalanaro, eyes charcoal-rimmed, wiry bodies covered with mud dimly glowing an eerie white, hair streamed back and waxed and gleaming. He stared at the *assegai*, aware of a sickness starting up from his stomach.

The Kalanaro laughed, then one picked up the pistol, and both went into the hut.

Erich watched the whitewashed buttocks disappear behind the tanhide, his hatred and anger mingled with a fear that set his heart pounding. He felt as unsure of himself as an adolescent—unable to consciously steel himself against the world around him.

But he knew he must.

He pulled himself to his feet and, furiously brushing off his uniform, glared toward the door and fought to still his shaking. A *Hamster*…a man who pedaled his bicycle out into the countryside to buy produce from farmers, and pedaled back to Berlin to resell it. The boot- and buttlickers of the earth. That's what his father had been, that was what Pleshdimer and the Kalanaro were.

The parlor magic he had witnessed in the hut might earn the loyalty of an idiot like Pleshdimer, but all it would earn the syphilitic was a place beside the major, before a firing squad. And the Kalanaro? They would make it five executions.

When Erich reached the compound gate, the guard was slow to salute. Erich grabbed him by the lapels. "When I so much as look at this gate, you get that arm up stiff as a cock in a whorehouse! Understand?"

With a look of dark timidity, the soldier raised his arm.

Erich knocked down the arm. "Don't waste the effort *now*, soldier! Just bolt the gate. No one is to come or go unless *I* say. That includes the Sturmbannführer. Got that? Anyone tries to force his way in, shoot to kill."

The soldier nodded fearfully as he hurried to shut and lock the gate.

"Consider that a command directly from the Führer!" Erich said over his shoulder as he stalked toward his tent.

The man snapped his heels together and his arm shot up.

That was the way to treat the Totenkopfverbände, Erich told himself: ferocity plus patriotism. Hadn't Hitler similarly summoned the devotion of millions? Now, *before* Hempel's arrest, was the time to re-establish command dominance.

For that, he had some magic of his own: eleven dark dogs and the barrel of his gun.

Johann yanked off his headphones and, looking confused, jumped to attention. He was trembling: eyes sunken, forehead wet with sweat. Malaria? Erich wondered.

"We just received a transmission, sir," Johann said. "The Russians have joined the Reich in freeing Poland. May I have the honor of informing the Sturmbannführer and the men of this glorious news?"

Fighting to control his own trembling, Erich poured brandy into his canteen cup and, gulping it down, slammed down the metal cup against the table. "First I have a message for Berlin." The sweet, burning liquor almost took his breath away. "To Gauleiter Josef Goebbels."

It was the camp's first outgoing transmission—radio silence was to be maintained until the Antongil region was secured. The ill, excited youth virtually panted as he transcribed the heading.

Erich downed another brandy. The alcohol settled him enough so that his mind burned with a clean, cunning wrath; the words flowed effortlessly as he paced. "Your worst fears confirmed. Stop. Officer in question indeed involved—make that intimately involved—with racial inferiors and guilty of murdering a soldier of the Reich. Stop. Treason no longer matter of conjecture. Stop. Possible sabotage attempt imminent. Stop. Will proceed per former instructions."

After several moments the youth set down his pencil, his sallow complexion dark with anxiety. "Is that all, sir?" he asked in a quivery voice.

"Isn't that enough?" Erich replied contemptuously.

His trembling now even more evident, the youth thumbed through *The German Dog in Word and Picture* for the page that corresponded with the date—figuring the numbers of the days of the year in reverse. He laboriously matched up the dictated words with those in the innocuous book Erich had chosen as his code book, each word having an in-text counterpart in a complex system based on the date and page, and tapped the coded message over the wireless to German contacts in Italian-held Ethiopia.

Laughing inwardly, Erich signed off with "Sachsenhausen" rather than with his own code name, *Hawk*. If the relayed transmission got through British jamming at Malta, Goebbels would hopefully believe the message had come from the major.

Meanwhile, the guards were sure to assume Hempel

was the officer in question. Any loyalty to the major would be severely strained if not severed. For once, Erich was glad the man liked being surrounded by the young and the stupid—and had recruited accordingly.

"See the corpsman about those chills." Erich sat down at the table. "Take the rest of the night off and get some sleep. I'll tend the wireless."

"Yes...*sir*!"

After Johann exited, Erich took a cheroot from the humidor Miriam had given him. He had to grasp one hand with the other to steady the match, but at last got the cigar lit and leaned back, sucking in the smoke deeply to calm himself. Well, he thought, the thing was done; the military shoring-up he would need to justify shooting a major would soon be firmly emplaced. HQ activities were top secret unless stipulated otherwise, but secrecy was the prerogative of old men and misers, not boys pretending to be soldiers. In an hour everyone in camp would know of the message. With luck, he would have little difficulty bringing the guards' always-simmering prejudices to a boil—against Hempel.

He reached into his footlocker for his MP 38 submachine gun and placed it across his lap. The metal with its light coating of oil felt comforting as he ran his hand from the barrel to the metal brace that served as a stock. He pictured himself squeezing off a round into Hempel's forehead. A powder-darkened hole between the eyes, the back of the skull burst open, a roar of approval from the men as he signaled for them to riddle the others. He would smile as the Zana-Malata screeched and Pleshdimer twitched and jerked, corpulent pig that he was. Blood would redden that eerily pulsing, whitish mud those shithole Kalanaro had smeared....

Glowing mud?

Something about that triggered a memory and sent him scavenging among his manuals. There *had* to be something about the Kalanaro in the military literature or the supplemental guides that he had missed before.

Glowing.

A memory tormented him, but he couldn't seem to recall it exactly. His mind felt fogged, and he kept seeing white buttocks and porcelain bowls. What was it? Something from physics, the only class he had liked at Goethe besides military history and biology—cutting up that calico cat. But what! He *knew* physics, and this was schoolboy stuff!

He remembered, and he uttered a triumphant chuckle as he leaned back and put his boots up on the locker.

Pitchblende.

Reports of Congolese crazies who smeared themselves with luminous tar in order to look like ferocious ghosts during battle had led to the discovery of the world's largest uranium deposit and, indirectly, to the physics of Einstein and Bohr. Now uranium was bound up in the incredible energy and wartime potential of Heisenberg's attempt to achieve critical mass. But there was a hitch: only three mining areas existed. The Czechoslovakian uranium mine was nearly exhausted; Canadian uranium was unavailable; and—for fear of aiding Hitler or angering him by selling to the Allies—

the Belgians had shut down their huge mine at Shinkolobwe in the Congo to *all* buyers.

Was that what Hempel had meant by the power of the Kalanaro? Was that why he had allied himself with the syphilitic?

Eliminate Hempel, Erich thought as he poured more alcohol, and play Gestapo with the monkeys. He had learned persuasion from the masters, hadn't he? That conniving Goebbels may have paper-shuffled him off to Madagascar, but Daniel was about to emerge from the den.

Find the pitchblende deposit, and he would be a force to be reckoned with. A man of means. Perhaps, given the war, a national hero. Like Foreign Minister Walther Rathenau had been, he told himself bitterly, and blew a stream of smoke.

CHAPTER TWENTY-TWO

"Drink."

Miriam lay in the nearly airless medical tent, so torporous that her limbs seemed without life. It was all she could do to open her eyes.

Above her, grinning down with rotted teeth, hovered a fat, oily face.

"Time for medicine," the Kapo said. Drool bubbled from his mouth and clung to his teeth like sea scum.

"Get away from me." She thought she had screamed, but the words emerged as a whisper.

"Drink," the Kapo said again. "Make the baby dream."

With a dirty finger, he pressed what looked like a liquid-filled thimble against her lips. She did not resist, because she could not.

Then he was gone, and she was staring at the knot

where the netting gathered above her and thinking of Luna Park, where Solomon had won a music box for her. In the distance she could hear "Glowworm" playing, broken by the howling of dogs.

The shadows began to spangle. *Franz,* her mind said. *Franz.*

Slow fire suffused her veins as the liquid took effect. Perhaps though I die the baby will live, she thought as her body heated up. Her breathing was shallow, yet the sound roared in her ears. Each blink of her eyes required enormous effort until, with absolute clarity, she saw herself at the age of eleven. She was huddled on the back seat of a speeding convertible, the head of her sheepdog in her lap. "She'll be all right," Mama was saying from the front seat as Papa raced the car along the tree-lined road toward Zurich. "Don't worry, darling, she'll be fine, the vet's not far now." Miriam could not stop sobbing. What did Mama or Papa know, what did anyone except a vet or Heidi herself know about having puppies! Tires screeched. The car slid on the icy road and flipped upside down. She flew against a hillside and, landing amid rocks but without pain, watched the convertible flip again and land right-side up. As if she were seeing spinning pictures on a zoetrope, she saw a man, a woman, and a dog tossed from side to side like ragdolls inside the vehicle. The stench of gasoline permeated the air; even on the hillside Miriam could smell it. Then flames burst throughout the car like a flower suddenly in bloom, bright as a sun shining on...

...a sea, calm and sparkling with light. A porpoise

surfaced as if through a mirror of liquid gold, flapping its fins and chittering at the *Altmark*. From the ship's rail, she saw people descend the rope rungs of the Jacob's ladder to dinghies manned by German seamen in white uniforms.

It was all familiar to her. Then it changed and no longer grew from her experience——

——*She sees Jews in black-striped pajamas, oars lifted, and other Jews, helping men, women, and children into the crafts.*

"Isn't it wonderful, Lise?" says a woman wearing a cloche. She is staring across the sun-burnished sea to the shore. "A homeland of our own. Just as the Führer promised."

"But we had to give so much," says a woman in a white lab coat.

"Our property, certainly," the first woman says. "But consider the alternative."

The woman in the lab coat looks at her with expressionless eyes. "I not only considered the alternative, I gave it to him. That's why you're here."

"I don't understand," says the woman in the hat.

"You don't want to understand," the other woman says. "Believe me, you don't want to understand anything."

The people on deck continue to press forward, and Miriam finds herself being pushed along with the crowd. She tries to extricate herself, but is so tightly wedged that she cannot move her arms. Immigrants keep moving relentlessly toward the rail and the Jacob's ladder. Their murmuring and quickened breathing rise in crescendo, and there is about them a smell that assails her senses. At first she thinks it the odor of people cramped in the hold during the long voyage. But it goes deeper than that.

The smell of fear. The smell of death.

"They have come to the island of lost souls to witness the birth of Deborah," Bruqah's voice says.

Someone places fingers on Miriam's bare arm, a sensation that chills her to the bone. The people press forward, eyes bulging, cheeks sunken, lips tight with determination.

"He kept his promise," someone says.

They are entering the rain forest. Despite the sun, mists curl up from among the foliage. Fruit bats by the thousands hang upside down, undisturbed by the gulls and paradise flycatchers that wheel in and out of the tendriled mists. The sea has turned the color of rust. The color of dried blood——

——"Your shepherd *bit* you?" Franz's voice. "That looks like more than a mere bite. Sagi tried to take your elbow off."

"Just bandage it."

Miriam recognized the voice as that of Holten-Pflug, the trainer who was always showing people pictures of his wife and daughter, back home in Weisbaden, sometimes showing the same people the same pictures over and over again.

"You tell the Oberst about this, and there'll be more than an elbow that'll need attention."

"Don't worry." The corpsman chuckled. "We'll get you fixed up—and the Oberst none the wiser."

"It was an accident! Sagi didn't mean to hurt me."

"I understand that. Just hold still, won't you?"

"He's a good dog. Wouldn't hurt a fly except on command."

"You trainers and your animals," the corpsman said in a light scoff that indicated affectionate respect. "Sometimes I think you believe the war was invented just so you could show off your pets. Like some others I know," he added, his voice low and irate, "who treat Jews the same way. Hold still, now. This is going to sting."

A grunt, followed by the rip of adhesive tape.

"There. That's it."

Canvas slapped. A third figure emerged into the haze of Miriam's vision, breathing heavily.

"Johann," the corpsman said. "Sounds as if you need some quinine."

"It's not malaria, I tell you," a youthful voice panted. "I won't be quarantined." His gasping grew louder. "Nothing's keeping *me* from doing my duty. Especially not tonight. You hear me, corpsman? You confine *me*, and I'll…"

"You'll do what?" Holten-Pflug taunted.

"Leave him alone. He's delirious."

"The hell I am!"

The sounds of scuffling ensued. Something hit the tent wall and she could see murky figures move with the same jerky chaos as the shadows she had once witnessed on that experimental gadget called television, installed under the stands during the Berlin Games.

From outside came a frenzied yapping and growling—a clamor that shook her as if Erich had seized her during one of his tantrums.

Holten-Pflug uttered "Holy God!" and the showcased figures of the three men ceased moving.

The barking that echoed in Miriam's ears made the hair along the back of her neck stand up. Groaning, she managed to roll onto her side, facing away from the tent opening. Something landed on her cheek. A grasshopper.

"I have she, Lady Miri," Bruqah said.

She had not heard him enter. She turned her head and watched him walk the grasshopper outside.

"*...it is the other one, the one called Bruqah of whom I speak.*"

The voice echoed in Miriam's memory. I refuse to believe that he is anything but what he has shown himself to be, she thought.

"Tell me again about Princess Ravalona," she said when he returned to her bedside like a child begging for a story. "What did she...does she have to do with you?"

"This my island. What affect island affect me." Bruqah perched at the edge of her cot. "My people await return of soul of Ravalona. Bruqah first man on island. They believe Ravalona first woman. My people believe soul wanders unless bones brought to proper homeland burial place. Ravalona die on Mauritius and not brought home."

He stood up and seemed to be deliberating whether or not he should continue.

"Bruqah male soul of Madagascar. Bruqah's wife female soul. So long she wanders, Bruqah incomplete. Count named vessel of woman, but because he false vessel, blood ran. Many people they die here."

"What does that have to do with me and with my child?" Miriam asked.

Bruqah looked surprised, though whether it was at her knowledge or her honesty, she did not know.

"If Zana-Malata wins—"

He stopped.

Miriam sat up with difficulty. "Are you saying that if your people mistake my child as the vessel that holds the soul of Ravalona, your island will run red with blood?"

"Even Bruqah cannot change history," he said, and as silently as he had appeared, he was gone.

CHAPTER TWENTY-THREE

The howling of the dogs made Solomon shiver despite the heat. Wrapped in his blanket to ward off the mosquitoes, he lay on the sleeping area's matted grass, experiencing a strange sense of compassion over the death of Aquarius.

Plaintive as a bird grieving for a mate, the sound of Bruqah's *vahila* rose from the foliage. As usual of late, he played "Glowworm."

Gradually the dogs quieted; a hush settled through the forest, as if the plinks of Bruqah's instrument had brought them a sense of calm. Sol found himself remembering and longing for the romance of Chopin, the sweet genius of Mozart, the order of Bach.

Droning, a mosquito landed on Solomon's neck. He slapped at the insect. At least, he thought wryly, putting his head down and pulling up the coarse blanket, the insects weren't racists. They fed as happily on Nazi as they did on Jew. Still, when the malaria hit—Bruqah had intimated that northeastern Madagascar was the worst place for the disease in all Africa—it would be the Jews who would die first. The quinine was certain to be distributed unequally.

He looked across the sleeping bodies, and cursed his pessimism. Hadn't they climbed out of Sachsenhausen and the *Altmark*'s hold? Didn't they have a canvas canopy that afforded some protection from the elements? Minimal though sufficient food? Fresh water from the water tank and from the spring at the bottom of the sentry-post hill that formed part of the compound?

Yet the mainland beckoned beyond the compound's barbed wire perimeter, beyond the shark-infested bay.

"You awake, Rabbi?" Goldman asked.

Sol groaned and rolled over. Lucius was a good man, but—

"I know this isn't a rest farm, but might I ask when you last slept?" Sol propped himself up on an elbow.

"Haven't been sleeping much...but I shouldn't trouble you."

Sol touched the back of the man's hand. "Tell me."

"It will soon be Yom Kippur."

"We're all aware of that," Sol said quietly.

"I've spoken to some of the others. They want you to lead another service."

"They all want that?"

Goldman hesitated. "Not all. Some say it would be too dangerous..."

"They are right, my friend. I believe that the Oberst's self-control—and his control of this compound—are near the breaking point. To push the matter would be...most unwise."

"If you won't help, I will lead a service myself."

Sol shook his head. "Perhaps next year it will be possible. This year we must ask God to hear the silent prayers in our hearts."

"We will pray together *this* year. My father and mother are still alive. Our prayers must reach God's ears *together*."

"God will understand, Lucius."

A tear rolled down Goldman's left cheek. Sol held the bristly head, comforting Goldman as he might a child. He felt a longing for his own family. Were his mother and sister safe in Amsterdam? "I need to think," he said. "Meantime, try to get some sleep."

Standing, Sol made his way across bodies lying tangled as lianas and, stepping out from beneath the canvas, walked over near the fence. He stared at the moon, wishing it could provide him with answers.

That Major Hempel and Colonel Alois hated one another was obvious. The prisoners had engaged in many intense, whispered debates about whether they could—and should—try to deepen that hatred and broaden the division between the Abwehr trainers and Hempel's Totenkopfverbände. Solomon had begged a halt to the discussions, for fear Jewish unity was itself being divided.

Regardless of what the others thought, to him the matter was clear. Should Otto Hempel seize control of the camp, all was lost. Helping Erich solidify his command, despite its making escape more difficult, was in the prisoners' best interest.

If Erich proved worthy of trust.

If.

Odd, he thought, that he should know Otto Hempel so well, while his former friend remained an enigma.

He heard footsteps behind him. "I told you that I need time to think," he said, expecting Goldman.

"I need your help, Solomon," Erich said.

"And I yours...Erich," Sol said, making his decision and risking the use of the familiar. "May I," he asked, thinking he might bring hope to Goldman and the others while simultaneously helping Erich put Hempel in his place, "make a request on behalf of the free laborers?"

"Give you a finger and you ask for a hand. Is that it?"

Solomon ignored the bait. "We would like permission to conduct a Kol Nidre service, and to complete the Yizkor service at sundown the following day."

"You had your prayers. There's been the devil to pay ever since." Looking toward Hempel's tent, Erich's eyes filled with a look of sly anger. "I'll consider it."

"We..."

"I said I'll consider it. Right now I have more urgent matters to attend to."

"You mentioned needing my help."

Erich hesitated. "Later," he said and strode off without mention of what had brought him to the Jewish quarters. Some advice to do with Miriam, perhaps?

"We heard everything," Goldman said, creeping into the moonlight. "Thank you. Perhaps even a Nazi heart can be opened."

"With a wooden stake," Solomon replied. What really lay within that heart, he wondered, watching the naked pygmies who had attached themselves to the camp during the past week leaping and cavorting among the shadows as they moved in a wild dance toward the Zana-Malata's hut. Glowworms?

Knowing he would find no rest that night, Solomon exercised the privilege that had, to his continued astonishment, not been removed, and made his way over to the medical tent. He found Miriam asleep, veiled by netting. Her eyes were squeezed shut; worry lines creased her forehead. She seemed oblivious to Taurus whimpering behind her, chest rising with each breath, fur rippling as if the muscle beneath were in constant spasm.

After a moment's hesitation—for fear of waking Miriam from the rest she so desperately needed, no matter how troubled it might be—Sol whispered *I love you*. For an instant she appeared to hover between sleep and waking. The worry lines deepened. Her hands tightened into fists.

Then she sighed and her shoulders sagged; her throat moved as she swallowed. In reflex action, her tongue touched her lips, like a small animal seeking moisture in the hot, oppressive tent. She turned on her side and put a hand protectively against her belly.

Solomon wondered if he had ever loved her as intensely as he did at this moment. Having been separated from her for so long, he had not fully internalized the changes her pregnancy had wrought. Until now, he had continued to think of her as his lithe dancer.

All this time, he realized, she had possessed what, despite his scholar's aptitude—or perhaps because of it—he had never learned. The ability to be practical. The ability not to question life but to live it. He felt ashamed of how little he knew compared to what she'd had to teach.

Some day, he vowed, we will be a family. With Misha as our eldest.

The boy, too, confounded him. Misha had had a chance to escape Berlin, had been almost aboard the train with Beadle Cohen. He had chosen to run from that, from someone who cared, back to danger and Miriam, whom he hardly knew. An eight-year-old, determined to find the parents who had been taken from him. Now he had run again, from Miriam who cared, to people and things too dreadful to contemplate.

Strangely, Taurus also fit in the picture of the household developing in his mind. Yet Erich's she was, and his she would remain.

He could never forgive Erich. Of that he was certain, though in fact he had learned that it was not Erich who had been directly responsible for his arrest. What Erich had done to earn Sol's contempt had happened long before that, while Solomon was safe in Amsterdam. It was then that the man he had once called friend had lied to Miriam, telling her that Solomon had been incarcerated. Lying again, this time about his own status in the Party, he had promised to keep Solomon alive, perhaps even have him released. Her part of the bargain was to live with Erich and prove that she loved him; prove that Solomon was but a friend by renouncing her religion, marrying Erich, and making Goebbels' precious propaganda film.

Now that he was free from Sachsenhausen but not from the Nazi threat, did the future hold any promise for Miriam and himself? He had traveled so far since attempting suicide in the camp, yet in some ways he had not moved a centimeter.

"Don't take the baby, Judith!" Miriam cried out in her sleep. "She's mine! She's mine! Bruqah, don't take her!" Her mouth looked pinched and narrow with terror. Her hair hung damp and lank, her forehead so pearled with sweat that her skin glistened in the lantern light.

Sol did not know if he should wake her. Even what to do with his hands baffled him; they felt too large and ungainly for the spare body the months in Sachsenhausen had bequeathed him.

Miriam opened her eyes. "Sol?" She blinked, glanced around, turned her gaze toward him again.

"I miss you so much!" he said.

"I miss you, too." She shut her eyes, and he thought she would nod off again. "I keep seeing...images. Erich says your dreams have infected me." She tried, unsuccessfully, to sit up. "I told him I was going to join you and the others."

So that was what Erich had intended to talk to him about, Sol thought. "I want you with me, you know that, but you need to be here." His words did not come easily. After a moment, he added, "I heard you calling out the name 'Judith.' Is she the same Judith who...." He did not know how to phrase it. "Whom I've seen?"

"Elderly...khaki clothes. She spoke of Ethiopia."

How many times had Judith visited him in dybbuk-borne visions—she, and half-a-dozen others? "Judith *told* you she was from Ethiopia. *She spoke to you?*"

"She warned me..."

She fell asleep again. He had to consciously stop himself from rousing her. How was it possible that Miriam was seeing his ghosts? Beadle Cohen, interpreting the mystic language of the Kabbalah, had said that the dybbuk opened doors to others' lives being lived in this and in other realities. In his, Sol's, case, the visions were complicated by his own power as a visionary. His ability to see randomly into what he supposed was the future, or a possible future, came in the form of psychic flashes, brought to him—as they were to Isaac Luria and others like him—in a halo of cobalt-blue light.

Their past had been brought to him by the dybbuk, which was no longer a part of him: Judith, speaking of the exodus of the Black Jews from Ethiopia, which gave Mussolini control of the southwestern edge of the Red Sea; Peta, the Ukrainian Jew whose people fought for Hitler against Stalin, in exchange for emigration; Lise, the physicist who cried about having sold the secret of something called critical mass. All so that German Jews might be released. And others, who had come to him repeatedly, showing him lives that, real or not, told of their hopes for a Jewish homeland in Madagascar, free from the evil of the Führer. If they gave Hitler what he wanted.

Was their present and future to be shown to him, too, by his own psychic force?

He had seen Judith so clearly on Rosh Hashanah. Was it possible that she was here, in the flesh, on Mangabéy? Had Miriam seen a real woman or a ghost? Perhaps both? And if so, by what possible means could Miriam be tied to her, perhaps even to the others?

Sol remembered the terrible night he had tried to have the dybbuk—and the dreams—exorcised. Under cover of night, the religious among Sachsenhausen's almost-dead had gathered outside Barracks 18 to pray for themselves. Sometimes they were led by a rabbi, though more often the task of leading the prayers fell to the physically strongest among them.

That night, he had found a rabbi, one schooled in such Kabbalistic rituals as exorcism.

The incongruity of an exorcism in a charnel house had been absurd.

Over and over, under the press of the rabbi's hands, he'd chanted the incantation born of King Solomon: *Lofaham, Solomon, Iyouel, Iyisebaiyu...*Leave this man..." Even now, he could taste the bile that had filled his mouth, feel the wave of nausea that engulfed him. Ultimately, he could hear only the ragged sound of his own voice, feel nothing but the throbbing in his head, see nothing but the sweep of the searchlight. Until, finally, the rabbi said, "All I can do for you, Solomon Freund, is ask for God's blessing. You had a dybbuk in you once. It is no longer there, but I believe it remains flesh of your flesh and blood of your blood. Whatever is in you *now* was always yours—and always will be."

"...*flesh of your flesh and blood of your blood....*"

The child.

Was the child the new vessel for the dybbuk, removed there through his seed and linked to Miriam through her unity with the infant?

If so, the child was his, in fact as well as in spirit.

Taurus' renewed whimpering commanded Sol's attention. Consciously drawing himself into the moment, he listened to the shepherd's faulty respiration.

What might Erich do to someone ministering—or failing to minister—to his prize pet? What might he, Solomon, feel if he did not try to help the so obviously failing animal?

He loosened her collar, but it didn't help. She lay on her side, eyes vacant, a deep *huuking* sounding in her throat, her chest heaving and her rear legs kicking spastically. He felt as useless as he had when Erich had begged him to help Grace, Achilles' mother. The dog had been dying after giving birth. Neither he nor Erich had been able to save her.

"Touching a *German* dog, Jew?"

A hand gripped his hair, and his head was wrenched back as Pleshdimer and the Zana-Malata materialized out of his peripheral blindness. He suddenly realized how very much the loss of his peripheral vision had increased his physical danger.

"Something's wrong with her breathing," he sputtered, pulling away and losing a handful of hair in the process. "You had better find the Oberst."

"Giving orders?" Pleshdimer's voice was heavy with menace. "A Jew giving orders!" He grinned at the Zana-Malata...then slapped Sol so hard across the temple that his head snapped sideways.

"What the hell's going on here?" Erich pushed aside the Kapo and the Zana-Malata and knelt beside Taurus. "What happened?" He lifted her head in his arms. He had been drinking again, Sol noticed—heavily, from the smell of him.

Taurus' tail flicked once, but otherwise she gave no sign of recognizing her master. Her weight went slack, and she slumped from Erich's hold.

"What can we do?" he asked Solomon.

We? Solomon's brows lifted. Suddenly it was "we"; everything had changed since their boyhood together, yet nothing had changed.

"Her breathing's labored," Sol said. "Why not talk to Bruqah? He has an amazing store of knowledge about..."

Erich put his head down on Taurus' chest. Apparently unable to hear a heartbeat, he kneaded the sternum with the heel of a hand, fingers interlocked, one hand behind the other. "Help me, Sol!"

Sol. Not *Solomon.* Nor, as he half expected, *Jew.*

In no position to refuse, Sol stooped beside Taurus, his hands awkward appendages disconnected from his desires. Ineffectually, he stroked the dog's coat. "Good girl." His voice sounded less than optimistic.

"Go back to your *books*," Erich said in disgust. "You always were useless in an emergency."

Sol's arms fell to his sides. A great stone upon his shoulders bore his head down.

"I suppose you're praying," Erich said. "You and your goddamned hocus-pocus, I swear you're as bad as…" He lifted his head, his gaze drilling the Zana-Malata. "What's that *filth* doing inside my compound!" He unsnapped his holster and brought his pistol up, leveling it at Pleshdimer's groin.

A shudder raced through Taurus. The *huuking* renewed. Fear clouded Erich's features; he thrust the gun back in the holster. "Get help!" he cried. "Get Bruqah…anyone!"

Sol turned to leave, but the Zana-Malata gripped his biceps.

"*Chi…en!*" the syphilitic hissed. He stooped and, shrugging off Sol's attempt to grab him, clenched shut the dog's frothing jaws. Erich frowned anxiously toward Sol, but kept massaging the heart as the Zana-Malata placed his mouth-hole over Taurus' nostrils and breathed into her, repeatedly raising up and sucking in air, only to utter "*Chi…en!*" and again lower his mouth over her nose.

Taurus gagged.

The syphilitic released his hold on the muzzle. The dog shook, opened her mouth—and began breathing.

"Her pulse feels stronger." Sol stooped to check the carotid artery. His eyes met Erich's, and the sense that the two men were remembering another dog, so many years ago, slammed into Sol like a fist. "The pain must have brought on a seizure. She'll be…fine," he tried to assure Erich.

"She'd better be." His head drooped, and he did not resist when Sol put a consoling hand on his shoulder. "Lose her, I lose everything."

The Zana-Malata straightened and touched the back of Erich's neck. "*Chi…en.*"

Erich batted away the man's hand.

Solomon clutched Erich's arm. "For heaven's sake! He saved Taurus. I think he's saying *chien*—French for dog! Maybe he's trying to tell you he can do something more for her."

"Don't be a fool!" Erich looked in disgust at the burbly, drooling hole. "Just because he grunted something you think is French doesn't mean I should put Taurus in his hands!"

Sol took hold of the black man's wrists. "*Vous parlez français?*"

The syphilitic nodded rapidly. "*Chi…en.*" He pointed toward Taurus.

"You studied a little French," Sol reminded Erich. Cocking an ear like a conductor listening for nuances from the violin section, he asked the syphilitic, "What *about* the dog?"

"*Chi…en. Beau.*"

"He says the dog is beautiful."

"So he knows two words. Madagascar is French territory."

"Maybe he can help Taurus. What harm could there

be in trying?" Sol put a gentle hand on the shepherd, which was panting softly and gazing up in bewilderment.

"Harm? Taurus could die."

"Looks like she could die anyway," Sol said.

After a moment, Erich said in a tone of resignation, "Ask him what he wants in return for his help."

"In return?"

"If you think that's the Good Samaritan, you'd better look again. The older you get, Solomon, the more ignorant you act."

Solomon spoke to the man, who responded with vowels and drool and vigorous headshaking.

"He doesn't want anything," Sol translated.

"He wants what we all want." Erich gave him a hard look. "Control."

Rising, the Zana-Malata pointed at Taurus and outside, in the direction of his shack. He repeated the gesture, then took off at a lope toward the gate, waving for them to follow. The gate guard jerked his Mauser to his shoulder and eyed the syphilitic through his rifle sight, but the Malagasy paid him no heed. Looking back over his shoulder, he continued to wave them onward.

Erich's gaze again met Sol's, and Sol felt the weight of what Erich demanded. He hadn't changed. Should something go wrong, it would be Solomon's fault.

"Get the stretcher," Erich instructed Pleshdimer. "We'll do whatever must be done to see her through this."

Together, Sol and the Kapo loaded the dog onto the stretcher and followed Erich across the compound. A small crowd of guards pressed forward to see what was being carried.

Hempel joined them. "Seems your brightest star has fallen from the zodiac, Herr Oberst." Lighting a cigarette, he nodded toward Taurus. "But don't worry, she'll be fine as long as *he* cares for her."

With his cigarette he pointed toward the hut. A sparking curl spiraled from the hole in the thatch. "Don't go blaming yourself for your dog's condition, Herr Oberst. Don't blame yourself for anything that goes wrong. It's just that caring and *caring for* are different entities."

"As are the ranks of Oberst and Sturmbannführer," Erich said. "Keep that in mind the next time you think about going near that boy."

Hempel touched his cap as if to acknowledge Erich's transient victory. "My men and I find the little animal—*entertaining*." His eyes gleamed. "So versatile. It's a rare pet, after all, that can spit-shine boots. But," he lifted his palm in compliance, "I shall procure a mascot more to your liking. You may have that one put to sleep."

"This isn't Sachsenhausen," Erich replied.

"Nor is it some Berlin suburb. Manicured lawns and delicate sensibilities have no place in the wild, Herr Oberst."

He saluted, did an about-face, and strode toward the mess, leaving Erich to glower, a hand on the grip of his pistol.

"Let's go," Erich said darkly, under his breath.

At the gate, the guard saluted listlessly. With Erich

in the lead, they hurried toward the hut. Grasshoppers sprayed out before them and crunched beneath their feet, and Sol could hear the rattle of Pleshdimer's breath as the fat man struggled to keep up. They moved along jerkily, Sol pulling at the front end of the stretcher and the Kapo yanking back, as if to slow their progress.

A searchlight illuminated the hut, and Sol witnessed a black arm reach around the tanhide door, urging them onward.

Taurus' breathing began to saw. "Faster!" Erich panted.

"No, Mister Germantownman."

The voice seem to hang disembodied in the air. Erich crouched, pistol ready. In the glare of the searchlight his face took on a look of irritated relief as Bruqah stepped from the shadows of the tanghin tree next to the hut.

"Help them with the stretcher," Erich ordered.

Bruqah shook his head. "This hut," with a knuckle he tapped the mud-and-wattle exterior, "no place for white men now human air has touched Benyowsky." He seemed to be struggling to translate his thoughts into words. "Kalanaro in there sometime do bad magic. They what you call cap...cap—"

"Capricious," Sol guessed, helping him out.

Bruqah nodded his thanks. "They happy to help Zana-Malata."

"Help him do what?" Sol asked.

"Control what you call spiritual realm, Sollyman.

Zana-Malata want child to live and major to succeed. He believe they help him kill those who ostra…ostra—"

"Ostracized," Sol said.

Again Bruqah nodded. "He believe child vessel for soul of Ravalona."

The man is afraid, Sol thought, disquieted. But of what exactly? Or perhaps it was more simple, a question of competition from someone who sought equal power.

Erich seized Bruqah by his *lamba*. "If anyone, or any*thing*, attempts to interfere with me, I'll consider it sabotage…an act of war. Understand one thing: Sturmbannführer Hempel and I are not all that different. Except I do not torture my enemies. I execute them."

He released Bruqah roughly. With a look of disgust, the Malagasy stepped back into the shadows of the tanghin.

"Just how many people *have* you killed, Herr Oberst?" Sol asked as he watched the Malagasy disappear into darkness.

Erich swiveled and jammed the barrel of the gun against Sol's cheek. Sol readjusted his hold on the stretcher, but otherwise did not move.

"Two," Erich said at last. "Both of them boys. The sons of fools who ran a cigar shop on Friedrich Ebert Strasse."

CHAPTER TWENTY-FOUR

The hut was sweltering. Eucalyptus branches glowed in a brazier, crackling and pouring off an oily smoke so thick it shellacked Erich's skin and smothered his forehead and cheeks with sweat. This is insanity, he thought, waiting for his burning eyes to adjust to the darkness.

He was almost sorry when they did. Chin against chest, shoulders sagged and arms hanging limply, the Zana-Malata sat behind the fire. He was staring lifelessly at the flames. Smoke seemed to curl from his peppercorn hair. He looked for all the world like a corpse that had died sitting upright. The two fossas crouched fearfully beside him, mewling and worming their noses against his shriveled legs.

He did not move.

Behind him a crudely woven raffia chair, hanging

from the ceiling by a plaited rope, swung slowly back and forth. Firelight glinted off three blackened cooking pans, and several zebu halters along the back wall. The flames of small, fat candles guttered in the empty sockets of a water buffalo skull that adorned an upper corner, its forehead painted with a swastika.

The fossas lifted their heads to survey the intruders. The fire popped, sparks cascading across the syphilitic's shoulders. Still he remained slumped. Filled with disgust and reluctance, Erich motioned with his pistol for Solomon and Pleshdimer to place the dog near the brazier and then go outside and wait. The fossas backed up, hackles raised; then, appearing to adopt a wait-and-see attitude, they hunkered down, watching suspiciously.

"What do you plan to do about the dysplasia?" Erich said, unable to control the ire in his voice as he crossed to the Zana-Malata.

Through glassy eyes the syphilitic continued peering into the flames.

Anguished that anyone could sit so mesmerized while Taurus lay so feebly, Erich put the gun close to the man's head. "Acknowledge me!" Erich fought to control his trembling. As if through someone else's eyes he watched the gun pull toward the syphilitic's head, like metal to a magnet.

"I said acknowledge me!"

When there was no response, a pressure that had been building inside him for a very long time erupted.

His finger squeezed.

Click.

The Zana-Malata sat impassive and unharmed. *My God*, Erich thought, ashamed at having actually pulled the trigger. He tried to reholster the gun, but instinctively jerked the trigger again. This time, the gun was pointed at the floor.

Click.

Stupefied, Erich stared at the pistol.

The Zana-Malata toppled onto his side and lay with his head near a shelf constructed of a mahogany plank placed across two rocks. On the plank sat three empty white bowls, cracked and stained and obviously very old, each painted with the scene of a clipper ship sailing through an Eden of leaves. Where, Erich wondered, had he seen those bowls before? He couldn't concentrate. All he could focus on was the syphilitic's arm, outstretched on the lashed-sapling floor, the biceps baggy with diseased skin, the fist without fingernails.

Blood drooled from the Zana-Malata's mouth.

"The gun didn't fire." Erich backed up. Filled with turmoil, he felt like retching. "I didn't shoot you." He turned toward Solomon, whose face, obscured by the haze, looked expressionless. "I didn't shoot any—"

Except it was not Solomon. He had ordered Solomon to stay outside. Hadn't he?

The fire snapped, and a curl of smoke rose from the brazier. The heat forced Erich to shield his eyes. When his vision returned, Pleshdimer was licking the blood from the saplings.

Erich grabbed the corporal by the hair. "He has syphilis, you imbecile!"

Pleshdimer grinned with reddened lips.

Erich shoved the man aside. The Kapo fell against Taurus and settled down with his head across her back. "If the dog dies, we feast," he said.

"Get up and out! You have five seconds!"

Pleshdimer folded his hands across his paunch.

"One!" Erich screamed.

A memory of Miriam seized him, making his head pound. "*Count!*" he had commanded that night he had lost his temper and taken her by force. "*Count!*"

"*One...two...three...*"

"*Slower!*"

"*Four...*"

"*Again! From the beginning!*"

"Five!" For an instant the face before him was Miriam's. He squeezed the trigger just as Sol's hand gripped his wrist.

"Erich!"

The explosion roared in his ears. A centimeter from Pleshdimer's jugular a black hole appeared in the floor, and a blue puff of smoke leapt up from the brazier.

"You could have killed Taurus!" Solomon shouted.

Erich blinked. *Taurus?* He twisted his hand from Sol's hold and watched the corporal lurch his bulk forward and cower in the corner. Too drained and displaced to aim again, he knelt beside the dog. He made no attempt to control his fierce trembling. "*Mein schatz,*" he murmured. "My love."

With a *plook* the Zana-Malata uncorked a crudely fashioned clay jug. The smell of chloroform pervaded the hut, and Solomon moved back toward the door and fresh air. Though the anesthetic made him dizzy and giddy, Erich remained near Taurus.

Pouring chloroform onto a ragged cloth and handing the cloth to Erich, the Zana-Malata indicated for him to hold it against the dog's nose. Erich signaled for the black man to recork the jug, the contents of which were making him dizzy. The syphilitic shook his head vehemently, lifted his gnarled, grotesque fist close to Erich's chin and opened the fingers. An ember burned on the palm. Erich pulled back from its heat. The fingers shut around the ember, the hideous mask that was the syphilitic's face registered no pain.

The hand reopened. In the palm lay what looked like a fruit pit. Propelled as if by a force not his own, Erich holstered the pistol and, taking the pit, stared at it stuporously, careful to keep his injured hand like a leaf-shaped paten below the other one, in case he dropped the thing.

"It's a tanghin pit," Solomon whispered, reappearing and squatting beside him, blending with the smoke as if he had lost all physical definition. "Bruqah says eating it induces a trance state."

The pit, fuzzed and creased, strangely fascinated Erich. "Tell him to get on with it."

Solomon gently took hold of the Zana-Malata's shoulders and spoke to him in French.

The Zana-Malata nodded, then crawled behind the dog and lifted her head. A small spasm rippled through the animal, and Erich shivered empathetically. He felt a vague sense of gratitude when the Zana-Malata directed him to cover Taurus' nose with the cloth.

Trying to keep his head as far away from it as possible changed the angle of his vision and he saw Pleshdimer in the corner, face chalk-white and arms slack. The thought drifted away from him as he watched a fossa pad forward to lick Pleshdimer's palm.

The smoke was no longer going up through the roof-hole. It had broken into blue crescents shaped like ferns and curled down around him. He blinked and looked toward Solomon for help, but the hut was wreathed in thick tendrils of smoke and he could not see beyond his hand.

Which still held the fruit pit.

He set it down near the brazier.

The pit was an eye, staring up at him. His lids felt weighted.

The Zana-Malata chanted something unintelligible. He held a knife that spangled like a sword in sunlight. Erich knew he should disarm the man, but he was in too much of a torpor to move or even care. He raised his hand, but his arm fell—slowly. Everything seemed to move through glue.

The syphilitic maneuvered the anesthetized dog onto her back, parted her hind legs, smeared something black and tarry onto the fur and shaved her thighs. After each stroke he ran the blade between his fingers to clean off the hair. Then he cleansed the skin with a rag that smelled of antiseptic and poised the knife above the left thigh.

Must be going to sever the pectineus muscle, Erich groggily understood. It was potentially a lethal or crippling operation, but what other course had Fate accorded them? Where could a hermit on a remote island the size of a pfennig have acquired the necessary knowledge and surgical skills?

In the smoky vertigo in which Erich floated, anything seemed possible.

The Zana-Malata sliced open and peeled back the skin. Erich averted his eyes. The sight of Taurus' tissue, red as uncooked biergarten meat, made his heart thud with fear. He would give the black man anything—*anything!*—he promised himself, were the operation successful. Regardless of the outcome, he would assuage her agony, for her pain was his pain.

Holding the chloroform-soaked rag, he searched the haze for some point of reference to help him keep his eyes open without having to watch the cutting. His gaze fastened on the bowls, and he remembered having associated them with Benyowsky.

From…the…*valavato*, he told himself.

The bowls were no longer empty. One contained dry-cooked rice; one, greasy morsels of what looked like uncooked chicken skin; one, a tiny, neat pile of brown-and-white gratings. The fourth, a calabash, held water. Solomon emerged from the smoke, picked up the third bowl, and said softly, "The grating's from two of the tanghin pits."

Puzzled, Erich wiped a bead of sweat from the end of his nose and stared dully into the fire. "How do you know?"

"Bruqah told me."

"Oh. I see."

Except he did not see. Smoke choked his mind;

Solomon's voice sounded as distant and disjointed as an echo in an abandoned sewer. The world around Erich seemed as wrong as a hailstorm in Paradise, wrong as a zebu stretching its black-and-white neck to feast on the weeping willow beside which he had carried out Hitler's order to shoot Achilles.

Solomon was bent over the mahogany plank, putting pinches from the first three bowls into the calabash. Turning, he offered Erich the concoction. "You must drink this."

"What is it?" Erich drew back.

"Justice," Hempel said as he pushed past the tanhide and entered the hut. "The tanghin tree's spirit will either kill you or protect you from the witchcraft the Zana-Malata must use to save Taurus." Apparently sensing Erich's confusion, he added, "The Malagasy assured me it's necessary. He tells me everything."

Malagasy? Erich wondered. Which Malagasy! The Zana-Malata spoke no German, Hempel no French; and he doubted that Bruqah would speak to Hempel at all. Was there some other language that Hempel and the hermit understood?

Placing the bowl in Erich's hands, Sol cupped Erich's fingers around it to make sure he would not spill the contents. "The Malagasy call the tanghin the 'ordeal tree.'" Solomon said.

"I suppose the Malagasy told you that," Erich muttered, fighting for his bearings, unable even to stand.

Solomon did not reply.

"Swallow it if you want to save the dog," Hempel insisted.

Shaking, Erich peered down at the bowl, stepping backwards with a cry of surprise as Solomon thrust one of the blackened cooking pans at him. Within it was what looked like gruel.

"Flour paste." Solomon scooped up some with a finger and held it, dripping and steaming, in front of Erich's nose. "Try to concentrate," he whispered. "I'm going to stuff this down your throat after the poison takes effect. Don't resist me. If you vomit, chances are you'll survive."

"You would save…me?" Try as he might, Erich was unable to speak without mumbling. A fog enveloped his will. He wondered why Solomon and Hempel, both of whom had reason to want him dead, would poison him and immediately administer an antidote. Then logic slipped away from him; he found himself mirrored in the ceramic bowl, and grinning.

"Bruqah says to tell you that to save an animal, you must be willing to sacrifice your humanness," Solomon explained.

Erich looked at Taurus. Beneath the Zana-Malata's knife the dog looked pitiful and hideous. Thighs parted and bloodied; a syphilitic surgeon; an operating room suffused with oil of eucalyptus. Erich wanted to howl at the absurdity.

Instead he took a deep breath to steel his resolve and brought the bowl to his lips. He gagged on the hot, thick mixture, but managed to swallow.

For a moment there was no sensation. He expected

to feel pain or to be gripped by a seizure, but there was nothing. He seemed to be apart from himself in a world without feeling or sound, save for the booming of his own heartbeat in his ears. Then, clutching his belly, he sagged to his knees as his brain exploded in a shower of sparks. He was trembling so violently that he seemed to set the buffalo skull spinning, its swastika pinwheeling like fireworks above Berlin's Luna Park. The hut's pans rattled and the thatch riffled. Fire pierced his belly and bowels and arrowed through his limbs, his skull a burning coal.

"Help me!" he begged. "Feed me the gruel!"

He clamped one arm around Solomon's ankles and with his free hand gripped Hempel's boot, but when he peered up to implore, their faces were lost behind a smokescreen that pulsed with laughter. He was going to die; Solomon and Hempel had, after all, conspired to kill him. Taurus' so-called operation was a ruse for Jew and jailer to trick him into taking poison.

Air. He needed air. If only he could crawl to the door, all would be well, but he could not get his knees under himself. The hut pitched and yawed, and Solomon's and Hempel's legs blocked the way. Bamboo legs.

He reached between the bars.

"*Miriam!*"

Taurus, not Miriam, emerged through the fog to face him. She poked an enormous head between the bars, dark eyes drinking him in. Thankfully he reached for her, knowing her warmth and compassion would quiet the pain....

She backed away.

Taurus?

Rolling onto her back and lifting her forepaws, she panted happily as the syphilitic sliced between her thighs.

"All those dog shows, Erich," he heard Solomon say. "All the Strongheart films. Rin Tin Tin a dozen times. Why do you spend so much time at the Marmorhaus?"

And echoing around the hut:

"Chi...en...beau. Chi...en...beau."

Erich covered his ears and put his forehead against the floor, but the words kept thrumming inside his skull. Sensing a presence before him, he looked up to find himself staring at the syphilitic's gleaming eyes. Smoke poured from the face-hole, smothering him in the stink of eucalyptus.

Stop! Erich shouted, but no sound came. He was a mute pleading for help in a world of the blind and the deaf. Only the fossas heard. They ambled forward curiously, garnet eyes shining in the firelight. Next to them, Achilles, dead three years, lay watching him while Taurus opened her jaws.

With the apathy of one about to be executed, Erich lowered his head and waited for her teeth to fasten around his neck.

I'm sorry, he wanted to say. *Forgive me.*

The blackened pan of gruel was shoved before him. He did not resist when hands forced down his head. As if the bitter paste were a last meal, he slurped and lapped. Taurus snarled and turned her muzzle sideways to bite, and darkness engulfed him....

"How do you feel?" Solomon asked.

Leaning against an outside wall of the shack, Erich retched. When the vomiting was over and he had stopped shaking, he watched the splay of searchlights sweeping across the camp and tried to remember what had happened inside the hut. The only thing he could clearly recall was holding a chloroform-soaked cloth over Taurus' nose. The rest was blurred and dim, as if *he*—instead of Taurus—had been anesthetized.

"She's all right?" he asked anxiously, trying to wave away a spotlight that zeroed in on them. In a low breath he swore at the effort it took to push himself from the shack's support.

"Seems to be fine," Solomon answered. "He was suturing her when I went in and brought you out here."

"You shouldn't have left her!" Erich started to move through the grass, but winced as pain pierced his hip. Limping, he re-entered the shack.

And stopped.

The fossas were gone. Lounging on the far side of the smoldering brazier were two puny, bald Kalanaro, asleep with their heads pillowed against the Zana-Malata's legs.

Taurus, too, was sleeping peacefully.

The syphilitic's eyes smiled. He rubbed each man's head as if for luck. They continued to snore softly as he shifted out from beneath them and checked Taurus' hind legs. They were bandaged with palm fronds covered with mud, and smelled of overripe bananas.

Erich clung to the door frame for support as a wave of intense pain attacked his hip and ran down the length of his legs, tearing at his nerves and muscles.

The syphilitic's eyes brightened. "*Chien...beau*," he said, this time pointing at Erich.

"Bruqah says to tell you that to save an animal, you must be willing to sacrifice your humanness."

The words came back to Erich on a renewed wave of pain. He gritted his teeth, waited for it to pass, and limped toward the outdoors.

In the morning, after a bottle of brandy, he would examine the price he had paid for Taurus' life.

CHAPTER TWENTY-FIVE

Most of the time, Miriam was grateful for the mosquito netting that was draped around her cot. At this moment, it felt like a shroud. If this is spring, she thought, just how bad is the full heat of summer going to be? She could tell by the movement of the netting that there was a breeze, but the same fabric that kept out small bugs also kept most of what little breeze there was from getting to her. This was compounded by the fact that there was little, if any, ventilation. Light shone through the tent opening, enhancing the contrast between the milky netting and the grasshoppers, moths, and crickets that perched on the outside of the gauzy fabric. There was even a stray butterfly, black with brilliant gold striations, and four times as big as any she had seen in Berlin.

She remembered once, when she was a little girl, saying that she wished she had been born a butterfly.

Now she wished for simpler things. Like a bath, or a good cup of coffee.

Or even just knowing if it was day or night.

Almost in self-defense, she drifted back into a drugged sleep. She dreamed of the Kalanaro, fourteen or fifteen of them, gyrating outside the ghetto fence. One man squatted and, cupping his hands, grinned with red-ochered lips and darkly painted eyes, his body whitewashed and glowing. The others ran at him one at a time and placed a foot in his hands. He lifted them, tossing them into a somersault. The landings were bone-jarring, onto buttocks or backs, but the Kalanaro squealed with delight and staggered to their feet again, to run full tilt toward the tosser.

A troop of ring-tailed lemurs wandered, tails lifted, into the frame of her dream. They padded along the fence's perimeter and sat down between the Kalanaro and the wire, watching the pygmies with benign curiosity. The Kalanaro drew away into a tighter semicircle, the smiles gone from their eyes. One or two, without taking their angry gazes from the lemurs, knelt and took hold of their spears.

The dream changed.

In Miriam's womb, hairless puppies writhed, then burst squirming in agony from the rumble seat of the burning convertible that held the charred bodies of her parents, her uncle, her dog who gave birth as it burned to a profusion of flaming, twisted creatures.

She twisted from side to side in her dream torment, awake enough to know that she was dreaming, asleep enough to experience the nightmare. Hands pressed against her belly mound, her mind roared with the names of men whose faces eluded her. *Help me, Solomon*, she cried out. *Come to me.* She heard a glass break, crunching as if underfoot. She saw a parade of faceless lovers—a pale mask named Solomon, a rumpled uniform with an Abwehr insignia, the Grecian features of a dancer with the Stuttgart who had loved her first, often and well, only to slap her and call her Jew when she said good-bye. She saw a loose-skinned black man stinking of eucalyptus, who took her only in her nightmares, mouth-hole pressing down over her lips so that she could struggle but not scream.

Miriam awoke again.

The haze created by the mosquito netting was clear compared with the murkiness in her mind. How many times, she wondered, had Pleshdimer been beside her in the past several days, forcing upon her the liquid that filled her throat with fire and brought the chaos of nightmare? She lay in a tent; of that she was reasonably certain. That, at least, was an improvement. Sometimes she awoke thinking that she was in her Swiss home, or at her uncle's estate in the Grünewald, or in a chittering jungle, or swathed in cloud.

There was one thing of which she was completely sure: she was within days, if not hours, of giving birth. She put her hand on her stomach, willing the child to kick and let her know that it was still alive, for in her stupor she could not recall recently having felt any movement.

"God help me," she said out loud.

"He will."

"Franz!" Miriam tried to sit up. "I thought I was alone. Very alone."

"Easy, Frau Alois." She saw a movement in the netting and felt the corpsman's warm, comforting hands on her shoulders. "Concentrate on keeping yourself mentally and physically prepared for the delivery."

"Maybe the child is dead. I can't feel it kicking."

"Don't you remember, Dr. Tyrolt said it would be quiet before the birth? Preparing itself for life, he said."

Miriam nodded, though she did not remember. She shook herself free of his grasp, reluctant to lie down again in the damp indentation in the cot. "It's so hot," she said, pushing her hair away from her face. "Always so hot." She parted the netting and angled her face in the direction of the breeze. "You cannot know how I long for the ice and snow of a Berlin winter." Come to me, Solomon, she thought. I need you here with me. Erich's orders had been explicit on that point. Sol was free to see her, until the birth.

"Where is my…my *husband!*"

"He'll be here soon enough, Frau Alois. Please, you must relax—"

"Don't patronize me!" She picked a grasshopper from her nightdress and tried to deposit it onto the floor. It headed for the entrance in a loud whirring of wings. She was annoyed, at Franz that he would naturally enough assume that she had been referring to Erich, and at herself for not having made her meaning clear. In fact, she thought, she was just plain irritated by everything.

"Patronize?" Franz shook his head. "I assure you, I'm just trying to—"

"And what's that God-awful stench!"

Franz walked around to face her. He tried to smile, but the effect was more like a grimace. "The smell of the tropics before the rain." He drifted to the entrance of the tent and stood leaning against the tent pole, looking out into the night, his body blocking her view. "Why would anyone want to bring a child into a world like…"

He looked at her, with embarrassment. "I didn't mean that, Frau Alois." Coming toward her, he took her hand as though he meant to kiss it. "Forgive me. I've tried to maintain a brave front in the face of things, but I guarantee you, you're not alone in being frightened. Like you, I wish Dr. Tyrolt were here."

"I have placed myself and my child in your care," Miriam said.

"I'm sorry, I…." He lifted his head and she could see that he was actively attempting to arrange his features into a mien of competence. He gave her a distant, detached look that was less than reassuring. "Things will work out," he said softly. "Everything will be fine. You'll see."

Miriam's head had begun to pound. Her breathing was shallow and irregular. She returned her hands to her belly. "We've an important curtain call to make," she said, trying to lighten things up.

"I will stay with you," Franz said. "Or do you wish me to find the Oberst?" He paused. "Or Solomon Freund?"

Miriam closed her eyes. She felt distanced from everyone, even Sol. She loved him now, more than ever, but that love seemed to draw strength from her that she needed to survive. That she and the baby needed. To survive. Maybe, she thought, it was as Erich had so often insisted—that pregnant women drew into themselves, shutting out the men they loved.

"I want to go to Solomon," she said suddenly. "I want to have the baby in there. With the Jews. Where I belong."

"I cannot let you do that, Frau Alois. My instructions—"

"Damn your instructions."

She swung heavily off the cot. Dusk had come and gone, and night was descending. She could sense the shadows creeping across the tent top, the sky darkening to ink. Would the stars be out tonight? Would it hold any meaning for her, for any of them, if they were?

She listened to the work-noise of the prisoners, to the talk of the guards, to the occasional laughter.

The baby kicked. For a time Miriam was very still, her mind at rest, then a wave of pain washed through her. She took several deep breaths, and moved toward the tent opening. Franz did not try to stop her. Cobalt-blue light spread like paint over her mind.

"Sol," she cried out, pushing away the vision that was trying to intrude upon her efforts. "Sol!"

Her gaze searched the Jewish quarters and she thought she saw him in the glare of the searchlight. Then it illuminated Hempel, who flicked a finger toward Solomon, indicating for him to come. Solomon did so, at a sprint. As he reached the major, he whipped off his cap, stuck it in his left armpit and stood at attention.

Together, they walked toward her, and she toward them, with Franz at her side. When they faced each other, Hempel directed Sol to stand shoulder-to-shoulder with her.

Do what he says, Sol's body language said to Miriam. For the baby. Lick Hempel's boots if you must. I did so at Sachsenhausen, and you must do so, too, if it is necessary for survival.

Hempel paced in front of the three of them. There was about him a particular arrogance that Miriam had not seen since meeting him on her uncle's estate, before the major's departure for Sachsenhausen. He was the supreme lord-overseer—lean without appearing hard-muscled, silver-haired without appearing elderly: the quintessential commander.

Abruptly he stopped pacing and looked directly into Solomon's eyes. Sol showed no fear. His life, Miriam was sure, depended on his being able to show self-respect and false respect for Hempel at the same time.

"Did you have sexual relations with this woman…the wife of Erich Alois?"

Fear seized Miriam. If Solomon told the truth, would Hempel kill him—and her? If he denied the charge, would he be killed for lying? She wanted to cry out that she had never really been Erich's wife except by right of paper, but she remained silent.

Sol remained frozen at attention, apparently afraid that Miriam would be killed if he admitted what Hempel probably already knew to be the truth.

"Answer me, Jew!"

"Yes," Miriam said. "Yes, we made love."

Hempel grabbed Solomon by the Adam's apple as though to tear it from his throat. "Jews do not know the meaning of love. Everyone knows that. You rut like animals. We proved that beyond dispute at Sachsenhausen!"

He released Solomon, who rocked back on his heels, eyes watering as he tried to catch his breath without choking. Miriam started to reach for him, but as Hempel turned her way Solomon shook his head.

Hempel looked at her and cocked a brow. "You let a Jew have you? You let a *Jew* inside you?"

She crossed her arms, mostly to stop the shaking of her body. She could feel none of the pain which she had earlier thought must be the start of labor. "I, too, am a Jew," she said.

"The Führer says otherwise. He proclaimed you not only Gentile, but German. Gauleiter Goebbels himself offered to assure your status by arranging for a complete blood transfusion for you."

"I am sorry that I could not accept the Gauleiter's generous offer. And I am sorry," she lowered her eyes, "that I have not lived up to the Führer's trust."

Hempel's eyes flashed.

This is it, Miriam thought. The day of our deaths. Without changing her line of sight, she made herself aware of the sky. It was a rarified blue-black, velvet and studded with diamonds.

Hempel unholstered his Mann and placed its barrel against Sol's temple. With the index finger of his other hand, he lifted Miriam's chin as though to assess her beauty. "You will be kept from harm," he said. "Until the child is born. After that," he looked back at Sol, "you can live wherever you please, with whomever you please. If you live at all."

"You are not in charge of me, Otto," Miriam said, her voice contemptuous. "What makes you think—"

A shadow stopped her. Shielding her eyes from the searchlight's glare, she looked upward at the darkening moon.

A sense of awe settled about the compound as even Hempel peered upward. The shepherds began to whine.

As if sensing that the guards' attention was no longer riveted upon their weapons, a group of Jews moved in unison toward the area of the gate.

"Activate the ghetto fence!" Hempel yelled.

Miriam, too, had seen the movement, but unlike Hempel it had not occurred to her that the Jews might try to make a spontaneous break for freedom. Sol would surely have told her if such a thing were imminent.

Still, anything was possible, she thought, as grasshoppers swarmed in from all sides, filling the air, sizzling into sparks on the fence around the Jewish quarters. Guards and prisoners alike danced and batted and cursed at the deluge. The insects covered Miriam's clothes and head, eyed her from the bridge of her nose before droning away, sought to invade her nostrils and ears. Through the whirring, maddening wings, she looked around at the Germans' maniacal antics, at the dogs leaping and snapping, at the Kalanaro who had dropped their spears to scoop up and devour the crisped insects near the fence.

"What the hell is going on?" Erich asked, staggering from his quarters.

Hempel moved in front of Erich, looked at him momentarily, without speaking, and stepped back formally, as though about to issue an edict. "Why don't you take a cold shower and sober up, Herr Oberst," he said. "I'll take care of things here."

Erich swayed. "I dis-distinctly told you that fence was not to be electrified," he said, pronouncing the words with difficulty.

"Nor was it," Hempel said. "Until now."

"You had no business...I promised the prisoners...."

"I did what I had to do, Herr Oberst. I would have consulted you, but you were...indisposed."

Erich started to argue, then apparently thought better of it. He turned around and began to limp toward the Jews who were clustered behind the wire. Halfway there, as if he had just realized that she was there, he turned around and stared at Miriam. "Get her to shelter," he called out.

He looked, Miriam thought, like anything but a commander. Head hanging. Pressing at his hip joint as if to grab hold of an all but unbearable pain as he walked out of sight. Despite everything, her heart wrenched with pity at Erich's plight, that part which had nothing to do with Solomon, or with her, but rather with his humiliation by Hempel. And with a hatred between Erich and Hempel that went back seventeen years, to when Erich had been a member of Hempel's Freikorps-Youth unit.

"I am going into the Jewish quarters," Miriam said to Franz. "That is where I wish to give birth."

"This is not possible, Frau Alois. Surely you can see that for yourself."

"I can see nothing," Miriam said quietly. "Are you saying that you will not assist me in there?" She held her hands palms upward, as if in supplication, and they were quickly covered by grasshoppers.

"I am saying that I cannot," Franz said. He sounded at the point of tears. "To help bring the Herr Oberst's child into the world is one thing. To bring a…a—"

"Say it, you coward! To bring the child of a Jew into the world would be, what? A sin against the Fatherland?"

Miriam felt herself sway. Her fingers closed around the insects, crunching them to a pulp. Battered by renewed pain, she collapsed onto the ground. In a state of semi-consciousness, she thought herself beneath the canopy of her bed in the villa. She thought she could see Erich Weisser peering in through the chiffoned French doors that led onto the balcony, while behind him the night was ablaze with Berlin burning. An acrid stench permeated everything, as though the villa itself were part of the conflagration, and for an instant she expected to see smoke roil beneath her bedroom door. "Papa," she tried to call out. "Papa?" But Erich had never been part of her life when Papa had been, and nothing made sense. Where was Papa! Down having one of those predawn breakfasts he and Uncle Walther so enjoyed, three-minute eggs and the *Tageblatt* spread out across the table, each complaining and commiserating about the state of the Fatherland what with the war reparations, while her dog lay between their feet, fitfully snoring?

Returning to full consciousness, Miriam fought to get a grip on reality. She dug her hands into her hair and pulled off squirming grasshoppers in each fist. Shuddering, she flipped the insects aside. They whirred away and sat twitching on the ground.

A cry followed by a crescendoing ululation of African voices rose to greet her. She heard footsteps crunch across the grass, followed by a series of excited yells and more laughter.

"What *is* it!" She clutched the neckline of her dress as if to cover herself more thoroughly and looked around for Sol.

"Hempel take Solly back to Jewish quarters. I watch. I come. Noise you hear is lemurs, Lady Miri." Bruqah leaned over her. "At the gate." He smiled as if to reassure her. "They all over out there, beyond the fence. Running around like little children, teasing the guards." He took a few steps in their direction, and she heard the crunching again. He looked up at the moon. "Kalanaro have full bellies tonight, all right, after eating they."

His face clouded as Miriam doubled up in pain. "Baby not come yet, but soon. This what you call pretend labor."

For the first time Miriam smiled. "*False* labor, Bruqah."

"Trouble coming. I feel it." He bent down and lowered his voice so that only she could hear him. Pointing up the hill toward the crypt, he said, "I take you there for birth of child."

Miriam started to argue. He placed his hand gently over her mouth. "Do not battle with me, Lady Miri. I carry you if need be."

The Malagasy's mouselemur crawled out of his *lamba*, peered at Miriam from behind Bruqah's head, and scuttled back within the cloth.

"You're not wanted here," Franz said, without conviction. "Herr Oberst Alois has said that you're troubling Frau Alois." The corpsman glanced with a certain sheepishness toward Miriam. "And the Sturmbannführer has told us privately that you're a threat to the entire operation."

"Has told *us?*" Bruqah asked, chin rising with the aristocratic arrogance of one severely slighted.

"Well, some of us," the corpsman said hesitantly. "Most of the guards, anyway. I wasn't there when he said that, but I heard. They still confide in me. Some of the others, I mean." Franz looked at Miriam, and nodded. "They do." His former look of confidence had dissipated.

Bruqah eyed Miriam anxiously. "We must leave here," he said.

"And go where?"

She realized that her hand was on her abdomen, and that there was an undertone of hysteria in her voice.

"Away."

"The hell she is," Franz stated, stepping between them and glaring up at the taller man.

"The Sturmbannführer is in power," Bruqah said to neither of them in particular.

"Does the Herr Oberst know that?" Miriam asked.

"If he does not yet, he will soon," Franz said. He made a sweeping gesture around the compound. "It's rather obvious, isn't it?"

"We really must go, Lady Miri," Bruqah said with greater need in his voice.

Franz seized Bruqah's arm. "Everything will be fine now!"

With apparent effortlessness Bruqah turned his wrist toward himself and disentangled himself from Franz' hold. "You not believe that," he said.

For a moment Franz said nothing, staring at some point beyond Bruqah. Then he shook his head. "No," he muttered.

"Erich would never stand aside and see his command usurped," Miriam said. "He'd die before that happened."

But she knew her assurance was a lie. In the sleeping area, the prisoners huddled in woeful-looking groupings. Even from a distance she could see that no one was speaking. They watched with forlorn expressions as the Kalanaro piled through the partly opened compound gate and, spears raised, ran through the kikuyu grass after the lemurs while the Nazis laughed and shouted catcalls as if they were at a wrestling match. In the distance, she could see Erich silhouetted in the moonlight. He sat slump-shouldered in the dirt near the sleeping-area gate, staring up at the water tower. His body spoke the language of a man who had lost everything, a man for whom the loss of power *was* everything.

She stood up with difficulty.

"We go now, Lady Miri," Bruqah put his hands on her shoulders and she was glad for the touch, glad there was someone to hold her up, "while there are lemurs still left to dance—and distract."

The blackness lifted from the face of the moon and Miriam saw a hint of a sad smile in Bruqah's eyes. With equal sadness, she nodded. She was being forced away from Solomon once again, this time for the sake of the child. Sol would understand.

He had always understood, she told herself. That was his greatest asset, and his greatest fault.

"I'll go with you," Franz whispered urgently. He eyed Bruqah with temerity. "Let me stop at the medical tent for cotton bandages and some other supplies—"

"No," Miriam said. "We will manage without you, Bruqah and I. If you are right and there is mutiny to come, you may be needed here."

Half carrying her, Bruqah led Miriam away from the compound toward the *valavato*, though she couldn't say exactly how they had passed the fence without going through the gate. The walking seemed to diminish her physical pain, and she attempted to alleviate the rest by thinking about Franz. She remembered what he had told her once while folding linens:

"I arrived at Sachsenhausen, unfortunately, only days before Hempel chose me for this assignment."

"Unfortunately?" she'd asked.

"I didn't have time to harden myself to the suffering, as the others did."

She glanced back at the compound. From the rear, shaded by the ragged collar of darkness beneath the limestone knoll, the night was crisscrossed with the searchlights beamed from the three sentry towers and from the knoll's crest. A large ruffled lemur darted into the light and went tumbling as a rifle shot rang out; the Kalanaro descended upon the victim, laughter shrilling and spears pinioning it to the earth as, caught within the spotlight, the animal squirmed and spasmed in its death throes.

Her gaze met Bruqah's.

His face was a mask, devoid of emotion. She tried to whisper a condolence but he put a finger to his lips, his eyes so expressionless that she wondered if he were capable of feeling grief or fear at all.

Then she realized that the mask of his face *was* his grief; the pain of knowing the lemurs were being killed had frozen his features. He tried to hide his feelings because that was his nature—or perhaps because he wished to protect her, in much the same way that she often tried to cover her fear with humor.

"Bruqah…"

A trickle of perspiration meandered down from her brow and into an eye. Though her mind, absorbed by the drama she was enacting, had not allowed the emotion to sink into her consciousness, her body responded to the fear.

She started to moan, not so much from pain but from exhaustion, and the fear she could no longer fight. Above her she could hear the low, excited voices of the two guards on duty atop a tower. A match was struck, and for a moment an oval of harshly yellow light glared against the night sky. She held her breath when the match went out.

Bruqah poked down the head of the mouselemur come up to inspect the world. The gesture reminded her of a young Solomon, pushing his glasses higher up the bridge of his nose in order to improve his clarity of vision. They moved up the hill under the moon-dappled overhang until they neared where the track connected to the two new roads. Bruqah looked left and right, shoulders raised and head swiveling stiffly as if he were a proper policeman in someone's colony, and then, arm also stiff, motioned her onto the path.

"You be all right?" he asked her.

"For a sack of potatoes that's fallen off the cart once too many times," she replied and hobbled onward.

"I carry you now," Bruqah said.

"I'll transport myself on my own legs, thank you, and if I fall down, you'll help me up again."

"Woman foolish creature," Bruqah said. "Pretty soon I pick you up anyhow."

Slowly they began the ascent up the road that led to the *valavato*. The further they drew from the meadow, the thicker and higher was the forest canopy. All they could see of the sky was a narrow blue-black avenue pebbled with stars, its northern edge tinged chartreuse by the moon.

CHAPTER TWENTY-SIX

"Herr Oberst!" Fermi shouted above the din. "It's the shepherds again!"

Erich blinked against his alcoholic daze and stared out at the compound. He swore, shouldered his MP-38 and, pain slicing up through his bad leg with each step, hurried as best he could toward the dog-runs, insects crunching beneath his feet. He could hear the animals barking and snapping. For the most part, the grasshoppers had stopped their descent, but they had apparently made the dogs crazy. In the moonlight, he could see the dogs tearing around, only to be yanked from their feet when they reached the end of the wires to which they were chained. Then in circles, then again the length of the wire, only to be pulled off their feet once more.

"I don't know what's gotten into the dogs!" Fermi said.

Other trainers were sprinting toward the yard, alternately cursing their shepherds and begging them for quiet. A knot of guards had formed at the gate. They were engaged in animated conversation, pointing toward the yard. Clusters of Jews peered around like drivers viewing an accident in the streets.

"Get them under control!" Erich screamed as he entered the yard, but he was uncertain if his men could obey. The animals were raging. Pisces had once again wrapped his chain around his run pole. Despite her bandages, Taurus lunged with full fury toward the gate, was jerked off her feet and rolled in the dust, only to charge again, oblivious to Erich's presence. Sagittarius was desperately tugging backward against the chain, trying to rid herself of her collar.

The others were similarly out of control but, to Erich's relief, none tried to attack the trainers. Rather, they acted as if their masters did not exist: struggling against confinement, glaring toward the gate, whining as if injured when the men snapped on choke chains. Aries' trainer had managed to muzzle his animal.

"He's feverish, sir," Fermi said. "What's wrong with them?"

"Who the hell knows!" Erich yelled over his shoulder as he hobbled toward Taurus, who was growling and straining at her bonds.

"Look!" Fermi pointed toward the Zana-Malata and the Kalanaro who were, in turn, watching Otto Hempel walk toward them. Misha trotted alongside him on a leash, the wolfhound's collar around his forehead like a flapper's headdress.

Hempel stopped and shook his fist toward the moon. A group of Kalanaro joined him. Carrying spears, they moved with feline grace across the *savoka*. Within the compound, guards scrambled from tents and, fumbling with web gear and grabbing Mausers, rushed to the fence and brought their rifles to their shoulders. Not a word was said. Like a pig shoot, Erich thought with a delight that surprised him. No more need to convince the guards that Hempel had overstepped. They might hesitate to shoot a fellow German, but they'd love to mow down Africans.

Except Erich couldn't allow it. He didn't believe Bruqah's talk about bad luck, but he could not afford to upset the Malagasy. Besides, once the shooting began there would be no stopping it, and first he had to learn where the pitchblende came from. And he would need miners. The Jews could hardly build the landing facility and mine the pitchblende at the same time, so he had to save the goddamn pygmies.

For now.

Involuntarily, he held his hand where the Zana-Malata had burned it with his African magic. Given what had happened the last time, he was loathe to let the little black men into the compound. Then again, what the hell, he thought. A man with uranium in his pocket could afford to be magnanimous.

"Let them in, but watch them!" he yelled to the men at the gate. He wanted to tell them not to let the major in, but would they obey him? Or would he be setting himself up for another defeat?

He petted Taurus, who strained but did not twist

against his hold. A calculating growl sounded in her throat, yet she no longer seemed out of control. Erich suppressed a smile. Now she was a predator awaiting prey. When it came to stopping the Kalanaro, the dogs would turn the trick with greater spectacle than bullets—and in their wake leave survivors who might, out of fear, prove quite amenable not only to revealing the pitchblende's location but to digging it from the ground.

With a creaking of hinges, two guards opened the entrance. Hempel entered first, followed by the Kalanaro, spears pointed outward.

The searchlights centered on Hempel, who snapped his heels together, arm springing into the air, chin lifted, eyes like obsidian. "*Sieg heil!*"

"*Sieg heil!*" Pleshdimer cried, stepping from behind the medical tent.

Hempel bellowed the greeting for a third time, and the men answered, visible excitement in their mien.

The Zana-Malata dramatically stretched out his hands. Small flames burned in his cupped palms. The men began to murmur, now and again looking toward the dog-runs. A couple patted the syphilitic on the shoulders.

Comrades all.

Squealing with joy and brandishing their spears, the Kalanaro darted toward the Jews, who backed abruptly from the fence.

"*Vahilo minihana! Vahilo minihana!*" Hempel shouted. "Attack and eat! Attack and eat!"

The guard at the ghetto entrance tugged up his heavy gloves and swung open the gate, only to be bowled over by an outrush of Jews. Erich saw the guard's gun fall.

The machine gunner in the northwestern tower laid down a peppery line of fire at the prisoners' feet, and the forward surge of captives halted. The guards stepped forward, Mausers raised. For a moment Jew and German looked at each other anxiously, and then the prisoners withdrew into the ghetto, leaving the fallen gun.

"*Vahilo minihana!*" Pleshdimer yelled, raising a fist.

The guards laughed at the Jews who were racing to get under their canopy, seeking the false safety of the shadows.

The Kalanaro did not enter the ghetto. Instead, they circled it, poking their spears between the electrified strands. Their movement sent the dogs into renewed frenzy.

"Control the dogs!" Erich hoarsely ordered the trainers. "They're no match for the Mausers!" Fighting to keep Taurus from charging, he swung the submachine pistol off his shoulder and, the choke chain wrapped around his forearm, lay down on the grass for a clear shot.

Trembling with excitement and fear, he zeroed in on Hempel's heart. He wondered if it might not be wiser to shoot the Zana-Malata, standing with his palm-cupped flames raised like some committeeman welcoming home a household of prodigals.

No, he decided. There was much greater purpose and pleasure in killing Hempel.

"Watch me bring the house down!" a guard loudly bragged, sighting toward the canopy. "See the guy ropes?"

The question momentarily shifted Erich's attention to the ghetto, and what he saw made him lift his cheek from against the gun's cool metal.

Stepping from beneath the canvas, Solomon Freund walked toward a leaping, howling Kalanaro on the other side of the fence.

The African poked at him with a spear from between the wire, but Solomon was out of reach. The Kalanaro withdrew the weapon and hissed, showing his teeth like a baboon, then danced back as Solomon kept coming toward him.

Other prisoners emerged from the shadows, but stayed well out of range of the spears, watching silently as the whitely pulsing African again pranced toward Solomon, feinting, jabbing, shrieking his torment.

The other Kalanaro, apparently sensing a drama developing, drew back. Stamping their feet and spear hafts against the ground, they hooted in derision at their comrade. The guards joined in, pointing and laughing.

When the one at the wire again tentatively stuck his spear between the strands, hesitant to draw closer to the lethal fence, two others rushed toward the wire, spears uplifted and faces contorted, only to retreat as quickly and burst into renewed mirth.

The Kalanaro lunged.

With an athleticism Erich would have thought impossible, Solomon dodged the speartip and grabbed the haft. The Kalanaro tried pulling back, but Solomon clung on and, for a moment, despite the wire between them, Jew and African were pitted like two children playing tug-of-war. The guards and the other Kalanaro roared with delight.

The spearman looked around. His grin remained, but his eyes filled with desperation, making everyone laugh the louder at his predicament.

Erich sighted on Solomon's tormentor. He knew that killing the pygmy would give Hempel an instant to react, but Solomon was one Jew who would not be destroyed unless *he*, Erich, said so.

They were *his* Jews.

Right! And this one fucked my wife, he thought.

His finger tightened on the trigger and he swung the barrel from the Kalanaro to Solomon. He was suddenly stone cold sober.

He fucked my wife, he thought again. Not only that, but she loves the son of a bitch.

Normally an expert and steady marksman, even when drunk, he was trembling. He imagined Miriam arched like a bow, face distorted with passion.

The barrel wavered. He fought to control his aim.

Trying to downthrust, the Kalanaro leaped onto the fence as Solomon let go of the spear.

Sparks jumped from the African's hair, hands, and feet as he hung twitching and spasming, eyes rolled up and head jerking. The acrid odor of burnt flesh mingled with the compound's other scents. With a loud pop, the cable from the generator to the fence exploded. The African's body dropped from the fence and lay tremoring. Erich swung the barrel back toward Hempel, only to find guards standing in the line of fire. Silently cursing his lapse of concentration, he forced himself to relax. And wait.

The camp fell silent. The dogs quieted, noses lifted and sniffing the unfamiliar scent of burnt flesh and hair. As the guards and other Kalanaro approached the body, Sol's face took on a look of disgust mixed with pity. He shook his head once, then turned and walked beneath the canopy.

One of the Africans stooped, ran a finger along a smoldering burn on the body, looked up—and grinned. "*Minihana!*" Light laughter rippled among the guards. Like a master of ceremonies, the black man responded to his audience. "*Minihana! Minihana!*" He looked up again, showing filed teeth as his grin widened. He leapt like a monkey around the body, motioning for the others to do the same. They finally did so, dancing and jumping, racing to the fence and prodding it with their spears as if to re-enact the event.

The Zana-Malata laughed, apparently much amused. Dousing his flames, he padded over to stand near the dead man's head. Hempel joined him, Mann pointed carelessly at the ground. The guards gathered behind him. Like Hitler Youth around a campfire, Erich thought with contempt.

In what appeared to be a benign moment, Hempel bent down and released Misha. The boy sat there, apparently not knowing quite what it was he was supposed to do. Hempel nudged him with his foot and Misha scampered away, out of Erich's line of sight.

More fortunately, Erich thought, out of the line of fire.

He turned to the trainers.

"Zodiac," he said softly.

"Sir?" Fermi had to tug his pawing dog sideways to get close enough to hear.

"Zodiac," Erich repeated, suddenly relieved that he had not executed Hempel...yet. He would send the dogs in; Zodiac was not only their best, and favorite, attack formation, it involved the trainers more than any other maneuver. Unless all the trainers were part of his putdown of Hempel's insubordination, killing the major might prove meaningless. Life after Hempel would never run smoothly as long as the Totenkopfverbände were in the majority, and to rectify that would require all the help he could get.

"Against our own, sir?"

"You call that rabble your own?" Erich eyed each trainer in turn, trying to draw them one by one back into his emotional camp.

"Killing the monkeys is one thing," Holten-Pflug whispered. "But other Germans..."

Erich knew that he could order the trainers to do his will and they almost certainly would comply, but he needed more than that. He needed to be sure of their loyalty.

"You all know that Müller's dead," he said quickly. "The guards killed him, and they're planning the same for the rest of us. Don't you know what's been going on in that goddamned hut over there?"

Though his mouth was open, he stopped speaking.

The men would never believe the truth even if he could explain it. He put a hand on Taurus to calm his frustration. When she looked back at him, straining and whining for the kill, he knew what he must say.

"I have known for some time that Sturmbannführer Hempel is a proven collaborator. During the Great War, he collaborated with the Senegalese."

The lie contained enough truth to be believable. The African blacks had been among France's fiercest fighters. After the war, the French had looked the other way when the Senegalese, and doubtless others, raped German girls in the Saar, the region both countries claimed. Hempel *had*, as the trainers knew, been drummed from the army under mysterious circumstances. Perhaps there was a connection....

The trainers' gazes flicked toward the major, and Erich saw that he had touched a nerve. "Goebbels found out the whole truth about Hempel's past a few months ago, and now Berlin wants Hempel forgotten. That's why we were all sent here...to be forgotten."

Anger, shock and despair registered on the trainers' faces.

"Now Hempel's collaborating with French Africans. You know what a pervert he is. He'll kill you and let his little black boyfriends feast on your shepherds."

Fermi's dark brows tugged down in concern, and for a moment Erich wondered if the trainers might also mutiny—in an effort to save their dogs. Then, with pleasure, he saw their faces harden like those of their shepherds.

"Zodiac!" Fermi uttered, and everyone murmured in assent.

"Who'll take one o'clock?" Holten-Pflug asked.

Erich patted his MP-38. "*This*," he said, "will take Aquarius' place."

"And the center position?"

"We are all the center. Or else there is no center."

Glancing toward the ghetto, he saw that the Zana-Malata was in that sector, and Hempel was at five o'clock—Taurus' area. How serendipitous, he thought, his excitement growing.

"Spread the dogs wide and let them ease in close so they can attack before too many guards can raise their weapons. When I signal, use your pistols to take out anyone else in your sector."

To hell with saving some of these Kalanaro, he told himself. There was a compound to control. If all the pygmies in the compound got killed, he would find some other way to acquire the pitchblende. Find other Kalanaro.

"Ready?"

The guards nodded. Erich could feel their resolve and the dogs' sense of battle. Just like during those early days at the estate. Unified.

He counted Mausers. Only ten guards were holding weapons, plus Hempel with his Mann. Perfect. Eleven dogs, eleven deaths. Glancing up anxiously toward the sentries in the towers, he saw that they too were watching the Kalanaro sideshow. Once the attack began they would initially withhold fire, he figured, to avoid hitting their comrades.

Taurus would tear out Hempel's throat before the major had time to utter much more than a strangled scream.

Erich smiled to himself as the trainers and dogs moved into position. It was going to be like wolves slaughtering sheep.

He made a small, circular motion with his hand, signaling the trainers to release their charges, then unhooked and patted Taurus. She perked up her ears when he unobtrusively pointed toward Hempel. *Good girl*, he said silently. *Kill him. Kill him for Papa.*

Their muzzles removed, the dogs hunkered down as they spread silently out along the edges of the light. Each is an extension of its trainer, Erich thought proudly, the culmination of years of effort and drill.

He lay down and, savoring the moment as the dogs closed upon the guards and Kalanaro, rested the submachine gun on a hillock of dirt and took aim on the syphilitic. He would shoot the bastard right in that stinking vagina he called a mouth.

He raised his left hand in signal and, as he jerked it down, felt a sense of power surge through him as he squeezed the trigger.

The gun did not fire.

The dogs did not move.

He swore under his breath and worked the action, but no round ejected. He heard another round chamber. If he fired now, the weapon was likely to explode. *Go!* he desperately, soundlessly commanded the dogs as he lurched to his knees and fought with the gun.

Around him, the trainers wrestled with their pistols.

Somewhere inside his head he heard the Zana-Malata's raucous laughter, and the gunmetal began to heat in his hands.

"Kill them!" he cried. "Kill them, Taurus!"

He thought he could smell the pungent odor of burnt flesh. He dropped the machine pistol and stared, stupefied, at his palms. The skin was severely burned, yet in his state of somnipathy he felt neither pain nor anxiety. Then he lifted his head and saw the dogs ease down from a crouch to their bellies, tails ticking as they crawled at an oblique angle away from the guards and Kalanaro and toward the ghetto. He tried to call the animals back, but no words formed. There was nothing: not hate or anger or sound, nothing within him save emptiness and a giddy sense of the searchlight's glow.

Taurus and the other dogs rose, shook themselves as if they had been swimming in the Wannsee. Heads down, they meandered around the outer fence until each stopped and lay down, facing the ghetto rather than the guards.

Each in its respective position on the clock. A Zodiac position, with the wrong targets. Watching the Jews.

"Vahilo minihana," his mind whispered. His mouth tasted the way it had after Taurus' surgery, of vomit and flour gruel.

"Vahilo minihana." Softer still. From deep inside. An animal hunger that he could not appease, like the throbbing pain of the dysplasia, somehow transferred to his hip after the surgery.

Slope-shouldered as a dullard, he started forward, holding the MP38 by its sling while the butt bounced along the ground. Grasshoppers sprayed up before him. He thought of stew made of dog meat, fruit bats, insects.

Hunger.

"Sagi?" he heard one of the trainers plead. The man had reached the dog, but the animal, watching the Jews, did not appear to notice. It eyed a prisoner who stepped forth from behind the mosquito netting.

The dog's tongue moved. Two licks, each beginning at the back end of the mouth and moving to the front.

Hunger.

The Kalanaro who had been killed struggled to his feet and steadied himself with his spear. He glanced at the burn stripes across his flesh, and managed a small, crooked grin as Erich strode past him.

Erich kept walking, eyes averted from the Kalanaro. He did not want to continue looking at the pygmy. Did not want to know that the dead had risen.

He reached the ghetto gate. The guard opened it for him. He stood at the entrance, staring, asking himself how he could have been so stupid as to want to save these wretches. He had lost his wife's love, almost lost Taurus, and now he was losing what shred of sanity he had left. And for what?

For *them*?

If they were so important to Hempel that the major would instigate mutiny, then Hempel could have them. He, Erich, would show them—show them all—just how little the Jews meant to him.

"Guard the prisoners!" he shouted at the dogs. "Kill any one of them that moves!"

Head held high, Solomon moved toward him.

Erich shouted again, and pointed, but the shepherds continued to mill, whining impatiently, looking toward the Zana-Malata.

At last, Erich realized his mistake. It was all so simple that he almost smiled at his own naïveté.

The dogs had never been his. Never been chattels of civilization. They belonged to themselves—and to the syphilitic, who demanded that the only law they or anything else adhere to was that of the jungle.

They too hungered as Erich did. They too felt an anger in the pit of their bellies that made them want to devour their enemies.

The Totenkopfverbände took positions around the ghetto, equidistant from one another, maddeningly precise in their deployment.

As a single being, the guards snapped their Mausers to their shoulders and sighted on the Jews.

Teutonic efficiency, Erich thought sardonically. The German mind so exactly ordered that the nation's children emerged, as if from an assembly line, as perfectly oiled killing machines.

Rather like the shepherds.

Just shoot the creatures that huddle in the ghetto, and save a bullet for me, he thought.

Anything to appease the hunger.

For a moment, he watched the dance of the Kalanaro along the outer perimeter of the fence, then he looked longingly at the gun, wondering if Benyowsky would consider him worthy of suicide.

CHAPTER TWENTY-SEVEN

When the shadow fell across the camp, Sol suffered the momentary terror of thinking he was losing the last of his sight. He was actually grateful for the reassurance of the searchlights cutting through the darkness. His participation in what followed was as much a function of relief and what felt like a reprieve with his vision, as it was a determination that he would not allow the Jews to be the butt of the Kalanaro's jokes. He did not really care what the little black men thought of them, if indeed they thought at all. But the fact was that the carnival event was put on for the amusement of Hempel and his men.

He cared about that.

To have had to leave Miriam in her fatigued state hurt greatly, and to his surprise seeing Erich so diminished hurt almost as much. It was clear to him, and not only because of the electrification of the fence, that Erich had lost control of the camp. He was drunk or hungover much of the time, he walked with difficulty and most often with a stick, bent over like an old man—or as if he would have preferred to drop to his knees and walk on all fours like his dogs.

Even now, reappearing around the Jewish quarters from the direction of the latrines, he looked aged and defeated.

Solomon looked at the shepherds and guards surrounding the ghetto and wondered if any prisoners would survive if Otto Hempel took full control of the camp, something he feared they would all soon have to face.

He watched Hempel saunter toward Erich, the major smiling suavely. When the two men were less than a meter apart, Hempel halted. Then he took another step forward, as though breaking through whatever aura of invulnerability Erich might think he still possessed, and another step. The men were nearly chest to chest, Hempel with his hands raised as if expecting the formal delivery of a sword of surrender. Even with his fading eyesight, Sol could tell that the smile on the major's lips—and doubtless in his eyes—was one of overbearing disdain.

For the first time in the more than two decades that Solomon had known him, Erich looked thoroughly defeated.

"Your aborted attempt on my life makes you guilty of treason," the major said. "I demand that you hand over your weapon."

Erich did not respond.

The trainers stepped forward, crowding around the officers. They were clearly dismayed and confused.

"Gefreiter?" Hempel asked. "*Private?* As of now I am your commanding officer. Obey me, or I will have you shot. You *and* your Jews."

Erich's lips remained clamped shut, but his facial muscles had gone slack; he appeared incapable of lifting his eyes above Hempel's belt buckle. With a shudder, Sol remembered where he'd seen that apathetic, wearied expression before. *Schmuckstück.* Costume jewelry: the living dead—those in Sachsenhausen who had given up hope.

"Gefreiter!"

Hempel's face had reddened with wrath. His eyes narrowed like those of a fossa. "Pick your targets," he hissed to the guards, without taking his gaze off Erich. "Choose any who appears weak or without proper respect toward the Reich. Fire in rotation. One round per Jew!"

Turning his head to compensate for his limited vision, Solomon watched his fellow prisoners straighten and draw into a tight circle, facing outward like musk ox to a storm, eyes cold with determination. Gone was the fear and the hope of the past. In place of both was the look of men for whom death held no mystery. Some gripped tent-pole spears—the canopy sagging where the poles had been removed—others had rocks and sharpened sticks retrieved from God knew where, still others held their wooden clogs like spanking paddles.

Even those with bare fists clearly intended to die fighting.

Or in the *pose* of fighting, Sol thought with a feeling of sad certainty. Of what value were such Maccabean heroics against Mausers?

He wondered if a scapegoat could satisfy the need for blood.

Could he trade his life for a reprieve, however temporary, for the lives of his fellow prisoners?

There was only one way to find out, and that was to find out. Bracing himself for the agony of a bullet, he took an exaggerated step toward the gate.

"Sturmbannführer Hempel!" he called out, watching with a kind of raw pleasure as the guard nearest the gate leveled his rifle.

"If you will kill but one Jew tonight—me, their leader, their rabbi—I will publicly renounce Judaism and all its evils."

The gasps behind him only served to steel his resolve. They will understand, he promised himself.

They will.

Hempel either did not hear the challenge or chose not to. Abruptly doing a right-face, he strode toward Taurus. With his arm stiff, he aimed his Mann toward the dog's neck.

Taurus lifted her head, sniffing the air.

"Don't hurt the dog," Erich said quietly.

"*All* inferiors are to be eliminated," Hempel replied. "Our work here in Madagascar will not be slowed down by those with physical problems."

Erich's head jerked up, and Sol saw him glance around uneasily, as though he had awakened in a strange place. "She's cured," he said in a boyish, petulant voice.

Hempel smiled and shook his head. "My friend the Zana-Malata has indicated to me that the affliction was merely diverted—into you, Gefreiter. Should your death be necessitated, the disorder will seek out its former host, thus again rendering the dog useless."

Sol watched Erich turn toward the Zana-Malata as if for confirmation. The syphilitic gave a slow, regal nod.

After staring at the shepherd for a long time—her tail wagging and her tongue hanging out as she lay panting—Erich lifted the MP38 and held it palms-up across his hands.

"Gefreiter." Hempel clicked his heels together, strode back to Erich, and again clicked his heels. Without any show of emotion, he ripped the colonel's insignia from Erich's blouse, then stepped back and handed the insignia, along with the weapon, to the nearest guard.

Pleshdimer came forward, saluted Hempel, and with theatrical flourish presented the major with a rolled-up paper tied with a black ribbon.

Hempel accepted the roll of paper almost absently, as though deep in thought. "The letting of blood is wholesome," he said, enunciating each word carefully. "It keeps the body politic in balance. The Medievalists knew that, but sometimes lately we seem to forget. Maybe the wound has been opened enough for now.

Maybe if...." He allowed his words to trail off, waited, and began again.

"If the men were reassured of your loyalty to the Reich." He paused. Holstering his pistol, he stepped forward and laid his hand on Erich's firearm. "The SS and Abwehr have never been friends," he said quietly. "The German race should be united, should it not, in its quest for its rightful destiny?"

Before Erich could reply, Hempel continued. "I can assure you that the first time you kill a Jew is like your first taste of fine cognac."

Erich took what appeared to be an involuntary step backwards.

"Watch," Hempel said. "I will show you how simple it is."

Once again he unholstered his Mann. Turning to face the Jews, he called out, "Bring one forward. Any one of them will do." A smile crossed his face. "On second thought, bring me Solomon Freund."

"This will stop. Now." Erich's voice rang with fury. "There will be no killing simply to prove a point. Not in my camp."

"*Your* camp? I think not, Gefreiter."

Without any further preliminaries, Hempel removed the ribbon from the paper-roll he had been handed. Holding the document at arm's length, he read in a deep voice: "In the judgment of a special court convened on this sovereign land of the German Isle of the Jews on this the twenty-second day of September in the year of our master and Führer, the vermin-monger Erich Alois né Weisser has been reduced to the rank of Gefreiter for crimes committed against the Fatherland and against humanity. All semblance of privilege, including that of leading the canine unit he attempted to pervert to his own Jew-inspired principles, has been revoked. He is to continue to serve the Reich and its Madagascar processing center, but he is to be considered by all other personnel, upon penalty of death for acting otherwise, as *persona non grata*. The command of the canine unit shall be placed in the hands of its rightful heir, Sturmbannführer Jurgens Otto von Hempel."

He looked around as if to see if anyone objected.

Pleshdimer hopped around like a child who needed to go to the bathroom. "And me," he said. "You promised."

"So I did." Hempel's voice was benign, his lips turned up in amusement. "The Sturmbannführer shall be assisted by Canine-Commander Rottenführer Wasj Hänkl Pleshdimer," he went on. "Signed, Sturmbannführer Jurgens Otto von Hempel, Commander-in-Chief of our master's and of the Führer's Southeast-African Felsennest Force, on behalf of Gauleiter Franz Josef Goebbels."

He released the lower end of the paper; it rolled upward with a crinkling. His arm stiff, he thrust the paper beneath his left armpit, did a right-face, and surveyed the Totenkopfverbände with a look of fatherly authority. "I will restate the order, so there can be no mistake," he snapped. "Gefreiter Alois is your servant," he told the guards. "Treat him as such!" His arm leaped up in salute. "*Sieg heil!*"

Those with the Mausers remained rigid—sighting like pointers on the prisoners. The rest of the Totenkopfverbände sprang into salute and answered in unison. Even the trainers lifted their arms, though their lack of zeal was apparent.

Raising their spears, the Kalanaro shouted, "*Minihana!*"

"Aim!" Hempel ordered the guards with the Mausers.

Mentally bracing for the blaze of a bullet, Solomon lifted his hand, fingers spread against the glare of the searchlights, and stepped closer to the gate. His head was bowed—as if to blunt the sacrilege he was about to commit: the denial of everything he held sacred.

"Sturmbannführer!" he called out to Hempel.

The major looked toward Solomon, diverting his attention from the guards, who grunted with dissatisfaction, having waited too long, heavy carbines in hand, for an order either to fire or to shoulder arms.

Solomon felt strangely apart from the happenings around him, ashamed and alone. Would Papa have been so quick to deny our faith? he asked himself.

Outside the fence Erich Alois stood motionless, head bowed, while a swarm of bats descended to feast, as they had done on the day of their arrival on the island.

"Solomon?"

Judith's voice, vague and distant, filtered through the frenzy. Sol dismissed it.

"Solomon...Freund."

Sol fought the buffeting waves of flying rodents as though pushing aside window curtains flapping against his face.

"It's time, Solomon!" Though Judith called his name, she seemed to be speaking to no one in particular. "It's time!"

The dogs pulled back from the fence, tails between their legs. Sol rushed toward the wire, but two of the guards jerked the muzzles of their Mausers in his direction despite the swirling bats, and he was forced back, hating his helplessness.

As if on impulse, Erich beat his way toward Solomon. Gagging on an insect, he stopped to spit it out.

"Gefreiter!" Hempel screamed. Pushing aside a curious Kalanaro, he jammed his Mann against Erich's neck. "Have you my permission to speak to the Jew? You are to stay away from them." He glared with newfound savagery toward the medical tent. "And from the woman."

Erich glared at his attacker. "She's my wife and will soon be in labor!"

"The Jews are all in labor, Gefreiter." The major's mocking tone made it clear that Erich's next word of insubordination would be his last. "Some are merely more productive than others. Now brush these goddamn grasshoppers off of my boots."

Hempel released the safety on his pistol. It made a resounding click in the quiet that had descended upon the camp.

"I said brush me off!"

Heart thudding, Sol watched as Erich backstepped, shaking his head in refusal, and Hempel stiffened his arm. Despite all that Erich had done to him, and to

Miriam, Sol could neither sit in judgment nor wish upon him so undignified an end.

"Ready!"

"For God's sake do whatever he asks, Erich!" Sol shouted.

Erich just stood there, as if he had no will at all: neither defiant nor compliant.

Sol sought desperately for any diversion, however temporary. He set his body to launch forward in a run toward the gate.

"Whaaa?" He felt a burning sensation in his throat and was jerked back, the front of his collar cutting off his windpipe.

He tried to sputter his rage. The one thing that remained within his control, the option of suicide, had for the second time in his life been wrested away.

"Look!" Max's voice bellowed in his ear. For an instant, Sol was too disoriented and the aperture of his vision too limited for him to understand.

"There!"

A second person held onto him, yelling in his other ear.

Goldman.

The farmer forced Sol's head around. For a moment Solomon relived another terrible time. Rathenau's assassination; Jacob Freund wrenching his son's head forward to see the death of the statesman they so admired and respected. He heard again his father's hoarse, whispered words, spoken through the ages in times of the death of a loved one: "I wish you long life."

The memory passed, and in its place Solomon saw what Goldman was pointing at.

The Zana-Malata was kneeling before one of Hempel's legs, picking grasshoppers off the major and stuffing them into his vertical mouth-slit, craning his neck and swallowing them like a long-throated bird.

At the other leg, Erich was brushing bugs from the trousers...the pistol still against his skull. His hands moved mechanically, as though connected to arms he did not control.

Hempel was grinning. An orgiastic, satiated face— tightened and twisted with pleasure. In the searchlight, even his hair appeared to shine with the intensity of his emotion, the silver the sheen of alpenglow.

"Now you." Hempel shoved the barrel of the pistol between Erich's eyes. "Just like the Zana-Malata. Eat!— or I'll turn woman and child over to the Kalanaro. Worse yet, to Wasj here."

He waved the pistol and began to laugh.

Erich remained poised for a moment above the trouser crease. Then he snatched at the grasshoppers, stuck them in his mouth, and began to chew.

The syphilitic drew back, chortling and whistling, as he watched Erich glean the major for his supper. Then, with hands that resembled claws, he pushed down Erich's head toward the major's boots.

Erich did not resist. His head remained bowed. As though peering into his own grave, Solomon thought.

What was it that had so separated them, he wondered. A uniform? Religion? Were they really so very different? Did they not love the same woman, and would they not soon earn a similar place in this island's ground, leaving behind...what?

Miriam and the child.

He glanced at his forearm.

37704.

Hölle....Hell.

Hempel had deliberately sought him out at Sachsenhausen. He had chosen the number with care—not because Sol was Jewish, but because of Sol's old friendship with Erich. Hempel's hatred of Erich Weisser Alois went back a long time, to the days when Erich was perhaps the only boy who had refused to go along with the former Freikorps-Youth leader's perversions—the same perversions that had caused Hempel to be drummed out of the army before the end of the Great War. Even then, he had been driven to prey on young boys.

He stared again at the number on his forearm: 37704.

Miriam carried his child, the first-born in this new Jewish homeland. With Erich and Solomon dead, would Hempel brand the child?

In a flash of ugly intuition, Solomon saw:

The number 1.

Chapter Twenty-Eight

The climb up the western hill proved after all too difficult for Miriam to manage alone. Her pregnancy seemed to bear her down much more than its actual weight and she did not resist when Bruqah dropped behind her and propelled her upward, hands flat on the small of her back.

Driven by his strength, she was able to take some note of her surroundings. A variety of growths rose in a dark gauntlet that brushed against her and appeared to block her way, only to open slightly as the two of them rounded each curve. For a while, the foliage almost enclosed the track, then the plant life abruptly gave way to a small, inclined meadow dotted with skinny totems. At its northern end, where the forest fell away, what looked like the ruins of a flat-roofed stone house cut into the grassy incline and stood sentry over the night. Far below lay the glistening sea.

Close to exhaustion, Miriam concentrated on the forward motion of her limbs. She did not look up again until she was parallel to the crypt site. With trepidation she moved toward the edifice, one hand supporting her abdomen. She wondered briefly why on earth Bruqah had brought her here to give birth, here to a place built for death.

"You be safe here," Bruqah said, answering her unspoken question. He smiled down at her as they halted before the stone face of the crypt.

A cold shiver traversed Miriam's spine, like a finger of frozen moonbeam. She glanced back and up over her shoulder.

"Nothing there, Lady Miri," Bruqah said. He pushed open the great stone door with his free hand and, the motion completed, rocked back on his heels. Seeing his tightened features she realized that opening the tomb was at least as troubling to him as it was to her.

The open crypt at once begged and forbade her entry. She drew back from the damp, stale air. She wanted to tell Bruqah that, regardless of the danger that Hempel represented, she would not hide within that place unless all traces of the body some of the men had said had been in there had been removed. If indeed it had been real, and not some trick to scare away intruders. Even with it gone, she was uncertain that she could sequester herself in a death chamber to await the birth of the child.

"It's gone, isn't it?" she asked.

Bruqah craned forward as if listening to the darkness. "It? You mean—?"

"Whatever it is, whoever it is...." She held out a hand. "Tell me it is no longer there. That it is gone." She tried without success to keep her voice level.

Smiling, Bruqah shook his head. "She spirit will never be gone, Lady Miri," he said. "Not from our hearts...or hopes, anyhow." His eyes took on a distant, determined look. "But rest easy. Body, *that* be gone. For now."

He started forward, then turned and, hands on her shoulders, eyed her soberly before stepping inside the tomb.

She could hear him rustle around, talking quietly to himself. There was a scratching noise, and a match flared. Through slanting shadows she saw him tilt the glass of a kerosene lamp and light the wick. Almost instanteously, lazy black smoke curled upward and the tomb was revealed. It reminded her of the tobacco-shop cellar, and she half expected to see a wall lined with shelves holding boxes of cigars and accoutrements, a rust-red seep from between the stones, a sewer grate recessed into the floor. But except for a stone bench, upon which Bruqah placed the lamp, the low ceiling, and the floor of black, tamped earth, the only thing of note in the room were two large eyehooks from which dangled the ends of ragged hemp. The ropes appeared to have been cut.

That, she supposed from the description she had heard, had been where Benyowsky's chair had hung. A corpse a hundred and fifty years old, greeting those intruding upon his grave.

Bruqah wiped the bench with his hand, as if to

prepare it for Miriam's arrival. Despite her trepidation, she smiled at the housekeeping gesture. Suddenly mindful of the weight she carried, she walked inside the crypt and allowed Bruqah to help her sit. At first she sat up demurely, feet together and toes pointed, then with the Malagasy's help she lay back, steeling her muscles for the shock of cold stone.

The bench was surprisingly comfortable. There were indentations which seemed to fit her form perfectly. Closing her eyes, she drew in a deep breath and tried to relax. She had reason to be grateful, she thought.

The baby was alive and she was, for the moment, safe from Pleshdimer and Hempel and the Zana-Malata.

Why then did she feel the sense of a corpse within her womb? Why the need to reach for the comfort of Bruqah's hand?

"Tell Solomon that I'm here," she begged in a whisper. She pushed back a sweat-dampened strand of hair from her forehead. "He needs to know. *I* need him to know that I'm...," she glanced around the crypt, "that I'm safe, for the time being." The words emerged with less certainty than she had intended.

"I do not think I should leave you here alone."

"Please, Bruqah. Go, now. Go to come back, as you say. Tell him I'm here and that...and that I love him."

Bruqah brought his lips to her fingers. Rising, he backed from the tomb. She heard him pad several steps across the grass, then the call of a night bird pierced the sound of insects outside and the strangeness of her situation pressed down upon her like a huge hand covering her mouth, trying to smother her. She tried to remember the good times. She with Sol at the shop, in the flat, in his arms.

The contractions began again, the "...*pretend labor*" as Bruqah had called it. A tightness twisted her body, lengthened it, forced her hips upward and her shoulders off her stone couch. Each wave of pain dissipated the memories she was attempting to hold onto so dearly, and she concentrated on making sure she did not crack her skull open when the contraction passed and her head became too heavy for her to hold up any longer.

She took in air hungrily, raggedly.

A form slipped through the entrance. At first she thought Bruqah had returned and, supporting herself with her elbows, she rose up, anxious for assurance that he had spoken to Solomon.

"Bru—"

"*Pour la petite enfant,*" the Zana-Malata said, peering at her from the shadows. *For the infant.*

To her astonishment, Miriam felt little fear. Perhaps, she thought, it was because the Zana-Malata had spoken the longest and most comprehensible phrase she had heard him utter. Or maybe, and far more likely, she was simply too tired to care. Even when she saw that, of all things possible, he held the Torah in his arms, she felt only a detached curiosity.

A huge raffia bag hung over his right shoulder. Over his left elbow was what looked like a sawhorse-crib.

He lowered himself to his knees and eased down the Torah until one end of the scroll touched the ground. "*Enfant...beau.*"

Happily, Miriam's pains had dissipated, and more

happily still, the Zana-Malata appeared to have no intention of harming her. She watched as he lifted the Torah and laid it in the sawhorse, unrolling part of the scroll and patting down the paper. She sensed a reverence in his handling of the scroll and felt no affront at his touching it.

"*Enfant...beau,*" he repeated, rocking his arms as if they held a baby.

It was only then that she understood that he had built a crib for the child.

From the raffia bag, he drew out a blood-red *lamba*. With a grand flourish—an upsweep of his arms—he unfurled the cloth and laid it on the dark, earthen floor.

He straightened out the corners with a toe.

Next he withdrew a small human-like skull, a lemur, Miriam figured, after an initial gasp of shock. Smoke spiraled from its eye sockets and filled the tomb with the smell of eucalyptus. She did not find the smell unpleasant.

He set the skull down on the *lamba*'s southwest corner. Additional entries to the collection on the cloth followed: a hoof from the slaughtered zebu claimed the northeast corner; on the northwest, a clump of bristly *savoka*; what appeared to be a dried fruit-pit on the southeast.

At last, the Zana-Malata settled himself onto the dirt in a cross-legged position, smiled his vertical smile, and blew a narrow stream of smoke toward the ceiling. He was acting for all the world, Miriam thought, like an expectant father.

"Lady Miri?" a voice called from outside the tomb.

"Bruqah!" Miriam answered. "I am glad you're back."

For what seemed like a long time there was no answer except for the call of the cicadas and the Zana-Malata's raspy breathing. Then Bruqah said in a hesitant voice, "I cannot enter. Do you not see the Kalanaro guarding the door?"

Miriam lugged herself from the bench and tottered to the entrance. Holding onto the lip of the rock, she strained outward into the starlit night.

She could see Bruqah near the edge of the clearing, a black figure before the dark indigo canvas of sea and sky. Around him, the trees and totems stood like mute, ebony sentinels. But no matter how carefully she squinted toward the brush, she could see nothing more than those and the dark and a covey of fireflies, hovering like guardians at the doorway to the crypt.

CHAPTER TWENTY-NINE

Bruqah pointed toward the Kalanaro who guarded the entrance to the crypt and watched Miriam crane toward the left and right.

"I have company," she said. "The Zana-Malata showed up, with a crib that he appears to have made for the child and all kinds of other things which I suppose make sense to him."

Though he could still not enter the cave, Bruqah felt better. That which he understood rarely caused him fear, and he understood this. The Zana-Malata had left the Kalanaro to guard the entrance to the crypt. Lady Miri could not see them because she did not understand how they could be fossas and men and fireflies, metamorphosing as the whim took them. But he understood. Was he not able, in his own way, to do the same thing? Was he not a traveler's tree for some, capable of giving sustenance, while for others he was at best a man?

Raising his voice but careful not to make his tone in any way threatening, he shouted at the Zana-Malata through the cave opening, asking to be allowed to enter. There were times, he thought, to forego anger. This was clearly one of those times.

"Why is he here, Bruqah?" Miriam asked, making her way slowly toward him.

"He waits for the child he thinks will be the vessel of the soul of Queen Ravalona."

"My child? Oh come now." Miriam laughed. "I've been willing to accept a lot of things you have said, Bruqah, but this is ridiculous."

"Do not laugh, Lady Miri. We must watch him very careful when the birthing time comes. He wishes to be there so that he can take the afterbirth."

"And do what with it!"

Bruqah hesitated before he answered her. He did not want to tell her too much, yet cared too much for her to tell her nothing. In the end, albeit an end that still lay in the far future, the child was what counted—to him, to the Zana-Malata, to Madagascar, and to whatever other future the child's life led her into.

He looked up at the sky and guessed it to be around three or four in the morning. The pains Miriam had experienced were not the real thing. He had induced them to ensure her safety. The actual birth of the child would not happen until the sun had come up and gone down again at least once, which left plenty of time for talk and more than enough time to rid themselves of the Zana-Malata's presence. Soon much would happen to change life on the island. For now, there was little reason why he and his old adversary could not, for a short while at least, declare a tenuous peace.

"I think that you had better answer me, Bruqah," Miriam said. Judging by her tone, curiosity and anxiety were becoming anger.

"He believe," Bruqah said, weighing his words carefully, "that if he eat the afterbirth he will gain power over the soul of the child." Which, he thought but chose not to say, was the soul of Ravalona, the soul of Madagascar. He deliberated whether or not to continue. "He believe," he went on, having made the decision, "that same give him power over life and death."

CHAPTER THIRTY

Released by the nudge from Hempel's boot, Misha wandered around aimlessly for a while, simply enjoying his freedom. Usually when he was not at Hempel's side, he made sure that he stayed within view of the compound, and of the activity around the shack. This time, he played on the beach in the moonlight, built a sand castle, caught one of the tiny sandcrabs that peeked out at him from a pinprick of a hole near the water's edge. He even dared a swim until the proximity of a small barracuda drove him out of the water.

Ultimately, he returned to the Storch to await Hempel, certain that the major would leash him to it like a guard dog. He had grown so accustomed to Hempel's sexual abuse and to Pleshdimer's cruelty, that he at first felt almost neglected. But as the hours passed, he began to enjoy his freedom from pain and to dread its return.

Comforted by the night breeze, he fell asleep under the wing of the plane. When he awoke, dawn had begun to lighten the sky. He lay on the sand until the sun rose, lazily contemplating the recent past. Most of all, he thought about how much Otto Hempel had changed since his, Misha's, voluntary return to the collar and the leash, leaving the boy pretty much to his own devices. He hadn't done the *thing* to him for days, nor had he given Pleshdimer permission to hurt him. This despite the Kapo's constant request that he be allowed to "…beat the little shit."

Rapidly, the sun heated up and crawled under the wing. Misha stood up and brushed himself off. Pretty soon, he figured, Hempel would come to the plane for his morning inspection. What better time than now to do what he had sworn to do, and kill the major? As far as Misha could tell, no one would miss Hempel, except maybe the Zana-Malata and Pleshdimer. Herr Alois would be happy, especially after yesterday. So would Miriam and Solomon. Maybe Bruqah would too, though it was hard to tell what he cared about.

His mind made up, Misha looked around for a weapon. The stones near the mangrove roots were either too little or too heavy. A stick, he decided. If he kept one hidden and at hand, he could plunge it into the major's black heart.

He picked up several sticks and tested them by stabbing them into the sand. The first two broke; the third bent into a bow.

Too tricky, he decided. If he chose the wrong stick, he'd end up not doing the job properly. He was going to have to find something more sophisticated. Something that couldn't miss, like a gun, or Pleshdimer's knife.

He found some shade under the second wing, lay down again, and looked up at the morning sky. He could see a raincloud approaching rapidly, bringing with it the day's first cloudburst. He didn't mind, in fact he rather enjoyed the momentary coolness that the sudden showers brought in their wake. But a gust of wind diverted the cloud, and it dropped its weather just to the right of him, onto the water.

With no other cloud in sight to distract him, he turned his thoughts to his list. He had neglected it of late because, truth to tell, it had grown a little confusing—what with Hempel racking up points on the plus side just by leaving him alone. That the major deserved to die hadn't changed, only the urgency of it.

The same was not true of Wasj Pleshdimer.

In his mind's eye, Misha walked through multiple possibilities: death by knife—a small boy might not get it through the fat; by bullet—he had no gun. By fire— now there was something to contemplate. Better yet, he would set fire to the Zana-Malata's hut while the two of them were asleep. That way the fat Kapo and the syphilitic could fry together, like the grasshoppers on the fence yesterday—

"You think you can hide from me?"

Misha jumped at the sound of the Kapo's voice, so alive for someone who, in Misha's imaginings, was at that very moment being reduced to ashes. Not only was he very much alive, he held Taurus by a leash, which he slung over one of the plane's struts.

Knotting it firmly, he knelt down and leaned over Misha, his face so close and his breath so acrid that it alone made the boy sick. Misha turned his head to avoid the stench.

With one hand, Pleshdimer turned Misha's face back toward him; with the other he gripped Misha's crotch and twisted.

The boy cried out and the Kapo smiled with pleasure. "Think you can fly the plane and get away, that it?" He released Misha and laughed heartily at his own humor.

Misha crouched in a ready position, determined to make a run for it if the Kapo came near him again. To his right and slightly behind him, Taurus growled and strained at her leash. If he could release the dog quickly enough, he thought, maybe Taurus would attack Pleshdimer and tear off his balls. Despite everything, he grinned at the image.

Then all notion of immediate revenge flew away as Pleshdimer's boot struck hard and accurately into the small of his back.

"I hate you!" Misha screamed, unwilling to control his fury and unable to control the pain. "Hate you, hate you, hate you."

Pleshdimer smiled benignly and let out a satisfied sigh, as if Misha's hatred had momentarily sated him. Then, eyes filled with renewed ugliness, he advanced upon the boy.

"Move it!" Otto Hempel's voice floated up from the beach that ran alongside the lagoon. "I don't have all day for this."

Pleshdimer stopped in his tracks.

Misha looked beyond the Kapo in the direction of the sound. He could see three figures walking along the beach. The major was in the lead. Behind him two men dragged their feet with the apparent weight of the wooden crate they were carrying. As they drew closer, Misha recognized Herr Alois and Herr Freund. The crate, about the size of a small coffin, was marked MUNITION in large black print.

"Over there," the major instructed, pointing at Misha. "Put it down in the shade. Be careful with it, or we'll all blow up."

Sweating profusely, the two men carried the crate the rest of the way and laid it gently on the sand. Herr Alois' face was scrunched up in pain.

"You, Jew, return to the compound. Gefreiter, you stay here."

Solomon's gaze caught Misha's and they nodded slightly at each other in greeting before Sol turned and headed toward the foliage at the edge of the sand. Misha watched him stop once and turn to stare at the group near the Storch. Then, apparently seeing that their attention was focused on the crate, Herr Freund moved quickly sideways into the greenery.

CHAPTER THIRTY-ONE

Erich stared incredulously at the bomb racks that had been rigged up underneath the Storch's wooden wings.

There were four wire-and-bracket clips on each side. A silver, crenellated cable ran the length of them and connected to eyehooks where each bomb would reside. The intent was clear: as the cable was engaged, the bombs would fall in sequence, beginning with the outermost ones.

Apparently, with forty barely pubescent camp guards, poorly trained for battle, less than a dozen dog handlers, who would probably bolt the moment they regained mastery over their charges, and a bunch of Kalanaro who seemed more monkey than human, Major Otto Hempel meant to take the war in Europe onto the mainland of Madagascar—without orders or proper ordnance, and with over a hundred and forty Jews itching to get their fingers around his neck. What could drive even a megalomaniac like Hempel to attempt something so extreme?

It took Erich only a moment to guess the answer.

What better way to hope to have one's ashes enshrined in one of Himmler's holy urns than to almost singlehandedly attempt an invasion? Erich would have laughed aloud were it not for the larger picture: he was supposed to be in command; he, not Hempel, would be blamed when the attempt failed. Goebbels would portray Hempel as a hero willing to sacrifice himself for the Reich's Greater Good—and would make scapegoats of the Jews.

He felt as if he were about to explode and clenched his fists, furious at his helplessness. Stripped of his rank, a private, a servant…forced to hand-carry bombs for Otto Hempel. He was hardly in a position to stop this, and yet stop it he must.

A muzzle touched the nape of his neck, making his hairs stand on end. "Straighten up, Gefreiter. You may be a private, but you are still a soldier in the German army."

Hempel stood on the seaward side, next to a growling Taurus. Erich stepped toward his animal, testing her response. The shepherd advanced to the end of her leash, savage-eyed, lowering her head in menace, the muscles along her back evident beneath her coat.

"In a few minutes, Gefreiter, the rest of my men will arrive. You will help them afix the bombs in this crate onto the apparatus we have rigged to the bottom of the wings. Is that clear?"

Erich continued to stare at Taurus.

"Answer me, Gefreiter."

"It is quite clear...Otto."

"Otto?" Hempel's face filled with rage. "*Otto!*"

His features smoothed and he smiled, the old feral smile Erich knew so well. "This is a private moment, so to speak," he said, pleased at his cleverness, "so I will allow your impudence to pass." He took a handmade pipe out of his pocket, tamped it, and lit it. "Not bad, these island leaves," he said, emitting a cloud of foul-smelling smoke.

He puffed for a while, then handed the pipe to Pleshdimer for safekeeping. The Kapo stared at it longingly but did not put it to his lips.

"I have often wondered, Weisser, whether you had any notion of the real mission of this contingent of Nazis and Jews. Did you really think that the Reich would allow Jew and Malagasy to live side-by-side? Are you that naïve?" Hempel looked at Erich with utter disdain. "Do you know what an affront a black Jew is to God? Why do you think the Führer so passionately supported Mussolini against the Ethiopians?"

Erich said nothing.

"We are here to test the effectiveness of tabun nerve-gas on isolated villages," Hempel said. Without waiting to judge the impact of his words, he went on. "As the Madagascar Homeland is implemented, the indigenous population will be eliminated rather than moved. This time, we will operate with real efficiency, against civilian populations, not just against soldiers—as was the case during the Great War."

He gazed dreamily across the water.

"Once I demonstrate how well the nerve gas works in warfare, I will at last, at the age of fifty-eight, realize my goal of becoming one of Himmler's Twelve Lieutenants. I intend to test the weapon on mainland villages immediately, and to use the dogs as perimeter guards to kill anyone attempting escape."

Erich could not even hazard a guess as to why Hempel had grown so expansive. He felt as trapped by the monologue as by the loss of the compound, and stupid for not having guessed that Himmler had intended from the start to sacrifice the Madagascar operation to the good of the Reich by making a martyr out of Hempel. That the Reichsführer had every intention of turning the Jews into scapegoats was no surprise. His method of doing so, however, filled Erich with renewed shock at the depths to which the Reich would descend to achieve its ends.

The existence of tabun, a new, highly lethal chemical weapon, was not news to him. Word of the nerve gas had filtered through the Abwehr's channels and corridors, but along with that had come a warning: tabun was so unstable and so deadly that even the most ardent nationalists among the scientists treated it with wary respect. One miscue, and a commander could wipe out his own force rather than that of the enemy.

Being neither chemist nor physician, Erich did not fully understand the science behind the gas, but he did recall his Abwehr briefing: tabun was an organophosphorous compound which inhibited the action of the body enzyme cholinesterase, and caused uncontrolled muscular contractions. Apparently, very small amounts resulted in paralysis, prostration, and death.

"After my men have taken body counts to determine gas-kill percentages, the Jews will bury the evidence," Hempel said. "I will get rid of *them* with the final bomb, and radio home to Berlin." He reached again for his pipe. Inhaled. Exhaled. "Yes, it's good enough. But I must confess that more than anything I long for a good cigar."

He removed the pipe from his mouth and stared at it intently.

"I wonder what your father would make of this," he said. "Did you know that he created a limited-edition cigar in my honor? *Rittmeister*, he called it, which of course is what I was at the time. He and I often sat in the tobacco shop, enjoying a cigar, a few cognacs. Reminiscing about the Great War, and about good German boys bewitched by Jewesses." He looked at Erich and shook his head, as if at a favorite but recalcitrant nephew. "It broke my heart to hear him go on about you, Erich. It really did. I told him I'd take care of you. As I do all my boys. There isn't *anything* I wouldn't do for your father." He gave Erich a knowing look. "Or he for me."

The man was deranged, over the brink of insanity, Erich thought. At this stage, killing him would be a kindness to Hempel and to humanity. He could do it here and now. Strangle him with his bare hands.

Why, then, did he not by now have Hempel's neck in his hands?

Because, unless he planned it right, it would be considered murder?

That was part, but not all of it, he told himself. There were other, more profound problems to be solved before dispatching the major. Like regaining control over the camp, and over the shepherds.

In the deepest part of his being, he could feel how torn Taurus was between her bloodlust and her desire to serve her former master. Somehow he had to break the hold the Zana-Malata had over her and over the other dogs.

He would need the trainers for that, as well as Solomon and the rest of the Jews. Until then, the death of the major would have to wait.

Hempel slipped an arm across Erich's shoulders and, contemplative, guided him toward the water's edge. Erich tried not to think of the pain in his hip and mind. Escape and vengeance: those were all that mattered now.

"How lucky we are to live in such a time as this!" Hempel swept an arm toward the box under the Storch's wing. "The day, Gefreiter, will come—and soon!—when *one* man," he lifted an index finger, "will control the world's destiny. One responsible, highly trained individual…," he paused for theatrical effect, "such as myself."

He held up both hands as if begging an enthusiastic audience to cease their applause. "I know, I know. You're wondering if I am worthy of such a challenge. I have asked myself that question many times. I am not always the man of action some people take me to be. In fact I am as committed to introspection and self-evaluation as any other officer of my caliber. Objective analysis—that's what sets men apart from women and Jews! I have assessed this situation with open eyes, and I tell you, the opportunity exists *here* for us to make a major moral contribution, not just to the world as we know it, but to all of history." He peered at the aircraft with an apparent sense of destiny. "The tides of men…you know what I mean." The timbre in his voice abruptly changed and he shook his head slightly, as though having awakened from daydream.

"So you're going to attempt to overthrow Madagascar," Erich said. "Now, *before* base camps are established."

For a moment Hempel appeared nonplussed and then gave Erich a loving, almost paternal look. He glanced around, as though to assure himself that no one else was within hearing range. "Had I fifty men such as myself I would attempt it. The balance of power in a backwater nation such as this could be tipped for the better with such a small fine force—but," he shook his head, "you know what abysmal men Reichsführer Himmler fettered me with for this operation. Not worth the price of the uniforms they wear." The smile, having wavered, returned. "Though they do have endearing qualities, especially the younger ones."

"You have no plans for an immediate attempt on the mainland?"

Hempel either did not notice or chose to ignore

Erich's tone. Lifting his gaze toward the larger island, a sense of imperious longing in his eyes, he said, "See where the massif rises to an apex?" He pointed toward the line of beige cliffs that jutted high above the swell of greenery along the shore. "Beyond that, the jungle is broken into small, sunken pockets surrounded by walls of limestone. I've flown over them three times, and each time I'm more impressed with just how cut off from the rest of the world those pockets really are. No way in or out except along narrow waterways— though I understand that a labyrinth of tunnels where underground rivers used to flow is also supposed to exist."

He looked at Erich and again put an arm across his shoulders. Erich stepped away from the embrace.

"That topography provides us with ideal testing conditions," Hempel continued. "Sometimes I think it was divinely ordained that we come here to Madagascar, you and I. Your rapport with the slave laborers, my science...and," he added, "my military strength. Himmler himself could not have created a better melding. So here's my actual plan." He relit the pipe. "We identify a dozen—no, *two* dozen villages in those isolated jungle pockets. I come in low," he made a flying motion with his hand, "barely above the massif. For accuracy, you see. No sense wasting ordnance by neutralizing jungle rather than the natives. Meanwhile, we station the dogs to block all avenues of escape. We don't want to endanger any of our own people, should the gas drift. After a few minutes, you and your Jews will go in, calculate the bomb-to-kill ratio, and bury or burn all evidence. Pity we don't have anybody around who could perform autopsies on the ones who're still twitching. The results would be of value—"

He gave Erich an amused look and added, "Don't worry. I've enough gas masks for your detail. Except for a few Jews we will dispose of as an example, I don't plan to eliminate any of your slave laborers until the experiment's been completed and I'm ready to report back to Himmler. The Jews and their military dupes may have stayed my hand when we gassed the enemy at Ypres, but this time I'll demonstrate the effectiveness of my ideas *before* we implement them in a crisis. The battlefield's no place for gas warfare...too many preventative measures exist! The *civilian* population— that's where we must hurt those who would harm the Reich!" He crabbed his fingers and pretended to reach for Erich's testicles. "Right down there where their gonads grow." He grinned. "You want a homeland for your Jew friends, Gefreiter?" Hempel pulled himself up straight, his chin set in triumph and his eyes uplifted in proud forebearance. "Fine. After the initial experiment is concluded and the Reichsführer has made me one of his trusted lieutenants for my efforts, I'll eradicate Madagascar of its former inhabitants—and without firing a shot. I'll give you and your Jews a land you can populate without further contagion."

"And your Zana-Malata?" Erich asked sarcastically. "You'll eliminate him as well? I thought perhaps he was the one holding your leash."

"We have an arrangement, he and I. I admire his

abilities, and he admires my strength. He helps to further our plans to ensure the progress toward perfection of an Aryan world in the knowledge that he will be provided for, and his enemies eliminated. Our syphilitic is of this land, but he holds no love for the people who have exiled him to this rock. Even a Jew lover such as yourself can appreciate that...or have I misread you?"

"Let me get this straight." Erich fought to maintain a calm posture. "After all the preparation and plans, what you want is to turn Madagascar into Sachsenhausen."

Hempel grinned. "Unless a simpler solution to the Jewish question can be found."

"Such as?" Erich's head was pounding, almost as much from the sun and his hangover as from the effort of keeping himself from making the futile gesture of breaking the major's neck with his bare hands.

"Don't look so distressed, Gefreiter. I will demonstrate how easy it is to kill, even when it is someone you know."

Calmly, he unholstered his Mann, released the safety, and cocked the pistol at Taurus. In the split-second before Erich could react, Hempel swiveled around, leveled the gun at Pleshdimer, and with a, "Sorry, Wasj," shot him through the chest.

An expression of absolute surprise crossed the Kapo's face before he fell. Erich watched the man twitch and the ground around him darken as blood seeped into the sand. Then he heard Misha let out a gurgle that contained more pain than joy and Taurus began to bark.

"Erich!" Solomon shouted, breaking through the bushes at a run.

He had covered half the distance before he stopped. "I thought he...you.... I couldn't see." He stared at Erich.

"Never mind *see*, Jew," Hempel said. He aimed the pistol at Solomon. "The question is, how much did you hear?"

CHAPTER THIRTY-TWO

"Let's go, Jew."

Hempel waved the pistol around in what seemed to Sol to be a far too casual manner. Sol tamed his instinct to duck. It was one thing to be shot by Hempel deliberately, another to be caught by a stray, careless bullet.

He glanced at Erich, who stood beside the Storch, facing Taurus, and wondered if Bruqah had told him, too, that Miriam was safely tucked away in the crypt and close to giving birth. His own conversation with Bruqah had of necessity been brief, and mostly composed of a vehement objection to her removal from the proximity of the corpsman and the medical tent. But that had given way quickly to gratitude that Bruqah was taking care of her.

"Walk!" Hempel prodded Sol in the back of the neck. "And you, Gefreiter, follow us."

Sol turned and trudged toward the path to the compound, Hempel close at his heels and uncharacteristically silent. As they approached the gate, the guards saluted with newfound enthusiasm. Trainers and guards alike looked away as Sol passed. He looked back to see how they reacted to Erich and found that, somewhere between the Storch and the camp, Erich had slipped away.

"Stop here," Hempel said, as they reached the inner gate that led into the Jewish quarters. "Gef—" He glanced over his shoulder and reddened as he discovered Erich's absence. He regained his composure with effort. "I have an announcement to make."

Hempel had uttered no word since his instructions to Sol and Erich. Unnerved, Sol looked at where the Kalanaro had fried himself upon the wire the previous night, and wished that the feeling of horror that had settled into the small of his back would resolve itself. He could see the African among his friends, chattering happily as though having returned from a successful hunt. Searching for a way to make sense of what he'd seen, Sol wondered if the white mud with which the Kalanaro had smeared themselves had something to do with the man's apparent imperviousness to electric shock.

"Gather your Jews over there." Hempel pointed to the open space where the Rosh Hashanah service had been held and where, tonight at sundown, they had planned to hold a Yom Kippur service.

While the Jews gathered—those of them who could be found within the compound—Hempel sent a runner for Johann, the wireless operator whom he had apparently pre-selected as his new adjutant. When the young Aryan corporal reached his side, the major assumed the same stance as when he had stripped Erich of rank, and held up his hand for silence.

"Your rabbi here," he pointed at Sol, "has, not for the first time, overstepped his boundaries. I would have shot him on the spot, but a better idea occurred to me. I have heard rumblings of your intention to hold a religious service tonight, with or without permission."

He would have made a fine actor, Sol thought, as Hempel paused.

"Let it be clear to you that I forbid you to hold your service," Hempel went on, obviously enjoying the drama of the moment. "In order to ensure that you take me at my word, I have my own new tradition to announce. Consider it my way to celebrate Yom Kippur. From now on, for each transgression, no matter how small, at least one Jew will be killed."

He paused again, looked around, and once more pointed his pistol at Solomon. "Shall I, after all, shoot your beloved rabbi, or is there one of you who will volunteer as his replacement? I frankly had other plans for him, but I could be persuaded to change my mind."

No one moved.

"The oldest among you, perhaps? Or the youngest?" Hempel looked around, like a butcher on a buying trip at the local abattoir.

A breathless silence seized the prisoners, during which Solomon heard the major tell Johann, "With so many to choose from it's like being a boy in a brothel, don't you think?"

Johann grinned.

"Must I repeat myself?" Hempel screamed.

The circle of guards who had followed the young corporal to the scene raised their Mausers and stood at attention.

"Take me!" someone called out from the back of the group of Jews. "No, take me!" another volunteered, and then another, until a chorus of voices offered themselves as Solomon's proxy.

"Stop this!" Sol shouted. "I will not allow any of you to die for me."

"The choice is not yours, Rabbi!"

David Kupke, a young man in his mid-twenties, stepped forward. Sol did not know him well, though people said he was once the finest young wheelwright ever to fire up a forge in Duderstadt, a strapping, happy youth given to swapping bierstube stories of hard labor and easy women. Two years in the camps had transformed him into a stooped husk who rarely spoke and spent every possible moment creating string-art masterpieces between his fingers.

He turned toward the other prisoners and—hands at chest height so the Nazis couldn't see—made a string-art piece which, though imaginary, had a clear purpose. A noose for Otto Hempel.

Angry chin held high, he turned to face the major.

"Do you serve Germany…or do you serve God!" Hempel demanded, a look of humor in his eyes.

"They are one and the same, Sturmbannführer!"

"You serve with every ounce of your filthy Jewish flesh?"

"Yes, Sturmbannführer!"

"Then prove your worth."

Hempel stuck his left foot forward. The prisoner dropped to his knees and kissed the toe of the major's boot.

"You seem to have been well schooled at Sachsenhausen," Hempel said. "Stand up. You serve a master well. From now on, you will serve the Kalanaro. Because your attitude has proved sufficient, you will not be eaten...while still alive."

The major made a sharp left-face as he leveled his pistol and fired point-blank into the young man's face. The body staggered back against the fence, and collapsed.

Solomon stared in horror at the blood. Goldman took half a step forward.

"You want something, Jew?" Hempel said to him. "Aren't you the one who blew the horn and turned my tank into a plow?"

Goldman stared the major down.

Hempel turned. "I'll be back at sundown. Anyone who looks like they're even thinking of a religious service will be fed to the dogs." He spun on his heel and was gone.

"Why, Lucius?" Sol asked. He thought of the child about to be born. Of Miriam and Misha who needed him, as did the others in the compound. "For God's sake, why did David do it?"

"For many reasons." Goldman looked toward the horizon. "They need you here, the others. You have always been there for us." He gazed at the dead man, then into Solomon's eyes. "Whether you wish it or not, I am going to sing *Kol Nidre* tonight."

Solomon began to object, but Goldman held up his hand. "Hear me out, Reb. I know how you feel about risking our lives for a tradition which God will surely forgive us for ignoring. I understand your logic, your reasoning. But what is in my heart is in my heart. Perhaps I have simply had enough of this struggle and this is my way to kill myself. A coward's way—to have it done for me and die a martyr. Whatever the reason, I shall sing *Kol Nidre* at sundown and mourn this young man's death. Should I survive until sundown tomorrow, I will blow the shofar after *Yiskor*."

"At least let us poll the others," Sol insisted.

"You know very well that they will say it must be my choice," Goldman said.

"I suppose I do." Sol's voice was heavy with sadness. "I suppose I do."

"He will kill us all eventually, Otto Hempel," Goldman said.

Sol shook his head. "I do not think so. Even a madman would recognize that he requires laborers. Besides, we will not let him. This is not Sachsenhausen. There are three times as many of us as them, and we are growing stronger daily." And he needs us to complete his private agenda, Sol thought, but was too weary to say. "Perhaps there can even be *L'shanah habaa* b'Yerushalayim...a next year in Jerusalem," he said instead.

A feeling of exhaustion dragged at him and he put his head in his hands——

——*In a flash of brilliant, cobalt-blue light, he enters the crypt and moves toward Miriam, who holds a blanket-wrapped baby in her arms.* He reaches out for her but she pulls away, staring at his hands. He looks down at them, and they are covered with blood.

"Deborah," he whispers. "We'll call her 'Deborah.'" He wishes he could close his eyes around that thought forever——

The Jews gathered in clusters, talking of choices and the lack of them, and of next year in Jerusalem.

"Before we do either," Max said, "we must bury David and go back to work, or feel Pleshdimer's stick in our ribs."

"Pleshdimer is dead," Solomon said quietly.

In the ensuing silence, he told the others what he had seen, and what he had overheard about Hempel's grand scheme.

"What are we to do, Rabbi?" someone asked.

"We wait," Sol answered before he realized he had spoken.

He focused on the faces before him. His decisions would come not from himself or from God, but from these men around him.

"They may make a show of strength by killing a few to frighten the many. Those without the brains or balls to be real men have to flex *something*," he said. There was a ripple of nervous, macabre chuckling. He waited until it had quieted before he went on. "The Nazis are madmen, but they are not inefficient. It is out of the question that they sailed the *Altmark* all the way here just to shoot us."

"Unless Hempel wants to end whatever was being attempted here, and have an excuse to go home," Goldman said.

Sol searched for a comeback that would combine logic and hope, but the logical answer was that Goldman was right—and hope wasn't logical.

"We must free ourselves and make a home here," Max said.

"A home*land*," someone argued.

"Jews! Back to work," the young voice of Johann called out, interrupting their discussions. "You think you're on holiday? You have a dock to finish."

Sol and Lucius headed for the wood-milling area. For the most part, it was not a rough detail, but it was noisy, and for Sol there were inherent dangers that caused him more pain than it might have the others. Standing a meter away and cradling a log end in his arms, he drew back as the two circular blades sent woodchips and sawdust flying. The spray beat against his face and invaded his eyes, bringing instant pain.

"Will you conduct the service?" Goldman whispered, in the momentary silence between cuts.

Sol shook his head and rushed to meet what the saws produced. Shouldering several planks, he walked across the compound, through the gate, and down the steep, rutted trail that led to the beach.

"Will you conduct the service?" Goldman asked

again, coming up behind him. "If not, say so and I shall find another!"

Goldman moved ahead. The two men concentrated on their loads as the trail steepened and their speed increased. When they came out of the forest and into the light, the sea breeze washed against their hot skin.

"It's much too risky," Sol said. But by then the sorghum farmer had pulled far ahead. They did not speak of the matter again until they had returned to the compound for lunch and Sol saw the older man moving from group to group, conferring with the others. Two strides and he was behind Goldman.

"If everyone can seem to be going about their business as normally as possible, I will lead all of you in words of prayer this holy day," he whispered, "but you must pray with me in silence, so as not to attract attention. Even saying one word is courting disaster, so I cannot conduct a full *Kol Nidre* service. In return for this concession, you must promise not to sing."

"I will do what I must," Goldman said.

Sol continued to drift from one small group to another. As he left each one, they in turn moved among other prisoners. The flicker of lifted eyes was enough to tell him which men were ready to receive whatever joy he could give them. How fine a congregation these men would have made, he thought, seated in the Grünewald Synagogue, wearing the traditional white of the Day of Atonement. How much finer they looked than had those businessmen in Berlin. Even dressed as they were, and enslaved, they were willing to risk their lives for one prayer. These men were indeed the children of God.

Sol walked among them, voice lower than a whisper. "As you know, Lucius Goldman insists upon singing *Kol Nidre* tonight. If Erich Weisser were still in command, we could safely hold a service. We could even, tomorrow, commemorate *Neilah*, and properly close the gates of Yom Kippur by blowing the shofar after the final saying of *Yizkor*, the prayer for the dead. But he is not. With Otto Hempel in command, who among us does not believe that that one long blast would bring retribution upon our heads? I am sure God sees, and understands our need to keep the horn wrapped in its rag and hidden away this year. Doubtless he will also forgive our lack of prayer shawls, *yarmulkes*, and candles."

He turned away from observing the others and, standing alone, thought about the death of a man and the coming of a child.

CHAPTER THIRTY-THREE

Certainly, Herr Sturmbannführer, I'll follow you to the camp like a good boy, Erich thought, staring at the back of Hempel's head. In a pig's eye, he would. A few minutes later he had sidestepped into the foliage and was watching Hempel and Solomon crest the rise and disappear into the compound area. The only possible reason for re-entering the compound would have been to find a bottle of schnapps. What had begun as general discomfort in his hip now ran like liquid fire up his back and down both legs. Even the last of what was in his flask might have served to dull the pain a little.

Worse than the pain, though, was the debasement. To think, he told himself, that he had actually begun to trail the pair, like a dog skulking after a master, or some pathetic camp follower trying to work her way toward the center of power—a whore sniffing for money.

Cat got your tongue? the hooker had mocked him that Christmas he had stood beneath the street lamp and imagined Solomon and Miriam in the flat across the street, sleeping in one another's arms. *I don't mind pain if the money's right....*

Taurus had shown her pain.

Taurus.

He glanced back at the Storch. All his life he had sacificed, and for what! All the years of athletic training and toil, only to have his chance for the Olympics snatched away by a scant two centimeters. Climbing the military ladder despite damaged fingers that should have kept him out of the service in the first place, only to find the platform at the top crowded with the likes of Heinrich Himmler and that clubfooted whoremonger, Josef Goebbels. Here, on an island in the backwater of nowhere, struggling to save the original intent of the mission and salvage what pride he had left, only to be usurped by one for whom service consisted of boys and young soldiers bending over and parting their buttocks.

He felt useless, used up. He had nothing more to give. Solomon could have Miriam; she had never been his anyway. And the baby, who knew whose child that was. Probably not even Miriam knew, he thought acidly. He turned and trundled back down toward the beach, reveling in the pain, wondering if Taurus would greet him, or if it would be like coming home to an empty house.

When the sea and the Storch were in full view, the water like crinkled aluminum in the breeze, he looked at the beautiful dog tethered beneath the wing. In a moment of icy clarity, he knew that there was one more sacrifice he had to make, one more trial he must endure. He supposed he had known it since that first day, when the Zana-Malata reduced the guard dogs to whimpering cowards beneath the hut; certainly he had known it, but refused to admit it, from the moment the pain in his hips was no longer sympathetic, but real.

According to the syphilitic, the transference of the dysplasia from Taurus to Erich was only temporary in that, if he died, it would return to the dog. And unless he regained his command, he was as good as dead. Killing Hempel wasn't enough—and could mean being hauled to Berlin in chains. Rather, he needed the men's acknowledgement, if not acclamation, of his leadership. Hempel might not have him physically leashed, like Taurus and Misha, but he was tethered just the same. When whatever purpose the major had for him was over, he would be discarded as surely and suddenly as Pleshdimer had been.

He touched the knife sheathed at his side and began a jerky hobble-run despite the pain. There was only one way he would have the emotional strength to manage this ultimate sacrifice, he thought. Somehow, he would have to force himself into a mental state that divorced him from his emotional attachment to Taurus.

The answer came to him more easily than he had anticipated: he would bring on an epileptic seizure. Berlin's dance marathons had intrigued him, but he'd had to stay out of ballrooms because of the lights that bounced off the mirrored globes revolving overhead; during his countless hours at the Marmorhaus, Strongheart and Rin Tin Tin flickering on the screen had placed him teetering on the abyss of an epileptic episode.

The pain and the satisfaction of having made a decision burned like a clean flame. He picked up speed, running now, an awkward gallop, winding in and out of the foliage and staring at the sunlight that strobed between the trees.

"Taurus," he said, bursting onto the beach.

Misha, sitting in the sand, looked up at him from near Pleshdimer's body. Taurus strained in excitement against her leash. She was his again, the connection renewed.

Something punched him in the small of his back with such force that he arched and, groaning, fell to his knees. The boy jumped up and started toward him, his face tight with concern.

Erich thought he saw the boy say something, but suddenly he was beyond sound. Instead of an aquamarine sea, he looked down upon a sea of vegetation, hunter green and painted with shadow. The sea rotated, above him now, while beneath him shone a puddled yellow moon.

His breathing returned to normal. He gained his feet and, brushing Misha aside, stumbled to the plane and clung to the prop. Losing his balance, he slid to the ground. Taurus padded forward, straining so hard to reach him that her collar must tear away from her neck.

He thought he could hear her barking as, on hands and knees, he fought for air, the world alternately tipping and spinning, light glinting dully off the blade of his knife.

He needed her power, her unthinking desire for vengeance and for blood, and there was only one way to get it. He fell sideways, twitching, her name on his lips.

As abruptly as it had begun, the seizure ended, and he was filled with a calm and a strength. His mind felt clear. He stood up slowly, feeling light yet strong, the air around him sweet and imbued with life. There had been a time, once, when he had believed that he and Taurus together could conquer the world. For a while, he had lost that conviction. It returned to him now, and he felt young again. He and Taurus, merged as one being, would be unstoppable except through the force of God. He remembered the many times that Bruqah had said that, in Africa, believing made it so. He could not believe more fervently than he did at that moment; all that was left was to make it so.

"C-cut the l-leash," he said, handing the knife to Misha, who was peering up at him. "So n-no one can ev-ever u-use it again."

Misha did as he was told, sawing earnestly at the leather. Then he held the knife to his side as the dog, freed not only from the tether but from the Zana-Malata's bonds, bounded toward her master.

Erich knelt, opening his arms, exultant not only from the sense of well-being which inevitably followed a seizure, but also from Taurus' return. She reached him, sliding to a stop, head lifted like a long-throated bird as she licked his face.

"M-my dearest l-love," he said.

He took her muzzle in one hand. With the other he clenched a thick fold of her neck, and jerked with all of his might.

The neck broke with an ease that surprised him.

She toppled with her head across his lap, staring blankly across the water. Her tail slapped once at a wavelet that reached her hind paws, and her whole body spasmed before the last of the air in her lungs was gone.

Misha dropped the knife and backed up so quickly that he bumped into the float and fell against the fuselage. He sat there in the sand, emitting tiny noises of disbelief.

Erich lifted Taurus' head from his leg and set it down gently. A final quiver passed through her. He stroked her, feeling the need to speak but unable to think of the right words.

When he rose, the dysplasia was gone. His hip sockets no longer ground in exquisite pain.

He picked up the knife from where Misha, in his shock, had dropped it onto the sand, passed it across his pants to wipe off the saltwater, and returned to the dog. Almost dispassionately, he wondered if he would be able to tell, now that she was gone, if the disease had again invaded her.

Turning her onto her back, he slit up from the soft, exposed belly to the rib cage, the skin so white in the sunlight it resembled purity itself. Truly the heritage of perfection, he told himself. Grace had mated with Harras, offspring of the German grand champion, Etzel von Oeringen. From her had come Achilles, whom Hitler had killed. From Achilles—Taurus, born during a blood-red May sunrise before the Nazis had come to power.

He could not recall having felt so physically and emotionally strong. He, Erich Weisser Alois, would be the last of the line.

He held the coat away from the flesh and finished slitting up to the throat and beneath the muzzle. Gripping with one hand and paring with the knife, he slid the dogskin backwards, the flesh and tissue white and pink and ropey with veins. He left the paws attached to the skin, sawing through the forelegs at the first joint. Finally he stood, put his foot against her neck, and pulled toward the tail. The dogskin slid free except at the hindlegs, which he quickly released.

For the first time since he had embarked on his course of action, remorse and compassion tugged at him as he held up the skin, the inside slick and gleaming. He fought the emotions, laid the skin across her body and pulled off his shirt and boots. Kneeling as if he were bowing before a lord, about to be knighted, he drew the skin over his back, shivering at the first touch of its moist warmth.

He stood up. From the corner of his eye he saw Misha scramble behind the float and stare in fear. The reaction made him feel electric. The skin hung like a cape, with the head hanging down his back. He secured it to himself with his boot laces. He tied it at his shoulders and beneath his biceps through holes he cut in the coat, then fastened it to his waist with his belt. Charged with power, he thought how puny and pathetic were the ways of humans. His eyesight was no longer sharp, but his other senses were keener than he had ever imagined possible. He smelled more than heard the Zana-Malata attempting to command him. The syphilitic's voice, if indeed it could be called that, hung in the oppressive air, before it drifted away on a sea breeze that wafted against the nape of his neck.

Feeling the need for ritual before he completed whatever transformation still lay in store for him, he sheathed the knife and, stooping, burrowed his hands into Taurus' body cavity. Pulling out the heart, the size of two melded fists, he tore it free. He turned to the breeze and lifted the heart to the sun, but said no words; he could think of no God worthy of prayer.

He lowered his hands to his chest and looked down at the heart, remembering Taurus running alongside him as he bicycled. Consciously, he put the nostalgia behind him and tore off a chunk of the heart with his teeth.

He did not bother chewing.

The meat slid, thick and rich, down his throat.

Screaming—exultant, emboldened, using two hands—he pitched the heart, still beating, in an arc into the sea.

CHAPTER THIRTY-FOUR

Misha huddled behind the float, comforted by the feel of the warm water of the lagoon moving around him. He stared in disbelief at Herr Alois, who appeared to have completely lost his mind. The thought occurred to him that he might be next; that in his feeding frenzy, the colonel would decide he had a hunger for consuming the flesh of young boys.

To his relief, Herr Alois, or Taurus, or whoever he thought he was, hardly gave him a second glance before he took off at a run in the direction of the encampment.

It was not until he was out of sight that Misha remembered the Kapo. Warily, he moved out of the water and across the sand, in the direction of the dead man.

"Help me. Please, help me."

Misha stopped in his tracks. At that moment, all he

wanted to do was scream that this could not be possible. The Kapo was dead. He had to be dead.

Pleshdimer moaned and opened his eyes. "A drink, Misha. A little water." He tried to move, cried out in pain, and covered his wound with his enormous hands.

Automatically, Misha took a step toward him. Then he stopped again. "No!" he shouted. "I want you to die!"

Half-crawling, passing out briefly at irregular intervals, Pleshdimer pulled himself around in the direction of the trail to the Zana-Malata's hut. Keeping some distance between them, Misha followed the Kapo and his trail of blood. Every now and again, when Pleshdimer came across some means of leverage, he attempted to get to his feet. A few times, he even managed to stagger forward for a step or two before falling to the ground.

Finally he tripped, tumbled, and lay still beneath the underbrush.

Misha waited, expecting to hear the Kapo call out or to see him emerge from cover like some lumbering boar. When what seemed like forever had passed in silence, he tiptoed closer. All he could see was the bottom half of the man's inert body.

He felt a surge of happiness, not entirely untinged by guilt at celebrating death—even this man's. Then he took off as fast as he could in the direction of the Zana-Malata's hut, keeping to the jungle so as not to be seen. He did not stop running until he was only a few feet away. He could smell the burning coals from the brazier inside.

Unsure whether or not the Zana-Malata was in the hut, he sat down on the grass and stared at the sunset. Soon it would be dark; soon it would be Yom Kippur.

He sat there unmoving until the onset of dusk. When he heard Herr Goldman's voice singing *Kol Nidre* he listened, recalling, dry-eyed, the last Yom Kippur he had spent with his mama and papa.

"Good Yomtov, Papa," he said softly. "Good Yomtov, Ma—"

He stopped, interrupted by gunshot and the insane barking of dogs. Even on Yom Kippur, he thought, as a plan formed in his mind. He would go inside and steal the Zana-Malata's magic. If he had that, he would never need to be afraid again. He ran up to the zebu-hide-covered doorway, stood still for a second to listen to the silence inside, and entered the hut.

The brazier burned, even in the Zana-Malata's absence. By its light, he looked around the room. Since he had last seen it, it had been emptied of much of its clutter. He felt a transient hope that the syphilitic had moved away for good, but though much was gone, too much still remained.

Tentatively, remembering his plan, he groped for the stack of tanghin pits that the syphilitic kept inside the buffalo skull on the shelf in the corner of the room. The skull was too high for him to reach, so he climbed into the suspended raffia chair and, balancing precariously, grasped one of the pits.

He opened his hand to look at his booty, and cried out as a flame burst into the air. The suddenness frightened him, but he felt no heat from the fire, which quickly went out when he dropped the pit. He examined his hand, expecting to see burn marks, but it was fine. He dug into the skull for a second pit and, holding it clenched in his fist, climbed off the chair.

Now what? he asked himself. Figuring he would go back outside and think while he listened for the sounds of the shofar from the compound, he stepped over the brazier and headed for the doorway. From outside he heard the renewed barking of the dogs. He stood with his back to the zebu-hide covering, wondering if there was anything else he should take. A knife glinted in the corner of the room.

He took a step forward—

Bloody fingers encircled his ankle from behind.

Groaning, using his elbows, the Kapo pulled himself into the hut.

"I want you to die!" Misha screamed like he had at the lagoon, lashing out with his foot.

Weakened by the loss of blood, Pleshdimer loosened his hold on the boy. Misha backed up against the far wall and watched as, impossibly, inch by inch, the Kapo crawled toward him.

Chapter Thirty-five

An hour or so before sundown, with the workday almost over, Sol saw Lucius Goldman take off for the spring. The farmer returned with his leather shoes knotted together and strung around his neck.

"I have prepared for Yom Kippur," Goldman told him.

The Hasid, Sol knew, was referring to the ritual cleansing, and to the fact that it was forbidden to wear leather shoes on the Day of Atonement.

"Walking on bare feet is a foolishness on a tropical island where such creatures as centipedes proliferate," Sol said.

Goldman laughed mirthlessly. "If they bite me, it will save the Sturmbannführer a bullet."

Sol avoided the man's eyes, for fear of seeing a mirror image of hopelessness. Instead, he looked at the horizon where the sun was about to be swallowed by the oncoming night.

As he had arranged with them, Sol's fellow prisoners did everything possible to create the illusion that tonight was no different from yesterday.

All except Goldman.

Apparently unable to live with the irreverence of praying with a bare head, he reached into his pocket and extracted a banyan leaf, which he placed on the crown of his skull. The gesture brought back memories for Sol—his father, donning his silk *tallit*, touching the Torah reverently with the prayer shawl's *tzitzit*, the soft fringes his mother had attached to the corners with blue thread, bending his head to recite the *Shema*.

"*Shema yisrael, adonai elohainu adonai echad,*" Sol began in a whisper. "Hear O Israel, the Lord is Our God, the Lord is One."

Unable to contain himself, Goldman's voice rang out. The first stanza of *Kol Nidre* coincided with his people's declaration of faith, their affirmation of God's unity.

Almost at once, a shadow fell across the congregation.

"*Manome!*" Hempel shouted, a word he had apparently practiced for the occasion. "*Sacrifice*! You want to pray? I'll give you a reason for prayer!"

Goldman continued to sing. Hempel unholstered his Mann and pointed it at the farmer.

"Leave him alone," Sol said. "This was my doing. You want me, so here I am."

Goldman tugged urgently at Solomon's arm. "Please, Rabbi."

Sol shook his head. "I can't let you die for me."

"Idiots! Now they're fighting to die." Hempel

laughed. "You'll both get it eventually. *Ve-la!*" he shouted. "Punishment."

"May the Lord comfort you, together with all who mourn—" Goldman said, as the shot reached its mark.

Dying, he fell to the ground and finished the ancient litany of mourning, "—and bring you peace." With enormous effort, he lifted his head and, gazing at Sol, said, "*L'shanah habaa b'Yerushalayim*, my friend." *Next year in Jerusalem.*

He shut his eyes, shuddered, and lay still.

Hot tears ran down Solomon's face. Looking directly at Hempel, he said, "*May God never forgive you.*"

Laughing, Hempel instructed two of the Jews to carry Goldman's body to one of the pandanus palms, its canopy a luxuriant umbrella in the bright light of the combined searchlights. There, the corpse was stripped naked. His hands were tied together with a length of concertina wire and he was hanged by them from one of the branches.

This can't be happening, Sol thought, looking around at the circle of Jews who had been led out of the ghetto to watch. He wanted to shriek aloud, to protest that he, and not his friend, should be the victim of this barbarism. It was only then that he noticed the continued absence of the Zana-Malata. The trainers had joined the spectacle, along with their dogs, which jumped and yelped around the body, tearing at their leashes and leaving Sol neither the time nor the stomach to speculate about the syphilitic's whereabouts.

"Release the dogs," Hempel commanded, from his favorite haunt beneath the tanghin tree.

The animals bounded forward. In a feeding frenzy, they tore at the bleeding body with savage intensity. Nothing was sacrosanct—head, hands, arms. In minutes, what was left of the legs was bloody and raw. One foot was gone, the other missing toes.

The guards shifted closer to the action, applauding and laughing whenever an animal made a particularly high leap. The trainers stood at the edge of the crowd, eyes expressionless and faces plaster-white in the glow of the moon and the searchlights, apparently unwilling to push past Hempel's men and attempt to control the shepherds.

The killings would go on and on, Sol thought, until the good Sturmbannführer denuded the island of Jews and all blacks except the Zana-Malata and the Kalanaro. Then the bloodlust would turn on itself, like a rabid dog chewing its own leg to the bone. In the end, Erich and the trainers would probably be impaled on sharpened poles, and Hempel would return to Goebbels to report how he had saved the Madagascar experiment from traitors, Jew-mongers, and dog-fuckers.

A dog pirouetted high in the air, tearing off a chunk of thigh as the guards roared their approval. Bright-eyed with self-satisfaction, the animal lifted its head and trotted off into the darkness, wolfing down the prize.

Chortling, a group of Kalanaro appeared. They danced around the body, kicking up clouds of dust and mimicking the shepherds. The dogs backed away, whimpering but persistent—hyenas hungry for a lion to finish with the kill.

"He who consumes his enemy, consumes power." Hempel meandered along the line of guards, smiling amiably. They parted as he came forward. The dogs padded to various points in their zodiac circle, lay down, and peered up at Goldman.

"So as our friend would say," he put an arm across Johann's shoulders, and pointed toward the Zana-Malata's hut. "*Mihinana!...Eat!*"

Nobody moved to accept the invitation.

"That the strong must cull the weak is a necessary evil." Hempel's familiar, paternal smile had returned. "It is a natural law which our modern society tries to circumvent—to their ultimate dissolution. Darwin and our Führer have shown us a better way. The rules of the animal world, where life is its most pristine, are pure and immutable. Humanity must renew and espouse its beginnings if it hopes to survive."

Sol averted his eyes from what was left of Lucius Goldman. He wanted to walk away, to mourn the Hasid in private, but Hempel had started on one of his monologues, and there was to be no escape from it.

"I am a self-educated man." Hempel waved his cigar and strode along the edge of the circle as he pontificated. "Unlike the effete intellectuals at the universities, I was wise enough to know that I could not read all the books, nor would I want to. I, therefore, thoroughly studied only those tomes beside which all other books pale by comparison. *Mein Kampf, The German Military Arms Manual, The Complete Stories of Sherlock Holmes.*

"Thus I have been spared from the *Bible*. From what I've been told, that novel," this to snickering from Johann and the other guards, "is filled with lost tribes, lost innocents, paradise lost. Also lost minds, from the kind of people I've witnessed fooled by it.

"One thing about it does intrigue me: the fiction about a barefooted runaway named Daniel who calms a den of lions.

"So here we have a Daniel." With his cigar he indicated Solomon, whose heart immediately started to pound. "As a true believer he must know that, should we command the animals to tear Daniel apart, the beasts will be calmed by the power of prayer."

The guards laughed heartily but the trainers, apparently with some sense of what was to come, blanched.

"Like any good story, ours of this modern Daniel has a twist." He held out his hand and Johann placed in it a roll of paper similar to the one Hempel had read to Erich.

"In the judgment of this impartial court," Hempel read, "convened this twenty-third day of September, nineteen hundred and thirty nine, on the German Isle of the Jews, we hereby condemn to death by dismemberment the subhuman known by the slave name Solomon Isaac Freund, prisoner three seven seven zero four. Dismemberment shall occur at the rate of one joint per hour, said body part to be fed to the canine unit while the prisoner watches. Signed, Sturmbannführer Jurgens Otto von Hempel,

Commander-in-Chief of our master and Führer's Southeast-African Felsennest Force, on behalf of Reichsführer Heinrich Himmler."

There was another enthusiastic round of applause. Sol, who had shut his eyes, opened them a slit. He could see only watery blues and yellows, for tears of mourning had obscured what sight the disease had not affected.

"But first, a little sport," Hempel continued. "We work hard enough teaching the Jews to work that we certainly deserve a little play!"

He moved toward Sol. The dogs edged forward, sniffing at Sol's legs and growling. He forced himself to stand his ground and not to look at them.

"That's it, my shepherds." Hempel reached down to pat a dog on the head. "Get a good whiff of Jew stench. Remember it." He took hold of Sol's shoulders, and his lips broke into a fatherly grin. "What the dogs don't eat, my little Jew boy will," he said softly. "We're aware you've a soft spot for him, so we'll save him...."

He seized Sol's genitals, and tugged. Groaning from the pain, Sol lurched forward.

"This will be less satisfying than hanging your father was," Hempel said, letting go. "But then we must take our pleasure where and when we can."

Sol was so filled with hatred at the confirmation of what, in his heart, he had always known, that he felt no more physical pain. He rocked back on his heels.

"This one likes to run at the mouth!" Hempel looked over his shoulder toward the guards, and grinned broadly. "Well, let's see how fast the rest of him can run! Any bettors among you?"

Within moments, he outlined the rules of his game. Sol would have about a hundred-meter head start. Bets were placed according to how far the men thought he would get before the dogs brought him down. The edge of the forest, various distances down the path, or the beach below. The *savoka* had the lowest odds at even money, the beach the highest at a hundred to one. At the men's insistence, side bets were also placed according to how many hours they thought Sol would live once the dismemberment began.

Hempel turned his grin toward Solomon. "We'll take your ears and nose—but not your eyes—then carve you down to head and torso before we cut off your jewels and feed them to Misha. Perhaps that will serve to improve his performance."

If Sachsenhausen had taught Sol anything, it had given him the ability to distinguish between truth and idle threat where the Nazis were concerned. He had no doubt that the major fully intended to do exactly as he said. Only by refusing to fight his fear and letting his shoulders sag was he able to remain upright at all.

Hempel pushed his face close to Sol's, his breath hot and rank. "Ever been attacked by a dog?" he screamed.

The ferocity caught Sol by surprise. He started to shake his head and then managed, "No, Sturmbannführer."

"I can't hear you, *Hundescheiss!*" Hempel stabbed his index finger against Sol's voice box.

The attack knocked Sol back a step. Only power of will kept him from grabbing his throat and dropping to the ground. He tried to blurt back the answer, but retched. Hans Hannes had told him about how Hempel had arranged his own Olympics, on the Oranienburg grainfields. A hundred prisoners condemned to death for trivial offenses had been lined up single file while the major stood a quarter-kilometer away, pistol in hand. The men had been made to sprint, tearing off their clothes as they ran. Arriving at the "finish," the naked man would fall to his knees and kiss the major's boots as Hempel checked his stopwatch. The reward for a good run was that Hempel shot the man immediately. A poor time, or failure to treat the major's boots with proper respect, meant the flogging bull followed by death by slow-hanging.

"No, Sturmbannführer. I have never been attacked by a dog."

"How about by ten, then?" The major turned his head slightly and nodded to acknowledge the guards' roar of laughter. "No need to worry, though." He drew a pair of leather gloves from his hip pocket and began sliding them on, the rolled-up paper tucked in his left armpit. "If you fight well, I may even order the dogs away quickly. Lie there like the cowardly Jew you are and I may not be so humane." He touched Solomon's shoulder, almost tenderly. "Run well! Make the Fatherland and our odds-makers proud!"

Sol lifted his chin. If the Nazis expected him to plead or physically ready himself in some way, they were mistaken. He leaned forward slightly, one hand on his forward knee. Eyes keened, he peered into the darkness, his tunnel vision defining for him a running lane to the rain forest. Everything outside that avenue was insignificant. Dodging would waste precious steps and seconds, given the shepherds' ability to change direction instantly. His only hope was to gain enough lead before they were loosed. If he could make it into the water, he might have a chance.

If.

If sharks weren't present—or hungry. Or if the dogs did not elect to follow him into the sea.

"Prepare to release the dogs," Hempel said. Then, to the animals, "*Mahlzeit!* Eat hearty! Now run, Jew. GO!"

Sol leapt forward, powered by desperation. For a time, all thought was gone. There was a dreamy quality to his running—an effortlessness despite the terror that squeezed at his diaphragm, draining him of oxygen. His legs pumped in fluid motion as he ran on feet made iron-hard by daily forty-kilometer agonies on the Sachsenhausen shoe-testing site. His breaths soughed from lungs strengthened and expanded by the *Altmark's* hellish heat. Though his awkwardness and Erich's jeers had kept him off the track team at Goethe, he was naturally blessed with a runner's lithe limbs.

On the wings of adrenaline, he headed for the jungle. Behind him, the dogs were barking, begging to be released, anxious for the chase and the kill. Once, he slowed just enough to glance over his shoulder. The guards and dogs were clustered together, within a blaze of searchlight. It surprised him somewhat that the searchlight was not attempting to track him, not that the dogs needed that kind of help. Other than his hope for the sea, he had no idea how to fool them or escape them, let alone defeat them.

With luck and a stick or stone, he might be able to fight off one or two, but eventually an animal would break through whatever makeshift defenses he might muster, and take him down. That would be the end of it, he thought, trying not to imagine what would come next.

If he only had time, a stone could be turned into a mace, a strip of branch a spear, a length of liana a garrotte.

If...

He ran.

The jungle loomed, an upsurge of bamboo and palm trunks interwined with lianas.

Then came the dogs. Their excited yelps hammered at him, spurring him, his running no longer smooth. He began to claw the air. His breathing raged like a bellows in his ears. When he glanced back over his shoulder, dark shapes with dark eyes bounded out of the light. Thorns tore at his calves and brambles ripped across his abdomen and chest as he raced onward, dodging sideways to skirt the larger, darker clumps, and using his arms to slash and bat away thinner shadows.

The dogs were right behind him, barking as they threw themselves through the stickers.

Sol squinted against the darkness and saw he would not make the forest edge before they were upon him. They would drag him down—here at the edge of the rain forest.

He spun, hoping he could fight hard enough that they would seize him by the throat and kill him. Not such a terrible way to die, he told himself. Hadn't Erich said that a dog bite could be so painful that it caused a form of paralysis?

The lead shepherd bounded out of the brush and leapt, sleek as an onrushing storm, its eyes dark-scarlet as the belly of a black widow. Sol stood his ground and prepared himself for the impact.

CHAPTER THIRTY-SIX

Erich had smelled Solomon before he had seen him, even amid the scent of fear and blood that came from the compound, odoriferous as old peat moss.

Drawn to the meadow by Goldman's voice, he had seen everything from a hunkering position amid ferns in the *savoka*—heard the pistol fire from near the tanghin tree, watched the shepherds leap and tear at the hanged man. What was left of his humanity was sickened, yet the scene increased the hunger in his belly.

Then a silhouette came charging out of the spotlight. He ducked instinctively, only to pull up his head again as the dogs, barking wildly, set off after the running man.

With an odd feeling of emotionlessness, he watched Solomon run toward him and the jungle. It all seemed to be happening outside himself, to some species with which he no longer felt close kinship. Solomon was nearly at the *savoka*, his breaths thundering through Erich's skull, before the dog-man reacted.

Prey, he thought.

A desire for blood coursed through him, along with a vague memory of teeth sinking into a whore's wrist, and his mouth was filled with a hot taste.

He gripped his knife and waited.

The figure came on, legs threshing through the grass. The dogs, released by the guards, bounded after him.

"Sol," Erich whispered, as Solomon stumbled forward several steps, caught himself with one hand as he started to fall, and staggered farther into the shadow of the rain forest. He glanced back just as Sagi, first of the dogs, crossed the remaining meters and leapt into the air.

Erich moved.

Without understanding why, he launched himself between Solomon and the dog, taking Sagi's charge full-force, then rolling with the animal and hitting its head with the haft of his knife. The dog pawed desperately, but Erich clung on. The man's mine! he wanted to say.

"Erich?" Sol asked as Sagi rolled off Erich and lay panting.

The other shepherds neared, slowing, sniffing, pacing.

Sol crawled through the *savoka*, reaching out to Erich. For an instant Erich started to back away, as if he were fearful of the man. Then the man's hands were on his back, clutching the fur, and Erich felt like whimpering with relief. He felt the pain where Sagi had bitten his hand and licked the wound, the desire for blood sated not by the taste of it, but by the hands of a friend.

"Erich?" Sol asked again.

The name sounded foreign, not a part of him at all. Sagi lay with paws outstretched, whining. He nuzzled his head beneath Erich's hand, also searching for comfort. The other shepherds moved closer, sniffing the dogskin, pressing their noses against Erich's bare chest.

He put his arms around their heads.

Home, he thought.

A spotlight, sweeping the area, found them. The dogs lifted their heads and looked into the glare, as if questioning what vile light dare disturb their gathering.

Erich looked between the animals to see Hempel and several guards coming slowly toward them, joking among themselves about how unfortunate it was for the dogs to be dining on a Jew.

He gripped Sol's wrist. "Go, Spatz!"

Even his own voice sounded strange to him.

For a moment, Sol did not move. Then the spotlight found him again, and he clutched Erich's wrist. A memory deeper even than the taste of blood seized Erich. He blinked and looked down at their joined hands, clasped in a way he had not experienced in decades. The *Wandervögel* handshake, he realized in a kind of dull comprehension that left him open-mouthed and brought his gaze up to meet Sol's.

"Keep Miriam alive," he found himself saying. Sagi

nudged him, again seeking affection. "Keep her safe."
He handed Sol the knife, haft first.

Sol took it, half-rising as the Nazis approached.

"Brothers in blood," Erich said.

Sol leaned over to touch Erich's cheek with the back
of his hand. "Blood brothers," he said. He reached
beneath the waist of his pants and drew out the Iron
Cross.

"Here," he said, handing it to Erich. Then he was
gone, lurching into the darkness of the jungle.

Let's go! Erich communicated the command
empathically to the other shepherds. He darted into the
foliage, reveling in the freedom from pain in his hip,
the dogs hard at his heels. He could hear Sol crashing
through the brush, working his way downhill toward
the beach.

You make damn sure she's safe, Erich thought toward
the retreating figure, as he worked his way east, along
the forest edge.

Spotlights and flashlights lanced amid the jungle. He
kept at a crouch, moving with an effortlessness that
made him giddy with excitement, sensing his way more
by smell than sight. With the other dogs close behind
him, he passed the path that led down the steepest part
of the hill and up again to the *valavato*. He could smell
the odor of sweat—human sweat, the stench left from
hours or perhaps even days ago.

Running freely, they explored the island's secret
places.

He was one with the pack.

CHAPTER THIRTY-SEVEN

"I play your glowworm song for you on *vahila*, Lady Miri?" Bruqah asked from his perch at the opening of the crypt. "You look too sad since you hear Farmer Goldman song."

Miriam walked toward him with difficulty. "I *am* sad, Bruqah," she said. "I should have been down there with Solomon tonight. It is Yom Kippur, a very special time for my people." She smiled at him, and he could see the effort that it took for her to do so. "I don't mean to sound ungrateful—"

"You not that," he assured her. "You want to speak to Bruqah of this Yom Kippur."

"You said that very well." She smiled again, more easily now. "But no, I don't really want to talk about it."

"I think you have been with me too much. You hold things inside like Bruqah."

She took enough steps forward so that she could see the encampment. "I heard shots. Now the dogs have gone crazy. What is happening, do you think?"

Bruqah hesitated. He did not have to be down there to know that there were great happenings afoot. The Zana-Malata had rarely left his post inside the crypt, and then only for minutes at a time. They had exchanged no more than a few brief words, yet Bruqah knew that the syphilitic had abandoned his game with the major for things of far greater consequence to him. Soon, Otto Hempel would feel the results of no longer having the sorcerer as his helpmate. As for the dogs, he could hear by their sounds that they were being governed by the smell of blood.

None of this was he willing to tell Miriam, for he knew equally well that within a few hours she would be in labor.

"Come, Lady Miri," he said, wanting to draw her back from her view of the compound. Solomon was in danger, he knew, and he did not want her so much as to catch a glimpse of him. If she guessed that he needed help, she would insist that Bruqah leave her and go down there.

Much as he would have liked to help Solomon, his duty—to himself and his people, as much as to Miriam—was to remain here at her side until the baby was born. He had left her twice since bringing her up here, the first time at her request to inform Solomon of her whereabouts, the second to take a sea bath and change into a fresh *lamba* and to fetch the gold earring which he wore upon ceremonial occasions.

Standing at Miriam's side, he watched the searchlights sweep the compound. Along the edge of the forest, three German guards with pistols ranged the area, as if they were searching for someone—or something. Leaving her, he walked to the edge of the cliff and peered down.

Below, a large pirogue with a lantern attached to a spar on the front was moving toward the island. He could make out half a dozen men, rowing steadily.

"Who are they?" Miriam asked, coming up behind him and clutching his arm.

"*Fokolana*," Bruqah explained. "Big council from tribe at southern part of bay. When Malagash king say, 'All to shave heads smooth as baby's butt to mourn son's death' those peoples say no. Many blood spill because of so, but those peoples keep hair and independence. Bruqah live with them sometime."

"Are they members of your tribe?"

"Vazimba no tribe, as I tell you. One here, one there, one there. So on." He made little gestures as if to indicate places on a map. "We special persons." He put his fist proudly against his chest. "No one walk in Vazimba shadow."

She glanced back toward the compound. "Look!" she said.

He followed her gaze. A Kalanaro appeared, then another and another, moving up the hill and halting behind the *valavato* totems as if they were trying to hide, even though the posts did little to conceal them.

Bruqah chuckled and turned back toward the sea as another shot resounded through the night. The guards had caught sight of the canoe. The second guard fired, and the oncoming lantern winked out. Now the pirogue was only a dark form on the water.

Both guards took aim. "No," Bruqah said quietly.

As he had that day, when Misha fell prey to the pitcher plant, he bowed his head and mumbled words Miriam could not comprehend. As if obeying a command, the guards relaxed and lowered their weapons. One of them lit a cigarette. When Bruqah lifted his head, they moved off toward the compound.

"How did you do that?" Miriam asked. "You stopped them from shooting. Sometimes you frighten me, Bruqah. You're as much a sorcerer as the Zana-Malata."

Bruqah nodded. "I tell you before, Africa she magical. You see. You believe. I am *mpanandro*-Vazimba. Zana-Malata takes power for self and punish people for making him alone. I wish only to preserve my people and she history. She die, I die, for never to return. With Vazimba, so long Germantownmen behave, they need be only afraid of smell." He craned his neck around and sniffed an armpit. "Phew! Bruqah *stink*!"

He was happy to hear Miriam laugh.

"You may play 'Glowworm' if it pleases you," she said, "but I must lie down. I'm very tired. Tired of waiting for this baby. I wish it would come, already."

Bruqah looked at her seriously. "Deborah come soon, Lady Miri. We are all children of the dusk on this island, but she will be child of the dawn." He took her arm to help her inside.

She pulled away from him. "I thought you could not pass by the guardians of the crypt," she said.

"Not alone, Lady Miri. They will not harm me if I am with you."

They walked inside together and he helped her onto her stone bed.

He ignored the Zana-Malata who, as usual, was seated in a cross-legged position, smoking and staring expectantly beyond the entrance to the crypt.

Chapter Thirty-Eight

Sol fought to still his noisy breathing and glanced over his shoulder to make certain that the dogs had stayed with Erich.

In front of him, splashed by moonlight, four large rubber dinghies floated on the bay. A fifth boat, half covered with planking that would form a floating dock once the Madagascar project moved to the mainland, was beached on the sand. On it, his back to Sol, sat a guard, his Mauser across his lap. His head lay forward against his chest, but from within the foliage Sol could not tell if the man were sleeping...and, if so, how deeply.

From up the hill, though muffled by the forest, came shouting and barking. By the sound of it, Hempel had realized that something had interfered with the shepherds' human retrieval. If Sol was going to take one of the dinghies and attempt escape, it would have to be now. The knife Erich had given him itched in his palm and he froze for a moment at what he was contemplating—to not only take a man's life, but to do so on Yom Kippur.

More than that, to abandon Miriam and the baby to Hempel, and Erich to madness. For the first time in many decades, he had heard his nickname on Erich's lips. Now, in his mind's eye, he heard the echo of the people in his dybbuk-inspired visions: Emanuel, Margabrook, Lise, all of whom had conspired to stop him from taking his own life at Sachsenhausen by telling him that he had a destiny to fulfil.

Was this that destiny, killing a man to save himself?

The images of David, his face blown away by Hempel's bullet, and of Lucius Goldman, shot to death and savaged, rose to remind him that Hempel had struck without mercy on this Day of Atonement.

Telling himself that only by surviving could he return to free the others, Sol squirmed forward on his belly, elbows and toes digging into the wet sand, fingers around the blade so that it would not glint. The boat guard, perhaps stirred by the noise from up the hill, shifted position, and the Mauser slipped from his grasp. He caught the weapon instinctively and sat up. Then his head lolled against his shoulder, and his snoring joined the other sounds of the night.

Sol released a slow breath, blinked against the assault of insects drawn by his sweat, and kept crawling toward the man's back. Huge, khaki-clad, unprotected, it seemed to be the only object in the universe.

Gripping the knife by the hasp, Sol covered the blade with his free hand and rose to a crouch. Pretend that you *are* Erich, he told himself. One hand over the guard's mouth and snap back the head at the same time you thrust.

Now!

The guard's breathing roared in Sol's ears, but he found himself unable to move the final step or to raise his arm. A small cry of despair passed through his lips and he stared down stupidly at his knife hand, wondering if his inability to kill was gallantry...or cowardice.

The sound was enough to awaken the man. Intuitively, he turned toward Sol. "What—?"

Sol's arm leapt up, and as if he were watching himself he saw himself backhand the man across the nose with the butt end of the knife. There was a crack as cartilage shattered. The guard moaned and crumpled into the boat's open half, blood streaming from both nostrils, rifle clattering against the planking.

Hands protecting his skull, Sol hit the ground and huddled beside the boat, expecting a bullet. He lay with his face in the sand, listening to the guard take what had to be his last labored breaths.

The sounds from the hill grew louder. Squinting toward the forest, Sol regained his feet. At this stage it was too late to worry about other guards, so he chose to decide that there were none. Erich had maintained two, and sometimes three, guards at the boats, but for Hempel the "enemy" was within the compound. He believed that he needed to keep the Jews corralled and the trainers scrutinized, not worry about mainlanders encroaching.

Deciding that for the moment he was safe, Sol straightened up and splashed into the water, moving toward the other dinghies. Staring at the boats and the black metal oars, he asked himself what he thought he was doing. Even if he did make it to the mainland without being riddled by rifle fire, where could he get help? If he found French authorities, would they risk their lives for the Jews when, according to Erich, the French had formulated the original Madagascar Plan?

He could hear people coming down the hill—the longer but easier way, by the path. They were talking and laughing. Taking their time. That meant they felt that they still had him under control.

Which they did, he thought disconsolately.

Unless...

He waded back to the landed boat and threw himself across the side, ready to smash down again with the knife. The guard was either still out cold, or dead. Sol lifted him in a fireman's carry and hustled him to the boat in the water. Cutting loose the lines that tied it to the others, he pushed the boat into the currents. It began at once to drift away from the island. He watched until the guard, sprawled in the bottom, was no longer in view, then he waded back to shore and ran up the beach and into the trees. Treasuring silence over distance, he eased between bamboo pickets and entered the foliage.

By then, he had formulated a plan. Without

questioning the odds of its working, he headed for the bottom of the strangler fig which abutted the jungle and whose branches overhung the gunner's station at the top of the limestone knoll.

The huge strangler fig's roots had sought the soil, creeping beneath the leaves of the forest floor. As it took of the food and water there, it killed the tree upon which it had germinated and became a gigantic, chaotic ladder.

There was a lesson there somewhere, Sol thought. He located a vine, tied on the knife, and looped it like a necklace around his head, with the knife hanging down his back. He spat upon his hands, rubbed them in the duff, and began to climb up into the thick overstory.

He had heard of South American Indians and African pygmies—the latter said to be the greatest tree climbers in the world—winding rope between their ankles to form a brace so that they could shimmy up the slickest trunks imaginable, climbing into the heavens in quest of fruits, insects, and honeycomb. The death wrought by the roots of the strangler fig made the goal more attainable to a city dweller like himself.

Still this was crazy, his trying to ascend the tree. Crazy even if he had daylight or lamplight by which to operate, given the tree's towering height. In fact, his whole plan was crazy. But escaping without trying to free Miriam and the others was crazier still.

In the darkness there was no way to measure distance. He had no way to tell how far he would climb, nor to determine how far he'd fall. Each handhold was a challenge; he could not discern if there would be another above it or if, sliding his fingers up the thick roots, he was pulling himself into a dead end and would have to descend and try another route. He attempted to pick bark off the roots as he went, thinking he might be able to locate the marks and thus better orient himself should he have to go down again, but the process slowed him, so he gave it up and concentrated on moving upward.

He reached leaves, leathery against his cheeks as he forced his head between the whorled foliage and supported his weight by hooking an arm, at the armpit, over a branch. Above the leaves a tiny breeze blew, and he could see a patch of sky. To his right loomed the pale, deeply convex cliff face. Peering up, he saw that the cliff bulged under the top branches of the tree; he had picked the correct strangler.

He took a breath and tried to get his bearings. Though some sounds, like the calling of birds and lemurs, carried remarkably well through the forest despite the natural buffer of the trees, others were evasive. He could hear the chugging of the generator, but it was impossible to tell if he was level with the camp, or if it was above or below him. High up through the seep of moonlight he could sometimes discern the side of the limestone chimney, a ghostly gray-green that bulked above the forest canopy. His goal, the small breastworks that formed the fourth sentry post, lay atop the hill.

Sol moved along steadily, with an agility that surprised him. He could only see his hand clearly when he held it close to his face, yet he felt a sense of comfort in these strange environs. This despite the danger of the climb and the almost deafening hiss of a million insects whose origins were foreign to him. Perhaps, he thought, it was his old friend, darkness, comforting him with the familiarity of his days and nights in the Berlin sewer beneath his father's tobacco shop.

Again, he tried to get his bearings. Toward the bottom, where the sunlight rarely reached, the foliage had been dense; here, higher up, where occasional patches of moonlight filtered through, the shadows formed patterns in chiaroscuro.

Something high in the canopy caught his eye. Face tilted up, for once blessing the tunnel vision that enabled him to concentrate on a tiny area or single object as though through a telescope, he caught the flashing signals of what had to be hundreds, if not thousands, of fireflies. Paul Lincke's melody began to play absurdly in his head.

"*Glühwürmchen, Glühwürmchen, Glimmre, Glimmre,*" he murmured, as he wiped sweat from his eyes and, parting a veil of loosely dangling lianas, struggled to see more clearly.

The moonlight increased, and climbing became easier. Every time he poked his head through the foliage, the fireflies loomed closer. Bright with promise, they blinked above him like the lights at KaDeWe department store during the holiday season. He almost felt as if he could reach up and capture them, and could not but wonder if the winking were a code to prevent just such a happening.

Twenty more meters, he guessed, anxiously peering up past the gnarled roots and foliage, and trying without success to see the top of the knoll. Here, higher than many surrounding trees, the effect of the moonlight was greater. He could see some of the overstory below, stippled in dark green. A fresh breeze blew, sending waves through the leaves like ripples on the surface of a lake.

Hearing a movement above him, he stopped climbing, put his face against the bark and drank in the air. Resting like that, he thought through more of his plan.

It was simple enough in concept.

He would knock out the sentry, secure the machine gun, and…what?

Free the entire camp?

He had never fired any kind of gun. Just how many of his own people would be killed or injured by his lack of experience?

What he had believed was an excellent idea became a jumble, and he was almost relieved when something growled above him. He was less relieved when he heard a jaw snap shut and felt teeth graze his fingertips. Yellow almond-shaped eyes with elliptical pupils glared down at him, and he reached for the knife.

The animal drew nearer. A foxlike head entered the weak light, and a fossa padded toward him, down the thick branch.

The knife felt suddenly clammy in his hands. He drew back, trying to get as much trunk as possible between them. The fossas had looked fierce enough on land;

they were the largest carnivores on Madagascar other than boars, Bruqah had said. Now it seemed both fierce and comfortable and in control, here, in its own milieu.

Snarling and hissing, it raised onto three legs and swiped at him with a forepaw. Sol parried, thrusting half-heartedly with the knife. The fossa slashed her claws across the back of his hand and leapt over his arm and onto the trunk, legs outstretched as she clung for balance, one back leg braced against a knot. Again she leapt, suspending herself between another branch and his head, squawling her rage at his intrusion, tearing at his shoulders and face with her claws. Drawing blood.

He twisted in terror, lost hold of the tree, and teetered in space, the rear legs of the huge cat scratching for purchase on his forehead and cheeks as the animal discovered itself in a similar predicament.

He screamed as the knife fell from his hands, and managed to clutch the tree, slamming himself against the trunk with such force that the fossa, spitting and caterwauling, toppled into his arms. For an instant he saw only fur and fury. Then, as quickly as it had attacked, it jumped back onto its branch.

Sol swiped angrily with a forearm at his bloodied face and stared away from the fossa, lest the meeting of eyes provoke another attack. As silent as it had earlier been furious, the fossa stalked along a branch and loped down to what appeared to be its mate.

He looked down into darkness and wondered if returning to the forest floor would not be wiser. Maybe he should, after all, attempt an escape to the mainland.

Both fossas began moving toward him—sleek shadows, upper lips curled back, incisors showing. He steeled himself, thinking that he could punch one hard enough to dissuade both from combat.

The fossas tilted their heads one way and another, snarling in displeasure. Two dozen pairs of eyes peered down from the dim heights. Lemurs. Defending the living coffin they called home against a common enemy.

The fossas glared at Solomon and made off into the foliage. Slowly the chittering declined, and the tiny lemurs, too, pattered away between the leaves.

Sol drew up his shirt tail and mopped his face before continuing. As he pulled himself upward, a pecking began. The vibration ticked through the roots as his hands touched them.

"*Ha-h'aye.*"

Sol saw the creature for only an instant, tapping its skeletal finger against the host tree's rotted trunk and looking for insect life in the dying wood. When it looked up, the eyes—betrayed by moonbeams breaking between the leaves—seemed to Sol as large and commanding as the radio speakers on the Funkturm. He shivered, and before the aye-aye disappeared among the maze of roots and lianas that encased the once-vital tree, it pointed at him with its skeletal finger. He began to climb again, faster this time, wondering what there was about the aye-aye's sound that filled him with hope rather than despair. Because the animal reminded him of Bruqah, despite the Malagasy's fear of it? Because he yearned for some foghorn to pipe him through his emotional storm?

What, he wondered, had caused the aye-aye to be branded as a harbinger of ill fortune? Bruqah said that his people believed it brought bad luck or death to any village where it appeared. The only escape was to kill it and if possible to burn down and relocate the village. Even dead, it was powerful magic. The sorcerer who dared to keep its finger gained occult strength which increased exponentially in power if he had the courage to twist or bite the finger from the still-living animal.

The limestone chimney bulked against the tree, so close to the trunk that Sol could touch it. He switched to the other side of the trunk and kept climbing, the going easier now despite the branches delaying him, the night clarifying his limited field of vision as he continued to rise above the surrounding canopy.

He was drawing closer to his goal: the sentry post was just overhead. Someone coughed. He strained to hear if there was more than one sentry, but couldn't tell. He could hear no voices except those that floated up to him from the main part of the compound.

Through the latticework, he thought he could see part of the northeast sentry tower and a section of the kennel area; the chimney of limestone blocked the rest. He heard shouted commands and saw a string of half a dozen lights as men—guards, he assumed—double-timed down the path that led into the forest and toward the beach.

He ascended with increased determination, making sure of his handholds as he moved up through the overstory. A snapped branch might alert a sentry.

Then the chimney appeared to fall away from the tree as though he were leaving the earth entirely, like the one time he had ridden in an airplane. The branches thinned out. Hunching his chest over a crotch of branches, he reached out and parted the foliage.

Perhaps it was the danger of falling and the vertigo—part of him wanted to step out and walk across the overstory, positive the sea of greenery would support him—but for an instant he felt closer to God than at any other time he could remember. Here where bromeliads bloomed like clusters of gemstones, the realm of God seemed more certain.

He moved downward until he reached a thick branch extending out over the chimney, and crawled out as far as he could without being seen. When the broad back of the sentry hunched over the machine gun atop the limestone chimney was directly below him, reality quickly cut Sol down to size.

Even given the element of surprise—assuming he managed to drop behind the guard before the man noticed him—the Nazi could probably overpower him easily. And even if that were not so, how was he to kill the guard?…throw him off the chimney? Go back and try to find the knife he had dropped?

Now that was a truly stupid idea, he thought, eyeing the bats that flitted around the knoll and envying them their ease of movement in the darkness. His lack of fear of the creatures surprised him.

The guard, apparently, felt differently. When one of

them flew too close to his head, he stood up abruptly and waved it away.

Sol seized the moment.

He fell upon the guard, knowing now that he was capable of killing and that he was strong, far stronger than he had realized. He also had the advantage of surprise. Sol landed just behind him. The man turned, eyes registering shock, and swung a fist. Sol ducked, searching for a weapon—anything! He shoved the ammo box, heavy with machine gun belts, at the guard. The man grabbed the box. He stumbled backwards, lost his balance, and plunged over the side of the knoll into the forest below, his cry like that of a bird. The belts, still attached to the gun, uncoiled from the box as he fell.

That's another one down, Sol thought, acknowledging to himself how much easier anything, even killing, was the second time. Feeling only relief that the other man and not he had been disposed of, he gathered the belts and squatted behind the machine gun. Now all he had to do was to figure out how to use it, and how to wipe out the encampment without also wiping out the Jewish contingent.

Leaning on the gun, he stared at the compound until his attention was drawn toward the Zana-Malata's hut. In the glare of a searchlight, he saw Misha's small figure disentangle itself from the zebu-hide. It tore from the door-frame as he fell down the steps and stumbled away from the hut. There was a loud series of pops and within moments the hut was ablaze. A second figure emerged.

Sol was shocked to recognize the huge form of the Kapo, staggering in a circle, his shirt aflame.

A siren blared and searchlights swept the area. Misha opened his hands. Immediately, a flame erupted from them. The boy froze like a mesmerized deer. There was a shot. The boy did not move.

"Run, Misha!" Sol shouted. He looked down at the machine gun. "Dear God," he whispered. "Show me how to do this."

And he began to fire.

Chapter Thirty-Nine

Frozen in the beam of the searchlight, Misha heard Herr Freund call out to him in warning from the top of the knoll.

Behind him, the Zana-Malata's hut crackled and roared as the fire set by the brazier sent sparks flying in all directions. Pleshdimer's dead, he thought. Dead, dead, dead! He felt no pang of conscience at having set the shack on fire with Pleshdimer inside it. If anything, he was sorry that it had been an accident, though no sorrier than he had felt when he'd discovered that the Kapo had, after all, not died at the hands of the major.

He could feel in his clenched fist the tanghin pit that had started the fire. Though he had no idea how the sorcery worked, he'd picked up the pit again before darting out of the hut, taking the syphilitic's magic and making it his own.

A shot broke through his hypnotic state. He looked up at the sentry tower, realized that they were shooting at him, and took a running dive into the closest bush.

Now what? he thought. He could go up to the crypt, where Bruqah had taken Miriam, but he had seen the Zana-Malata headed in that direction. The last thing he needed was punishment for having destroyed the syphilitic's home. He knew the major was in the mess tent because he had watched him go in there, but he wasn't about to go to *him*, especially after what he had done to Herr Goldman. As for Herr Freund, who was up there shooting, he was afraid to go to him in case he was hit by a stray bullet on the way.

The first searchlight went out, destroyed by the machine gun fire from the knoll. Crouching there, Misha thought about one of the stories his papa had told him—all about an ancient city somewhere in Palestine, near the Dead Sea. Just like here, the Jews were looking for a homeland. They had found it in Jericho, by making the walls of the city come tumbling down so that they could go in—even if their enemies didn't want them to.

That gave him an idea; he was amazed that he hadn't thought of it before.

He would go into the Jewish quarters, find the zebu horn that he had given Herr Goldman to use as a shofar, and blow it. The fence that formed the Jewish sleeping area would tumble down—and the outside fence—and everyone would be free.

He parted the branches and peered at the compound. Ahead of him, and slightly to the left, he could see Herr Alois and the rest of the shepherds. The colonel was still dressed in Taurus' skin. He was hauling a section of the punishment cage.

Ignoring the spray of bullets from the knoll and from the sentry towers, Misha sprinted toward the dogs. As he ran, the American Negro song that his father had taught him rang softly inside his head, and in his mind's eye he saw the walls of Jericho come tumbling down.

CHAPTER FORTY

Keeping carefully within the jungle, Erich and his dogs circumnavigated the meadow. When they were near the ruins of Benyowsky's hospital, he found a vantage point which allowed him to observe Hempel without being seen.

The major, probably thinking that the pack was still chasing Sol, was returning triumphantly to the camp. The guards gathered around as he entered with the air of a conqueror. In a group, they ducked into the mess tent.

Erich looked around. The overhang of vermiliads and orchids would afford him and the dogs protection from the knoll and sentry towers, allowing them to get to the compound unseen.

He led the way. With the pack behind him, he dropped to his belly and crawled toward the fence.

The smell of smoke stopped them. Turning around,

he saw a spiral of smoke coming from the Zana-Malata's hut, and watched as the shack burst into flames. He didn't have time to wonder who, if anyone, was inside, before he saw Misha run and stop, caught in the beam of the sentry towers' searchlights. He heard Solomon's shouted warning, and a burst of fire from the sentry station atop the knoll.

Misha scooted toward the bushes.

Spatz! His *Spatz*! Solomon Freund...*wise friend*, Erich thought. Who would have credited him with the balls?

As the other sentry posts returned fire, Erich acted. He dragged part of the collapsed punishment cage over to a small natural cavity at the base of the fence. The other shepherds looked at him expectantly as he shoved the lashed bamboo under the fence to pry it up. One by one, they crawled forward as if to be petted, and passed safely beneath. He smiled when he saw that Misha was last in line behind them.

When they were all inside, Erich led the way to the area behind the supply tent, keeping to the shadows as the spotlights swept the compound.

The trainers could join him if they wanted to, he thought. Right now, all they had were empty dog runs. They could all be a unit again until the *Altmark* returned, at which time some if not all them might try to head back to Germany.

He would not miss them.

The shepherds were really the only friends he had left. His true friends.

My friends, he heard the syphilitic call from the top of the hill. *My Sagittarius, my Pisces, my Erich....*

He put his hands over his ears and listened only to the pounding of his heart. Hempel and the guards had burst from the mess tent and were near the Panzer shooting toward the knoll. Machine-gun fire spat from above them, and they dove to the ground.

Bullets ricocheted off the tank. One man screamed and fell, clutching himself. Hempel rolled behind the tank as another spray of bullets stitched a line toward him. A searchlight shattered. The remaining two swung chaotically from the sentry towers, searching for the enemy and finally realizing it came from one of their own positions. They fired toward the limestone chimney, and Solomon retaliated. A second light went out in response.

Misha and the dogs drew close as the guards opened fire on anyone and anything that moved. Erich put an arm for comfort around the nearest neck. *Stay calm*, he told them, though he knew he was incapable of taking his own advice.

Solomon fired a burst toward the generator, but hit the water tower, which was in the way. Water streamed from it.

Just shoot the spotlights, Spatz. Don't worry about the power! Erich thought.

He looked over at the Jewish quarters, knowing intuitively that Hempel's boys would have re-electrified the wire around the sleeping area while the major was down at the beach.

What he saw made him want to stand up and cheer.

The Jews had torn down the canopy that he had

given them and thrown it over the fence. Four or five of them were beating down the wire with the poles that had held up the tent. Having broken the circuit, they poured over the fence. What was left of it buckled under their weight.

Solomon laid down peppery fire. The sentry towers fired back, and the guards near the tank blasted at the human wave heading toward them. The front line of Jews fell back, their agonized screams filling the night, only to have more Jews rush on.

Turning to Misha, Erich gave him quick instructions. "Go into the munitions tent. Open one of the small wooden crates marked *Granate*. It'll be on the right, near the entrance. Bring me a grenade. And be careful," he added as an afterthought.

Before he had finished the sentence, Misha was headed around the tent.

Erich and the shepherds followed, staying close to the canvas. He could see in the dark far better than his adversaries, and he was surprised to find himself without fear and also without bloodlust. He operated on animal instinct alone, but there was still the hunger with which to contend. He looked around, fearing the Zana-Malata's presence. He could feel the sorcerer's voice calling to him, but it was weak and distant. Then the voice was gone.

The dogs would not obey the syphilitic any more. Will they obey me? Erich wondered. He didn't know, but he had to try. Silently, he gave the command: *Zodiac*.

The dogs fanned out. As if the animals had reversed roles and called out to them, the trainers moved from various points of the encampment to join their charges.

Ready, Erich commanded.

The spotlight sighted the boy at the same time as the guard who had stayed at his post outside the munitions supply tent.

"Kill him!" Hempel screamed.

"*No!*" Franz burst from the medical tent, flailing his arms as he ran. "Don't shoot the boy!"

A volley from half a dozen guards caught the corpsman with such force that he left his feet. When he hit the ground, his legs flopped toward his head and down again like a rag doll. His arms splayed out, his head turned at an unnatural angle, and blood ran in a jagged line from his mouth.

As if by silent command, all carbines snapped toward the boy, who stood motionless within the searchlight's glare. He had stretched out his arm. Elongated flames rose from his palm into the night sky.

"Shoot him!" Hempel screamed again, but no one moved. Erich could almost taste the fear and frustration in the major's voice. Where is your precious syphilitic now? he thought sarcastically.

Attack! Erich mentally commanded Pisces and, trusting in the animal, jumped up in full sight of everyone. "Shoot *me*, you bastards! Kill a colonel!" he yelled.

"It's Alois!" someone shouted. "Dressed as a dog!"

Shooting started again. Solomon fired as the spotlight moved toward the new target. No more than a split-second later, Pisces was upon the man. As a rain of bullets took man and beast, the boy tore at the tent-flap ties and dashed inside. He emerged moments later holding two grenades.

"Here! Bring them here!" Erich yelled. "Roll them if you have to! We've got to blow up the generator!"

Misha started forward, half running, half staggering, then stuttery fire kicked up the dirt before him and he was running the other way, toward the power plant. He dropped one grenade and wheeled around to retrieve it, only to see the ground behind him erupt with bullets. He leapt and rolled. Erich saw him yank out the pin, and then the boy screamed as he charged, arm lifted.

A bullet spun him around before he reached the generator. The grenade fell from his hand, bounced as though striking a rock, and rolled down the incline that Jews in their work had worn smooth of grass. Misha lay in a heap as the grenade came to rest against one leg of the water tower.

The explosion shook the ground, pelting Erich with rocks and debris. When it was over, he rolled onto his back, trying to spot Solomon but instead seeing the tripod topple.

Everything seemed to happen in slow motion. The bottom of one leg of the tower was missing—jagged where it had been blown off—and the whole thing leaned drunkenly, water fountaining from the holes Solomon had shot in it in his attempt to destroy the generator.

Another leg snapped beneath the weight and the structure tipped. Water cascaded as the tower fell onto the generator and the headquarters tent. The generator sizzled—and shorted. There were several sharp pops, then darkness.

No more shots came from the limestone chimney.

Hempel climbed onto the Panzer and entered the turret. There was a growl and a metallic whirr, and the tank swung around to face the Jews. Their knot spread out into a line.

Hempel stuck up his head. "I warned you and yours against any insurrection, Rabbi!" he screamed.

In a shower of sparks, the roof of the hut collapsed. The major ducked down again into the Panzer.

Erich looked up, positioning his body. If only Solomon would give covering fire…if he was still alive.

He tensed himself, and felt the dogs tense in response. His years of track and field, their years of training with the Abwehr and then in the specialized program he had set up on the Rathenau estate, it was all culminating here.

Fire spewed from the barrel of the tank's gun. Perhaps a fourth of the Jews were mown down, limbs scattered like tenpins, as the .50 caliber machine gun traced through their line.

The remainder swarmed upon the tank, so close to it now as to render it ineffective. The guards shot them at point-blank range but they kept coming, one or two wrestling the Mausers from the hands of sadistic boys who thought themselves soldiers, and returning the fire.

The shepherds leapt, tearing at throats and testicles. Erich speared his hand into an eye with a satisfaction he would not have dreamed possible; the guard staggered back, falling against Johann, who was wrestling with Max, each ripping savagely at the other. Someone rifle-butted Erich in the back. He went down hard, and glanced up just in time to see the tank swivel toward the melee.

He's going to shoot us all, he thought, even if it means killing his own men.

Hempel popped his head out of the turret to look around. Bullets rang against the armor as Fermi and Holten-Pflug knelt and fired, forcing the major back inside. A wave of Jews reached the tank and began, by force of numbers, to overturn it.

The Totenkopfverbände threw down their weapons and ran toward the jungle, closely pursued by dogs, trainers, and Jews. Those still alive in the sentry towers raised their hands in surrender. The tank growled and lurched forward, spitting clods of dirt as the rocking treads grappled for purchase.

Jews and guards screamed as the tank crushed them in Hempel's haste to exit the camp and save himself.

The machine was halfway to the road leading down the hill when it stalled. Erich ran toward it, leaped on and peered inside, expecting to get shot by Hempel's pistol. He had done what he had set out to do. He had saved the Jews. Now there was only one thing left. Rid himself and the world of Hempel.

A mouselemur, the tank's sole occupant, gazed up at him with doleful eyes.

Instinctively, Erich knew that Hempel was headed

toward the Storch. He let Taurus' spirit course through him. Immediately he sensed the shortcut the major had taken. He sniffed the air, consciously attempting to cease thinking in human terms. The world was sapped of all pigments, the jungle a hothouse of orchids gone to gray, but the forest was rich with odors. His hearing was likewise acute. The rumble of a centipede across a leaf; the storm of Hempel's breaths a hundred meters down the hill.

As he dashed among the trees and ferns, Erich could still hear sporadic shooting behind him. He moved laterally along the hillside until the desire to stop seized him and he sniffed the air a second time. He could smell them. The Kalanaro, their body heat aromatic strata he could read like a geological map. Those monkey-men were old, it occurred to him for some reason he could not explain but which he had already begun to trust: old as Benyowsky's diary, perhaps old when it was written. Had they been the ones who stood, three thousand strong, as Benyowsky and the King of the North sliced their own chests with the royal *assegai* and sucked each other's blood?

Ampanzanda-be!

Where was the meaning to Benyowsky's life? The writing of the country's first constitution? The attempt to save Ravalona, only to be betrayed by friends and his own idealistic ambition? What joy could have come to the Count in the cool darkness of the crypt?

Perhaps only the grasshoppers and the centipedes held meaning. Perhaps only footfalls through the woods at the first light of dawn. All else, he told himself, must be nothingness, must be chaos. The only real advice worth listening to was the sound of his own heart, where the voices of dogs dwelled.

"Taurus," he said.

And then: "Miriam."

Sensing her presence within the *valavato* and knowing that if he neared it he might lose all control, he continued to descend the hill, slipping effortlessly between lianas and brambles. With his newfound senses had come surety of foot. At the base of the hill a tidal pond loomed like a moat, but he danced across the line of stumps and sprang to a grassy dune. Digging his hands into the sand he scrambled to the top and peered over.

The Storch, two small tabun bombs emplaced beneath the wings, was turning, taxiing hard, prop wash dimpling the water. He set his sights on the white September moon above the western tree line. Only a low spine of beach ridge blocked the pilot's view of him as he sprinted across the sand, heading for the short spit that arced into the sea at the open end of the lagoon.

Ducking his head, he ran in a half-crouch for the end of the spit. The dogskin slapped against him, the foliage cast crenellated shadows across the sand, enabling him to run in relative secrecy. The last twenty meters, though, was fully exposed, an apron of wet beach studded with sharp, dark stones. He hit the area at top stride, so charged with anger and power that he sailed painlessly across the rocks, laughing as Hempel aimed the Mann.

The plane whipped toward him as the first shot zinged past his ear.

He splashed out into the lagoon. Hempel waved his right arm as he attempted another shot and jerked the craft to the left, revving as he headed into the bay. The floats sluiced across wavelets, spray rooster-tailing behind.

Erich threw himself into a surface dive.

He caught the right float's tail fin. Its force whipped his body out straight. As water pelted over him and the plane picked up speed, he grabbed the strut. The left float lifted off the water and the right, lower due to his weight, followed suit. He saw the major jerk the controls to the left, trying to compensate as the aircraft pitched to the right. The machine yawed crazily and slowly corrected.

Hempel's feet were directly above him, soles against the wraparound window. He looked down, eyes angry.

Erich bared his teeth and grinned up at him.

The major, swearing inaudibly, reached across to the passenger seat and picked up his gun. As he maneuvered in his chair to get a clear shot down through the glass, Erich took a firm grip on the sponson and heaved himself left, caught the strut that ran to the left wing, and pulled himself up toward the passenger hatch. He heard the gun fire—twice, like someone cracking walnuts—but he was beyond fear, beyond caring. Physical action subordinated thought.

He shouted, smashing at the hatch with his fist.

The window splintered into a spiderweb of shattered glass. He wrenched at the door handle so hard that the door slammed open and caught the airflow. The momentum knocked him against the fuselage.

Another shot rang out. "You should have shot me long ago, when you had the chance," Erich shouted, as the plane dipped to one side and the pistol flew from Hempel's hand.

Laughing, Erich placed the arch of his foot into the V of the strut joint and swung up to look the pilot in the eyes.

Hempel threw the plane into a turn. Greenery displaced the blue of the sea as they banked back toward Mangabéy. Erich clutched the top of the hatch frame and, raising and tucking his legs as though he were about to pole vault, hurled himself inside and lashed out with both feet, catching the major squarely on the jaw.

Hempel lurched backwards against the pilot's window. His head thudded twice against the pane and the Storch veered sharply left, bringing Erich fully inside the cockpit. He landed crossways over the seats, legs in Hempel's lap, and snapped his left knee up against the major's chin. Hempel sighed, and slumped in the seat.

The plane nose-dived.

As the ground slanted closer, Hempel came to with a groan. He squinted through the window beneath his feet, paled—and pulled back on the wheel. The plane began a roller-coaster climb.

Hempel reached for the loop of black wire that ran along the top of the front window and out to the bombs.

Erich seized him by the shoulders, twisting and wrenching as he dug his nails into the man's flesh.

Hempel pawed at the air, trying to grab the wire loop, but Erich shoved him back, hard, into the pilot's seat, driving his full force into him. Without thinking, he leaned forward and sank his teeth deep into the man's neck.

The major gurgled and slammed his fists against the back of Erich's head. "Bastard! You bas...!"

The sound ceased. The resistance stopped.

Erich felt the plane bank—too far. The blue of the bay was framed in the passenger window and the moon showed silver on the bottom front of the nose.

So be it! he thought. Damn them all!

Hempel hit him again but it was like a friend chucking another on the shoulder in greeting. His arms slid down Erich's back and sagged to his sides. His mouth was open and he was staring blankly.

When Erich pulled the Iron Cross from his pocket and put it around Hempel's neck, the major did not resist.

Erich patted the medal once against the man's chest, and smiled. With one hand, he took hold of Hempel's neck, and twisted. The major's eyes protruded. A blood bubble formed on his lips, popped, and meandered down his chin. He slumped in the seat. Erich spat out Hempel's blood and flesh, and laughed again, a cackle that seemed to emanate from outside himself.

The plane had begun to spiral, but Erich made no attempt to gain the controls; control, he realized, was the last thing he wanted.

He lay with the crown of his skull against the window as the plane dipped. The only thing that mattered to him now was the redolent green of the Antabalana River region below. He thought he could hear the voices of thousands of Jews as they unloaded from ships, their cries in his honor like the adulation of tribesmen, hurrahs spilling like tumbling jungle waters into the bay.

He could see the moon, a silver wafer on a velvet sky. Perhaps, he thought, the Bushmen were right and that really was where the soul went. Leni had told him that one parched night as they sat on the edge of an African desert.

He laughed again and the moon spun, melting into madness.

CHAPTER FORTY-ONE

Chaos reigned in the encampment. In the melee—which he had started, Sol admitted to himself freely—it was hard if not impossible to tell who was winning and who was losing. The compound was no longer guarded against incursion from within or attack from without. The generator had been rendered useless by the collapsing water tower, the fences were for the most part shredded, and the searchlights were no longer operable.

Which meant that Sol no longer had even the vaguest idea of which targets he was hitting.

Having acknowledged all of that, he ceased firing and climbed down from behind the breastworks. His intent was to go down the south side of the limestone chimney, sprint through the clearing that Miriam called the grotto, and emerge well past the camp and the carnage.

From there, a reasonably short and not all that unpleasant run up the next hill would take him to the crypt.

A surge of pleasure reminded him that for the first time in his adult life he would be running to and not from—not away, not between sewer walls, not along the well-laid-out hell of the Sachsenhausen shoe-testing course that he'd had to endure for weeks on end.

Seeing the boy fall near the water tank and not get up had changed that plan. Misha lay somewhere down there, among the shots and the screams and the growling of both men and dogs.

Keeping as close as possible to the limestone chimney, Sol descended the front of the chimney rather than its rear, and climbed down into the camp. Once he was inside the compound, he found that most of the fighting was concentrated in the area near the main gate. He moved between the tents with comparative ease, as long as he kept his head down when he ran to avoid the natural traps of the tent lines. With the exception of tripping once, over a dead guard, he reached the boy without mishap.

Misha lay where Sol had last spotted him, crumpled in a small heap near the water tank. Sol turned him over carefully. Blood had welled up in a wound on the boy's forehead. Sol spat on his fingers and wiped it away. It was no more than a graze.

He touched the carotid artery and, to his great relief, found a pulse.

"Misha," he said in a hoarse voice. "It's Herr Freund. Open your eyes and speak to me, young man."

The boy's eyes fluttered open and he took a shallow breath. "Don't make me go back to the hut," he mumbled. "I don't want to go back any more."

Sol glanced up at what was left of the shack. "I don't think that you need worry about that." He ruffled the boy's hair. His fingers came in contact with a lump. "Try to sit up, Mishele," he said.

Misha sat up with no trouble, but his hand shot to his head and he scrunched up his face.

"Head hurt?" Sol asked.

Misha nodded gently, as if to minimize the movement. "I thought I was dead."

Sol chuckled. "You must have hit your head when you fell, but I am happy to be able to tell you that you are very much alive. Now let's see if we can get you out of here that way."

He started to bundle up the boy in his arms, but Misha shook him off. "I can walk myself, Herr Freund," he said, though he did reach for Sol's hand.

In that way, man and boy together, they walked between the tents and headed for the front of the camp. Everywhere Sol looked there were bodies, many of them dead or almost dead, others being attended to by their friends as best they could. Those guards whom he had seen earlier running for the forest had apparently not returned, nor had the dogs who had chased them. Nevertheless, there were enough of Hempel's men alive and around that the occasional shooting broke out. Hempel and the tank were gone, and Erich was nowhere to be seen.

Worried about Miriam's safety, he hastened his steps.

There was no real reason now not to exit through the gate, but it would make him and the boy easy targets for any sniper who might be hiding and waiting.

Apparently sensing Sol's hesitation, Misha tugged at his hand. "We could go out the way I came in," he said.

Sol followed the boy, and soon he was arching his back as he crawled beneath the fence, which was amazingly intact on that side. Misha was already under the wire. They ran hand-in-hand for several meters before machine-gun fire burst from one of the sentry towers. The boy stumbled. This time brooking no argument, Sol swept him into his arms. He did not stop running until they were well up the western track.

He set the boy down and turned to look at the encampment. Dawn had begun to lighten the sky. The hut was little more than a pile of embers, the compound a shambles.

Beside him, the boy began to cough.

Sol crouched down and removed the dog collar from Misha's neck. He pitched it into the bushes and placed his arm across the boy's narrow shoulders. They stayed motionless for a moment, surveying the manmade chaos below. They leaned against each other as if for support—though whether for physical or emotional support, Sol was not sure. He had the feeling that he had escaped not only from the Nazis, but from a life of dread lived on a predetermined road. His belief that everything happened for a reason was unshaken, for God, unlike man, did not roll dice. But how much of a part was he expected to play in God's plan? And how much of *that* was predetermined?

He stood up, brushing off his knees. There was a great sadness in him for those of his fellow Jews who'd had to lose their lives in this battle, but his overwhelming feelings were of gratitude that he was alive, and pride that he had helped to free his people.

"I think that you should tell me a story, Herr Freund," Misha said, once more taking Sol's hand. "Rabbi Freund." He seemed to be testing the words. "I think that you are a much better rabbi than you know."

Solomon laughed. "Better yet," he said, "let us sing."

Misha looked startled. "Sing? Someone will hear us."

"I do not think there are many left who care what we do. But perhaps you are right, so we shall sing softly. *"Da-da-yenu,"* he began. *"Da-da-yenu, Da-da-yenu, Da-yenu, Da-ye-nu."*

The boy grinned and joined in and they sang the song which, traditionally, was heard at Passover and was everyone's favorite because of its optimism and its happy beat.

Dayenu. Enough. We are slaves no longer. We are free.

When they had stopped singing, Misha tugged at Solomon's hand. Sol wiped away the tears that had formed as he'd remembered sitting at the Seder with his parents and his sister, Recha, vying for who could sing the song with the most ferocity.

"What is it, Misha?" he asked. "Another song?"

"The Kapo," Misha said. "He wasn't dead down there on the beach. I...I tripped over the brazier and started the fire—"

"Slow down, Mishele."

The boy took a deep breath. "I went back to the hut to steal the Zana-Malata's magic. When I was leaving, he...the Kapo...he came after me. I was so scared, Herr Freund. He was blocking my way and then he saw the knife lying there—" He shuddered.

"You don't have to talk about it," Sol said.

"I want to tell you," the boy insisted. "He reached for the knife. That was when I ran. I tripped over the brazier and the coals spilled all over. I knew they were burning, Herr Freund. I did. I knew they would start a fire." The boy was silent for a moment. "But I'm not sorry. I'm glad he's dead."

"I'm glad he's dead, too, Mishele. He was a very bad man."

"I wish I could kill the Sturmbahnführer, too," Misha went on.

Sol squeezed the boy's hand. "Who could blame you for feeling that way? Not even God, I think."

"I love you, Herr Freund," the boy said suddenly. "Not as much as I love Papa, but I do love you."

His thin little face was serious, his eyes held a hint of tears. Sol picked him up and hugged him. "And I love you, too, Misha. Very much."

They had stopped walking and were halfway up the hill that led to the crypt. Sol looked out over the trees toward the eastern edge of the lagoon, trying to keep himself from crying. He heard the thrum of the Storch, and hugged the boy tighter. In an instant the plane appeared, its spray like an elaborate headdress as it moved at a rapid rate past the spit and toward open water. He could see a figure, recognizable only because it was a man dressed in dogskin, running along the sand.

Erich.

Like a champion swimmer he dove, flat out onto a float as the plane passed. The aircraft lifted. Erich dangled for a moment, but quickly pulled himself up.

The Storch came around in a sharp turn and flew overhead, not much higher than the trees. Erich threw himself into the machine through the hatch door.

The plane sputtered twice, banked, and flew on, completing the arc and heading toward the mainland, its drone diminishing as it grew smaller.

Not wanting to lose sight of it, Sol cupped a hand above his eyes. Then he spied its silhouette against the moon.

The Storch fell, spinning like a ride at Luna Park. At first Sol thought that it would pull out, that Hempel—who was surely the pilot—would right the craft and swoop in for an effortless landing.

But the angle of descent was too steep and he watched helplessly as the plane disappeared into the trees.

The boy was looking up at him, knowledge that the plane had crashed evident in his young face.

"I do not think that Otto Hempel will ever hurt you again," Sol said.

Nor Erich, me, he thought, staring at the place where the plane had gone down.

Misha kicked a stone. Smiled. Kicked another. Sol

tried to return the smile, but his heart was too filled with tears.

"*Dayenu*," he said softly. "Goodbye, old friend. May you rest in peace."

Chapter Forty-Two

Miriam let out a slow breath and chewed down hard on the leaf that Bruqah had placed in her mouth to help her through labor. She could see the pre-dawn sky through the open doorway, cobalt-blue and studded with stars. She could not recall having seen a sky that color, but then she had never really spent much time looking at the sky, she thought, especially not one so early in the morning, especially not during the throes of labor.

"Soon, Lady Miri." Bruqah wiped her forehead with a damp cloth.

"Soon!" Miriam shouted. "I'm tired of hearing you say that. Can't you find something else to say?" She lowered her voice. "I'm sorry, Bruqah. I shouldn't be shouting at *you*. It's not like you did this to me, and if it weren't for you—"

She gasped as another round of pain tore at her. Bruqah signaled the Zana-Malata to hold her by the ankles to steady her until the wave passed. When it had, she swore silently at the sky and everything that walked the earth beneath it. The God who condemned women to this was certainly male and had no sense of humor whatsoever; of that she was damn sure.

"Solomon!" she hissed between gritted teeth, not knowing if she wanted to kill him or have him at her side supporting her.

"We will find Mister Sollyman!" Bruqah said. "As soon baby is here. Chew the leaf, Lady Miri. It will help. It is the way of our women."

She breathed rapidly, hyperventilating as the next contraction rolled from her womb. Arched in agony, she wondered why sex had been invented in the first place—and why she had been so foolish as to partake.

Bruqah put a hand against her cheek. The coolness of his flesh startled her, and for a moment she looked up without pain at his white teeth and shining eyes.

"We have a saying for such times," he whispered, running his hand up across her forehead and gently pushing her hair back, "'Where childbirth blooms, the indri watches.'"

"What's that supposed to mean!"

"Mean, Lady Miri?"

She shook her head in exasperation. "You and your goddamn sayings." Another contraction was coming on; she prepared herself for its fury. "Your people are as bad as…" she released a slow groan, "…the Germans. A saying for everything."

He grinned. "We have one for that too, Lady Miri."

Sitting up, she seized his shoulder. "Solomon!"

He pressed her back down. "In good time. For now you have the baby to worry you about."

"There!"

Sol and Misha stood framed in the doorway, as if by a horseshoe of sky. Fireflies winked around their heads like sequins.

"Miriam!"

She chewed down on the leaf.

"You and the boy stay outside, please, Rabbi," Bruqah said.

Before Miriam could argue, another wave of pain rose through her. She gasped and bit down hard. The leaf tasted slightly bitter, like dried coffee.

"Push!" Bruqah said.

"I am pushing, damn you!"

"Not hard enough. Bite on the leaf."

She bit down again. Suddenly lightheaded, she drifted down a stream into a realm where pain existed, real, but apart from her. Solomon and Bruqah stood behind a shimmery curtain, smiling and speaking to her in soundless voices. She attempted to return the smile, to assure them that everything was all right, that she was quite adept at delivering this baby or any other, but her facial muscles refused to respond.

It did not matter. Nothing was important except the child. They knew that, surely; even men could understand such things.

She heard a woman thanking and praising her; and for an instant she was certain she saw several dozen natives, naked and coated with white mud, cheer and lift gleaming spear blades into the air—but it was only a trick of the breeze and the breaking dawn.

And she saw fireflies.

Glowworms…was that Lincke's melody tinkling across her mind? She glanced up at Bruqah. He was cranking her music box, cradled in the crook of his arm. He raised a eucalyptus branch and shook it above her head, then executed an abrupt turn and shook the branch toward the door.

"Only a moment more."

The voice was Judith's. Miriam reached out for her hand.——

——*"I can't help you, Miriam. You must do this on your own. When you see me again, it will be in the flesh. For now, we belong to the child, the others and I."*——

——One more time, the pain intruded. Miriam braced against the rough surface of the rock wall with her hand and bore down until it seemed as if she would turn herself inside out. Three quick breaths, and she pushed down again. She tried for more breaths but the waves of pain were too close, each one greater and rolling over its predecessor. The agony seemed to rip her groin asunder.

"Solly! Misha! Come! She is here, the baby."

"A…what? You mean the baby's here already? I…"

Bruqah wrapped the infant in a *lamba*. A layer of blue-veined flesh veiled the upper half of the baby's face. Plastered from the top of the totally bald head to the nose, it looked like a bandit's mask.

With infinite care, Bruqah cut the umbilical cord and

slipped the caul from the child's head. She could see the Zana-Malata behind him, hear him babbling something unintelligible.

"What is he saying?" she asked.

"He praise the spirit child of Ravalona." Bruqah handed the child to her and placed his hand over hers. She felt his sincerity. "Though he praises true, he seeks the afterbirth. He wishes to eat it, for strength—and seeing face of death."

"He wants to die?"

"He wishes to recognize she face so to dance out of she path."

At any other time Miriam might have chuckled at Bruqah's convoluted language. "The man helped me," she said simply. "Give it to him."

"No can do," Bruqah said.

At that, the Zana-Malata darted forward. Grabbing the caul, he began to stuff it hungrily into his mouth. When Bruqah lunged for him, the syphilitic sidestepped neatly and darted out of the crypt.

"Get him, Solly!" Bruqah shouted. But he was too late.

Bruqah veiled the eucalyptus branch in purple gossamer and, sticking his head outside the door and jamming the branch into a crack in the rockwork, struck a match and set afire each dangling cloth-end. Quickly the flames spread; leaves crackled. He re-entered the crypt and, squatting by her side, took her hands between his palms.

"Bruqah inform the Kalanaro. They will help drive demons away."

She wanted to smile but, realizing Bruqah was serious, instinctively put her hand on the child's back. Then she called out to Sol and Misha, for it was time they too saw the child of the dawn.

Epilogue

Because it was so interpreted from the Talmud by some of them, the Jews buried their dead in the four days between the Day of Atonement and Succot.

Because it is written that the building of the *Succah*, the hut which commemorates the season of rejoicing—*zman simhatainu*—must begin immediately after Yom Kippur, they mourned privately and joined together to erect the tabernacle. For this, they gathered the traditional citron, the branches of palm trees, the boughs of thick-leaved trees, and the willows where the spring emptied at the bottom of the cliff. One hundred surviving Jews, and the two dog trainers, Fermi and the family man, Holten-Pflug.

Having built three walls, they left the fourth one open and began on the roof, using only that which grows from the ground and has been cut off from the ground. They left a space in the roof, no more than ten inches wide, yet large enough to see the stars and let in the rain, thus showing that they trusted in God to provide and to keep them safe.

From the roof they hung decorations of fruit and flowers. In the same way they decorated the walls. A child and a young man named Max retrieved a zebu-horn shofar from the debris of the encampment and placed it in a position of honor.

At dusk on the fourth day after Yom Kippur, a holiday was declared, and the Festival of Succot began. They sang and they danced, and they expressed joy in God and in their newfound, hard-earned, freedom.

While they sang and they danced, the Kalanaro poled from Nosy Mangabéy to the mainland. In the light of the rising moon, their pirogue looked like it was overflowing with glowworms. The fireflies winked on and off in unison.

A man watched them. In his arms he held an infant, wrapped in a *lamba*, perfectly content.

When he could no longer see the pirogue, he looked down at the beach and listened to the chanting that floated up to him.

Baruch ata adonai elohainu melech ha-olam shesheheyanu v'kee-y'manu v'hee-gee-anu lazman hazeh.

"Blessed art Thou, Lord our God, King of the universe who has imparted His wisdom to those who revere Him," he echoed softly, so that the child would not become alarmed. "Sweet Deborah," he crooned, and stared down at her in the light of the quarter moon.

Swept up by the power of the benediction, he entered the child's mind. There, in the flesh of his flesh, he rediscovered the dybbuk that had been in him for most of his life.

Entering Deborah's consciousness, he found himself back where the dybbuk began: with the nurse, Judith, who was killed by the grenade that took the life of Walther Rathenau. Entering the woman's cobalt-blue eyes, he discovered that Judith could have stopped the assassination through the conscious giving of her own life. Instead, she chose to live—and lost her life and her soul as well.

Unlike the five sparrows—Rathenau, Erich, Emanuel, Margabrook, and Lise, those who lost their lives to help others—Judith was never willing even to risk hers for someone else.

Ironically, though he was once nicknamed *Spatz*—"Sparrow"—this man was not one of them. Unlike them, he had not lost his life. His gift, or curse, was to see into the future. Since boyhood, he has been able to see glimpses of what the dybbuk will bring.

Returning to the present—to the hilltop—he wondered if it were possible to change history so that the dybbuk that was now within his infant daughter had no chance to alter events in devastating ways.

He wrestled with the ultimate moral dilemma.

Staring out over the bay, he made his choice: He would watch over Deborah and make sure the dybbuk was not exorcised. He would teach her what wisdom he could, in the hope that her actions would allow the dybbuk to atone for its sins, and find rest at last.

A woman called out to him from the beach. He did not answer, for there was one more thing he must do before joining the others.

He held the infant against his chest. Her heart beat against his. Though he promised himself he would never deliberately ask to be shown the future, he invited it to come to him.

"Please," he begged——

——*Please....*

The word snakes from the mouth of a girl of perhaps eight, wreathed in cobalt-blue light. She is tied naked to a carved wooden post by ropes wound among the water buffalo horns nailed above her head. Behind her, the vent of a volcano boils against the dusk. Her face quivers, her eyes are huge with terror. Suddenly her body sags, and only the ropes that bind her fast keep her from slumping to the ground.

Bruqah help me, she mutters, almost as if out of old habit. *Papa help me. I'm here. I'm here.* Then her voice is lost beneath the sputter and pop of red-orange lava fingers crawling among the stone menhirs and monoliths that surround her.

The eight-year-old glances between the sawtoothed leaves of the tanghin tree.

"Leave me alone, Jehuda!" she shouts.

Why Deborah! Do I offend you? You who deny my existence?

The voice comes from inside the girl's head.

In front of her, a thin spiral of smoke rises from black lava, and heat-charred snags smolder like damp torches. Out of that comes a snarling, a growling, and figures appear, men dressed in skins and carrying rifles and axes. Hunchbacked, they move across the landscape.

Making wide ambulatory crossings along the hillside to avoid a molten area, stopping every now and then to shoot back down the hill, the figures close in. It is almost impossible to tell them apart, for their heads are draped with the heads of dogs.

Squatting, concentrating their firepower on the brush below, the bizarre coven watch in silence as a skin-dressed man emerges from a thicket of thorns. He, too, wears a dog head, but it lies upside-down between his shoulder-blades. Around his neck, he wears an Iron Cross.

He sits down and starts to beat a weir drum. The others dance. Slowly. All elbows and shoulders, moving clockwise along the swamp that edges the rain forest. Now counterclockwise, soundless except for the occasional slapping of guns and sheathed knives against their skin.

The drummer rises. Passing between the others, he trudges up the black pumice and threads his way through the huge gravestones to stoop before the unconscious girl.

Taloned fingers lift her chin. Her eyes blink open and her facial muscles constrict with fear. Whimpering quietly, she tries to work her arms free. The rope scrapes uselessly against the totem and the dog-man raises his head and laughs——

Laughter from the beach and the whimpering of the child who was being held too close drew the man out of the vision.

"I'll be right down," he said, but he did not move. "It is not over yet, is it...Erich?" he whispered.

He stared at the Madagascar mainland, toward the rain forest, where four days ago he saw a plane spiral down to earth.

Afterword

The Madagascar Plan—the basis of The Madagascar Manifesto, of which *Children of the Dusk* is part—was first proposed by Napoleon's staff. The German High Command adopted it in 1938. Shortly thereafter, Eichmann embraced it as the "solution" to the "Jewish Question." The Plan's many supporters included the U.S. Congress and France's Baron von Rothchild, the Jewish cognac magnate who offered to buy the island in a desperate attempt to help save his people.

Walther Rathenau did have a niece; whether she knew Solomon Freund is doubtful. Sol's father, Jacob, who figures largely in the first book of this trilogy, is based on Janet's grandfather. He was co-owner, together with a Gentile, of a tobacco shop in Berlin.

Wanda Pollock, along with an American student and an Iranian wrestler, was instrumental in keeping the

Nazis from assassinating Churchill, Stalin, and Roosevelt in one fell swoop in Tehran, after the magician, Jean-Jacques Beguin, inadvertently used his "clairvoyance" to reveal the location of the Big Three's upcoming meeting.

Tabun was developed by the Nazis in 1937. Why Hitler did not use it is a matter of conjecture, though perhaps even he was afraid of its instability—and of bringing nerve-gas warfare to his own country.

The *Altmark* was in the area during the time of the novel, as was the *Graf Spee*. The *Spee* would later be scuttled by its crew in Montevideo, Uruguay, after a raging battle with British ships. The *Altmark* would eventually be boarded by British marines in a daring raid near Norway. The British seamen-prisoners she housed were released. Captain Dau committed suicide the day after WWII ended. As of now, the authors have been unable to find out what happened to Doctor Tyrolt.

The Vazimba and Zana-Malata are real peoples, as are the Betsileo and Antakarana; reports differ as to whether the Kalanaro exist in reality or are a synonym for the Tanal, the legendary People of the Forest. Trial by ordeal, using the pit of the tanghin fruit, is accurately described, as is the ceremony for opening a *valavato* tomb. No crypt exists on Mangabéy, though the Ravalona legend is well known in the region.

Today, Nosy Mangabéy is the world's only official refuge for the aye-aye. Fossas, mysterious pitcher plants, and other unique flora and fauna are endemic to the region. The elephant bird—source of the Roc legend of the Sinbad tales—pygmy hippos, and other seemingly fantastic creatures inhabited Madagascar until a few hundred years ago. Priceless elephant bird eggs are occasionally still found. Under certain circumstances, some fireflies are known to blink in unison.

THE END

Biography

In 1935, Janet Berliner's parents fled Berlin to escape the Nazi terror. In 1961, Janet left her native South Africa in protest against apartheid. After living and teaching in New York, she moved to San Francisco's Bay Area; started her own business as an editorial consultant, lecturer, and writer; and wrote *Rite of the Dragon*, which got her banned from South Africa. She now lives and works in Las Vegas.

Aside from more than twenty-five short stories, fifteen of them in the last year-and-a-half, Janet is the co-creator and coeditor of such projects as *Peter S. Beagle's Immortal Unicorn* and *David Copperfield's Tales of the Impossible* (HarperPrism, Fall '95). She co-created Peter S. Beagle's *Unicorn Sonata* (Turner Publishing, Fall '96), and recently completed work on *The Michael Crichton Companion* for Ballantine Books. For more information on her current projects, visit the Berliner-Philes web site at http://members.aol.com/BerlPhil/

In 1982 George Guthridge accepted a teaching position in a Siberian-Yupik Eskimo village on a stormswept island in the Bering Sea, in a school so troubled it was under threat of closure. Two years later his students made educational history by winning two national academic championships in one year—a feat that resulted in his being named one of 78 top educators in the nation. Journalists have written about his teaching techniques in such books as *SuperLearning 2000*.

As a writer, he has authored or coauthored six novels, including the acclaimed Holocaust novel *Child of the Light* (with Janet Berliner) and the Western *The Bloodletter* (Northwest Books, 1994). He also has published over sixty short stories in major magazines and anthologies, and has been a finalist for the prestigious Nebula and Hugo awards. He currently teaches English and Eskimo education at the University of Alaska Fairbanks, Bristol Bay. In his spare time he enjoys karate, exploring caves, and traveling in Thailand with his wife, Noi. His website is at http://www.uaf.alaska.edu/bbc/Guthridge.html

We at White Wolf are constantly striving to bring you revolutionary fiction from the hottest new writers and the legendary voices of the past. Filling out this form will help us better to deliver our unique stories to the places where you go for books. And if our undying gratitude is not enough to get you to respond, we will send a **FREE WHITE WOLF NOVEL OR ANTHOLOGY** to everyone who returns this form with a self addressed envelope.

BUT ENOUGH ABOUT US, TELL US A LITTLE ABOUT YOURSELF...

NAME_____

ADDRESS_____

_____

WHERE DO YOU GO TO BUY NEW BOOKS? CHECK THE TYPE OF STORE YOU SHOP. IF YOUR ANSWER IS A CHAIN STORE, PLEASE LIST YOUR FAVORITE CHAINS.

__CHAINSTORES_____

__ INDEPENDENT BOOKSELLER

__ COMIC OR HOBBY STORES

__ MAIL ORDER FROM PUBLISHER

__ MAIL ORDER HOUSE

__ INTERNET BOOKSTORE

HOW DO YOU FIND OUT ABOUT NEW BOOK RELEASES THAT YOU WANT TO READ?

__ PUBLISHED REVIEWS

    __ IN MAGAZINES (PLEASE LIS

    __ IN NEWSPAPERS (PLEASE LIST)

__ ADVERTISEMENTS IN MAGAZINES

__ RECOMMENDATIONS BY A FRIEND

__ LOOK OF COVER

__ BACK COVER TEXT/REVIEW QUOTES ON COVER

THAT'S IT. SEND COMPLETED FORM TO—WHITE WOLF PUBLISHING
                        ATTN: FREE BOOK
                        735 PARK NORTH BLVD.
                        SUITE 128
                        CLARKSTON, GA 30021